## *An Expensive Place to Die*

Len Deighton was trained as an illustrator at the Royal College of Art in London. His writing career began with *The Ipcress File* which was a spectacular success and was made into a classic film starring Michael Caine.

Since then he has written many books of fiction and non-fiction. These include spy stories and war novels such as *Goodbye Mickey Mouse* and *Bomber* which the BBC recently made into a day-long radio drama in 'real time'. Last year Deighton's history of World War Two, *Blood, Tears and Folly*, was published to wide acclaim – Jack Higgins called it 'an absolute landmark'.

Three of his Bernard Samson stories – *Game*, *Set* and *Match* – were made into an internationally aired thirteen-hour television series. These were followed by *Hook*, *Line* and *Sinker*. He is at present working on the third Samson trilogy, *Faith*, *Hope* and *Charity*.

BY LEN DEIGHTON

# LEN DEIGHTON

# AN EXPENSIVE PLACE TO DIE

HarperCollins*Publishers*

HarperCollins*Publishers*
77–85 Fulham Palace Road,
Hammersmith, London W6 8JB

This paperback edition 1995
1  3  5  7  9  8  6  4  2

Previously published in paperback by Grafton 1977
Reprinted fourteen times

First published in Great Britain by
Jonathan Cape Ltd 1967

Copyright © Vico Patentverwertungs- und
Vermögensverwaltungs GMBH 1967

ISBN 0 586 02671 1

Set in Times

Printed and bound in Great Britain by
Caledonian International Book Manufacturing Ltd, Glasgow

Do not disturb the President of the Republic
except in the case of world war.
*Instructions for night duty officers
at the Élysée Palace*

You should never beat a woman,
not even with a flower.
*The Prophet Mohammed*

Dying in Paris is a terribly expensive
business for a foreigner.
*Oscar Wilde*

# 1

The birds flew around for nothing but the hell of it. It was that sort of day: a trailer for the coming summer. Some birds flew in neat disciplined formations, some in ragged mobs, and higher, much higher, flew the loner who didn't like corporate decisions.

I turned away from the window. My visitor from the Embassy was still complaining.

'Paris lives in the past,' said the courier scornfully. 'Manet is at the opera and Degas at the ballet. Escoffier cooks while Eiffel builds, lyrics by Dumas, music by Offenbach. Oo-là-là our Paree is gay, monsieur, and our private rooms discreet, our coaches call at three, monsieur, and Schlieffen has no plans.'

'They're not all like that,' I said. Some birds hovered near the window deciding whether to eat the seed I'd scattered on the window-sill.

'All the ones I meet are,' said the courier. He too stopped looking across the humpty-backed rooftops, and as he turned away from the window he noticed a patch of white plaster on his sleeve. He brushed it petulantly as though Paris was trying to get at him. He pulled at his waistcoat – a natty affair with wide lapels – and then picked at the seat of the chair before sitting down. Now that he'd moved away from the window the birds returned, and began fighting over the seed that I had put there.

I pushed the coffee pot to him. 'Real coffee,' he said. 'The French seem to drink only instant coffee nowadays.' Thus reassured of my decorum he unlocked the briefcase that rested upon his knees. It was a large black case and

1

contained reams of reports. One of them he passed across to me.

'Read it while I'm here. I can't leave it.'

'It's secret?'

'No, our document copier has gone wrong and it's the only one I have.'

I read it. It was a 'stage report' of no importance. I passed it back. 'It's a lot of rubbish,' I said. 'I'm sorry you have to come all the way over here with this sort of junk.'

He shrugged. 'It gets me out of the office. Anyway it wouldn't do to have people like you in and out of the Embassy all the time.' He was new, this courier. They all started like him. Tough, beady-eyed young men anxious to prove how efficient they can be. Anxious too to demonstrate that Paris could have no attraction for them. A near-by clock chimed 2 P.M. and that disturbed the birds.

'Romantic,' he said. 'I don't know what's romantic about Paris except couples kissing on the street because the city's so overcrowded that they have nowhere else to go.' He finished his coffee. 'It's terribly good coffee,' he said. 'Dining out tonight?'

'Yes,' I said.

'With your artist friend Byrd?'

I gave him the sort of glance that Englishmen reserve for other Englishmen. He twitched with embarrassment. 'Look here,' he said, 'don't think for a moment . . . I mean . . . we don't have you . . . that is . . .'

'Don't start handing out indemnities,' I said. 'Of course I am under surveillance.'

'I remembered your saying that you always had dinner with Byrd the artist on Mondays. I noticed the Skira art book set aside on the table. I guessed you were returning it to him.'

'All good stuff,' I said. 'You should be doing my job.'

He smiled and shook his head. 'How I'd hate that,' he said. 'Dealing with the French all day; it's bad enough having to mix with them in the evening.'

'The French are all right,' I said.

'Did you keep the envelopes? I've brought the iodine in pot iodide.' I gave him all the envelopes that had come through the post during the previous week and he took his little bottle and painted the flaps carefully.

'Resealed with starch paste. Every damn letter. Someone here, must be. The landlady. Every damned letter. That's too thorough to be just nosiness. *Prenez garde.*' He put the envelopes, which had brown stains from the chemical reaction, into his case. 'Don't want to leave them around.'

'No,' I said. I yawned.

'I don't know what you do all day,' he said. 'Whatever do you find to do?'

'I do nothing all day except make coffee for people who wonder what I do all day.'

'Yes, well thanks for lunch. The old bitch does a good lunch even if she does steam your mail open.' He poured both of us more coffee. 'There's a new job for you.' He added the right amount of sugar, handed it to me and looked up. 'A man named Datt who comes here to Le Petit Légionnaire. The one that was sitting opposite us at lunch today.' There was a silence. I said:

'What do you want to know about him?'

'Nothing,' said the courier. 'We don't want to know anything about him, we want to give him a caseful of data.'

'Write his address on it and take it to the post office.'

He gave a pained little grimace. 'It's got to sound right when he gets it.'

'What is it?'

'It's a history of nuclear fall-out, starting from New Mexico right up to the last test. There are reports from

3

the Hiroshima hospital for bomb victims and various stuff about its effect upon cells and plant-life. It's too complex for me but you can read it through if your mind works that way.'

'What's the catch?'

'No catch.'

'What I need to know is how difficult it is to detect the phoney parts. One minute in the hands of an expert? Three months in the hands of a committee? I need to know how long the fuse is, if I'm the one that's planting the bomb.'

'There is no cause to believe it's anything other than genuine.' He pressed the lock on the case as though to test his claim.

'Well that's nice,' I said. 'Who does Datt send it to?'

'Not my part of the script, old boy. I'm just the errand boy, you know. I give the case to you, you give it to Datt, making sure he doesn't know where it came from. Pretend you are working for CIA if you like. You are a clean new boy, it should be straightforward.'

He drummed his fingers to indicate that he must leave.

'What am I expected to do with your bundle of papers – leave it on his plate one lunchtime?'

'Don't fret, that's being taken care of. Datt will know that you have the documents, he'll contact you and ask for them. Your job is just to let him have them . . . reluctantly.'

'Was I planted in this place six months ago just to do this job?'

He shrugged, and put the leather case on the table.

'Is it that important?' I asked. He walked to the door without replying. He opened the door suddenly and seemed disappointed that there was no one crouching outside.

'Terribly good coffee,' he said. 'But then it always is.' From downstairs I could hear the pop music on the radio.

It stopped. There was a fanfare and a jingle advertising shampoo.

'This is your floating favourite, Radio Janine,' said the announcer. It was a wonderful day to be working on one of the pirate radio ships: the sun warm, and three miles of calm blue sea that entitled you to duty-free cigarettes and whisky. I added it to the long list of jobs that were better than mine. I heard the lower door slam as the courier left. Then I washed up the coffee cups, gave Joe some fresh water and cuttlefish bone for his beak, picked up the documents and went downstairs for a drink.

# 2

Le Petit Légionnaire ('*cuisine faite par le patron*') was a plastic-trimmed barn glittering with mirrors, bottles and pin-tables. The regular lunchtime customers were local businessmen, clerks from a near-by hotel, two German girls who worked for a translation agency, a couple of musicians who slept late every day, two artists and the man named Datt to whom I was to offer the nuclear fall-out findings. The food was good. It was cooked by my landlord who was known throughout the neighbourhood as *la voix* – a disembodied voice that bellowed up the lift shaft without the aid of a loudspeaker system. *La voix* – so the stories went – once had his own restaurant in Boul. Mich. which during the war was a meeting place for members of the Front National.[1] He almost got a certificate signed by General Eisenhower but when his political past became clearer to the Americans he got his restaurant declared out of bounds and searched by the MPs every week for a year instead.

*La voix* did not like orders for *steck bien cuit, charcuterie* as a main dish or half-portions of anything at all. Regular customers got larger meals. Regular customers also got linen napkins but were expected to make them last all the week. But now lunch was over. From the back of the café I could hear the shrill voice of my landlady and the soft voice of Monsieur Datt who was saying, 'You might be making a mistake, you'll pay one hundred and ten thousand francs in Avenue Henri Martin and never see it come back.'

[1] Politically mixed but communist-dominated underground anti-Nazi organization.

'I'll take a chance on that,' said my landlord. 'Have a little more cognac.'

M. Datt spoke again. It was a low careful voice that measured each word carefully, 'Be content, my friend. Don't search for the sudden flashy gain that will cripple your neighbour. Enjoy the smaller rewards that build imperceptibly towards success.'

I stopped eavesdropping and moved on past the bar to my usual table outside. The light haze that so often prefaces a very hot Paris day had disappeared. Now it was a scorcher. The sky was the colour of well-washed *bleu de travail*. Across it were tiny wisps of cirrus. The heat bit deep into the concrete of the city and outside the grocers' fruit and vegetables were piled beautifully in their wooden racks, adding their aroma to the scent of a summer day. The waiter with the withered hand sank a secret cold lager, and old men sat outside on the *terrasse* warming their cold bones. Dogs cocked their legs jauntily and young girls wore loose cotton dresses and very little make-up and fastened their hair with elastic bands.

A young man propped his *moto* carefully against the wall of the public baths across the road. He reached an aerosol can of red paint from the pannier, shook it and wrote '*lisez l'Humanite nouvelle*' across the wall with a gentle hiss of compressed air. He glanced over his shoulder, then added a large hammer and sickle. He went back to his *moto* and sat astride it surveying the sign. A thick red dribble ran down from the capital H. He went back to the wall and dabbed at the excess paint with a piece of rag. He looked around, but no one shouted to him, so he carefully added the accent to the *e* before wrapping the can into the rag and stowing it away. He kicked the starter, there was a puff of light-blue smoke and the sudden burp of the two-stroke motor as he roared away towards the Boulevard.

I sat down and waved to old Jean for my usual Suze.

The pin-table glittered with pop-art-style illuminations and click-clicked and buzzed as the perfect metal spheres touched the contacts and made the numbers spin. The mirrored interior lied about the dimensions of the café and portrayed the sunlit street deep in its dark interior. I opened the case of documents, smoked, read, drank and watched the life of the *quartier*. I read ninety-three pages and almost understood by the time the rush-hour traffic began to thicken. I hid the documents in my room. It was time to visit Byrd.

I lived in the seventeenth arrondissement. The modernization project that had swept up the Avenue Neuilly and was extending the smart side of Paris to the west had bypassed the dingy Quartier des Ternes. I walked as far as the Avenue de la Grande Armée. The Arc was astraddle the Étoile and the traffic was desperate to get there. Thousands of red lights twinkled like bloodshot stars in the warm mist of the exhaust fumes. It was a fine Paris evening, Gauloises and garlic sat lightly on the air, and the cars and people were moving with the subdued hysteria that the French call *élan*.

I remembered my conversation with the man from the British Embassy. He seemed upset today, I thought complacently. I didn't mind upsetting him. Didn't mind upsetting all of them, come to that. No cause to believe it's anything other than genuine. I snorted loudly enough to attract attention. What a fool London must think I am. And that stuff about Byrd. How did they know I'd be dining with him tonight? Byrd, I thought, art books from Skira, what a lot of cock. I hardly knew Byrd, even though he was English and did lunch in Le Petit Légionnaire. Last Monday I dined with him but I'd told no one that I was dining with him again tonight. I'm a professional. I wouldn't tell my mother where I keep the fuse wire.

# 3

The light was just beginning to go as I walked through the street market to Byrd's place. The building was grey and peeling, but so were all the others in the street. So, in fact, were almost all the others in Paris. I pressed the latch. Inside the dark entrance a twenty-five-watt bulb threw a glimmer of light across several dozen tiny hutches with mail slots. Some of the hutches were marked with grimy business cards, others had names scrawled across them in ball-point writing. Down the hall there were thick ropes of wiring connected to twenty or more wooden boxes. Tracing a wiring fault would have proved a remarkable problem. Through a door at the far end there was a courtyard. It was cobbled, grey and shiny with water that dripped from somewhere overhead. It was a desolate yard of a type that I had always associated with the British prison system. The concierge was standing in the courtyard as though daring me to complain about it. If mutiny came, then that courtyard would be its starting place. At the top of a narrow creaking staircase was Byrd's studio. It was chaos. Not the sort of chaos that results from an explosion, but the kind that takes years to achieve. Spend five years hiding things, losing things and propping broken things up, then give it two years for the dust to settle thickly and you've got Byrd's studio. The only really clean thing was the gigantic window through which a sunset warmed the whole place with rosy light. There were books everywhere, and bowls of hardened plaster, buckets of dirty water, easels carrying large half-completed canvases. On the battered sofa were the two posh English Sunday papers still pristine and unread. A huge enamel-topped table that Byrd used as a palette was sticky with patches of colour, and across one wall was a fifteen-foot-high hardboard construction upon which Byrd was painting a mural. I walked straight in – the door was always open.

'You're dead,' called Byrd loudly. He was high on a ladder working on a figure near the top of the fifteen-foot-high painting.

'I keep forgetting I'm dead,' said the model. She was nude and stretched awkwardly across a box.

'Just keep your right foot still,' Byrd called to her. 'You can move your arms.'

The nude girl stretched her arms with a grateful moan of pleasure.

'Is that okay?' she asked.

'You've moved the knee a little, it's tricky . . . Oh well, perhaps we'll call that a day.' He stopped painting. 'Get dressed, Annie.' She was a tall girl of about twenty-five. Dark, good-looking, but not beautiful. 'Can I have a shower?' she asked.

'The water's not too warm, I'm afraid,' said Byrd, 'but try it, it may have improved.'

The girl pulled a threadbare man's dressing-gown around her shoulders and slid her feet into a pair of silk slippers. Byrd climbed very slowly down from the ladder on which he was perched. There was a smell of linseed oil and turpentine. He rubbed at the handful of brushes with a rag. The large painting was nearly completed. It was difficult to put a name to the style; perhaps Kokoschka or Soutine came nearest to it but this was more polished, though less alive, than either. Byrd tapped the scaffolding against which the ladder was propped.

'I built that. Not bad, eh? Couldn't get one like it anywhere in Paris, not anywhere. Are you a do-it-yourself man?'

'I'm a let-someone-else-do-it man.'

10

'Really,' said Byrd and nodded gravely. 'Eight o'clock already, is it?'

'Nearly half past,' I said.

'I need a pipe of tobacco.' He threw the brushes into a floral-patterned chamber-pot in which stood another hundred. 'Sherry?' He untied the strings that prevented his trouser bottoms smudging the huge painting, and looked back towards the mural, hardly able to drag himself away from it. 'The light started to go an hour back. I'll have to repaint that section tomorrow.' He took the glass from an oil lamp, lit the wick carefully and adjusted the flame. 'A fine light these oil lamps give. A fine silky light.' He poured two glasses of dry sherry, removed a huge Shetland sweater and eased himself into a battered chair. In the neck of his check-patterned shirt he arranged a silk scarf, then began to sift through his tobacco pouch as though he'd lost something in there.

It was hard to guess Byrd's age except that he was in the middle fifties. He had plenty of hair and it was showing no sign of grey. His skin was fair and so tight across his face that you could see the muscles that ran from cheekbone to jaw. His ears were tiny and set high, his eyes were bright, active and black, and he stared at you when he spoke to prove how earnest he was. Had I not known that he was a regular naval officer until taking up painting eight years ago I might have guessed him to be a mechanic who had bought his own garage. When he had carefully primed his pipe he lit it with slow care. It wasn't until then that he spoke again.

'Go to England at all?'

'Not often,' I said.

'Nor me. I need more baccy; next time you go you might bear that in mind.'

'Yes,' I said.

'This brand,' he held a packet for me to see. 'Don't seem to have it here in France. Only stuff I like.'

He had a stiff, quarter-deck manner that kept his elbows at his waist and his chin in his neck. He used words like 'roadster' that revealed how long it was since he had lived in England.

'I'm going to ask you to leave early tonight,' he said. 'Heavy day tomorrow.' He called to the model, 'Early start tomorrow, Annie.'

'Very well,' she called back.

'We'll call dinner off if you like.' I offered.

'No need to do that. Looking forward to it to tell the truth.' Byrd scratched the side of his nose.

'Do you know Monsieur Datt?' I asked. 'He lunches at the Petit Légionnaire. Big-built man with white hair.'

'No,' he said. He sniffed. He knew every nuance of the sniff. This one was light in weight and almost inaudible. I dropped the subject of the man from the Avenue Foch.

Byrd had asked another painter to join us for dinner. He arrived about nine thirty. Jean-Paul Pascal was a handsome muscular young man with a narrow pelvis who easily adapted himself to the cowboy look that the French admire. His tall rangy figure contrasted sharply with the stocky blunt rigidity of Byrd. His skin was tanned, his teeth perfect. He was expensively dressed in a light-blue suit and a tie with designs embroidered on it. He removed his dark glasses and put them in his pocket.

'An English friend of Monsieur Byrd,' Jean-Paul repeated as he took my hand and shook it. 'Enchanted.' His handshake was gentle and diffident as though he was ashamed to look so much like a film star.

'Jean-Paul speaks no English,' said Byrd.

'It is too complicated,' said Jean-Paul. 'I speak a little but I do not understand what you say in reply.'

'Precisely,' said Byrd. 'That's the whole idea of English. Foreigners can communicate information to us but Englishmen can still talk together without an outsider being able to comprehend.' His face was stern, then he smiled

12

primly. 'Jean-Paul's a good fellow just the same: a painter.' He turned to him. 'Busy day, Jean?'

'Busy, but I didn't get much done.'

'Must keep at at, my boy. You'll never be a great painter unless you learn to apply yourself.'

'Oh but one must find oneself. Proceed at one's own speed,' said Jean-Paul.

'Your speed is too slow,' Byrd pronounced, and handed Jean-Paul a glass of sherry without having asked him what he wanted. Jean turned to me, anxious to explain his apparent laziness. 'It is difficult to begin a painting – it's a statement – once the mark is made one has to relate all later brush-strokes to it.'

'Nonsense,' said Byrd. 'Simplest thing in the world to begin, tricky though pleasurable to proceed with, but difficult – dammed difficult – to end.'

'Like a love affair,' I said. Jean laughed. Byrd flushed and scratched the side of his nose.

'Ah. Work and women don't mix. Womanizing and loose living is attractive at the time, but middle age finds women left sans beauty, and men sans skills; result misery. Ask your friend Monsieur Datt about that.'

'Are you a friend of Datt?' Jean-Paul asked.

'I hardly know him,' I said. 'I was asking Byrd about him.'

'Don't ask too many questions,' said Jean. 'He is a man of great influence; Count of Périgord it is said, an ancient family, a powerful man. A dangerous man. He is a doctor and a psychiatrist. They say he uses LSD a great deal. His clinic is as expensive as any in Paris, but he gives the most scandalous parties there too.'

'What's that?' said Byrd. 'Explain.'

'One hears stories,' said Jean. He smiled in embarrassment and wanted to say no more, but Byrd made an impatient movement with his hand, so he continued. 'Stories of gambling parties, of highly placed men who have got into financial trouble and found themselves . . .' he paused '. . . in the bath.'

'Does that mean dead?'

'It means "in trouble", idiom,' explained Byrd to me in English.

'One or two important men took their own lives,' said Jean. 'Some said they were in debt.'

'Damned fools,' said Byrd. 'That's the sort of fellows in charge of things today, no stamina, no fibre; and that fellow Datt is a party to it, eh? Just as I thought. Oh well, chaps won't be told today. Experience better bought than taught they say. One more sherry and we'll go to dinner. What say to La Coupole? It's one of the few places still open where we don't have to reserve.'

Annie the model reappeared in a simple green shirt-waist dress. She kissed Jean-Paul in a familiar way and said good evening to each of us.

'Early in the morning,' Byrd said as he paid her. She nodded and smiled.

'An attractive girl,' Jean-Paul said after she had gone.

'Yes,' I said.

'Poor child,' said Byrd. 'It's a hard town for a young girl without money.'

I'd noticed her expensive crocodile handbag and Charles Jourdan shoes, but I didn't comment.

'Want to go to an art show opening Friday? Free champagne.' Jean-Paul produced half a dozen gold-printed invitations, gave one to me and put one on Byrd's easel.

'Yes, we'll go to that,' said Byrd; he was pleased to be organizing us. 'Are you in your fine motor, Jean?' Byrd asked.

Jean nodded.

Jean's car was a white Mercedes convertible. We drove down the Champs with the roof down. We wined and dined well and Jean-Paul plagued us with questions like

14

do the Americans drink Coca-Cola because it's good for their livers.

It was nearly one A.M. when Jean dropped Byrd at the studio. He insisted upon driving me back to my room over Le Petit Légionnaire. 'I am especially glad you came tonight,' he said. 'Byrd thinks that he is the only serious painter in Paris, but there are many of us who work equally hard in our own way.'

'Being in the navy,' I said, 'is probably not the best of training for a painter.'

'There is no training for a painter. No more than there is training for life. A man makes as profound a statement as he is able. Byrd is a sincere man with a thirst for knowledge of painting and an aptitude for its skills. Already his work is attracting serious interest here in Paris and a reputation in Paris will carry you anywhere in the world.'

I sat there for a moment nodding, then I opened the door of the Mercedes and got out. 'Thanks for the ride.'

Jean-Paul leaned across the seat, offered me his card and shook my hand. 'Phone me,' he said, and – without letting go of my hand – added, 'If you want to go to the house in the Avenue Foch I can arrange that too. I'm not sure I can recommend it, but if you have money to lose I'll introduce you. I am a close friend of the Count; last week I took the Prince of Besacoron there – he is another very good friend of mine.'

'Thanks,' I said, taking the card. He stabbed the accelerator and the motor growled. He winked and said, 'But no recriminations afterward.'

'No,' I agreed. The Mercedes slid forward.

I watched the white car turn on to the Avenue with enough momentum to make the tyres howl. The Petit Légionnaire was closed. I let myself in by the side entrance. Datt and my landlord were still sitting at the same table as they had been that afternoon. They were still playing Monopoly. Datt was reading from his Community Chest card, '*Allez en prison. Avancez tout droit en prison. Ne passez pas par la case "Départ". Ne recevez pas Frs 20.000.*' My landlord laughed, so did M. Datt.

'What will your patients say?' said my landlord.

'They are very understanding,' said Datt; he seemed to take the whole game seriously. Perhaps he got more out of it that way.

I tiptoed upstairs. I could see right across Paris. Through the dark city the red neon arteries of the tourist industry flowed from Pigalle through Montmartre to Boul. Mich., Paris's great self-inflicted wound.

Joe chirped. I read Jean's card. '"Jean-Paul Pascal, artist painter". And good friend to princes,' I said. Joe nodded.

# 4

Two nights later I was invited to join the Monopoly game. I bought hotels in rue Lecourbe and paid rent at the Gare du Nord. Old Datt pedantically handled the toy money and told us why we went broke.

When only Datt remained solvent he pushed back his chair and nodded sagely as he replaced the pieces of wood and paper in the box. If you were buying old men, then Datt would have come in a box marked White, Large and Bald. Behind his tinted spectacles his eyes were moist and his lips soft and dark like a girl's, or perhaps they only seemed dark against the clear white skin of his face. His head was a shiny dome and his white hair soft and wispy like mist around a mountain top. He didn't smile much, but he was a genial man, although a little fussy in his mannerisms as people of either sex become when they live alone.

Madame Tastevin had, upon her insolvency, departed to the kitchen to prepare supper.

I offered my cigarettes to Datt and to my landlord. Tastevin took one, but Datt declined with a theatrical gesture. 'There seems no sense in it,' he proclaimed, and again did that movement of the hand that looked like he was blessing a multitude at Benares. His voice was an upper-class voice, not because of his vocabulary or because he got his conjugations right but because he sang his words in the style of the Comédie Française, stressing a word musically and then dropping the rest of the sentence like a half-smoked Gauloise. 'No sense in it,' he repeated.

'Pleasure,' said Tastevin, puffing away. 'Not sense.'
His voice was like a rusty lawn-mower.

'The pursuit of pleasure,' said Datt, 'is a pitfall-studded route.' He removed the rimless spectacles and looked up at me blinking.

'You speak from experience?' I asked.

'I've done everything,' said Datt. 'Some things twice. I've lived in eight different countries in four continents. I've been a beggar and I've been a thief. I've been happy and sad, rich and poor, master and manservant.'

'And the secret of happiness,' mocked Tastevin, 'is to refrain from smoking?'

'The secret of happiness,' Datt corrected, 'is to refrain from wishing to.'

'If that's the way you feel,' said Tastevin, 'why do you come to my restaurant almost every day?'

At that moment Madame Tastevin came in with a tray holding a coffee jug and plates of cold chicken and terrine of hare.

'There's your reason for not smoking,' said Datt. 'I would never let tobacco mar the taste of the food here.' Madame Tastevin purred with delight. 'I sometimes think my life is too perfect. I enjoy my work and never wish to do less of it, and I eat your wonderful food. What a perfect life.'

'That's self-indulgent,' said Tastevin.

'Perhaps it is – so what? Isn't your life self-indulgent? You could make far more money working in one of the three-star restaurants but you spend your life running this small one – one might almost say for your friends.'

'I suppose that's true,' said Tastevin. 'I enjoy cooking, and my customers appreciate my work I think.'

'Quite so. You are a sensible man. It's madness to go every day to work at something you do not enjoy.'

'But suppose,' asked Madame Tastevin, 'that such a

18

job brought us a lot of money that would enable him to retire and then do as he wishes?'

'Madame,' said Datt. His voice took on that portentous, melodious quality that narrators on arty French films employ. 'Madame Tastevin,' he said again, 'there is a cave in Kashmir – Amarnath cave – the most sacred spot on earth to a worshipper of the Hindu god Siva. The pilgrims who journey there are old; sometimes sick too. Many of them die on the high passes, their tiny tents swept away by the sudden rainstorms. Their relatives do not weep. To them this does not matter; even the arrival – which must always be on a night of full moon – is not more vital than the journey. Many know they will never arrive. It is the journey that is holy, and so it is to Existentialists: life is more important than death. Whatever they do, men are too anxious to get to the end. The sex act, eating a fine meal, playing golf, there is a temptation to rush, gobble or run. That is foolish, for one should move at a relaxed pace through life doing the work one enjoys instead of chasing ambition helter-skelter, pursuing one's ultimate death.'

Tastevin nodded sagely and I stopped gobbling the cold chicken. Datt tucked a napkin in his collar and savoured a little terrine, pursing his lips and remarking on the salt content. When he had finished he turned to me. 'You have a telephone, I believe,' he said, and without waiting for my reply was already on his feet and moving towards the door.

'By all means use it,' I told him and by a burst of speed was able to get upstairs before him. Joey blinked in the sudden electric light. Datt dialled a number and said 'Hello, I am at the Petit Légionnaire and I am ready for the car in about five minutes.' He hung up. Datt came over to where I was standing with Joey. 'It's my belief,' said Datt, 'that you are making inquiries about me.'

I didn't answer.

19

'It would be a fruitless task.'

'Why?'

'Because no matter what you discover it will not harm me.'

'The art of Zen in clandestine behaviour?'

Datt smiled. 'The art of Zen in having influential friends,' he said.

I didn't answer him. I pushed open the shutters and there was Paris. Warm streets, a policeman, two lovers, four cats, fifty dented *deux-chevaux* cars and a pavement full of garbage bins. The life of Paris centres on its streets; its inhabitants sit at the windows gazing down upon people as they buy, sell, thieve, drive, fight, eat, chat, posture, cheat or merely stand looking, upon the streets of Paris. Its violence too centres upon the streets and outside the public baths the previous night M. Picard, who owned the laundry, was robbed and knifed. He died twitching his own blood into ugly splashes that could still be seen upon the torn election posters flapping from the ancient shutters.

A black Daimler came down the road and stopped with a tiny squeak.

'Thank you for the use of your telephone,' said Datt. At the door he turned. 'Next week I should like to talk with you again,' he said. 'You must tell me what you are curious about.'

'Any time,' I agreed. 'Tomorrow if you wish.'

Datt shook his head. 'Next week will be soon enough.'

'As you wish.'

'Yes,' said Datt. He walked out without saying good night.

After Datt left Joey took a brief swing. I checked that the documents were still in their hiding-place. Perhaps I should have given them to Datt a few minutes before, but I looked forward to seeing him again next week. 'It seems to me, Joe,' I said, 'that we are the only people in town who don't have powerful friends.' I put the cover on him before he could answer.

# 5

Faubourg St Honoré, seven thirty P.M. Friday. The tiny art gallery was bursting at the seams. Champagne, free champagne, was spilling over high suede boots and broken sandals. I had spent twenty-five minutes prising triangular pieces of smoked salmon away from circular pieces of toast, which is not a rewarding experience for a fully grown human male. Byrd was talking to Jean-Paul and rapping at one of the abstract panels. I edged towards them, but a young woman with green eye-shadow grabbed my arm. 'Where's the artist?' she asked. 'Someone's interested in "Creature who fears the machine" and I don't know if it's one hundred thousand francs or fifty.' I turned to her but she had grabbed someone else already. Most of my champagne was lost by the time I got to Byrd and Jean-Paul.

'There's some terrible people here,' said Jean-Paul.

'As long as they don't start playing that dashed rock-and-roll music again,' said Byrd.

'Were they doing that?' I asked.

Byrd nodded. 'Can't stand it. Sorry and all that, but can't stand it.'

The woman with green eye-shadow waved across a sea of shoulders, then cupped her mouth and yelled to me. 'They have broken one of the gold chairs,' she said. 'Does it matter?'

I couldn't stand her being so worried. 'Don't worry,' I called. She nodded and smiled in relief.

'What's going on?' said Jean-Paul. 'Do you own this gallery?'

'Give me time,' I said, 'and maybe I'll give you a one-man show.'

Jean-Paul smiled to show that he knew it was a joke, but Byrd looked up suddenly. 'Look here, Jean-Paul,' he said severely, 'a one-man show would be fatal for you right now. You are in no way prepared. You need time, my boy, time. Walk before you run.' Byrd turned to me. 'Walk before you run, that's right, isn't it?'

'No,' I said. 'Any mother will tell you that most kids can run before they can walk; it's walking that's difficult.'

Jean-Paul winked at me and said, 'I must decline, but thank you anyway.'

Byrd said, 'He's not ready. You gallery chappies will just have to wait. Don't rush these young artists. It's not fair. Not fair to them.'

I was just going to straighten things out when a short thickset Frenchman with a Légion d'Honneur in his buttonhole came up and began to talk to Byrd.

'Let me introduce you,' said Byrd. He wouldn't tolerate informality. 'This is Chief Inspector Loiseau. Policeman. I went through a lot of the war with his brother.'

We shook hands, and then Loiseau shook hands with Jean-Paul, although neither of them showed a great deal of enthusiasm for the ritual.

The French, more particularly the men, have developed a characteristic mouth that enables them to deal with their language. The English use their pointed and dexterous tongues, and their mouths become pinched and close. The French use their lips and a Frenchman's mouth becomes loose and his lips jut forward. The cheeks sink a little to help this and a French face takes on a lean look, back-sloping like an old-fashioned coal-scuttle. Loiseau had just such a face.

'What's a policeman doing at an art show?' asked Byrd.

'We policemen are not uncultured oafs,' said Loiseau

with a smile. 'In our off-duty hours we have even been known to drink alcohol.'

'You are never off duty,' said Byrd. 'What is it? Expecting someone to make off with the champagne buckets?' Loiseau smiled slyly. A waiter nearly passed us with a tray of champagne.

'One might ask what you are doing here?' said Loiseau to Byrd. 'I wouldn't think this was your sort of art.' He tapped one of the large panels. It was a highly finished nude, contorted in pose, the skin shiny as though made from polished plastic. In the background there were strange pieces of surrealism, most of them with obvious Freudian connotations.

'The snake and the egg are well drawn,' said Byrd. 'The girl's a damn poor show though.'

'The foot is out of drawing,' said Jean-Paul. 'It's not well observed.'

'A girl that could do that would have to be a cripple,' said Byrd.

Still more people crowded into the room and we were being pushed closer and closer to the wall.

Loiseau smiled. 'But a *poule* that could get into that position would earn a fortune on the rue Godot de Mauroy,' said the Chief Inspector.

Loiseau spoke just like any police officer. You can easily recognize them by their speech, to which a lifetime of giving evidence imparts a special clarity. The facts are arranged before the conclusions just like a written report, and certain important words – bus route numbers and road names – are given emphasis so that even young constables can remember them.

Byrd turned back to Jean-Paul: he was anxious to discuss the painting. 'You've got to hand it to him though, the *trompe l'œil* technique is superb, the tiny brushwork. Look at the way the Coca-Cola bottle is done.'

23

'He's copied that from a photo,' said Jean-Paul. Byrd bent down for a close look.

'Damn me! The rotten little swine!' said Byrd. 'It *is* a bloody photo. It's stuck on. Look at that!' He picked at the corner of the bottle and then appealed to the people around him. 'Look at that, it's been cut from a coloured advert.' He applied himself to other parts of the painting. 'The typewriter too, and the girl . . .'

'Stop picking at that nipple,' said the woman with green eye-shadow. 'If you touch the paintings once more you'll be asked to leave.' She turned to me. 'How can you stand there and let them do it? If the artist saw them he'd go mad.'

'Gone mad already,' said Byrd curtly. 'Thinking chaps are going to pay money for bits cut out of picture books.'

'It's quite legitimate,' said Jean-Paul. 'It's an *objet trouvé* . . .'

'Rot,' said Byrd. 'An *objet trouvé* is a piece of driftwood or a fine stone – it's something in which an artist has found and seen otherwise unnoticed beauty. How can an advert be found? How can you find an advert – the damned things are pushed under your noses every way you look, more's the pity.'

'But the artist must have freedom to . . .'

'Artist?' snorted Byrd. 'Damned fraud. Damned rotten little swine.'

A man in evening dress with three ballpoint pens in his breast pocket turned round. 'I haven't noticed you decline any champagne,' he said to Byrd. He used the intimate *tu*. Although it was a common form of address among the young arty set, his use of it to Byrd was offensive.

'What I had,' interrupted Jean-Paul – he paused before delivering the insult – 'was Sauternes with Alka Seltzer.'

The man in the dinner suit leaned across to grab at

him, but Chief Inspector Loiseau interposed himself and got a slight blow on the arm.

'A thousand apologies, Chief Inspector,' said the man in the dinner suit.

'Nothing,' said Loiseau. 'I should have looked where I was going.'

Jean-Paul was pushing Byrd towards the door, but they were moving very slowly. The man in the dinner suit leaned across to the woman with the green eye-shadow and said loudly, 'They mean no harm, they are drunk, but make sure they leave immediately.' He looked back towards Loiseau to see if his profound understanding of human nature was registering. '*He's* with them,' the woman said, nodding at me. 'I thought he was from the insurance company when he first came.' I heard Byrd say, 'I will not take it back; he's a rotten little swine.'

'Perhaps,' said dinner-jacket tactfully, 'you would be kind enough to make sure that your friends come to no harm in the street.'

I said, 'If they get out of here in one piece they can take their own chances in the street.'

'Since you can't take a hint,' said dinner-jacket, 'let me make it clear . . .'

'He's with me,' said Loiseau.

The man shied. 'Chief Inspector,' said dinner-jacket, 'I am desolated.'

'We are leaving anyway,' said Loiseau, nodding to me. Dinner-jacket smiled and turned back to the woman with green eye-shadow.

'You go where you like,' I said. 'I'm staying right here.'

Dinner-jacket swivelled back like a glove puppet.

Loiseau put a hand on my arm. 'I thought you wanted to talk about getting your *carte de séjour* from the Prefecture.'

'I'm having no trouble getting my *carte de séjour*,' I said.

'Exactly,' said Loiseau and moved through the crowd towards the door. I followed.

Near the entrance there was a table containing a book of newspaper clippings and catalogues. The woman with green eye-shadow called to us. She offered Loiseau her hand and then reached out to me. She held the wrist limp as women do when they half expect a man to kiss the back of their hand. 'Please sign the visitors' book,' she said.

Loiseau bent over the book and wrote in neat neurotic writing 'Claude Loiseau'; under comments he wrote 'stimulating'. The woman swivelled the book to me. I wrote my name and under comments I wrote what I always write when I don't know what to say – 'uncompromising'.

The woman nodded. 'And your address,' she said.

I was about to point out that no one else had written their address in the book, but when a shapely young woman asks for my address I'm not the man to be secretive. I wrote it: 'c/o Petit Légionnaire, rue St Ferdinand, 17ième.'

The woman smiled to Loiseau in a familiar way. She said, 'I know the Chief Inspector's address: Criminal Investigation Department, Sûreté Nationale, rue des Saussaies.'[1]

---

[1] France has a particularly complex police system. The Sûreté Nationale is the police system for all France that operates directly for the Minister of the Interior in the Ministry at rue des Saussaies. At Quai des Orfèvres there is the Prefecture which does the same job for Paris. There is also the Gendarmerie – recognized by their khaki coats in summer – who police the whole of France under the orders of the Army Ministry and are, in effect, soldiers. As well as this there are special groups – Gardes Mobiles and CRS (Compagnie Républicaine de Sécurité) companies – which are highly mobile and have violent striking power. Loiseau worked for the first-named, the Sûreté

Loiseau's office had that cramped, melancholy atmosphere that policemen relish. There were two small silver pots for the shooting team that Loiseau had led to victory in 1959 and several group photos – one showed Loiseau in army uniform standing in front of a tank. Loiseau brought a large M 1950 automatic from his waist and put it into a drawer. 'I'm going to get something smaller,' he said. 'This is ruining my suits.' He locked the drawer carefully and then went through the other drawers of his desk, riffling through the contents and slamming them closed until he laid a dossier on his blotter.

'This is your dossier,' said Loiseau. He held up a print of the photo that appears on my *carte de séjour*. '"Occupation,"' he read, '"travel agency director".' He looked up at me and I nodded. 'That's a good job?'

'It suits me,' I said.

'It would suit me', said Loiseau. 'Eight hundred new francs each week and you spend most of your time amusing yourself.'

'There's a revived interest in leisure,' I said.

'I hadn't noticed any decline among the people who work for me.' He pushed his Gauloises towards me. We lit up and looked at each other. Loiseau was about fifty years old. Short muscular body with big shoulders. His face was pitted with tiny scars and part of his left ear was missing. His hair was pure white and very short. He had plenty of energy but not so much that he was prepared to waste any. He hung his jacket on his chair back and rolled up his shirtsleeves very neatly. He didn't look like a policeman now, more like a paratroop colonel planning a coup.

---

Nationale, who as well as all standard police work also attend to counter-espionage, economic espionage (unions and potential strikes etc.), frontier policing and gaming. The sixty CRS units are also controlled by one of the directorates (Public Security) of the Sûreté Nationale.

'You are making inquiries about Monsieur Datt's clinic on the Avenue Foch.'

'Everyone keeps telling me that.'

'Who for?'

I said, 'I don't know about that place, and I don't want to know about it.'

'I'm treating you like an adult,' said Loiseau. 'If you prefer to be treated like a spotty-faced j.v. then we can do that too.'

'What's the question again?'

'I'd like to know who you are working for. However, it would take a couple of hours in the hen cage to get that out of you. So for the time being I'll tell you this: I am interested in that house and I don't want you to even come downwind of it. Stay well away. Tell whoever you are working for that the house in Avenue Foch is going to remain a little secret of Chief Inspector Loiseau.' He paused, wondering how much more to tell me. 'There are powerful interests involved. Violent groups are engaged in a struggle for criminal power.'

'Why do you tell me that?'

'I thought that you should know.' He gave a Gallic shrug.

'Why?'

'Don't you understand? These men are dangerous.'

'Then why aren't you dragging them into your office instead of me?'

'Oh, they are too clever for us. Also they have well-placed friends who protect them. It's only when the friends fail that they resort to . . . coercion, blackmail, killing even. But always skilfully.'

'They say it's better to know the judge than to know the law.'

'Who says that?'

'I heard it somewhere.'

'You're an eavesdropper,' said Loiseau.

28

'I am,' I said. 'And a damned good one.'

'It sounds as though you like it,' said Loiseau grimly.

'It's my favourite indoor sport. Dynamic and yet sedentary; a game of skill with an element of chance. No season, no special equipment . . .'

'Don't be so clever,' he said sadly. 'This is a political matter. Do you know what that means?'

'No. I don't know what that means.'

'It means that you might well spend one morning next week being lifted out of some quiet backwater of the St Martin canal and travelling down to the Medico-Legal Institute[2] where the boys in butchers' aprons and rubber boots live. They'll take an inventory of what they find in your pockets, send your clothes to the Poor Law Administration Office, put a numbered armband on you, freeze you to eight degrees centigrade and put you in a rack with two other foolish lads. The superintendent will phone me and I'll have to go along and identify you. I'll hate doing that because at this time of year there are clouds of flies as large as bats and a smell that reaches to Austerlitz Station.' He paused. 'And we won't even investigate the affair. Be sure you understand.'

I said, 'I understand all right. I've become an expert at recognizing threats no matter how veiled they are. But before you give a couple of cops tape measures and labels and maps of the St Martin canal, make sure you choose men that your department doesn't find indispensable.'

'Alas, you have misunderstood,' said Loiseau's mouth, but his eyes didn't say that. He stared. 'We'll leave it like that, but . . .'

'Just leave it like that,' I interrupted. 'You tell your cops to carry the capes with the lead-shot hems and I'll wear my water-wings.'

---

[2] An old building on a prison site adjacent to Mazas Square near Austerlitz Station. It is used as a mortuary.

Loiseau allowed his face to become as friendly as it could become.

'I don't know where you fit into Monsieur Datt's clinic, but until I do know I'll be watching you very closely. If it's a political affair, then let the political departments request information. There's no point in us being at each other's throat. Agreed?'

'Agreed.'

'In the next few few days you might be in contact with people who claim to be acting for me. Don't believe them. Anything you want to know, come back to me directly. I'm 22.22.[3] If you can't reach me here then this office will know where I am. Tell the operator that "*Un sourire est différent d'un rire*".'

'Agreed,' I said. The French still use those silly code words that are impossible to use if you are being overheard.

'One last thing,' said Loiseau. 'I can see that no advice, however well meant, can register with you, so let me add that, should you tackle these men and come off best . . .' he looked up to be sure that I was listening, '. . . then I will personally guarantee that you'll *manger les haricots* for five years.'

'Charged with . . .?'

'Giving Chief Inspector Loiseau trouble beyond his normal duties.'

'You might be going further than your authority permits,' I said, trying to give the impression that I too might have important friends.

Loiseau smiled. 'Of course I am. I have gained my present powerful position by always taking ten per cent more authority than I am given.' He lifted the phone and jangled the receiver rest so that its bell tinkled in the outer office. It must have been a prearranged signal

---

[3] Senior police officers in France are assigned their own private lines.

because his assistant came quickly. Loiseau nodded to indicate the meeting was over.

'Goodbye,' he said. 'It was good to see you again.'

'Again?'

'NATO conference on falsification of cargo manifests, held in Bonn, April 1956. You represented BAOR, if I remember rightly.'

'You talk in endless riddles,' I said. 'I've never been in Bonn.'

'You are a glib fellow,' said Loiseau. 'Another ten minutes and you'd convince me I'd never been there.' He turned to the assistant who was waiting to conduct me downstairs. 'Count the fire extinguishers after he's left,' said Loiseau. 'And on no account shake hands with him; you might find yourself being thrown into the Faubourg St Honoré.'

Loiseau's assistant took me down to the door. He was a spotty-faced boy with circular metal-framed spectacles that bit deep into his features like pennies that had grown into the trunk of a tree. 'Goodbye,' I said as I left him, and gave him a brief smile. He looked through me, nodding to the policeman on sentry who eased the machine gun on his shoulder. Abandoning the *entente cordiale* I walked towards the Faubourg St Honoré looking for a taxi. From the gratings in the road there came the sound of a Métro train, its clatter muffled by four huddled *clochards* anxious for the warmth of the sour subterranean air. One of them came half-awake, troubled by a bad dream. He yelled and then mumbled.

On the corner an E-type was parked. As I turned the corner the headlights flashed and it moved towards me. I stood well back as the door swung open. A woman's voice said, 'Jump in.'

'Not right now,' I said.

# 6

Maria Chauvet was thirty-two years old. She had kept
her looks, her gentleness, her figure, her sexual optimism,
her respect for men's cleverness, her domestication. She
had lost her girlhood friends, her shyness, her literary
aspirations, her obsession with clothes and her husband.
It was a fair swop, she decided. Time had given her a
greater measure of independence. She looked around the
art gallery without seeing even one person that she really
desired to see again. And yet they were her people: the
ones she had known since her early twenties, the people
who shared her tastes in cinema, travel, sport and books.
Now she no longer wished to hear their opinions about
the things she enjoyed and she only slightly wished to
hear their opinions about the things she hated. The
paintings here were awful, they didn't even show a
childish exuberance; they were old, jaded and sad. She
hated things that were too real. Ageing was real; as things
grew older they became more real, and although age
wasn't something she dreaded she didn't want to hurry in
that direction.

Maria hoped that Loiseau wasn't going to be violent
with the Englishman that he had taken away. Ten years
ago she would have said something to Loiseau, but now
she had learned discretion, and discretion had become
more and more vital in Paris. So had violence, come to
that. Maria concentrated on what the artist was saying to
her. '. . . the relationships between the spirit of man and
the material things with which he surrounds himself . . .'

Maria had a slight feeling of claustrophobia; she also
had a headache. She should take an aspirin, and yet she

didn't, even though she knew it would relieve the pain. As a child she had complained of pain and her mother had said that a woman's life is accompanied by constant pain. That's what it's like to be a woman, her mother had said, to know an ache or a pain all day, every day. Her mother had found some sort of stoic satisfaction in that statement, but the prospect had terrified Maria. It still terrified her and she was determined to disbelieve it. She tried to disregard all pains, as though by acknowledging them she might confess her feminine frailty. She wouldn't take an aspirin.

She thought of her ten-year-old son. He was living with her mother in Flanders. It was not good for the child to spend a lot of time with elderly people. It was just a temporary measure and yet all the time he was there she felt vaguely guilty about going out to dinner or the cinema, or even evenings like this.

'Take that painting near the door,' said the artist. '"Holocaust quo vadis?" There you have the vulture that represents the ethereal and . . .'

Maria had had enough of him. He was a ridiculous fool; she decided to leave. The crowd had become more static now and that always increased her claustrophobia, as did people in the Métro standing motionless. She looked at his flabby face and his eyes, greedy and scavenging for admiration among this crowd who admired only themselves. 'I'm going now,' she said. 'I'm sure the show will be a big success.'

'Wait a moment,' he called, but she had timed her escape to coincide with a gap in the crush and she was through the emergency exit, across the *cour* and away. He didn't follow her. He probably already had his eye on some other woman who could become interested in art for a couple of weeks.

Maria loved her car, not sinfully, but proudly. She looked after it and drove it well. It wasn't far to the rue

33

des Saussaies. She positioned the car by the side of the Ministry of the Interior. That was the exit they used at night. She hoped Loiseau wouldn't keep him there too long. This area near the Élysée Palace was alive with patrols and huge Berliot buses, full of armed cops, the motors running all night in spite of the price of petrol. They wouldn't do anything to her, of course, but their presence made her uncomfortable. She looked at her wristwatch. Fifteen minutes the Englishman had been there. Now, the sentry was looking back into the courtyard. This must be him. She flashed the headlights of the E-type. Exactly on time; just as Loiseau had told her.

# 7

The woman laughed. It was a pleasant musical laugh. She said, 'Not in an E-type. Surely no whore solicits from an E-type. Is it a girl's car?' It was the woman from the art gallery.

'Where I come from,' I said, 'they call them hairdressers' cars.'

She laughed. I had a feeling that she had enjoyed my mistaking her for one of the motorized prostitutes that prowled this district. I got in alongside her and she drove past the Ministry of the Interior and out on to the Malesherbes. She said,

'I hope Loiseau didn't give you a bad time.'

'My resident's card was out of date.'

'Poof!' she scoffed. 'Do you think I'm a fool? You'd be at the Prefecture if that was the case, not the Ministry of the Interior.'

'So what do *you* think he wanted?'

She wrinkled her nose. 'Who can tell? Jean-Paul said you'd been asking questions about the clinic on the Avenue Foch.'

'Suppose I told you I wish I'd never heard of the Avenue Foch?'

She put her foot down and I watched the speedometer spin. There was a screech of tyres as she turned on to the Boulevard Haussmann. 'I'd believe you,' she said. 'I wish I'd never heard of it.'

I studied her. She was no longer a girl – perhaps about thirty – dark hair and dark eyes; carefully applied make-up; her clothes were like the car, not brand-new but of good quality. Something in her relaxed manner told me that she had been married and something in her overt friendliness told me she no longer was. She came into the Étoile without losing speed and entered the whirl of traffic effortlessly. She flashed the lights at a taxi that was on a collision course and he sheered away. In the Avenue Foch she turned into a driveway. The gates opened.

'Here we are,' she said. 'Let's take a look.'

The house was large and stood back in its own piece of ground. At dusk the French shutter themselves tightly against the night. This gaunt house was no exception.

Near to, the cracks in the plaster showed like wrinkles in a face carelessly made-up. The traffic was pounding down the Avenue Foch but that was over the garden wall and far away.

'So this is the house on the Avenue Foch,' I said.

'Yes,' said the girl.

The big gates closed behind us. A man with a flashlight came out of the shadows. He had a small mongrel dog on a chain.

'Go ahead,' said the man. He waved an arm without exerting himself. I guessed that the man was a one-time cop. They are the only people who can stand motionless without loitering. The dog was a German Shepherd in disguise.

We drove down a concrete ramp into a large underground garage. There were about twenty cars there of various expensive foreign makes: Ford GTs, Ferraris, a Bentley convertible. A man standing near the lift called, 'Leave the keys in.'

Maria slipped off her soft driving shoes and put on a pair of evening shoes. 'Stay close,' she said quietly.

I patted her gently. 'That's close enough,' she said.

When we got out of the lift on the ground floor, everything seemed red plush and cut glass – *un décor maison-fin-de-siècle* – and all of it was tinkling: the

36

laughter, the medals, the ice cubes, the coins, the chandeliers. The main lighting came from ornate gas lamps
with pink glass shades; there were huge mirrors and
Chinese vases on plinths. Girls in long evening dresses
were seated decorously on the wide sweep of the staircase,
and in an alcove a barman was pouring drinks as fast as
he could work. It was a very fancy affair; it dididn't have
the Republican Guard in polished helmets lining the
staircase with drawn sabres, but you had the feeling that
they'd wanted to come.

Maria leaned across and took two glasses of champagne
and some biscuits heaped with caviare. One of the men
said, 'Haven't seen you for ages.' Maria nodded without
much regret. The man said, 'You should have been in
there tonight. One of them was nearly killed. He's hurt;
badly hurt.'

Maria nodded. Behind me I heard a woman say, 'He
must have been in agony. He wouldn't have screamed
like that unless he had been in agony.'

'They always do that, it doesn't mean a thing.'

'I can tell a real scream from a fake one,' said the
woman.

'How?'

'A real scream has no music, it slurs, it . . . screeches.
It's ugly.'

"The cuisine,' said a voice behind me, 'can be superb;
the very finely sliced smoked pork served hot, cold citrus
fruits divided in half, bowls of strange hot grains with
cream upon it. And those large eggs that they have here
in Europe, skilfully fried crisp on the outside and yet the
yolk remains almost raw. Sometimes smoked fish of
various kinds.' I turned to face them. The speaker was a
middle-aged Chinese in evening dress. He had been
speaking to a fellow countryman and as he caught my eye
he said, 'I am explaining to my colleague the fine Anglo-
Saxon breakfast that I always enjoy so much.'

37

'This is Monsieur Kuang-t'ien,' said Maria, introducing us.

'And you, Maria, are exquisite this evening,' said M. Kuang-t'ien. He spoke a few lines of soft Mandarin.

'What's that?' asked Maria.

'It is a poem by Shao Hsŭn-mei, a poet and essayist who admired very much the poets of the West. Your dress reminded me of it.'

'Say it in French,' said Maria.

'It is indelicate, in parts.' He smiled apologetically and began to recite softly.

> 'Ah, lusty May is again burning,
> A sin is born of a virgin's kiss;
> Sweet tears tempt me, always tempt me
> To feel between her breasts with my lips.
>
> Here life is as eternal as death,
> As the trembling happiness on a wedding night;
> If she is not a rose, a rose all white,
> Then she must be redder than the red of blood.'

Maria laughed. 'I thought you were going to say "she must be redder than the Chinese People's Republic".'

'Ah. Is not possible,' said M. Kuang-t'ien, and laughed gently.

Maria steered me away from the two Chinese. 'We'll see you later,' she called over her shoulder. 'He gives me the creeps,' she whispered.

'Why?'

'"Sweet tears", "if she isn't white she'll be red with blood", death "between breasts".' She shook away the thought of it. 'He has a sick sadistic streak in him that frightens me.'

A man came pushing through the crowd. 'Who's your friend?' he asked Maria.

'An Englishman,' said Maria. 'An old friend,' she added untruthfully.

38

'He looks all right,' said the man approvingly. 'But I wished to see you in those high patent shoes.' He made a clicking sound and laughed, but Maria didn't. All around us the guests were talking excitedly and drinking. 'Excellent,' said a voice I recognized. It was M. Datt. He smiled at Maria. Datt was dressed in a dark jacket, striped trousers and black tie. He looked remarkably calm; unlike so many of his guests, his brow was not flushed nor his collar wrinkled. 'Are you going in?' he asked Maria. He looked at his pocket watch. 'They will begin in two minutes.'

'I don't think so,' said Maria.

'Of course you are,' said Datt. 'You know you will enjoy it.'

'Not tonight,' said Maria.

'Nonsense,' said Datt gently. 'Three more bouts. One of them is a gigantic Negro. A splendid figure of a man with gigantic hands.'

Datt lifted one of his own hands to demonstrate, but his eyes watched Maria very closely. She became agitated under his gaze and I felt her grip my hand tightly as though in fear. A buzzer sounded and people finished their drinks and moved towards the rear door.

Datt put his hands on our shoulders and moved us the way the crowd went. As we reached the large double doors I saw into the salon. A wrestling ring was set up in the centre and around it were folding chairs formed up in rows. The salon itself was a magnificent room with golden caryatids, a decorated ceiling, enormous mirrors, fine tapestry and a rich red carpet. As the spectators settled the chandeliers began to dim. The atmosphere was expectant.

'Take a seat, Maria,' said Datt. 'It will be a fine fight; lots of blood.' Maria's palm was moist in mine.

'Don't be awful,' said Maria, but she let go of my hand and moved towards the seats.

'Sit with Jean-Paul,' said Datt. 'I want to speak with your friend.'

Maria's hand trembled. I looked around and saw Jean-Paul for the first time. He was seated alone. 'Go with Jean-Paul,' said Datt gently.

Jean-Paul saw us, he smiled. 'I'll sit with Jean-Paul,' said Maria to me.

'Agreed,' I said. By the time she was seated, the first two wrestlers were circling each other. One was an Algerian I would guess, the other had bright dyed yellow hair. The man with straw hair lunged forward. The Algerian slid to one side, caught him on the hip and butted him heavily with the top of his head. The crack of head meeting chin was followed by the sharp intake of breath by the audience. On the far side of the room there was a nervous titter of laughter. The mirrored walls showed the wrestlers repeated all around the room. The central light threw heavy shadows under their chins and buttocks, and their legs, painted dark with shadow, emerged into the light as they circled again looking for an opening. Hanging in each corner of the room there was a TV camera linked by landline to monitor screens some distance away. The screens were showing the recorded image.

It was evident that the monitor screens were playing recordings, for the pictures were not clear and the action on the screen took place a few seconds later than the actual fighting. Because of this time-lag between recording and playing back the audience were able to swing their eyes to the monitors each time there was an attack and see it take place again on the screen.

'Come upstairs,' said Datt.

'Very well.' There was a crash; they were on the mat and the fair man was in a leg lock. His face was contorted. Datt spoke without turning to look. 'This fighting is rehearsed. The fair-haired man will win after being nearly throttled in the final round.'

I followed him up the magnificent staircase to the first floor. There was a locked door. Clinic. Private. He unlocked the door and ushered me through. An old woman was standing in the corner. I wondered if I was interrupting one of Datt's interminable games of Monopoly.

'You were to come next week,' said Datt.

'Yes he was,' said the old woman. She smoothed her apron over her hips like a self-conscious maidservant.

'Next week would have been better,' said Datt.

'That's true. Next week – without the party – would have been better,' she agreed.

I said, 'Why is everyone speaking in the past tense?'

The door opened and two young men came in. They were wearing blue jeans and matching shirts. One of them was unshaven.

'What's going on now?' I asked.

'The footmen,' said Datt. 'Jules on the left. Albert on the right. They are here to see fair play. Right?' They nodded without smiling. Datt turned to me. 'Just lie down on the couch.'

'No.'

'What?'

'I said no I won't lie down on the couch.'

Datt tutted. He was a little put out. There wasn't any mockery or sadism in the tutting. 'There are four of us here,' he explained. 'We are not asking you to do anything unreasonable, are we? Please lie down on the couch.'

I backed towards the side table. Jules came at me and Albert was edging around to my left side. I came back until the edge of the table was biting my right hip so I knew exactly how my body was placed in relation to it. I watched their feet. You can tell a lot about a man from the way he places his feet. You can tell the training he

41

has had, whether he will lunge or punch from a stationary position, whether he will pull you or try to provoke you into a forward movement. Jules was still coming on. His hands were flat and extended. About twenty hours of gymnasium karate. Albert had the old *course d'échalotte* look about him. He was used to handling heavyweight, over-confident drunks. Well, he'd find out what I was; yes, I thought: a heavyweight, over-confident drunk. Heavyweight Albert was coming on like a train. A boxer; look at his feet. A crafty boxer who would give you all the fouls; the butts, kidney jabs and back of the head stuff, but he fancied himself as a jab-and-move-around artist. I'd be surprised to see him aim a kick in the groin with any skill. I brought my hands suddenly into sparring position. Yes, his chin tucked in and he danced his weight around on the balls of his feet. 'Fancy your chances, Albert?' I jeered. His eyes narrowed. I wanted him angry. 'Come on soft boy,' I said. 'Bite on a piece of bare knuckle.'

I saw the cunning little Jules out of the corner of my eye. He was smiling. He was coming too, smooth and cool inch by inch, hands flat and trembling for the killer cut.

I made a slight movement to keep them going. If they once relaxed, stood up straight and began to think, they could eat me up.

Heavyweight Albert's hands were moving, foot forward for balance, right hand low and ready for a body punch while Jules chopped at my neck. That was the theory. Surprise for Albert: my metal heelpiece going into his instep. You were expecting a punch in the buffet or a kick in the groin, Albert, so you were surprised when a terrifying pain hit your instep. Difficult for the balancing too. Albert leaned forward to console his poor hurt foot. Second surprise for Albert: under-swung flat hand on the nose; nasty. Jules is coming, cursing Albert for forcing his hand. Jules is forced to meet me head down. I felt the edge of the table against my hip. Jules thinks I'm going to lean into him. Surprise for Jules: I lean back just as he's getting ready to give me a hand edge on the corner of the neck. Second surprise for Jules: I do lean in after all and give him a fine glass paperweight on the earhole at a range of about eighteen inches. The paperweight seems none the worse for it. Now's the chance to make a big mistake. Don't pick up the paperweight. Don't pick up the paperweight. Don't pick up the paperweight. I didn't pick it up. Go for Datt, he's standing he's mobile and he's the one who is mentally the driving force in the room.

Down Datt. He's an old man but don't underrate him. He's large and weighty and he's been around. What's more he'll use anything available; the old maidservant is careful, discriminating, basically not aggressive. Go for Datt. Albert is rolling over and may come up to one side of my range of vision. Jules is motionless. Datt is moving around the desk; so it will have to be a missile. An inkstand, too heavy. A pen-set will fly apart. A vase: unwieldy. An ashtray. I picked it up, Datt was still moving, very slowly now, watching me carefully, his mouth open and white hair disarrayed as though he had been in the scuffle. The ashtray is heavy and perfect. Careful, you don't want to kill him. 'Wait,' Datt says hoarsely. I waited. I waited about ten seconds, just long enough for the woman to come behind me with a candlestick. She was basically not aggressive, the maidservant. I was only unconscious thirty minutes, they told me.

# 8

I was saying 'You are not basically aggressive' as I regained consciousness.

'No,' said the woman as though it was a grave shortcoming. 'It is true.' I couldn't see either of them from where I was full length on my back. She switched the tape recorder on. There was the sudden intimate sound of a girl sobbing. 'I want it recording,' she said, but the sound of the girl became hysterical and she began to scream as though someone was torturing her. 'Switch that damn thing off,' Datt called. It was strange to see him disturbed, he was usually so calm. She turned the volume control the wrong way and the sound of the screams went right through my head and made the floor vibrate.

'The other way,' screamed Datt. The sound abated, but the tape was still revolving and the sound could just be heard; the girl was sobbing again. The desperate sound was made even more helpless by its diminished volume, like someone abandoned or locked out.

'What is it?' asked the maidservant. She shuddered but seemed reluctant to switch off; finally she did so and the reels clicked to a standstill.

'What's it sound like?' said Datt. 'It's a girl sobbing and screaming.'

'My God,' said the maidservant.

'Calm down,' said Datt. 'It's for amateur theatricals. It's just for amateur theatricals,' he said to me.

'I didn't ask you,' I said.

'Well, I'm telling you.' The servant woman turned the reel over and rethreaded it. I felt fully conscious now and

44

I sat up so that I could see across the room. The girl Maria was standing by the door, she had her shoes in her hand and a man's raincoat over her shoulders. She was staring blankly at the wall and looking miserable. There was a boy sitting near the gas fire. He was smoking a small cheroot, biting at the end which had become frayed like a rope end, so that each time he pulled it out of his mouth he twisted his face up to find the segments of leaf and discharge them on the tongue-tip. Datt and the old maidservant had dressed up in those old-fashioned-looking French medical gowns with high buttoned collars. Datt was very close to me and did a patent-medicine commercial while sorting through a trayful of instruments.

'Has he had the LSD?' asked Datt.

'Yes,' said the maid. 'It should start working soon.'

'You will answer any questions we ask,' said Datt to me.

I knew he was right: a well-used barbiturate could nullify all my years of training and experience and make me as co-operatively garrulous as a tiny child. What the LSD would do was anyone's guess.

What a way to be defeated and laid bare. I shuddered, Datt patted my arm.

The old woman was assisting him. 'The Amytal,' said Datt, 'the ampoule, and the syringe.'

She broke the ampoule and filled the syringe. 'We must work fast,' said Datt. 'It will be useless in thirty minutes; it has a short life. Bring him forward, Jules, so that she can block the vein. Dab of alcohol, Jules, no need to be inhuman.'

I felt hot breath on the back of my neck as Jules laughed dutifully at Datt's little joke.

'Block the vein now,' said Datt. She used the arm muscle to compress the vein of the forearm and waited a moment while the veins rose. I watched the process with interest, the colours of the skin and the metal were shiny

45

and unnaturally bright. Datt took the syringe and the old woman said, 'The small vein on the back of the hand. If it clots we've still got plenty of patent ones left.'

'A good thought,' said Datt. He did a triple jab under the skin and searched for the vein, dragging at the plunger until the blood spurted back a rich gusher of red into the glass hypodermic. 'Off,' said Datt. 'Off or he'll bruise. It's important to avoid that.'

She released the arm vein and Datt stared at his watch, putting the drug into the vein at a steady one cc per minute.

'He'll feel a great release in a moment, an orgastic response. Have the Megimide ready. I want him responding for at least fifteen minutes.'

M. Datt looked up at me. 'Who are you?' he asked in French. 'Where are you, what day is it?'

I laughed. His damned needle was going into someone else's arm, that was the only funny thing about it. I laughed again. I wanted to be absolutely sure about the arm. I watched the thing carefully. There was the needle in that patch of white skin but the arm didn't fit on to my shoulder. Fancy him jabbing someone else. I was laughing more now so that Jules steadied me. I must have been jostling whoever was getting the injection because Datt had trouble holding the needle in.

'Have the Megimide and the cylinder ready,' said M. Datt, who had hairs – white hairs – in his nostrils. 'Can't be too careful. Maria, quickly, come closer, we'll need you now, bring the boy closer; he'll be the witness if we need one.' M. Datt dropped something into the white enamel tray with a tremendous noise. I couldn't see Maria now, but I smelled the perfume – I'd bet it was *Ma Griffe*, heavy and exotic, oh boy! It's orange-coloured that smell. Orange-coloured with a sort of silky touch to it. 'That's good,' said M. Datt, and I heard Maria say orange-coloured too. Everyone knows, I thought, everyone knows the colour of *Ma Griffe* perfume.

The huge glass orange fractured into a million prisms, each one a brilliant, like the Sainte Chapelle at high noon, and I slid through the coruscating light as a punt slides along a sleepy bywater, the white cloud low and the colours gleaming and rippling musically under me.

I looked at M. Datt's face and I was frightened. His nose had grown enormous, not just large but enormous, larger than any nose could possibly be. I was frightened by what I saw because I knew that M. Datt's face was the same as it had always been, and that it was my awareness that had distorted. Yet even knowing that the terrible disfigurement had happened inside my mind, not on M. Datt's face, did not change the image; M. Datt's nose had grown to a gigantic size.

'What day is it?' Maria was asking. I told her. 'It's just a gabble,' she said. 'Too fast to really understand.' I listened but I could hear no one gabbling. Her eyes were soft and unblinking. She asked me my age, my date of birth and a lot of personal questions. I told her as much, and more, than she asked. The scar on my knee and the day my uncle planted the pennies in the tall tree. I wanted her to know everything about me. 'When we die,' my grandmother told me, 'we shall all go to Heaven,' she surveyed her world, 'for surely this is Hell?' 'Old Mr Gardner had athlete's foot, whose was the other foot?' Recitation: 'Let me like a soldier fall . . .'

'A desire,' said M. Datt's voice, 'to externalize, to confide.'

'Yes,' I agreed.

'I'll bring him up with the Megimide if he goes too far,' said M. Datt. 'He's fine like that. Fine response. Fine response.'

Maria repeated everything I said, as though Datt could not hear it himself. She said each thing not once but twice. I said it, then she said it, then she said it again differently; sometimes very differently so that I corrected her, but she was indifferent to my corrections and spoke in that fine voice she had; a round reed-clear voice full of song and sorrow like an oboe at night.

Now and again there was the voice of Datt deep and distant, perhaps from the next room. They seemed to think and speak so slowly. I answered Maria leisurely but it was ages before the next question came. I tired of the long pauses eventually. I filled the gaps telling them anecdotes and interesting stuff I'd read. I felt I'd known Maria for years and I remember saying 'transference', and Maria said it too, and Datt seemed very pleased. I found it was quite easy to compose my answers in poetry – not all of it rhymed, mind you – but I phrased it carefully. I could squeeze those damned words like putty and hand them to Maria, but sometimes she dropped them on to the marble floor. They fell noiselessly, but the shadows of them reverberated around the distant walls and furniture. I laughed again, and wondered whose bare arm I was staring at. Mind you, that wrist was mine, I recognized the watch. Who'd torn that shirt? Maria kept saying something over and over, a question perhaps. Damned shirt cost me £3.10s and now they'd torn it. The torn fabric was exquisite, detailed and jewel-like. Datt's voice said, 'He's going now: it's very short duration, that's the trouble with it.'

Maria said, 'Something about a shirt, I can't understand, it's so fast.'

'No matter,' said Datt. 'You've done a good job. Thank God you were here.'

I wondered why they were speaking in a foreign language. I had told them everything. I had betrayed my employers, my country, my department. They had opened me like a cheap watch, prodded the main spring and

48

laughed at its simple construction. I had failed and failure closed over me like a darkroom blind coming down.

Dark. Maria's voice said, 'He's gone,' and I went, a white seagull gliding through black sky, while beneath me the even darker sea was welcoming and still. And deep, and deep and deep.

# 9

Maria looked down at the Englishman. He was contorted and twitching, a pathetic sight. She felt inclined to cuddle him close. So it was as easy as that to discover a man's most secret thoughts – a chemical reaction – extraordinary. He'd laid his soul bare to her under the influence of the Amytal and LSD, and now, in some odd way, she felt responsible – guilty almost – about his well-being. He shivered and she pulled the coat over him and tucked it around his neck. Looking around the damp walls of the dungeon she was in, she shivered too. She produced a compact and made basic changes to her make-up: the dramatic eye-shadow that suited last night would look terrible in the cold light of dawn. Like a cat, licking and washing in moments of anguish or distress. She removed all the make-up with a ball of cotton-wool, erasing the green eyes and deep red lips. She looked at herself and pulled that pursed face that she did only when she looked in a mirror. She looked awful without make-up, like a Dutch peasant; her jaw was beginning to go. She followed the jawbone with her finger, seeking out that tiny niche halfway along the line of it. That's where the face goes, that niche becomes a gap and suddenly the chin and the jawbone separate and you have the face of an old woman.

She applied the moisture cream, the lightest of powder and the most natural of lipstick colours. The Englishman stirred and shivered; this time the shiver moved his whole body. He would become conscious soon. She hurried with her make-up, he mustn't see her like this. She felt a strange physical thing about the Englishman. Had she spent over thirty years not understanding what physical attraction was? She had always thought that beauty and physical attraction were the same thing, but now she was unsure. This man was heavy and not young – late thirties, she'd guess – and his body was thick and uncared for. Jean-Paul was the epitome of masculine beauty: young, slim, careful about his weight and his hips, artfully tanned – all over, she remembered – particular about his hairdresser, ostentatious with his gold wristwatch and fine rings, his linen, precise and starched and white, like his smile.

Look at the Englishman: ill-fitting clothes rumpled and torn, plump face, hair moth-eaten, skin pale; look at that leather wristwatch strap and his terrible old-fashioned shoes – so English. Lace-up shoes. She remembered the lace-up shoes she had as a child. She hated them, it was the first manifestation of her claustrophobia, her hatred of those shoes. Although she hadn't recognized it as such. Her mother tied the laces in knots, tight and restrictive. Maria had been extra careful with her son, he never wore laced shoes. Oh God, the Englishman was shaking like an epileptic now. She held his arms and smelled the ether and the sweat as she came close to him.

He would come awake quickly and completely. Men always did, they could snap awake and be speaking on the phone as though they had been up for hours. Man the hunter, she supposed, alert for danger; but they made no allowances. So many terrible rows with men began because she came awake slowly. The weight of his body excited her, she let it fall against her so that she took the weight of it. He's a big ugly man, she thought. She said 'ugly' again and that word attracted her, so did 'big' and so did 'man'. She said 'big ugly man' aloud.

I awoke but the nightmare continued. I was in the sort of dungeon that Walt Disney dreams up, and the woman

51

was there saying 'Big ugly man' over and over. Thanks a lot, I thought, flattery will get you nowhere. I was shivering, and I came awake carefully; the woman was hugging me close, I must have been cold because I could feel the warmth of her. I'll settle for this, I thought, but if the girl starts to fade I'll close my eyes again, I need a dream.

It was a dungeon, that was the crazy thing. 'It really is a dungeon,' I said.

'Yes,' said Maria, 'it is.'

'What are *you* doing here then?' I said. I could accept the idea of me being in a dungeon.

'I'm taking you back,' she said. 'I tried to lift you out to the car but you were too heavy. How heavy are you?'

'Never mind how heavy I am,' I said. 'What's been going on?'

'Datt was questioning you,' she said. 'We can leave now.'

'I'll show you who's leaving,' I said, deciding to seek out Datt and finish off the ashtray exercise. I jumped off the hard bench to push open the heavy door of the dungeon. It was as though I was descending a non-existent staircase and by the time I reached the door I was on the wet ground, my legs twitching uselessly and unable to bear my weight.

'I didn't think you'd get even this far,' said Maria, coming across to me. I took her arm gratefully and helped myself upright by clawing at the door fixtures. Step by difficult step we inched through the cellar, past the rack, pincers and thumbscrews and the cold fireplace with the branding irons scattered around it. 'Who lives here?' I asked. 'Frankenstein?'

'Hush,' said Maria. 'Keep your strength for walking.'

'I had a terrible dream,' I said. It had been a dream of terrible betrayal and impending doom.

'I know,' said Maria. 'Don't think about it.'

The dawn sky was pale as though the leeches of my night had grown fat upon its blood. 'Dawns should be red,' I said to Maria.

'You don't look so good yourself,' she said, and helped me into the car.

She drove a couple of blocks from the house and parked under the trees amid the dead motor cars that litter the city. She switched the heater on and the warm air suffused my limbs.

'Do you live alone?' she asked.

'What's that, a proposal?'

'You aren't fit enough to be left alone.'

'Agreed,' I said. I couldn't shake off the coma of fear and Maria's voice came to me as I had heard it in the nightmare.

'I'll take you to my place, it's not far away,' she said.

'That's okay,' I said. 'I'm sure its worth a detour.'

'It's worth a journey. Three-star food and drink,' she said. 'How about a *croque monsieur* and a baby?'[1]

'The *croque monsieur* would be welcome,' I agreed.

'But having the baby together might well be the best part,' she said.

She didn't smile, she kicked the accelerator and the power surged through the car like the blood through my reviving limbs. She watched the road, flashing the lights at each intersection and flipping the needle around the clock at the clear stretches. She loved the car, caressing the wheel and agog with admiration for it; and like a clever lover she coaxed it into effortless perfomance. She came down the Champs for speed and along the north side of the Seine before cutting up through Les Halles. The last of the smart set had abandoned their onion soup and now the lorries were being unloaded. The *fortes* were working like looters, stacking the crates of vegetables

---

[1] baby: a small whisky.

and boxes of fish. The lorry-drivers had left their cabs to patronize the brothels that crowd the streets around the Square des Innocents. Tiny yellow doorways were full of painted whores and arguing men in *bleu de travail*. Maria drove carefully through the narrow streets.

'You've seen this district before?' she asked.

'No,' I said, because I had a feeling that she wanted me to say that. I had a feeling that she got some strange titillation from bringing me this way to her home. 'Ten new francs,' she said, nodding towards two girls standing outside a dingy café. 'Perhaps seven if you argued.'

'The two?'

'Maybe twelve if you wanted the two. More for an exhibition.'

She turned to me. 'You are shocked.'

'I'm only shocked that you want me to be shocked,' I said.

She bit her lip and turned on to the Sebastopol and speeded out of the district. It was three minutes before she spoke again. 'You are good for me,' she said.

I wasn't sure she was right but I didn't argue.

That early in the morning the street in which Maria lived was little different from any other street in Paris; the shutters were slammed tight and not a glint of glass or ruffle of curtain was visible anywhere. The walls were colourless and expressionless as though every house in the street was mourning a family death. The ancient crumbling streets of Paris were distinguished socially only by the motor cars parked along the gutters. Here the R4s, corrugated *deux chevaux* and dented Dauphines were outnumbered by shiny new Jags, Buicks and Mercs.

Inside, the carpets were deep, the hangings lush, the fittings shiny and the chairs soft. And there was that symbol of status and influence: a phone. I bathed in hot perfumed water and sipped aromatic broth, I was tucked into crisp sheets, my memories faded and I slept a long dreamless sleep.

When I awoke the radio was playing Françoise Hardy in the next room and Maria was sitting on the bed. She looked at me as I stirred. She had changed into a pink cotton dress and was wearing little or no make-up. Her hair was loose and combed to a simple parting in that messy way that takes a couple of hours of hairdressing expertise. Her face was kind but had the sort of wrinkles that come when you have smiled cynically about ten million times. Her mouth was small and slightly open like a doll, or like a woman expecting a kiss.

'What time is it?' I asked.

'It's past midnight,' she said. 'You've slept the clock round.'

'Get this bed on the road. What's wrong, have we run out of feathers?'

'We ran out of bedclothes; they are all around you.'

'Fill her up with bedclothes mister and if we forget to check the electric blanket you get a bolster free.'

'I'm busy making coffee. I've no time to play your games.'

She made coffee and brought it. She waited for me to ask questions and then she answered deftly, telling me as much as she wished without seeming evasive.

'I had a nightmare and awoke in a medieval dungeon.'

'You did,' said Maria.

'You'd better tell me all about it,' I said.

'Datt was terrified that you were spying on him. He said you have documents he wants. He said you had been making inquiries so he had to know.'

'What did he do to me?'

'He injected you with Amytal and LSD (it's the LSD that takes time to wear off). I questioned you. Then you went into a deep sleep and awoke in the cellars of the house. I brought you here.'

'What did I say?'

'Don't worry. None of those people speak English. I'm the only one that does. Your secrets are safe with me. Datt usually thinks of everything, but he was disconcerted when you babbled away in English. I translated.'

So that was why I'd heard her say everything twice. 'What did I say?'

'Relax. It didn't interest me but I satisfied Datt.'

I said, 'And don't think I don't appreciate it, but why should you do that for me?'

'Datt is a hateful man. I would never help him, and anyway, I took you to that house, I felt responsible for you.'

'And . . . ?'

'If I had told him what you really said he would have undoubtedly used amphetamine on you, to discover more and more. Amphetamine is dangerous stuff, horrible. I wouldn't have enjoyed watching that.'

'Thanks,' I said. I reached towards her, took her hand, and she lay down on the bed at my side. She did it without suspicion or arch looks, it was a friendly, rather than a sexual gesture. She lit a cigarette and gave me the packet and matches. 'Light it yourself,' she said. 'It will give you something to do with your hands.'

'What did I say?' I asked casually. 'What did I say that you didn't translate into French for Datt?'

'Nothing,' Maria said immediately. 'Not because you said nothing, but because I didn't hear it. Understand? I'm not interested in what you are or how you earn your living. If you are doing something that's illegal or dangerous, that's your worry. Just for the moment I feel a little responsible for you, but I've nearly worked off that feeling. Tomorrow you can start telling your own lies and I'm sure you will do it remarkably well.'

'Is that a brush-off?'

She turned to me. 'No,' she said. She leaned over and kissed me.

'You smell delicious,' I said. 'What is it you're wearing?'

'Agony,' she said. 'It's an expensive perfume, but there are few humans not attracted to it.'

I tried to decide whether she was geeing me up, but I couldn't tell. She wasn't the sort of girl who'd help you by smiling, either.

She got off the bed and smoothed her dress over her hips.

'Do you like this dress?' she asked.

'It's great,' I said.

'What sort of clothes do you like to see women in?'

'Aprons,' I said. 'Fingers a-shine with those marks you get from handling hot dishes.'

'Yes, I can imagine,' she said. She stubbed out her cigarette.

'I'll help you if you want help but don't ask too much, and remember that I am involved with these people and I have only one passport and it's French.'

I wondered if that was a hint about what I'd revealed under the drugs, but I said nothing.

She looked at her wristwatch. 'It's very late,' she said. She looked at me quizzically. 'There's only one bed and I need my sleep.' I had been thinking of having a cigarette but I replaced them on the side table. I moved aside. 'Share the bed,' I invited, 'but I can't guarantee sleep.'

'Don't pull the Jean-Paul lover-boy stuff,' she said, 'it's not your style.' She grabbed at the cotton dress and pulled it over her head.

'What is my style?' I asked irritably.

'Check with me in the morning,' she said, and put the light out. She left only the radio on.

# 10

I stayed in Maria's flat but the next afternoon Maria went back to my rooms to feed Joey. She got back before the storm. She came in blowing on her hands and complaining of the cold.

'Did you change the water and put the cuttlefish bone in?' I asked.

'Yes,' she said.

'It's good for his beak,' I said.

'I know,' she said. She stood by the window looking out over the fast-darkening boulevard. 'It's primitive,' she said without turning away from the window. 'The sky gets dark and the wind begins to lift hats and boxes and finally dustbin lids, and you start to think this is the way the world will end.'

'I think politicians have other plans for ending the world,' I said.

'The rain is beginning. Huge spots, like rain for giants. Imagine being an ant hit by a . . .'

The phone rang. '. . . raindrop like that.' Maria finished the sentence hurriedly and picked up the phone.

She picked it up as though it was a gun that might explode by accident. 'Yes,' she said suspiciously. 'He's here.' She listened, nodding, and saying 'yes'. 'The walk will do him good,' she said. 'We'll be there in about an hour.' She pulled an agonized face at me. 'Yes,' she said to the phone again. 'Well you must just whisper to him and then I won't hear your little secrets, will I?' There was a little gabble of electronic indignation, then Maria said, 'We'll get ready now or we'll be late,' and firmly replaced the receiver. 'Byrd,' she said. 'Your countryman

Mr Martin Langley Byrd craves a word with you at the Café Blanc.' The noise of rain was like a vast crowd applauding frantically.

'Byrd,' I explained, 'is the man who was with me at the art gallery. The art people think a lot of him.'

'So he was telling me,' said Maria.

'Oh, he's all right,' I said. 'An ex-naval officer who becomes a bohemian is bound to be a little odd.'

'Jean-Paul likes him,' said Maria, as though it was the epitome of accolades. I climbed into my newly washed underwear and wrinkled suit. Maria discovered a tiny mauve razor and I shaved millimetre by millimetre and swamped the cuts with cologne. We left Maria's just as the rain shower ended. The concierge was picking up the potted plants that had been standing on the pavement.

'You are not taking a raincoat?' she asked Maria.

'No,' said Maria.

'Perhaps you'll only be out for a few minutes,' said the concierge. She pushed her glasses against the bridge of her nose and peered at me.

'Perhaps,' said Maria, and took my arm to walk away.

'It will rain again,' called the concierge.

'Yes,' said Maria.

'Heavily,' called the concierge. She picked up another pot and prodded the earth in it.

Summer rain is cleaner than winter rain. Winter rain strikes hard upon the granite, but summer rain is sibilant soft upon the leaves. This rainstorm pounced hastily like an inexperienced lover, and then as suddenly was gone. The leaves drooped wistfully and the air gleamed with green reflections. It's easy to forgive the summer rain; like first love, white lies or blarney, there's no malignity in it.

Byrd and Jean-Paul were already seated at the café. Jean-Paul was as immaculate as a shop-window dummy but Byrd was excited and dishevelled. His hair was awry and his eyebrows almost non-existent, as though he'd been too near a water-heater blow-back. They had chosen a seat near the side screens and Byrd was wagging a finger and talking excitedly. Jean-Paul waved to us and folded his ear with his fingers. Maria laughed. Byrd was wondering if Jean-Paul was making a joke against him, but deciding he wasn't, continued to speak.

'Simplicity annoys them,' Byrd said. 'It's just a rectangle, one of them complained, as though that was a criterion of art. Success annoys them. Even though I make almost no money out of my painting, that doesn't prevent the critics who feel my work is bad from treating it like an indecent assault, as though I have deliberately chosen to do bad work in order to be obnoxious. They have no kindness, no compassion, you see, that's why they call them critics – originally the word meant a captious fool; if they had compassion they would show it.'

'How?' asked Maria.

'By painting. That's what a painting is, a statement of love. Art is love, stricture is hate. It's obvious, surely. You see, a critic is a man who admires painters (he wants to be one) but cares little for paintings (which is why he isn't one). A painter, on the other hand, admires paintings, but doesn't like painters.' Byrd, having settled that problem, waved to a waiter. 'Four grands crèmes and some matches,' he ordered.

'I want black coffee,' said Maria.

'I prefer black too,' said Jean-Paul.

Byrd looked at me and made a little noise with his lips. 'You want black coffee?'

'White will suit me,' I said. He nodded an appreciation of a fellow countryman's loyalty. 'Two crèmes – grands crèmes – and two small blacks,' he ordered. The waiter arranged the beer mats, picked up some ancient checks and tore them in half. When he had gone Byrd leaned towards me. 'I'm glad,' he said – he looked around to see that the other two did not hear. They were talking to each other – 'I'm glad you drink white coffee. It's not good for the nerves, too much of this very strong stuff.' He lowered his voice still more. 'That's why they are all so argumentative,' he said in a whisper. When the coffees came Byrd arranged them on the table, apportioned the sugar, then took the check.

'Let me pay,' said Jean-Paul. 'It was my invitation.'

'Not on your life,' said Byrd. 'Leave this to me, Jean-Paul. I know how to handle this sort of thing, it's my part of the ship.'

Maria and I looked at each other without expression. Jean-Paul was watching closely to discover our relationship.

Byrd relished the snobbery of certain French phrases. Whenever he changed from speaking French into English I knew it was solely because he intended to introduce a long slab of French into his speech and give a knowing nod and slant his face significantly, as if we two were the only people in the world who understood the French language.

'Your inquiries about this house,' said Byrd. He raised his forefinger. 'Jean-Paul has remarkable news.'

'What's that?' I asked.

'Seems, my dear fellow, that there's something of a mystery about your friend Datt and that house.'

'He's not a friend of mine,' I said.

'Quite quite,' said Byrd testily. 'The damned place is a brothel, what's more . . .'

'It's not a brothel,' said Jean-Paul as though he had explained this before. 'It's a *maison de passe*. It's a house that people go to when they already have a girl with them.'

'Orgies,' said Byrd. 'They have orgies there. Frightful

61

goings on Jean-Paul tells me, drugs called LSD, pornographic films, sexual displays . . .'

Jean-Paul took over the narrative. 'There are facilities for every manner of perversion. They have hidden cameras there and even a great mock torture-chamber where they put on shows . . .'

'For masochists,' said Byrd. 'Chaps who are abnormal, you see.'

'Of course he sees,' said Jean-Paul. 'Anyone who lives in Paris knows how widespread are such parties and exhibitions.'

'*I* didn't know,' said Byrd. Jean-Paul said nothing. Maria offered her cigarettes around and said to Jean-Paul, 'Where did Pierre's horse come in yesterday?'

'A friend of theirs with a horse,' Byrd said to me.

'Yes,' I said.

'Nowhere,' said Jean-Paul.

'Then I lost my hundred nouveaux,' said Maria.

'Foolish,' said Byrd to me. He nodded.

'My fault,' said Jean-Paul.

'That's right,' said Maria. 'I didn't give it a second look until you said it was a certainty.'

Byrd gave another of his conspiratorial glances over the shoulder.

'You,' he pointed to me as though he had just met me on a footpath in the jungle, 'work for the German magazine *Stern*.'

'I work for several German magazines,' I admitted. 'But not so loud, I don't declare all of it for tax.'

'You can rely upon me,' said Byrd. 'Mum's the word.'

'Mum's the word,' I said. I relished Byrd's archaic vocabulary.

'You see,' said Byrd, 'when Jean-Paul told me this fascinating stuff about the house on Avenue Foch I said that you would probably be able to advance him a little of the ready if you got a story out of it.'

'I might,' I agreed.

'My word,' said Byrd, 'what with your salary from the travel agency and writing pieces for magazines you must be minting it. Absolutely minting it, eh?'

'I do all right,' I admitted.

'All right, I should think you do. I don't know where you stack it all if you are not declaring it for tax. What do you do, hide it under your bed?'

'To tell you the truth,' I said, 'I've sewn it into the seat of my armchair.'

Byrd laughed. 'Old Tastevin will be after you, tearing his furniture.'

'It was his idea,' I joked, and Byrd laughed again, for Tastevin had a reputation for being a skinflint.

'Get you in there with a camera,' mused Byrd. 'Be a wonderful story. What's more it would be a public service. Paris is rotten to the core you see. It's time it was given a shaking up.'

'It's an idea,' I agreed.

'Would a thousand quid be too much?' he asked.

'Much too much,' I said.

Byrd nodded. 'I thought it might be. A hundred more like it eh?'

'If it's a good story with pictures I could get five hundred pounds out of it. I'd pay fifty for an introduction and guided tour with co-operation, but the last time I was there I was persona non grata.'

'Precisely, old chap,' said Byrd. 'You were man-handled, I gather, by that fellow Datt. All a mistake, wasn't it?'

'It was from my point of view,' I said. 'I don't know how Monsieur Datt feels about it.'

'He probably feels *désolé*,' said Byrd. I smiled at the idea.

'But really,' said Byrd, 'Jean-Paul knows all about it. He could arrange for you to do your story, but meanwhile

63

mum's the word, eh? Say nothing to anyone about any aspect. Are we of one mind?'

'Are you kidding me?' I said. 'Why would Datt agree to expose his own activities?'

'You don't understand the French, my boy.'

'So everyone keeps telling me.'

'But really. This house is owned and controlled by the Ministry of the Interior. They use it as a check and control on foreigners – especially diplomats – blackmail you might almost say. Bad business, shocking people, eh? Well they are. Some other French johnnies in government service – Loiseau is one – would like to see it closed down. Now do you see, my dear chap, now do you see?'

'Yes,' I said. 'But what's in it for you?'

'Don't be offensive, old boy,' said Byrd. 'You asked me about the house. Jean-Paul is in urgent need of the ready; ergo, I arrange for you to make a mutually beneficial pact.' He nodded. 'Suppose we say fifty on account, and another thirty if it gets into print?'

A huge tourist bus crawled along the boulevard, the neon light flashing and dribbling down its glasswork. Inside, the tourists sat still and anxious, crouching close to their loudspeakers and staring at the wicked city.

'Okay,' I said. I was amazed that he was such an efficient bargain-maker.

'In any magazine anywhere,' Byrd continued. 'With ten per cent of any subsequent syndication.'

I smiled. Byrd said, 'Ah, you didn't expect me to be adept at bargaining, did you?'

'No,' I said.

'You've a lot to learn about me. Waiter,' he called. 'Four kirs.' He turned to Jean-Paul and Maria. 'We have concluded an agreement. A small celebration is now indicated.'

The white wine and cassis came. 'You will pay,' Byrd said to me, 'and take it out of our down payment.'

'Will we have a contract?' asked Jean-Paul.

'Certainly not,' said Byrd. 'An Englishman's word is his bond. Surely you know that, Jean-Paul. The whole essence of a contract is that it's mutually beneficial. If it isn't, no paper in the world will save you. Besides,' he whispered to me in English, 'give him a piece of paper like that and he'll be showing everyone; he's like that. And that's the last thing you want, eh?'

'That's right,' I said. That's right, I thought. My employment on a German magazine was a piece of fiction that the office in London had invented for the rare times when they had to instruct me by mail. No one could have known about it unless they had been reading my mail. If Loiseau had said it, I wouldn't have been surprised, but Byrd . . . !

Byrd began to explain the theory of pigment to Jean-Paul in the shrill voice that he adopted whenever he talked art. I bought them another kir before Maria and I left to walk back to her place.

We picked our way through the dense traffic on the boulevard.

'I don't know how you can be so patient with them,' Maria said. 'That pompous Englishman Byrd and Jean-Paul holding his handkerchief to protect his suit from wine stains.'

'I don't know them well enough to dislike them,' I explained.

'Then don't believe a word they say,' said Maria.

'Men were deceivers ever.'

'You are a fool,' said Maria. 'I'm not talking about amours, I'm talking about the house on Avenue Foch; Byrd and Jean-Paul are two of Datt's closest friends. Thick as thieves.'

'Are they?' I said. From the far side of the boulevard I looked back. The wiry little Byrd – as volatile as when we'd joined him – was still explaining the theory of pigment to Jean-Paul.

'*Comédiens*,' Maria pronounced. The word for 'actor' also means a phoney or impostor. I stood there a few minutes, looking. The big Café Blanc was the only brightly lit place on the whole tree-lined boulevard. The white coats of the waiters gleamed as they danced among the tables laden with coffee pots, *citron pressé* and soda siphons. The customers were also active, they waved their hands, nodded heads, called to waiters and to each other. They waved ten-franc notes and jangled coins. At least four of them kissed. It was as though the wide dark boulevard was a hushed auditorium, respecting and attentive, watching the drama unfold on the stage-like *terrasse* of the Café Blanc. Byrd leaned close to Jean-Paul. Jean-Paul laughed.

# 11

We walked and talked and forgot the time. 'Your place,' I said finally to Maria. 'You have central heating, the sink is firmly fixed to the wall, you don't share the w.c. with eight other people and there are gramophone records I haven't even read the labels on yet. Let's go to your place.'

'Very well,' she said, 'since you are so flattering about its advantages.' I kissed her ear gently. She said, 'But suppose the landlord throws you out?'

'Are you having an affair with your landlord?'

She smiled and gave me a forceful blow that many French women conveniently believe is a sign of affection.

'I'm not washing any more shirts,' she said. 'We'll take a cab to your place and pick up some linen.'

We bargained with three taxi-drivers, exchanging their directional preferences with ours; finally one of them weakened and agreed to take us to the Petit Légionnaire.

I let myself into my room with Maria just behind me. Joey chirped politely when I switched on the light.

'My God,' said Maria, 'someone's turned you over.'

I picked up a heap of shirts that had landed in the fireplace.

'Yes,' I said. Everything from the drawers and cupboards had been tipped on to the floor. Letters and cheque stubs were scattered across the sofa and quite a few things were broken. I let the armful of shirts fall to the floor again, I didn't know where to begin on it. Maria was more methodical, she began to sort through the clothes, folding them and putting trousers and jackets on

67

the hangers. I picked up the phone and dialled the number Loiseau had given me.

'*Un sourire est différent d'un rire,*' I said. France is one place where the romance of espionage will never be lost, I thought. Loiseau said 'Hello.'

'Have you turned my place over, Loiseau?' I said.

'Are you finding the natives hostile?' Loiseau asked.

'Just answer the question,' I said.

'Why don't you answer mine?' said Loiseau.

'It's my jeton,' I said. 'If you want answers you buy your own call.'

'If my boys had done it you wouldn't have noticed.'

'Don't get blasé. Loiseau. The last time your boys did it – five weeks back – I did notice. Tell 'em if they must smoke, to open the windows; that cheap pipe tobacco makes the canary's eyes water.'

'But they are very tidy,' said Loiseau. 'They wouldn't make a mess. If it's a mess you are complaining of.'

'I'm not complaining about anything,' I said. 'I'm just trying to get a straight answer to a simple question.'

'It's too much to ask of a policeman,' said Loiseau. 'But if there is anything damaged I'd send the bill to Datt.'

'If anything gets damaged it's likely to be Datt,' I said.

'You shouldn't have said that to me,' said Loiseau. 'It was indiscreet, but *bonne chance* anyway.'

'Thanks,' I said and hung up.

'So it wasn't Loiseau?' said Maria, who had been listening.

'What makes you think that?' I asked.

She shrugged. 'The mess here. The police would have been careful. Besides, if Loiseau admitted that the police have searched your home other times why should he deny that they did it this time?'

'Your guess is as good as mine,' I said. 'Perhaps Loiseau did it to set me at Datt's throat.'

'So you were deliberately indiscreet to let him think he'd succeeded?'

'Perhaps.' I looked into the torn seat of the armchair. The horse-hair stuffing had been ripped out and the case of documents that the courier had given me had disappeared. 'Gone,' said Maria.

'Yes,' I said. 'Perhaps you did translate my confession correctly after all.'

'It was an obvious place to look. In any case I was not the only person to know your "secret": this evening you told Byrd that you kept your money there.'

'That's true, but was there time for anyone to act on that?'

'It was two hours ago,' said Maria. 'He could have phoned. There was plenty of time.'

We began to sort out the mess. Fifteen minutes passed, then the phone rang. It was Jean-Paul.

'I'm glad to catch you at home,' he said. 'Are you alone?'

I held a finger up to my lips to caution Maria. 'Yes,' I said. 'I'm alone. What is it?'

'There's something I wanted to tell you without Byrd hearing.'

'Go ahead.'

'Firstly. I have good connections in the underworld and the police. I am certain that you can expect a burglary within a day or so. Anything you treasure should be put into a bank vault for the time being.'

'You're too late,' I said. 'They were here.'

'What a fool I am. I should have told you earlier this evening. It might have been in time.'

'No matter,' I said. 'There was nothing here of value except the typewriter.' I decided to solidify the freelance-writer image a little. 'That's the only essential thing. What else did you want to tell me?'

'Well that policeman, Loiseau, is a friend of Byrd.'

'I know,' I said. 'Byrd was in the war with Loiseau's brother.'

'Right,' said Jean-Paul. 'Now Inspector Loiseau was asking Byrd about you earlier today. Byrd told Inspector Loiseau that . . .'

'Well, come on.'

'He told him you are a spy. A spy for the West Germans.'

'Well that's good family entertainment. Can I get invisible ink and cameras at a trade discount?'

'You don't know how serious such a remark can be in France today. Loiseau is forced to take notice of such a remark no matter how ridiculous it may seem. And it's impossible for you to *prove* that it's not true.'

'Well thanks for telling me,' I said. 'What do you suggest I do about it?'

'There is nothing you can do for the moment,' said Jean-Paul. 'But I shall try to find out anything else Byrd says of you, and remember that I have very influential friends among the police. Don't trust Maria whatever you do.'

Maria's ear went even closer to the receiver. 'Why's that?' I asked. Jean-Paul chuckled maliciously. 'She's Loiseau's ex-wife, that's why. She too is on the payroll of the Sûreté.'

'Thanks,' I said. 'See you in court.'

Jean-Paul laughed at that remark – or perhaps he was still laughing at the one before.

# 12

Maria applied her make-up with unhurried precision. She was by no means a cosmetics addict but this morning she was having lunch with Chief Inspector Loiseau. When you had lunch with an ex-husband you made quite sure that he realized what he had lost. The pale-gold English wool suit that she had bought in London. He'd always thought her a muddle-headed fool so she'd be as slick and businesslike as possible. And the new plain-front shoes; no jewellery. She finished the eyeliner and the mascara and began to apply the eye-shadow. Not too much; she had been wearing much too much the other evening at the art gallery. You have a perfect genius, she told herself severely, for getting yourself involved in situations where you are a minor factor instead of a major factor. She smudged the eye-shadow, cursed softly, removed it and began again. Will the Englishman appreciate the risk you are taking? Why not tell M. Datt the truth of what the Englishman said? The Englishman is interested only in his work, as Loiseau was interested only in *his* work. Loiseau's love-making was efficient, just as his working day was. How can a woman compete with a man's work? Work is abstract and intangible, hypnotic and lustful; a woman is no match for it. She remembered the nights she had tried to fight Loiseau's work, to win him away from the police and its interminable paperwork and its relentless demands upon their time together. She remembered the last bitter argument about it. Loiseau had kissed her passionately in a way he had never done before and they had made love and she had clung to him, crying silently in the sudden release of

71

tension, for at that moment she knew that they would separate and divorce, and she had been right.

Loiseau still owned a part of her, that's why she had to keep seeing him. At first they had been arranging details of the legal separation, custody of the boy, then agreements about the house. Then Loiseau had asked her to do small tasks for the police department. She knew that he could not face the idea of losing her completely. They had become dispassionate and sincere, for she no longer feared losing him; they were like brother and sister now, and yet . . . she sighed. Perhaps it all could have been different; Loiseau still had an insolent confidence that made her pleased, almost proud, to be with him. He was a man, and that said everything there was to say about him. Men were unreasonable. Her work for the Sûreté had become quite important. She was pleased with the chance to show Loiseau how efficient and businesslike she could be, but Loiseau would never acknowledge it. Men were unreasonable. All men. She remembered a certain sexual mannerism of his, and smiled. All men set tasks and situations in which anything a woman thinks, says, or does will be wrong. Men demand that women should be inventive, shameless whores, and then reject them for not being motherly enough. They want them attract their men friends and then they get jealous about it.

She powdered her lipstick to darken it and then pursed her lips and gave her face one final intent glare. Her eyes were good, the pupils were soft and the whites gleaming. She went to meet her ex-husband.

# 13

Loiseau had been smoking too much and not getting enough sleep. He kept putting a finger around his metal wristwatch band; Maria remembered how she had dreaded those nervous mannerisms that always preceded a row. He gave her coffee and remembered the amount of sugar she liked. He remarked on her suit and her hair and liked the plain-fronted shoes. She knew that sooner or later he would mention the Englishman.

'Those same people have always fascinated you,' he said. 'You are a gold-digger for brains, Maria. You are drawn irresistibly to men who think only of their work.'

'Men like you,' said Maria. Loiseau nodded.

He said, 'He'll just bring you trouble, that Englishman.'

'I'm not interested in him,' said Maria.

'Don't lie to me,' said Loiseau cheerfully. 'Reports from seven hundred policemen go across this desk each week. I also get reports from informers and your concierge is one of them.'

'The bitch.'

'It's the system,' said Loiseau. 'We have to fight the criminal with his own weapons.'

'Datt gave him an injection of something to question him.'

'I know,' said Loiseau.

'It was awful,' said Maria.

'Yes, I've seen it done.'

'It's like a torture. A filthy business.'

'Don't lecture me,' said Loiseau. 'I don't like Amytal injections and I don't like Monsieur Datt or that clinic, but there's nothing I can do about it.' He sighed. 'You

73

know that, Maria.' But Maria didn't answer. 'That house is safe from even my wide powers.' He smiled as if the idea of him endangering anything was absurd. 'You deliberately translated the Englishman's confession incorrectly, Maria,' Loiseau accused her.

Maria said nothing. Loiseau said, 'You told Monsieur Datt that the Englishman is working under my orders. Be careful what you say or do with these people. They are dangerous – all of them are dangerous; your flashy boy-friend is the most dangerous of all.'

'Jean-Paul you mean?'

'The playboy of the Buttes Chaumont,' said Loiseau sarcastically.

'Don't keep calling him my boy-friend,' said Maria.

'Come come, I know all about you,' said Loiseau, using a phrase and a manner that he employed in interrogations. 'You can't resist these flashy little boys and the older you get the more vulnerable you become to them.' Maria was determined not to show anger. She knew that Loiseau was watching her closely and she felt her cheeks flushing in embarrassment and anger.

'He wants to work for me,' said Loiseau.

'He likes to feel important,' explained Maria, 'as a child does.'

'You amaze me,' said Loiseau, taking care to be unamazed. He stared at her in a way that a Frenchman stares at a pretty girl on the street. She knew that he fancied her sexually and it comforted her, not to frustrate him, but because to be able to interest him was an important part of their new relationship. She felt that in some ways this new feeling she had for him was more important than their marriage had been, for now they were friends, and friendship is less infirm and less fragile than love.

'You mustn't harm Jean-Paul because of me,' said Maria.

74

'I'm not interested in Drugstore cowboys,' said Loiseau. 'At least not until they are caught doing something illegal.'

Maria took out her cigarettes and lit one as slowly as she knew how. She felt all the old angers welling up inside her. This was the Loiseau she had divorced; this stern, unyielding man who thought that Jean-Paul was an effeminate gigolo merely because he took himself less seriously than Loiseau ever could. Loiseau had crushed her, had reduced her to a piece of furniture, to a dossier – the dossier on Maria; and now the dossier was passed over to someone else and Loiseau thought the man concerned would not handle it as competently as he himself had done. Long ago Loiseau had produced a cold feeling in her and now she felt it again. This same icy scorn was poured upon anyone who smiled or relaxed; self-indulgent, complacent, idle – these were Loiseau's words for anyone without his self-flagellant attitude to work. Even the natural functions of her body seemed something against the law when she was near Loiseau. She remembered the lengths she went to to conceal the time of her periods in case he should call her to account for them, as though they were the mark of some ancient sin.

She looked up at him. He was still talking about Jean-Paul. How much had she missed – a word, a sentence, a lifetime? She didn't care. Suddenly the room seemed cramped and the old claustrophobic feeling that made her unable to lock the bathroom door – in spite of Loiseau's rages about it – made this room unbearably small. She wanted to leave.

'I'll open the door,' she said. 'I don't want the smoke to bother you.'

'Sit down,' he said. 'Sit down and relax.'

She felt she must open the door.

'Your boy-friend Jean-Paul is a nasty little casserole,'[1] said Loiseau, 'and you might just as well face up to it. You accuse me of prying into other people's lives: well perhaps that's true, but do you know what I see in those lives? I see things that shock and appal me. That Jean-Paul. What is he but a toe-rag for Datt, running around like a filthy little pimp. He is the sort of man that makes me ashamed of being a Frenchman. He sits all day in the Drugstore and the other places that attract the foreigners. He holds a foreign newspaper pretending that he is reading it – although he speaks hardly a word of any foreign language – hoping to get into conversation with some pretty little girl secretary or better still a foreign girl who can speak French. Isn't that a pathetic thing to see in the heart of the most civilized city in the world? This lout sitting there chewing Hollywood chewing-gum and looking at the pictures in *Playboy*. Speak to him about religion and he will tell you how he despises the Catholic Church. Yet every Sunday when he's sitting there with his hamburger looking so *transatlantique*, he's just come from Mass. He prefers foreign girls because he's ashamed of the fact that his father is a metal-worker in a junk yard and foreign girls are less likely to notice his coarse manners and phoney voice.'

Maria had spent years hoping to make Loiseau jealous and now, years after their divorce had been finalized, she had succeeded. For some reason the success brought her no pleasure. It was not in keeping with Loiseau's calm, cold, logical manner. Jealousy was weakness, and Loiseau had very few weaknesses.

Maria knew that she must open the door or faint. Although she knew this slight dizziness was claustrophobia she put out the half-smoked cigarette in the hope that it would make her feel better. She stubbed it

[1] Informer.

out viciously. It made her feel better for about two minutes. Loiseau's voice droned on. How she hated this office. The pictures of Loiseau's life, photos of him in the army: slimmer and handsome, smiling at the photographer as if to say 'This is the best time of our lives, no wives, no responsibility.' The office actually smelled of Loiseau's work; she remembered that brown card that wrapped the dossiers and the smell of the old files that had come up from the cellars after goodness knows how many years. They smelled of stale vinegar. It must have been something in the paper, or perhaps the fingerprint ink.

'He's a nasty piece of work, Maria,' said Loiseau. 'I'd even go so far as to say evil. He took three young German girls out to that damned cottage he has near Barbizon. He was with a couple of his so-called artist friends. They raped those girls, Maria, but I couldn't get them to give evidence. He's an evil fellow; we have too many like him in Paris.'

Maria shrugged, 'The girls should not have gone there, they should have known what to expect. Girl tourists – they only come here to be raped; they think it's romantic to be raped in Paris.'

'Two of these girls were sixteen years old, Maria, they were children; the other only eighteen. They'd asked your boy-friend the way to their hotel and he offered them a lift there. Is this what has happened to our great and beautiful city, that a stranger can't ask the way without risking assault?'

Outside the weather was cold. It was summer and yet the wind had an icy edge. Winter arrives earlier each year, thought Maria. Thirty-two years old, it's August again but already the leaves die, fall and are discarded by the wind. Once August was hot midsummer, now August was the beginning of autumn. Soon all the seasons would

77

merge, spring would not arrive and she would know the menopausal womb-winter that is half-life.

'Yes,' said Maria. 'That's what has happened.' She shivered.

# 14

It was two days later when I saw M. Datt again. The
courier was due to arrive any moment. He would probably
be grumbling and asking for my report about the house
on the Avenue Foch. It was a hard grey morning, a slight
haze promising a scorching hot afternoon. In the Petit
Légionnaire there was a pause in the business of the day,
the last *petit déjeuner* had been served but it was still too
early for lunch. Half a dozen customers were reading
their newspapers or staring across the street watching the
drivers argue about parking space. M. Datt and both the
Tastevins were at their usual table, which was dotted
with coffee pots, cups and tiny glasses of Calvados. Two
taxi-drivers played 'ping-foot', swivelling the tiny wooden
footballers to smack the ball across the green felt cabinet.
M. Datt called to me as I came down for breakfast.

'This is terribly late for a young man to wake,' he
called jovially. 'Come and sit with us.' I sat down,
wondering why M. Datt had suddenly become so
friendly. Behind me the 'ping-foot' players made a sudden
volley. There was a clatter as the ball dropped through
the goal-mouth and a mock cheer of triumph.

'I owe you an apology,' said M. Datt. 'I wanted to wait
a few days before delivering it so that you would find it in
yourself to forgive me.'

'That humble hat doesn't fit,' I said. 'Go a size larger.'

M. Datt opened his mouth and rocked gently. 'You
have a fine sense of humour,' he proclaimed once he had
got himself under control.

'Thanks,' I said. 'You are quite a joker yourself.'

M. Datt's mouth puckered into a smile like a carelessly

ironed shirt-collar. 'Oh I see what you mean,' he said suddenly and laughed. 'Ha-ha-ha,' he laughed. Madame Tastevin had spread the Monopoly board by now and dealt us the property cards to speed up the game. The courier was due to arrive, but getting closer to M. Datt was the way the book would do it.

'Hotels on Lecourbe and Belleville,' said Madame Tastevin.

'That's what you always do,' said M. Datt. 'Why don't you buy railway stations instead?'

We threw the dice and the little wooden discs went trotting around the board, paying their rents and going to prison and taking their chances just like humans. 'A voyage of destruction,' Madame Tastevin said it was.

'That's what all life is,' said M. Datt. 'We start to die on the day we are born.'

My chance card said '*Faites des réparations dans toutes vos maisons*' and I had to pay 2,500 francs on each of my houses. It almost knocked me out of the game but I scraped by. As I finished settling up I saw the courier cross the *terrasse*. It was the same man who had come last time. He took it very slow and stayed close to the wall. A coffee crème and a slow appraisal of the customers before contacting me. Professional. Sift the tails off and duck from trouble. He saw me but gave no sign of doing so.

'More coffee for all of us,' said Madame Tastevin. She watched the two waiters laying the tables for lunch, and now she called out to them, 'That glass is smeary', 'Use the pink napkins, save the white ones for evening', 'Be sure there is enough terrine today. I'll be angry if we run short.' The waiters were keen that Madame shouldn't get angry, they moved anxiously, patting the cloths and making microscopic adjustments to the placing of the cutlery. The taxi-drivers decided upon another game and there was a rattle of wooden balls as the coin went into the slot.

The courier had brought out a copy of *L'Express* and was reading it and sipping abstractedly at his coffee. Perhaps he'll go away, I thought, perhaps I won't have to listen to his endless official instructions. Madame Tastevin was in dire straits, she mortgaged three of her properties. On the cover of *L'Express* there was a picture of the American Ambassador to France shaking hands with a film star at a festival.

M. Datt said, 'Can I smell a terrine cooking? What a good smell.'

Madame nodded and smiled. 'When I was a girl all Paris was alive with smells; oil paint and horse sweat, dung and leaky gas lamps and everywhere the smell of superb French cooking. Ah!' She threw the dice and moved. 'Now,' she said, 'it smells of diesel, synthetic garlic, hamburgers and money.'

M. Datt said, 'Your dice.'

'Okay,' I told him. 'But I must go upstairs in a moment. I have so much work to do.' I said it loud enough to encourage the courier to order a second coffee.

Landing on the Boul des Capucines destroyed Madame Tastevin.

'I'm a scientist,' said M. Datt, picking up the pieces of Madame Tastevin's bankruptcy. 'The scientific method is inevitable and true.'

'True to what?' I asked. 'True to scientists, true to history, true to fate, true to what?'

'True to itself,' said Datt.

'The most evasive truth of all,' I said.

M. Datt turned to me, studied my face and wet his lips before beginning to talk. 'We have begun in a bad . . . a silly way.' Jean-Paul came into the café – he had been having lunch there every day lately. He waved airily to us and bought cigarettes at the counter.

'But there are certain things that I don't understand,' Datt continued. 'What are you doing carrying a case-load of atomic secrets?'

'And what are you doing stealing it?'

Jean-Paul came across to the table, looked at both of us and sat down.

'Retrieving,' said Datt. 'I retrieved it for you.'

'Then let's ask Jean-Paul to remove his gloves,' I said.

Jean-Paul watched M. Datt anxiously. 'He knows,' said M. Datt. 'Admit it, Jean-Paul.'

'On account,' I explained to Jean-Paul, 'of how we began in a bad and silly way.'

'I said that,' said M. Datt to Jean-Paul. 'I said we had started in a bad and silly way and now we want to handle things differently.'

I leaned across and peeled back the wrist of Jean-Paul's cotton gloves. The flesh was stained violet with 'nin'.[1]

'Such an embarrassment for the boy,' said M. Datt, smiling. Jean-Paul glowered at him.

'Do you want to buy the documents?' I asked.

M. Datt shrugged. 'Perhaps. I will give you ten thousand new francs, but if you want more than that I would not be interested.'

'I'll need double that,' I said.

'And if I decline?'

'You won't get every second sheet, which I removed and deposited elsewhere.'

'You are no fool,' said M. Datt. 'To tell you the truth the documents were so easy to get from you that I suspected their authenticity. I'm glad to find you are no fool.'

[1] Ninhydrine: a colour reagent, reddish-black powder. Hands become violet because of amino acid in the skin. It takes three days before it comes off. Washing makes it worse.

'There are more documents,' I said. 'A higher percentage will be Xerox copies but you probably won't mind that. The first batch had a high proportion of originals to persuade you of their authenticity, but it's too risky to do that regularly.'

'Whom do you work for?'

'Never mind who I work for. Do you want them or not?'

M. Datt nodded, smiled grimly and said, 'Agreed, my friend. Agreed.' He waved an arm and called for coffee. 'It's just curiosity. Not that your documents are anything like my scientific interests. I shall use them merely to stimulate my mind. Then they will be destroyed. You can have them back . . .' The courier finished his coffee and then went upstairs, trying to look as though he was going no farther than the toilets on the first floor.

I blew my nose noisily and then lit a cigarette. 'I don't care what you do with them, monsieur. My fingerprints are not on the documents and there is no way to connect them with me; do as you wish with them. I don't know if these documents connect with your work. I don't even know what your work is.'

'My present work is scientific,' explained Datt. 'I run my clinic to investigate the patterns of human behaviour. I could make much more money elsewhere, my qualifications are good. I am an analyst. I am still a good doctor. I could lecture on several different subjects: upon oriental art, Buddhism or even Marxist theory. I am considered an authority on Existentialism and especially upon Existentialist psychology; but the work I am doing now is the work by which I will be known. The idea of being remembered after death becomes important as one gets old.' He threw the dice and moved past Départ. 'Give me my twenty thousand francs,' he said.

'What do you do at this clinic?' I peeled off the toy

83

money and passed it to him. He counted it and stacked it up.

'People are blinded by the sexual nature of my work. They fail to see it in its true light. They think only of the sex activity.' He sighed. 'It's natural, I suppose. My work is important merely because people cannot consider the subject objectively. I can; so I am one of the few men who can control such a project.'

'You analyse the sexual activity?'

'Yes,' said Datt. 'No one does anything they do not wish to do. We do employ girls but most of the people who go to the house go there as couples, and they leave in couples. I'll buy two more houses.'

'The same couples?'

'Not always,' said Datt. 'But that is not necessarily a thing to be deplored. People are mentally in bondage, and their sexual activity is the cipher which can help to explain their problems. You're not collecting your rent.' He pushed it over to me.

'You are sure that you are not rationalizing the ownership of a whorehouse?'

'Come along there now and see,' said Datt. 'It is only a matter of time before you land upon my hotels in the Avenue de la République.' He shuffled his property cards together. 'And then you are no more.'

'You mean the clinic is operating at noon?'

'The human animal,' said Datt, 'is unique in that its sexual cycle continues unabated from puberty to death.' He folded up the Monopoly board.

It was getting hotter now, the sort of day that gives rheumatism a jolt and expands the Eiffel Tower six inches. 'Wait a moment,' I said to Datt. 'I'll go up and shave. Five minutes?'

'Very well,' said Datt. 'But there's no real need to shave, you won't be asked to participate.' He smiled.

84

I hurried upstairs, the courier was waiting inside my room. 'They bought it?'

'Yes,' I said. I repeated my conversation with M. Datt.

'You've done well,' he said.

'Are you running me?' I lathered my face carefully and began shaving.

'No. Is that where they took it from, where the stuffing is leaking out?'

'Yes. Then who is?'

'You know I can't answer that. You shouldn't even ask me. Clever of them to think of looking there.'

'I told them where it was. I've never asked before,' I said, 'but whoever is running me seems to know what these people do even before I know. It's someone close, someone I know. Don't keep poking at it. It's only roughly stitched back.'

'That at least is wrong,' said the courier. 'It's no one you know or have ever met. How did you know who took the case?'

'You're lying. I told you not to keep poking at it. Nin; it colours your flesh. Jean-Paul's hands were bright with it.'

'What colour?'

'You'll be finding out,' I said. 'There's plenty of nin still in there.'

'Very funny.'

'Well who told you to poke your stubby peasant fingers into my stuffing?' I said. 'Stop messing about and listen carefully. Datt is taking me to the clinic, follow me there.'

'Very well,' said the courier without enthusiasm. He wiped his hands on a large handkerchief.

'Make sure I'm out again within the hour.'

'What am I supposed to do if you are not out within the hour?' he asked.

'I'm damned if I know,' I said. They never ask questions

85

like that in films. 'Surely you have some sort of emergency procedure arranged?'

'No,' said the courier. He spoke very quietly. 'I'm afraid I haven't. I just do the reports and pop them into the London dip mail secret tray. Sometimes it takes three days.'

'Well this could be an emergency,' I said. 'Something should have been arranged beforehand.' I rinsed off the last of the soap and parted my hair and straightened my tie.

'I'll follow you anyway,' said the courier encouragingly. 'It's a fine morning for a walk.'

'Good,' I said. I had a feeling that if it had been raining he would have stayed in the café. I dabbed some lotion on my face and then went downstairs to M. Datt. Upon the great bundle of play-money he had left the waiter's tip: one franc.

Summer was here again; the pavement was hot, the streets were dusty and the traffic cops were in white jackets and dark glasses. Already the tourists were everywhere, in two styles: beards, paper parcels and bleached jeans, or straw hats, cameras and cotton jackets. They were sitting on benches complaining loudly. 'So he explained that it was one hundred new francs or it would be ten thousand old francs, and I said, "Gracious me I sure can understand why you people had that revolution."'

Another tourist said, 'But you don't speak the language.'

A man replied, 'I don't have to speak the language to know what that waiter meant.'

As we walked I turned to watch them and caught sight of the courier strolling along about thirty yards behind us.

'It will take me another five years to complete my

work,' said Datt. 'The human mind and the human body; remarkable mechanisms but often ill-matched.'

'Very interesting,' I said. Datt was easily encouraged.

'At present my researches are concerned with stimulating the registering of pain, or rather the excitement caused by someone pretending to have sudden physical pain. You perhaps remember that scream I had on the tape recorder. Such a sound can cause a remarkable mental change in a man if used in the right circumstances.'

'The right circumstances being that film-set-style torture chamber where I was dumped after treatment.'

'Exactly,' said Datt. 'You have hit it. Even if they can see that it's a recording and even if we tell them that the girl was an actress, even then the excitement they get from it is not noticeably lessened. Curious, isn't it?'

'Very,' I said.

The house on the Avenue Foch quivered in the heat of the morning. The trees before it moved sensuously as though anxious to savour the hot sun. The door was opened by a butler; we stepped inside the entrance hall. The marble was cold and the curve of the staircase twinkled where sunbeams prodded the rich colours of the carpeting. High above us the chandeliers clinked with the draught from the open door.

The only sound was a girl's scream. I recognized it as the tape-recording that Datt mentioned. The screams were momentarily louder as a door opened and closed again somewhere on the first floor beyond the top of the staircase.

'Who is up there?' said Datt as he handed his umbrella and hat to the butler.

'Monsieur Kuang-t'ien,' said the butler.

'A charming fellow,' said Datt. 'Major-domo of the Chinese Embassy here in Paris.'

Somewhere in the house a piano played Liszt, or perhaps it was a recording.

I looked towards the first floor. The screams continued, muffled by the door that had now closed again. Suddenly, moving noiselessly like a figure in a fantasy, a young girl ran along the first-floor balcony and came down the stairs, stumbling and clinging to the banister rail. She half-fell and half-ran, her mouth open in that sort of soundless scream that only nightmares produce. The girl was naked but her body was speckled with patches of bright wet blood. She must have been stabbed twenty, perhaps thirty times, and the blood had produced an intricate pattern of rivulets like a tight bodice of fine red lace. I remembered M. Kuang-t'ien's poem: 'If she is not a rose all white, then she must be redder than the red of blood.'

No one moved until Datt made a half-hearted attempt to grab her, but he was so slow that she avoided him effortlessly and ran through the door. I recognized her face now; it was the model that Byrd had painted, Annie.

'Get after her.' Datt called his staff into action with the calm precision of a liner captain pulling into a pier. 'Go upstairs, grab Kuang-t'ien, disarm him, clean the knife and hide it. Put him under guard, then phone the Press Officer at the Chinese Embassy. Don't tell him anything, but he must stay in his office until I call him to arrange a meeting. Albert, get on my personal phone and call the Ministry of the Interior. Tell them we'll need some CRS policemen here. I don't want the Police Municipale poking around too long. Jules, get my case and the drug box and have the transfusion apparatus ready; I'll take a look at the girl.' Datt turned, but stopped and said softly, 'And Byrd, get Byrd here immediately; send a car for him.'

He hurried after the footmen and butler who were running across the lawn after the bleeding girl. She glanced over her shoulder and gained fresh energy from the closeness of the pursuit. She grabbed at the gatepost and swung out on to the hot dusty pavement of the

Avenue Foch, her heart pumping the blood patches into shiny bulbous swellings that burst and dribbled into vertical stripes.

'Look!' I heard the voices of passers-by calling.

Someone else called 'Hello darling', and there was a laugh and a lot of wolf-whistles. They must have been the last thing the girl heard as she collapsed and died on the hot, dusty Parisian pavement under the trees in the Avenue Foch. A bewhiskered old crone carrying two *baguettes* came shuffling in her threadbare carpet-slippers. She pushed through the onlookers and leaned down close to the girl's head. 'Don't worry chérie, I'm a nurse,' she croaked. 'All your injuries are small and superficial.' She pushed the loaves of bread tighter under her armpit and tugged at her corset bottom. 'Just superficial,' she said again, 'so don't make so much fuss.' She turned very slowly and went shuffling off down the street muttering to herself.

There were ten or twelve people around her by the time I reached the body. The butler arrived and threw a car blanket over her. One of the bystanders said '*Tant pis*', and another said that the *jolie pépée* was well barricaded. His friend laughed.

A policeman is never far away in Paris and they came quickly, the blue-and-white corrugated van disgorging cops like a gambler fanning a deck of cards. Even before the van came to a halt the police were sorting through the bystanders, asking for papers, detaining some, prodding others away. The footmen had wrapped the girl's body in the blanket and began to heave the sagging bundle towards the gates of the house.

'Put it in the van,' said Datt. One of the policemen said, 'Take the body to the house.' The two men carrying the dead girl stood undecided.

'In the van,' said Datt.

'I get my orders from the Commissaire de Police,' said

the cop. 'We are on the radio now.' He nodded towards the van.

Datt was furious. He struck the policeman a blow on the arm. His voice was sibilant and salivatory. 'Can't you see that you are attracting attention, you fool? This is a political matter. The Ministry of the Interior are concerned. Put the body in the van. The radio will confirm my ruling.' The policeman was impressed by Datt's anger. Datt pointed at me. 'This is one of the officers working with Chief Inspector Loiseau of the Sûreté. Is that good enough for you?'

'Very well,' said the policeman. He nodded to the two men, who pushed the body on to the floor of the police van. They closed the door.

'Journalists may arrive,' said Datt to the policeman. 'Leave two of your men on guard here and make sure they know about article ten.'

'Yes,' said the policeman docilely.

'Which way are you going?' I asked the driver.

'The meat goes to the Medico-Legal,' he said.

'Ride me to the Avenue de Marigny,' I said. 'I'm going back to my office.'

By now the policeman in charge of the vehicle was browbeaten by Datt's fierce orders. He agreed to my riding in the van without a word of argument. At the corner of the Avenue de Marigny I stopped the van and got out. I needed a large brandy.

# 15

I expected the courier from the Embassy to contact me again that same day but he didn't return until the next morning. He put his document case on top of the wardrobe and sank into my best armchair.

He answered an unasked question. 'It's a whorehouse,' he pronounced. 'He calls it a clinic but it's more like a whorehouse.'

'Thanks for your help,' I said.

'Don't get snotty – you wouldn't want me telling you what to say in your reports.'

'That's true,' I admitted.

'Certainly it's true. It's a whorehouse that a lot of the Embassy people use. Not just our people – the Americans, etc., use it.'

I said, 'Straighten me up. Is this just a case of one of our Embassy people getting some dirty pictures back from Datt? Or something like that?'

The courier stared at me. 'I'm not allowed to talk about anything like that,' he said.

'Don't give me that stuff,' I said. 'They killed that girl yesterday.'

'In passion,' explained the courier. 'It was part of a kinky sex act.'

'I don't care if it was done as a publicity stunt,' I said. 'She's dead and I want as much information as I can get to avoid trouble. It's not just for my own skin; it's in the interests of the department that I avoid trouble.'

The courier said nothing, but I could see he was weakening.

I said, 'If I'm heading into that house again just to

recover some pictures of a secretary on the job, I'll come back and haunt you.'

'Give me some coffee,' said the courier, and I knew he had decided to tell me whatever he knew. I boiled the kettle and brewed up a pint of strong black coffee.

'Kuang-t'ien,' said the courier, 'the man who knifed the girl: do you know who he is?'

'Major-domo at the Chinese Embassy, Datt said.'

'That's his cover. His name is Kuang-t'ien, but he's one of the top five men in the Chinese nuclear programme.'

'He speaks damn good French.'

'Of course he does. He was trained at the Laboratoire Curie, here in Paris. So was his boss, Chien San-chiang, who is head of the Atomic Energy Institute in Peking.'

'You seem to know a lot about it,' I said.

'I was evaluating it this time last year.'

'Tell me more about this man who mixes his sex with switchblades.'

He pulled his coffee towards his and stirred it thoughtfully. Finally he began.

'Four years ago the U2 flights picked up the fourteen-acre gaseous diffusion plant taking hydro-electric power from the Yellow River not far from Lanchow. The experts had predicted that the Chinese would make their bombs as the Russians and French did, and as we did too: by producing plutonium in atomic reactors. But the Chinese didn't; our people have been close. I've seen the photos. Very close. That plant proves that they are betting all or nothing on hydrogen. They are going full steam ahead on their hydrogen research programme. By concentrating on the light elements generally and by pushing the megaton instead of the kiloton bomb they could be the leading nuclear power in eight or ten years if their hydrogen research pays off. This man Kuang-t'ien is their best authority on hydrogen. See what I mean?'

I poured more coffee and thought about it. The courier

got his case down and rummaged through it. 'When you left the clinic yesterday did you go in the police van?'

'Yes.'

'Um. I thought you might have. Good stunt that. Well, I hung around for a little while, then when I realized that you'd gone I came back here. I hoped you'd come back, too.'

'I had a drink,' I said. 'I put my mind in neutral for an hour.'

'That's unfortunate,' said the courier. 'Because while you were away you had a visitor. He asked for you at the counter, then hung around for nearly an hour, but when you didn't come back he took a cab to the Hotel Lotti.'

'What was he like?'

The courier smiled his mirthless smile and produced some ten-by-eight glossy pictures of a man drinking coffee in the afternoon sunlight. It wasn't a good-quality photograph. The man was about fifty, dressed in a light-weight suit with a narrow-brimmed felt hat. His tie had a small monogram that was unreadable and his cufflinks were large and ornate. He had large black sunglasses which in one photo he had removed to polish. When he drank coffee he raised his little finger high and pursed his lips.

'Ten out of ten,' I said. 'Good stuff: waiting till he took the glasses off. But you could use a better D and P man.'

'They are just rough prints,' said the courier. 'The negs are half-frame but they are quite good.'

'You are a regular secret agent,' I said admiringly. 'What did you do – shoot him in the ankle with the toe-cap gun, send out a signal to HQ on your tooth and play the whole thing back on your wristwatch?'

He rummaged through his papers again, then slapped a copy of *L'Express* upon the table top. Inside there was a photo of the US Ambassador greeting a group of American businessmen at Orly Airport. The courier looked up at me briefly.

'Fifty per cent of this group of Americans work – or did work – for the Atomic Energy Commission. Most of the remainder are experts on atomic energy or some allied subject. Bertram: nuclear physics at MIT. Bestbridge: radiation sickness of 1961. Waldo: fall-out experiments and work at the Hiroshima hospital. Hudson: hydrogen research – now he works for the US Army.' He marked Hudson's face with his nail. It was the man he'd photographed.

'Okay,' I said. 'What are you trying to prove?'

'Nothing. I'm just putting you in the picture. That's what you wanted, isn't it?'

'Yes,' I said. 'Thanks.'

'I'm just juxtaposing a hydrogen expert from Peking with a hydrogen expert from the Pentagon. I'm wondering why they are both in the same city at the same time and especially why they both cross your path. It's the sort of thing that makes me nervous.' He gulped down the rest of his coffee.

'You shouldn't drink too much of that strong black coffee,' I said. 'It'll be keeping you awake at night.'

The courier picked up his photos and copy of L'Express. 'I've got a system for getting to sleep,' he said. 'I count reports I've filed.'

'Watch resident agents jumping to conclusions,' I said.

'It's not soporific.' He got to his feet. 'I've left the most important thing until last,' he said.

'Have you?' I said, and wondered what was more important than the Chinese People's Republic preparing for nuclear warfare.

'The girl was ours.'

'What girl was whose?'

'The murdered girl was working for us, for the department.'

'A floater?'

'No. Permanent; warranty contract, the lot.'

'Poor kid,' I said. 'Was she pumping Kuang-t'ien?'

'It's nothing that's gone through the Embassy. They know nothing about her there.'

'But you knew?'

'Yes.'

'You are playing both ends.'

'Just like you.'

'Not at all. I'm just London. The jobs I do for the Embassy are just favours. I can decline if I want to. What do London want me to do about this girl?'

He said, 'She has an apartment on the left bank. Just check through her personal papers, her possessions. You know the sort of thing. It's a long shot but you might find something. These are her keys – the department held duplicates for emergencies – small one for mail box, large ones front door and apartment door.'

'You're crazy. The police were probably turning it over within thirty minutes of her death.'

'Of course they were. I've had the place under observation. That's why I waited a bit before telling you. London is pretty certain that no one – not Loiseau nor Datt nor anyone – knew that the girl worked for us. It's probable that they just made a routine search.'

'If the girl was a permanent she wouldn't leave anything lying around,' I said.

'Of course she wouldn't. But there may be one or two little things that could embarrass us all . . .' He looked around the grimy wallpaper of my room and pushed my ancient bedstead. It creaked.

'Even the most careful employee is tempted to have something close at hand.'

'That would be against orders.'

'Safety comes above orders,' he said. I shrugged my grudging agreement. 'That's right,' he said. 'Now you see why they want you to go. Go and probe around there as though it's your room and you've just been killed. You might find something where anyone else would fail. There's an insurance of about thirty thousand new francs if you find someone who you think should get it.' He wrote the address on a slip of paper and put it on the table. 'I'll be in touch,' he said. 'Thanks for the coffee, it was very good.'

'If I start serving instant coffee,' I said, 'perhaps I'll get a little less work.'

# 16

The dead girl's name was Annie Couzins. She was twenty-four and had lived in a new piece of speculative real estate not far from the Boul. Mich. The walls were close and the ceilings were low. What the accommodation agents described as a studio apartment was a cramped bed-sitting room. There were large cupboards containing a bath, a toilet and a clothes rack respectively. Most of the construction money had been devoted to an entrance hall lavished with plate glass, marble and bronze-coloured mirrors that made you look tanned and rested and slightly out of focus.

Had it been an old house or even a pretty one, then perhaps some memory of the dead girl would have remained there, but the room was empty, contemporary and pitiless. I examined the locks and hinges, probed the mattress and shoulder pads, rolled back the cheap carpet and put a knife blade between the floorboards. Nothing. Perfume, lingerie, bills, a postcard greeting from Nice, '. . . some of the swimsuits are divine . . .', a book of dreams, six copies of *Elle*, laddered stockings, six medium-price dresses, eight and a half pairs of shoes, a good English wool overcoat, an expensive transistor radio tuned to France Musique, tin of Nescafé, tin of powdered milk, saccharine, a damaged handbag containing spilled powder and a broken mirror, a new saucepan. Nothing to show what she was, had been, feared, dreamed of or wanted.

The bell rang. There was a girl standing there. She may have been twenty-five but it was difficult to say. Big cities leave a mark. The eyes of city-dwellers scrutinize rather than see; they assess the value and the going-rate and try to separate the winners from the losers. That's what this girl tried to do.

'Are you from the police?' she asked.

'No. Are you?'

'I'm Monique. I live next door in apartment number eleven.'

'I'm Annie's cousin, Pierre.'

'You've got a funny accent. Are you a Belgian?' She gave a little giggle as though being a Belgian was the funniest thing that could happen to anyone.

'Half Belgian,' I lied amiably.

'I can usually tell. I'm very good with accents.'

'You certainly are,' I said admiringly. 'Not many people detect that I'm half Belgian.'

'Which half is Belgian?'

'The front half.'

She giggled again. 'Was your mother or your father Belgian, I mean.'

'Mother. Father was a Parisian with a bicycle.'

She tried to peer into the flat over my shoulder. 'I would invite you in for a cup of coffee,' I said, 'but I musn't disturb anything.'

'You're hinting. You want me to invite you for coffee.'

'Damned right I do.' I eased the door closed. 'I'll be there in five minutes.'

I turned back to cover up my searching. I gave a last look to the ugly cramped little room. It was the way I'd go one day. There would be someone from the department making sure that I hadn't left 'one or two little things that could embarrass us all'. Goodbye, Annie, I thought. I didn't know you but I know you now as well as anyone knows me. You won't retire to a little *tabac* in Nice and get a monthly cheque from some phoney insurance company. No, you can be resident agent in hell, Annie, and your bosses will be sending directives from Heaven telling you to clarify your reports and reduce your expenses.

I went to apartment number eleven. Her room was like Annie's: cheap gilt and film-star photos. A bath towel on the floor, ashtrays overflowing with red-marked butts, a plateful of garlic sausage that had curled up and died.

Monique had made the coffee by the time I got there. She'd poured boiling water on to milk powder and instant coffee and stirred it with a plastic spoon. She was a tough girl under the giggling exterior and she surveyed me carefully from behind fluttering eyelashes.

'I thought you were a burglar,' she said, 'then I thought you were the police.'

'And now?'

'You're Annie's cousin Pierre. You're anyone you want to be, from Charlemagne to Tin-Tin, it's no business of mine, and you can't hurt Annie.'

I took out my notecase and extracted a one-hundred-new-franc note. I put it on the low coffee table. She stared at me thinking it was some kind of sexual proposition.

'Did you ever work with Annie at the clinic?' I asked.

'No.'

I placed another note down and repeated the question.

'No,' she said.

I put down a third note and watched her carefully. When she again said no I leaned forward and took her hand roughly. 'Don't no me,' I said. 'You think I came here without finding out first?'

She stared at me angrily. I kept hold of her hand. 'Sometimes,' she said grudgingly.

'How many?'

'Ten, perhaps twelve.'

'That's better,' I said. I turned her hand over, pressed my fingers against the back of it to make her fingers open and slapped the three notes into her open palm. I let go of her and she leaned back out of reach, rubbing the back of her hand where I had held it. They were slim, bony hands with rosy knuckes that had known buckets of cold water and Marseilles soap. She didn't like her hands. She put them inside things and behind them and hid them under her folded arms.

'You bruised me,' she complained.

'Rub money on it.'

'Ten, perhaps twelve, times,' she admitted.

'Tell me about the place. What went on there?'

'You are from the police.'

'I'll do a deal with you, Monique. Slip *me* three hundred and I'll tell you all about what *I* do.'

She smiled grimly. 'Annie wanted an extra girl sometimes, just as a hostess . . . the money was useful.'

'Did Annie have plenty of money?'

'Plenty? I never knew anyone who had plenty. And even if they did it wouldn't go very far in this town. She didn't go to the bank in an armoured car if that's what you mean.' I didn't say anything.

Monique continued, 'She did all right but she was silly with it. She gave it to anyone who spun her a yarn. Her parents will miss her, so will Father Marconi; she was always giving to his collection for kids and missions and cripples. I told her over and over, she was silly with it. You're not Annie's cousin, but you throw too much money around to be the police.'

'The men you met there. You were told to ask them things and to remember what they said.'

'I didn't go to bed with them . . .'

'I don't care if you took *thé anglais* with them and dunked the *gâteau sec*, what were your instructions?' She hesitated, and I placed five more one-hundred-franc notes on the table but kept my fingers on them.

'Of course I made love to the men, just as Annie did, but they were all refined men. Men of taste and culture.'

'Sure they were,' I said. 'Men of real taste and culture.'

'It was done with tape recorders. There were two switches on the bedside lamps. I was told to get them talking about their work. So boring, men talking about their work, but are they ready to do it? My God they are.'

'Did you ever handle the tapes?'

'No, the recording machines were in some other part of the clinic.' She eyed the money.

'There's more to it than that. Annie did more than that.'

'Annie was a fool. Look where it got her. That's where it will get me if I talk too much.'

'I'm not interested in you,' I said. 'I'm only interested in Annie. What else did Annie do?'

'She substituted the tapes. She changed them. Sometimes she made her own recordings.'

'She took a machine into the house?'

'Yes. It one of those little ones, about four hundred new francs they cost. She had it in her handbag. I found it there once when I was looking for her lipstick to borrow.'

'What did Annie say about it?'

'Nothing. I never told her. And I never opened her handbag again either. It was her business, nothing to do with me.'

'The miniature recorder isn't in her flat now.'

'I didn't pinch it.'

'Then who do you think did?'

'I told her not once. I told her a thousand times.'

'What did you tell her?'

She pursed up her mouth in a gesture of contempt. 'What do you think I told her, M. Annie's cousin Pierre? I told her that to record conversations in such a house was a dangerous thing to do. In a house owned by people like those people.'

'People like what people?'

101

'In Paris one does not talk of such things, but it's said that the Ministry of the Interior or the SDECE[1] own the house to discover the indiscretions of foolish aliens.' She gave a tough little sob, but recovered herself quickly.

'You were fond of Annie?'

'I never got on well with women until I got to know her. I was broke when I met her, at least I was down to only ten francs. I had run away from home. I was in the laundry asking them to split the order because I didn't have enough to pay. The place where I lived had no running water. Annie lent me the money for the whole laundry bill – twenty francs – so that I had clean clothes while looking for a job. She gave me the first warm coat I ever had. She showed me how to put on my eyes. She listened to my stories and let me cry. She told me not to live the life that she had led, going from one man to another. She would have shared her last cigarette with a stranger. Yet she never asked me questions. Annie was an angel.'

'It certainly sounds like it.'

'Oh I know what you're thinking. You're thinking that Annie and I were a couple of Lesbians.'

'Some of my best lovers are Lesbians,' I said.

Monique smiled. I thought she was going to cry all over me, but she sniffed and smiled. 'I don't know if we were or not,' she said.

'Does it matter?'

'No, it doesn't matter. Anything would be better than to have stayed in the place I was born. My parents are still there; it's like living through a siege, besieged by the cost of necessities. They are careful how they use detergent, coffee is measured out. Rice, pasta and potatoes eke out tiny bits of meat. Bread is consumed, meat is revered and Kleenex tissues never afforded.

[1] Service de Documentation Extérieure et Contre-Espionage.

Unnecessary lights are switched off immediately, they put on a sweater instead of the heating. In the same building families crowd into single rooms, rats chew enormous holes in the woodwork – there's no food for them to chew on – and the w.c. is shared by three families and it usually doesn't flush. The people who live at the top of the house have to walk down two flights to use a cold water tap. And yet in this same city I get taken out to dinner in three-star restaurants where the bill for two dinners would keep my parents for a year. At the Ritz a man friend of mine paid nine francs a day to them for looking after his dog. That's just about half the pension my father gets for being blown up in the war. So when you people come snooping around here flashing your money and protecting the République Française's rocket programme, atomic plants, supersonic bombers and nuclear submarines or whatever it is you're protecting, don't expect too much from my patriotism.'

She bit her lip and glared at me, daring me to contradict her, but I didn't contradict. 'It's a lousy rotten town,' I agreed.

'And dangerous,' she said.

'Yes,' I said. 'Paris is all of those things.'

She laughed. 'Paris is like me, cousin Pierre; it's no longer young, and too dependent upon visitors who bring money. Paris is a woman with a little too much alcohol in her veins. She talks a little too loud and thinks she is young and gay. But she has smiled too often at strange men and the words "I love you" trip too easily from her tongue. The ensemble is chic and the paint is generously applied, but look closely and you'll see the cracks showing through.'

She got to her feet, groped along the bedside table for a match and lit her cigarette with a hand that trembled very slightly. She turned back to me. 'I saw the girls I knew taking advantage of offers that came from rich men

103

they could never possibly love. I despised the girls and wondered how they could bring themselves to go to bed with such unattractive men. Well, now I know.' The smoke was getting in her eyes. 'It was fear. Fear of being a woman instead of a girl, a woman whose looks are slipping away rapidly, leaving her alone and unwanted in this vicious town.' She was crying now and I stepped closer to her and touched her arm. For a moment she seemed about to let her head fall upon my shoulder, but I felt her body tense and unyielding. I took a business card from my top pocket and put it on the bedside table next to a box of chocolates. She pulled away from me irritably. 'Just phone if you want to talk more,' I said.

'You're English,' she said suddenly. It must have been something in my accent or syntax. I nodded.

'It will be strictly business,' she said. 'Cash payments.'

'You don't have to be so tough on yourself,' I said. She said nothing.

'And thanks,' I said.

'Get stuffed,' said Monique.

# 17

First there came a small police van, its klaxon going. Co-
operating with it was a blue-uniformed man on a motor-
cycle. He kept his whistle in his mouth and blew repeat-
edly. Sometimes he was ahead of the van, sometimes
behind it. He waved his right hand at the traffic as if by
just the draught from it he could force the parked cars up
on the pavement. The noise was deafening. The traffic
ducked out of the way, some cars went willingly, some
grudgingly, but after a couple of beeps on the whistle
they crawled up on the stones, the pavement and over
traffic islands like tortoises. Behind the van came the
flying column: three long blue buses jammed with Garde
Mobile men who stared at the cringing traffic with a
bored look on their faces. At the rear of the column
came a radio car. Loiseau watched them disappear down
the Faubourg St Honoré. Soon the traffic began to move
again. He turned away from the window and back to
Maria. 'Dangerous,' pronounced Loiseau. 'He's playing a
dangerous game. The girl is killed in his house, and Datt
is pulling every political string he can find to prevent an
investigation taking place. He'll regret it.' He got to his
feet and walked across the room.

'Sit down, darling,' said Maria. 'You are just wasting
calories in getting annoyed.'

'I'm not Datt's boy,' said Loiseau.

'And no one will imagine that you are,' said Maria.
She wondered why Loiseau saw everything as a threat to
his prestige.

'The girl is entitled to an investigation,' explained
Loiseau. 'That's why I became a policeman. I believe in

equality before the law. And now they are trying to tie my hands. It makes me furious.'

'Don't shout,' said Maria. 'What sort of effect do you imagine that has upon the people that work for you, hearing you shouting?'

'You are right,' said Loiseau. Maria loved him. It was when he capitulated so readily like that that she loved him so intensely. She wanted to care for him and advise him and make him the most successful policeman in the whole world. Maria said, 'You are the finest policeman in the whole world.'

He smiled. 'You mean with your help I could be.' Maria shook her head. 'Don't argue,' said Loiseau. 'I know the workings of your mind by now.'

Maria smiled too. He did know. That was the awful thing about their marriage. They knew each other too well. To know all is to forgive nothing.

'She was one of my girls,' said Loiseau. Maria was surprised. Of course Loiseau had girls, he was no monk, but it surprised her to hear him talk like that to her. 'One of them?' She deliberately made her voice mocking.

'Don't be so bloody arch, Maria. I can't stand you raising one eyebrow and adopting that patronizing tone. One of my girls.' He said it slowly to make it easy for her to understand. He was so pompous that Maria almost giggled. 'One of my girls, working for me as an informant.'

'Don't all the tarts do that?'

'She wasn't a tart, she was a highly intelligent girl giving us first-class information.'

'Admit it, darling,' Maria cooed, 'you were a tiny bit infatuated with her.' She raised an eyebrow quizzically.

'You stupid cow,' said Loiseau. ''What's the good of treating you like an intelligent human.' Maria was shocked by the rusty-edged hatred that cut her. She had made a kind, almost loving remark. Of course the girl had fascinated Loiseau and had in turn been fascinated by him. The fact that it was true was proved by Loiseau's anger. But did his anger have to be so bitter? Did he have to wound her to know if blood flowed through her veins?

Maria got to her feet. 'I'll go,' she said. She remembered Loiseau once saying that Mozart was the only person who understood him. She had long since decided that that at least was true.

'You said you wanted to ask me something.'

'It doesn't matter.'

'Of course it matters. Sit down and tell me.'

She shook her head. 'Another time.'

'Do you have to treat me like a monster, just because I won't play your womanly games?'

'No,' she said.

There was no need for Maria to feel sorry for Loiseau. He didn't feel sorry for himself and seldom for anyone else. He had pulled the mechanism of their marriage apart and now looked at it as if it were a broken toy, wondering why it didn't work. Poor Loiseau. My poor, poor, darling Loiseau. I at least can build again, but you don't know what you did that killed us.

'You're crying, Maria. Forgive me. I'm so sorry.'

'I'm not crying and you're not sorry.' She smiled at him. 'Perhaps that's always been our problem.'

Loiseau shook his head but it wasn't a convincing denial.

Maria walked back towards the Faubourg St Honoré. Jean-Paul was at the wheel of her car.

'He made you cry,' said Jean-Paul. 'The rotten swine.'

'I made myself cry,' said Maria.

Jean-Paul put his arm around her and held her tight. It was all over between her and Jean-Paul, but feeling his arm around her was like a shot of cognac. She stopped feeling sorry for herself and studied her make-up.

'You look magnificent,' said Jean-Paul. 'I would like to take you away and make love to you.'

There was a time when that would have affected her, but she had long since decided that Jean-Paul seldom *wanted* to make love to anyone, although he did it often enough, heaven knows. But it was a good thing to hear when you have just argued with an ex-husband. She smiled at Jean-Paul and he took her hand in his large tanned one and turned it around like a bronze sculpture on a turntable. Then he released it and grabbed at the controls of the car. He wasn't as good a driver as Maria was, but she preferred to be his passenger rather than drive herself. She lolled back and pretended that Jean-Paul was the capable tanned he-man that he looked. She watched the pedestrians, and intercepted the envious glances. They were a perfect picture of modern Paris: the flashy automobile, Jean-Paul's relaxed good looks and expensive clothes, her own well-cared-for appearance – for she was as sexy now as she had ever been. She leaned her head close upon Jean-Paul's shoulder. She could smell his after-shave perfume and the rich animal smell of the leather seats. Jean-Paul changed gear as they roared across the Place de la Concorde. She felt his arm muscles ripple against her cheek.

'Did you ask him?' asked Jean-Paul.

'No,' she said. 'I couldn't. He wasn't in the right mood.'

'He's never in the right mood, Maria. And he's never going to be. Loiseau knows what you want to ask him and he precipitates situations so that you never will ask him.'

'Loiseau isn't like that,' said Maria. She had never thought of that. Loiseau was clever and subtle; perhaps it was true.

'Look,' said Jean-Paul, 'during the last year that house on the Avenue Foch has held exhibitions, orgies, with perversions, blue movies and everything, but has never had any trouble from the police. Even when a girl dies there, there is still little or no trouble. Why? Because it has the protection of the French Government. Why does it have protection? Because the activities at the house are filmed and photographed for official dossiers.'

'I'm not sure you're right. Datt implies that, but I'm not sure.'

'Well I am sure,' said Jean-Paul. 'I'll bet you that those films and photos are in the possession of the Ministry of the Interior, Loiseau probably sees every one of them. They probably have a private showing once a week. Loiseau probably saw that film of you and me within twenty-four hours of its being taken.'

'Do you think so?' said Maria. A flash of fear rose inside her, radiating panic like a two-kilowatt electric fire. Jean-Paul's large cool hand gripped her shoulder. She wished he would grip her harder. She wanted him to hurt her so that her sins would be expiated and erased by the pain. She thought of Loiseau seeing the film in the company of other policemen. Please God it hadn't happened. Please please God. She thought she had agonized over every aspect of her foolishness, but this was a new and most terrible one.

'But why would they keep the films?' Maria asked, although she knew the answer.

'Datt selects the people who use that house. Datt is a psychiatrist, a genius . . .'

'. . . an evil genius.'

'Perhaps an evil genius,' said Jean-Paul objectively. 'Perhaps an evil genius, but by gathering a select circle of people – people of great influence, of prestige and diplomatic power – Datt can compile remarkable assessments and predictions about their behaviour in everything they do. Many major shifts of French Government policy have been decided by Datt's insights and analysis of sexual behaviour.'

'It's vile,' said Maria.

'It's the world in our time.'

'It's France in our time,' Maria corrected. 'Foul man.'

'He's not foul,' said Jean-Paul. 'He is not responsible for what those people do. He doesn't even encourage them. As far as Datt is concerned his guests could behave with impeccable decorum; he would be just as happy to record and analyse their attitudes.'

'*Voyeur.*'

'He's not even a *voyeur*. That's the odd thing. That's what makes him of such great importance to the Ministry. And that's why your ex-husband could do nothing to retrieve that film even if he wished to.'

'And what about you?' asked Maria casually.

'Be reasonable,' said Jean-Paul. 'It's true I do little jobs for Datt but I am not his *confidant*. I've no idea of what happens to the film . . .'

'They burn them sometimes,' Maria remembered. 'And often they are taken away by the people concerned.'

'You have never heard of duplicate prints?'

Maria's hopes sank. 'Why didn't you ask for that piece of film of us?'

'Because you said let them keep it. Let them show it every Friday night, you said.'

'I was drunk,' said Maria. 'It was a joke.'

'It's a joke for which we are both paying dearly.'

Maria snorted. 'You love the idea of people seeing the film. It's just the image you love to project. The great lover . . .' She bit her tongue. She had almost added that the film was his sole documentary proof of heterosexuality, but she closed her eyes. 'Loiseau could get the film back,' she said. She was sure, sure, sure that Loiseau hadn't seen that piece of film, but the memory of the fear remained.

'Loiseau *could* get it,' she said desperately, wanting Jean-Paul to agree on this one, very small point.

'But he won't,' said Jean-Paul. 'He won't because I'm involved and your ex-husband hates me with a deep and illogical loathing. The trouble is that I can understand why he does. I'm no good for you, Maria. You would probably have managed the whole thing excellently except that Loiseau is jealous of your relationship with me. Perhaps we should cease to see each other for a few months.'

'I'm sure we should.'

'But I couldn't bear it, Maria.'

'Why the hell not? We don't love each other. I am only a suitable companion and you have so many other women you'd never even notice my absence.' She despised herself even before she'd completed the sentence. Jean-Paul detected her motive immediately, of course, and responded.

'My darling little Maria.' He touched her leg lightly and sexlessly. 'You are different from the others. The others are just stupid little tarts that amuse me as decorations. They are not women. You are the only real woman I know. You are the woman I love, Maria.'

'Monsieur Datt himself,' said Maria, '*he* could get the film.' Jean-Paul pulled into the side of the road and double parked.

'We've played this game long enough, Maria,' he said.

'What game?' asked Maria. Behind them a taxi-driver swore bitterly as he realized they were not going to move.

'The how-much-you-hate-Datt game,' said Jean-Paul.

'I do hate him.'

'He's your father, Maria.'

'He's not my father, that's just a stupid story that he told you for some purpose of his own.'

'Then where is your father?'

'He was killed in 1940 in Bouillon, Belgium, during the fighting with the Germans. He was killed in an air raid.'

'He would have been about the same age as Datt.'

'So would a million men,' said Maria. 'It's such a stupid lie that it's not worth arguing about. Datt hoped I'd swallow that story but now even he no longer speaks of it. It's a stupid lie.'

Jean-Paul smiled uncertainly. 'Why?'

'Oh Jean-Paul. Why. You know how his evil little mind works. I was married to an important man in the Sûreté. Can't you see how convenient it would be to have me thinking he was my father? A sort of insurance, that's why.'

Jean-Paul was tired of this argument. 'Then he's not your father. But I still think you should co-operate.'

'Co-operate how?'

'Tell him a few snippets of information.'

'Could he get the film if it was really worth while?'

'I can ask him.' He smiled. 'Now you are being sensible, my love,' he said. Maria nodded as the car moved forward into the traffic. Jean-Paul planted a brief kiss on her forehead. A taxi-driver saw him do it and tooted a small illegal toot on the horn. Jean-Paul kissed Maria's forehead again a little more ardently. The great Arc de Triomphe loomed over them as they roared around the Étoile like soapsuds round the kitchen sink. A hundred tyres screamed an argument about centrifugal force, then they were into the Grande Armée. The traffic had stopped at the traffic lights. A man danced nimbly between the cars, collecting money and whipping newspapers from window to window like a fan dancer. As the traffic lights changed the cars slid forward. Maria opened her paper; the ink was still wet and it smudged under her thumb. 'American tourist disappears,' the headline said. There was a photograph of Hudson, the American hydrogen-research man. The newspaper said he was a frozen foods executive named Parks, which was the story the US Embassy had given out. Neither the face nor either name meant anything to Maria.

'Anything in the paper?' asked Jean-Paul. He was fighting a duel with a Mini-Cooper. 'No,' said Maria. She rubbed the newsprint on her thumb. 'There never is at this time of year. The English call it the silly season.'

# 18

Les Chiens is everything that delights the yeh yeh set. It's dark, hot, and squirming like a tin of live bait. The music is ear-splitting and the drink remarkably expensive even for Paris. I sat in a corner with Byrd.

'Not my sort of place at all,' Byrd said. 'But in a curious way I like it.'

A girl in gold crochet pyjamas squeezed past our table, leaned over and kissed my ear. 'Chéri,' she said. 'Long time no see,' and thereby exhausted her entire English vocabulary.

'Dash me,' said Byrd. 'You can see right through it, dash me.'

The girl patted Byrd's shoulder affectionately and moved on.

'You do have some remarkable friends,' said Byrd. He had ceased to criticize me and begun to regard me as a social curiosity well worth observing.

'A journalist must have contacts,' I explained.

'My goodness yes,' said Byrd.

The music stopped suddenly. Byrd mopped his face with a red silk handkerchief. 'It's like a stokehold,' he said. The club was strangely quiet.

'Were you an engineer officer?'

'I did gunnery school when I was on lieutenants' list. Finished a Commander; might have made Captain if there'd been a little war, Rear-Admiral if there'd been another big one. Didn't fancy waiting. Twenty-seven years of sea duty is enough. Right through the hostilities and out the other side, more ships than I care to remember.'

'You must miss it.'

'Never. Why should I? Running a ship is just like running a small factory; just as exciting at times and just as dull for the most part. Never miss it a bit. Never think about it, to tell you the truth.'

'Don't you miss the sea, or the movement, or the weather?'

'Good grief, laddie, you've got a nasty touch of the Joseph Conrads. Ships, especially cruisers, are large metal factories, rather prone to pitch in bad weather. Nothing good about that, old boy – damned inconvenient, that's the truth of it! The Navy was just a job of work for me, and it suited me fine. Nothing against the Navy mind, not at all, owe it an awful lot, no doubt of it, but it was just a job like any other; no magic to being a sailor.' There was a plonking sound as someone tapped the amplifier and put on another record. 'Painting is the only true magic,' said Byrd. 'Translating three dimensions into two – or if you are a master, four.' He nodded suddenly, the loud music started. The clientèle, who had been stiff and anxious during the silence, smiled and relaxed, for they no longer faced the strain of conversing together.

On a staircase a wedge of people were embracing and laughing like advertising photos. At the bar a couple of English photographers were talking in cockney and an English writer was explaining James Bond.

A waiter put four glasses full of ice cubes and a half-bottle of Johnnie Walker on the table before us. 'What's this?' I asked.

The waiter turned away without answering. Two Frenchmen at the bar began to argue with the English writer and a bar stool fell over. The noise wasn't loud enough for anyone to notice. On the dance floor a girl in a shiny plastic suit was swearing at a man who had burned a hole in it with his cigarette. I heard the English writer behind me say, 'But I have always immensely adored violence. His violence is his humanity. Unless you understand that you understand nothing.' He wrinkled his nose and smiled. One of the Frenchmen replied, 'He suffers in translation.' The photographer was clicking his fingers in time to the music.

'Don't we all?' said the English writer, and looked around.

Byrd said, 'Shocking noise.'

'Don't listen,' I said.

'What?' said Byrd.

The English writer was saying '. . . a violent Everyman in a violent but humdrum . . .' he paused, 'but humdrum world.' He nodded agreement to himself. 'Let me remind you of Baudelaire. There's a sonnet that begins . . .'

'So this bird wants to get out of the car . . .' one of the photographers was saying.

'Speak a little more quietly,' said the English writer. 'I'm going to recite a sonnet.'

'Belt up,' said the photographer over his shoulder. 'This bird wanted to get out of the car . . .'

'Baudelaire,' said the writer. 'Violent, macabre and symbolic.'

'You leave bollicks out of this,' said the photographer, and his friend laughed. The writer put a hand on his shoulder and said, 'Look my friend . . .' The photographer planted a right jab into his solar plexus without spilling the drink he was holding. The writer folded up like a deckchair and hit the floor. A waiter grabbed towards the photographer but stumbled over the English writer's inert body.

'Look here,' said Byrd, and a passing waiter turned so fast that the half-bottle of whisky and the four glasses of ice were knocked over. Someone aimed a blow at the photographer's head. Byrd got to his feet saying quietly and reasonably, 'You spilled the drink on the floor. Dash me, you'd better pay for it. Only thing to do. Damned rowdies.' The waiter pushed Byrd violently and he fell back and disappeared among the densely packed dancers. Two or three people began to punch each other. A wild blow took me in the small of the back, but the attacker had moved on. I got both shoulder-blades rested against the nearest piece of wall and braced the sole of my right foot for leverage. One of the photographers came my way, but he kept going and wound up grappling with a waiter. There was a scuffle going on at the top of the staircase, and then violence travelled through the place like a flash flood. Everyone was punching everyone, girls were screaming and the music seemed to be even louder than before. A man hurried a girl along the corridor past me. 'It's those English that make the trouble,' he complained.

'Yes,' I said.

'You look English.'

'No, I'm Belgian,' I said. He hurried after the girl. When I got near the emergency exit a waiter was barring the way. Behind me the screaming, grunting and breaking noises continued unabated. Someone had switched the music to top volume.

'I'm coming through,' I said to the waiter.

'No,' he said. 'No one leaves.'

A small man moved quickly alongside me. I flinched away from what I expected would be a blow upon my shoulder but it was a pat of encouragement. The man stepped forward and felled the waiter with two nasty karate cuts. 'They are all damned rude,' he said, stepping over the prostrate waiter. 'Especially waiters. If they showed a little good manners their customers might behave better.'

'Yes,' I said.

'Come along,' said Byrd. 'Don't moon around. Stay close to the wall. Watch the rear. You!' he shouted to a man with a ripped evening suit who was trying to open the emergency doors. 'Pull the top bolt, man, ease the mortice at the same time. Don't hang around, don't want to have to disable too many of them, this is my painting hand.'

We emerged into a dark side-street. Maria's car was drawn up close to the exit. 'Get in,' she called.

'Were you inside?' I asked her.

She nodded. 'I was waiting for Jean-Paul.'

'Well, you two get along,' said Byrd.

'What about Jean-Paul?' Maria said to me.

'You two get along,' said Byrd. 'He'll be quite safe.'

'Can't we give you a lift?' asked Maria.

'I'd better go back and see if Jean-Paul is all right,' said Byrd.

'You'll get killed,' said Maria.

'Can't leave Jean-Paul in there,' explained Byrd. 'Close ranks, Jean-Paul's got to stop hanging around in these sort of places and get to bed early. The morning light is the only light to paint in. I wish I could make him understand that.'

Byrd hurried back towards the club. 'He'll get killed,' said Maria.

'I don't think so,' I said. We got into Maria's E-type.

Hurrying along the street came two men in raincoats and felt hats.

'They are from the PJ crime squad,' said Maria. One of the men signalled to her. She wound the window down. He leaned down and touched his hat in salute. 'I'm looking for Byrd,' he said to Maria.

'Why?' I asked, but Maria had already told them he was the man who had just left us.

'Police judiciaire. I'm arresting him for the murder of Annie Couzins,' he said. 'I've got sworn statements from witnesses.'

'Oh God,' said Maria. 'I'm sure he's not guilty, he's not the violent type.'

I looked back to the door but Byrd had disappeared inside. The two policemen followed. Maria revved the motor and we bumped off the pavement, skimmed past a *moto* and purred into the Boul. St Germain.

The sky was starry and the air was warm. The visitors had spread through Paris by now and they strolled around entranced, in love, jilted, gay, suicidal, inspired, bellicose, defeated; in clean cotton St Trop, wine-stained Shetland, bearded, bald, bespectacled, bronzed. Acned little girls in bumbag trousers, lithe Danes, fleshy Greeks, nouveau-riche communists, illiterate writers, would-be directors – Paris had them all that summer; and Paris can keep them.

'You didn't exactly inspire me with admiration,' said Maria.

'How was that?'

'You didn't exactly spring to the aid of the ladies.'

'I didn't exactly know which ones were ladies,' I said.

'All you did was to save your own skin.'

'It's the only one I've got left,' I explained. 'I used the others for lampshades.' The blow I'd had in my kidneys hurt like hell. I'm getting too old for that sort of thing.

'Your funny time is running out,' said Maria.

'Don't be aggressive,' I said. 'It's not the right mood for asking favours.'

'How did you know I was going to ask a favour?'.

'I can read the entrails, Maria. When you mistranslated my reactions to the injections that Datt gave me you were saving me up for something.'

'Do you think I was?' she smiled. 'Perhaps I just salvaged you to take home to bed with me.'

'No, it was more than that. You are having some sort of trouble with Datt and you think – probably wrongly – that I can do something about it.'

'What makes you think so?' The streets were quieter at the other end of St Germain. We passed the bomb-scarred façade of the War Ministry and raced a cab over

119

the river. The Place de la Concorde was a great concrete field, floodlit like a film set.

'There's something in the way you speak of him. Also that night when he injected me you always moved around to keep my body between you and him. I think you had already decided to use me as a bulwark against him.'

'Teach Yourself Psychiatry, volume three.'

'Volume five. The one with the Do-It-Yourself Brain Surgery Kit.'

'Loiseau wants to see you tonight. He said it's something you'll enjoy helping him with.'

'What's he doing – disembowelling himself?' I said.

She nodded. 'Avenue Foch. Meet him at the corner at midnight.' She pulled up outside the Café Blanc.

'Come and have coffee,' I suggested.

'No. I must get home,' she said. I got out of the car and she drove away. Jean-Paul was sitting on the terrace drinking a Coca-Cola. He waved and I walked over to him. 'Were you in Les Chiens this evening?' I asked.

'Haven't been there for a week,' he said. 'I was going tonight but I changed my mind.'

'There was a *bagarre*. Byrd was there.'

Jean-Paul pulled a face but didn't seem interested. I ordered a drink and sat down. Jean-Paul stared at me.

# 19

Jean-Paul stared at the Englishman and wondered why he had sought him out. It was more than a coincidence. Jean-Paul didn't trust him. He thought he had seen Maria's car in the traffic just before the Englishman sat down. What had they both been plotting? Jean-Paul knew that no woman could be trusted. They consumed one, devoured one, sapped one's strength and confidence and gave no reassurance in return. The very nature of women made them his . . . was 'enemy' too strong a word? He decided that 'enemy' wasn't too strong a word. They took away his manhood and yet demanded more and more physical love. 'Insatiable' was the only word for them. The other conclusion was not worth considering – that his sexual prowess was under par. No. Women were hot and lustful and, if he was truthful with himself, evil. His life was an endless struggle to quench the lustful fires of the women he met. And if he ever failed they would mock him and humiliate him. Women were waiting to humiliate him.

'Have you seen Maria lately?' Jean-Paul asked.

'A moment ago. She gave me a lift here.'

Jean-Paul smiled but did not comment. So that was it. At least the Englishman had not dared to lie to him. He must have read his eyes. He was in no mood to be trifled with.

'How's the painting going?' I asked. 'Were the critics kind to your friend's show the other day?'

'Critics,' said Jean-Paul, 'find it quite impossible to separate modern painting from teenage pregnancy, juvenile delinquency and the increase in crimes of violence.

They think that by supporting the dull repetitious, representational type of painting that is out of date and unoriginal, they are also supporting loyalty to the flag, discipline, a sense of fair play and responsible use of world supremacy.'

I grinned. 'And what about those people that like modern painting?'

'People who buy modern paintings are very often interested only in gaining admittance to the world of the young artists. They are often wealthy vulgarians who, terrified of being thought old and square, prove that they are both by falling prey to quick-witted opportunists who paint modern – very modern – paintings. Provided that they keep on buying pictures they will continue to be invited to bohemian parties.'

'There are no genuine painters?'

'Not many,' said Jean-Paul. 'Tell me, are English and American exactly the same language, exactly the same?'

'Yes,' I said. Jean-Paul looked at me. 'Maria is very taken with you.' I said nothing. 'I despise all women.'

'Why?'

'Because they despise each other. They treat each other with a cruelty that no man would inflict upon another man. They never have a woman friend who they can be sure won't betray them.'

'That sounds like a good reason for men to be kind to them,' I said.

Jean-Paul smiled. He felt sure it was not meant seriously.

'The police have arrested Byrd for murder,' I said.

Jean-Paul was not surprised. 'I have always thought of him as a killer.'

I was shocked.

'They all are,' said Jean-Paul. 'They are all killers for their work. Byrd, Loiseau, Datt, even you, my friend, are killers if work demands.'

'What are you talking about? Whom did Loiseau kill?'

'He killed Maria. Or do you think she was always like she is now – treacherous and confused, and constantly in fear of all of you?'

'But you are not a killer?'

'No,' said Jean-Paul. 'Whatever faults I have I am not a killer, unless you mean . . .' He paused before carefully pronouncing the English word, 'a "lady-killer"'

Jean-Paul smiled and put on his dark glasses.

# 20

I got to the Avenue Foch at midnight.

At the corner of a narrow alley behind the houses were four shiny motor-cycles and four policemen in crash helmets, goggles and short black leather coats. They stood there impassively as only policemen stand, not waiting for anything to happen, not glancing at their watches or talking, just standing looking as though they were the only people with a right to be there. Beyond the policemen there was Loiseau's dark-green DS 19, and behind that red barriers and floodlights marked the section of the road that was being evacuated. There were more policemen standing near the barriers. I noticed that they were not traffic policemen but young, tough-looking cops with fidgety hands that continually tapped pistol holsters, belts and batons to make sure that everything was ready.

Inside the barriers twenty thick-shouldered men were bent over road-rippers. The sound was deafening, like machine-guns firing long bursts. The generator trucks played a steady drone. Near to me the ripper operator lifted the handles and prised the point into a sunsoft area of tar. He fired a volley and the metal buried its point deep, and with a sigh a chunk of paving fell back into the excavated area. The operator ordered another man to take over, and turned towards us mopping his sweaty head with a blue handkerchief. Under the overalls he wore a clean shirt and a silk tie. It was Loiseau.

'Hard work,' he said.

'You are going into the cellars?'

'Not the cellars of Datt's place,' Loiseau said to me.

'We're punching a hole in these cellars two doors away, then we'll mousehole through into Datt's cellars.'

'Why didn't you ask these people?' I pointed at the house behind which the roadwork was going on. 'Why not just ask them to let you through?'

'I don't work that way. As soon as I ask a favour I show my hand. I hate the idea of *you* knowing what we are doing. I may want to deny it tomorrow.' He mopped his brow again. 'In fact I'm damned sure I will be denying it tomorrow.' Behind him the road-ripper exploded into action and the chiselled dust shone golden in the beams of the big lights, like illustrations for a fairy story, but from the damp soil came that sour aroma of death and bacteria that clings around a bombarded city.

'Come along,' said Loiseau. We passed three huge Berliot buses full of policemen. Most were dozing with their képis pulled forward over their eyes; a couple were eating crusty sandwiches and a few were smoking. They didn't look at us as we passed by. They sat, muscles slack, eyes unseeing and minds unthinking, as experienced combat troops rest between battles.

Loiseau walked towards a fourth bus; the windows were of dark-blue glass and from its coachwork a thick cable curved towards the ground and snaked away into a manhole cover in the road. He ushered me up the steps past a sentry. Inside the bus was a brightly lit command centre. Two policemen sat operating radio and teleprinter links. At the back of the bus a large rack of MAT 49 sub-machine guns was guarded by a man who kept his silver-braided cap on to prove he was an officer.

Loiseau sat down behind a desk, produced a bottle of Calvados and two glasses. He poured a generous measure and pushed one across the desk to me. Loiseau sniffed at his own drink and sipped it tentatively. He drank a mouthful and turned to me. 'We hit some old *pavé* just under the surface. The city engineer's department didn't

125

know it was there. That's what slowed us down, otherwise we'd be into the cellars by now, all ready for you.'

'All ready for me,' I repeated.

'Yes,' said Loiseau. 'I want you to be the first into the house.'

'Why?'

'Lots of reasons. You know the layout there, you know what Datt looks like. You don't look too much like a cop – especially when you open your mouth – and you can look after yourself. And if something's going to happen to the first man in I'd rather it wasn't one of my boys. It takes a long time to train one of my boys.' He allowed himself a grim little smile.

'What's the real reason?'

Loiseau made a motion with the flattened hand. He dropped it between us like a shutter or screen. 'I want you to make a phone call from inside the house. A clear call for the police that the operator at the Prefecture will enter in the log. We'll be right behind you, of course, it's just a matter of keeping the record straight.'

'Crooked, you mean,' I said. 'It's just a matter of keeping the record crooked.'

'That depends where you are sitting,' said Loiseau.

'From where I'm sitting, I don't feel much inclined to upset the Prefecture. The *Renseignements généraux* are there in that building and they include dossiers on us foreigners. When I make that phone call it will be entered on to my file and next time I ask for my *carte de séjour* they will want to deport me for immoral acts and goodness knows what else. I'll never get another alien's permit.'

'Do what all other foreigners do,' said Loiseau. 'Take a second-class return ticket to Brussels every ninety days. There are foreigners who have lived here for twenty years who still do that rather than hang around for five hours at the Prefecture for a *carte de séjour*.' He held his flat hand

126

high as though shielding his eyes from the glare of the sun.

'Very funny,' I said.

'Don't worry,' Loiseau said. 'I couldn't risk your telling the whole Prefecture that the Sûreté had enlisted you for a job.' He smiled. 'Just do a good job for me and I'll make sure you have no trouble with the Prefecture.'

'Thanks,' I said. 'And what if there is someone waiting for me at the other side of the mousehole? What if I have one of Datt's guard dogs leap at my throat, jaws open wide? What happens then?'

Loiseau sucked his breath in mock terror. He paused. 'Then you get torn to pieces,' he said and laughed, and dropped his hand down abruptly like a guillotine.

'What do you expect to find there?' I asked. 'Here you are with dozens of cops and noise and lights – do you think they won't get nervous in the house?'

'You think they will?' Loiseau asked seriously.

'Some will,' I told him. 'At least a few of the most sophisticated ones will suspect that something's happening.'

'Sophisticated ones?'

'Come along, Loiseau,' I said irritably. 'There must be quite a lot of people close enough to your department to know the danger signals.'

He nodded and stared at me.

'So that's it,' I said. 'You were ordered to do it like this. Your department couldn't issue a warning to its associates but it could at least warn them by handling things noisily.'

'Darwin called it natural selection,' said Loiseau. 'The brightest ones will get away. You can probably guess my reaction, but at least I shall have the place closed down and may catch a few of the less imaginative clients. A little more Calvados.' He poured it.

I didn't agree to go, but Loiseau knew I would. The

127

wrong side of Loiseau could be a very uncomfortable place to reside in Paris.

It was another half-hour before they had broken into the cellars under the alley and then it took twenty minutes more to mousehole through into Datt's house. The final few demolitions had to be done brick by brick with a couple of men from a burglar-alarm company tapping around for wiring.

I had changed into police overalls before going through the final breakthrough. We were standing in the cellar of Datt's next-door neighbour under the temporary lights that Loiseau's men had slung out from the electric mains. The bare bulb was close to Loiseau's face, his skin was wrinkled and grey with brick dust through which little rivers of perspiration were shining bright pink.

'My assistant will be right behind you as far as you need cover. If the dogs go for you he will use the shot-gun, but only if you are in real danger, for it will alert the whole house.'

Loiseau's assistant nodded at me. His circular spectacle lenses flashed in the light of the bare bulb and reflected in them I could see two tiny Loiseaus and a few hundred glinting bottles of wine that were stacked behind me. He broke the breach of the shotgun and checked the cartridges even though he had only loaded the gun five minutes before.

'Once you are into the house, give my assistant your overalls. Make sure you are unarmed and have no compromising papers on you, because once we come in you might well be taken into custody with the others and it's always possible that one of my more zealous officers might search you. So if there's anything in your pockets that would embarrass you . . .'

'There's a miniaturized radio transmitter inside my denture.'

'Get rid of it.'

'It was a joke.'

Loiseau grunted and said, 'The switchboard at the Prefecture is being held open from now on' – he checked his watch to be sure he was telling the truth – 'so you'll get through very quickly.'

'You told the Prefecture?' I asked. I knew that there was bitter rivalry between the two departments. It seemed unlikely that Loiseau would have confided in them.

'Let's say I have friends in the Signals Division,' said Loiseau. 'Your call will be monitored by us here in the command vehicle on our loop line.'[1]

'I understand,' I said.

'Final wall going now,' a voice called softly from the next cellar. Loiseau smacked me lightly on the back and I climbed through the small hole that his men had made in the wall. 'Take this,' he said. It was a silver pen, thick and clumsily made. 'It's a gas gun,' explained Loiseau. 'Use it at four metres or less but not closer than one, or it might damage the eyes. Pull the bolt back like this and let it go. The recess is the locking slot; that puts it on safety. But I don't think you'd better keep it on safety.'

'No,' I said, 'I'd hate it to be on safety.' I stepped into the cellar and picked my way upstairs.

The door at the top of the service flight was disguised as a piece of panelling. Loiseau's assistant followed me. He was supposed to have remained behind in the cellars but it wasn't my job to reinforce Loiseau's discipline. And anyway I could use a man with a shotgun.

I stepped out through the door.

One of my childhood books had a photo of a fly's eye magnified fifteen thousand times. The enormous glass chandelier looked like that eye, glinting and clinking and unwinking above the great formal staircase. I walked

---

[1] Paris police have their own telephone system independent of the public one.

across the mirror-like wooden floor feeling that the chandelier was watching me. I opened the tall gilded door and peered in. The wrestling ring had disappeared and so had the metal chairs; the salon was like the carefully arranged rooms of a museum: perfect yet lifeless. Every light in the place was shining bright, the mirrors repeated the nudes and nymphs of the gilded stucco and the painted panels.

I guessed that Loiseau's men were moving up through the mouseholed cellars but I didn't use the phone that was in the alcove in the hall. Instead I walked across the hall and up the stairs. The rooms that M. Datt used as offices – where I had been injected – were locked. I walked down the corridor trying the doors. They were all bedrooms. Most of them were unlocked; all of them were unoccupied. Most of the rooms were lavishly rococo with huge four-poster beds under brilliant silk canopies and four or five angled mirrors.

'You'd better phone,' said Loiseau's assistant.

'Once I phone the Prefecture will have this raid on record. I think we should find out a little more first.'

'I think . . .'

'Don't tell me what you think or I'll remind you that you're supposed to have stayed down behind the wainscoting.'

'Okay,' he said. We both tiptoed up the small staircase that joined the first floor to the second. Loiseau's men must be fretting by now. At the top of the flight of steps I put my head round the corner carefully. I put my head everywhere carefully, but I needn't have been so cautious, the house was empty. 'Get Loiseau up here,' I said.

Loiseau's men went all through the house, tapping panelling and trying to find secret doors. There were no documents or films. At first there seemed to be no secrets of any kind except that the whole place was a kind of

130

secret: the strange cells with the awful torture instruments, rooms made like lush train compartments or Rolls Royce cars, and all kinds of bizarre environments for sexual intercourse, even beds.

The peep-holes and the closed-circuit TV were all designed for M. Datt and his 'scientific methods'. I wondered what strange records he had amassed and where he had taken them, for M. Datt was nowhere to be found. Loiseau swore horribly. 'Someone,' he said, 'must have told Monsieur Datt that we were coming.'

Loiseau had been in the house about ten minutes when he called his assistant. He called long and loud from two floors above. When we arrived he was crouched over a black metal device rather like an Egyptian mummy. It was the size and very roughly the shape of a human body. Loiseau had put cotton gloves on and he touched the object briefly.

'The diagram of the Couzins girl,' he demanded from his assistant.

It was obtained from somewhere, a paper pattern of Annie Couzins's body marked in neat red ink to show the stab wounds, with the dimensions and depth written near each in tiny careful handwriting.

Loiseau opened the black metal case. 'That's it,' he said. 'Just what I thought.' Inside the case, which was just large enough to hold a person, knife points were positioned exactly as indicated on the police diagram. Loiseau gave a lot of orders and suddenly the room was full of men with tape-measures, white powder and camera equipment. Loiseau stood back out of their way. 'Iron maidens I think they call them,' he said. 'I seem to have read about them in some old schoolboy magazines.'

'What made her get into the damn thing?' I said.

'You are naïve,' said Loiseau. 'When I was a young officer we had so many deaths from knife wounds in brothels that we put a policeman on the door in each

131

one. Every customer was searched. Any weapons he carried were chalked for identity. When the men left they got them back. I'll guarantee that not one got by that cop on the door but still the girls got stabbed, fatally sometimes.'

'How did it happen?'

'The girls – the prostitutes – smuggled them in. You'll never understand women.'

'No,' I said.

'Nor shall I,' said Loiseau.

# 21

Saturday was sunny, the light bouncing and sparkling as it does only in impressionist paintings and Paris. The boulevard had been fitted with wall-to-wall sunshine and out of it came the smell of good bread and black tobacco. Even Loiseau was smiling. He came galloping up my stairs at 8.30 A.M. I was surprised; he had never visited me before, at least not when I was at home.

'Don't knock, come in.' The radio was playing classical music from one of the pirate radio ships. I turned it off.

'I'm sorry,' said Loiseau.

'Everyone's at home to a policeman,' I said, 'in this country.'

'Don't be angry,' said Loiseau. 'I didn't know you would be in a silk dressing-gown, feeding your canary. It's very Noël Coward. If I described this scene as typically English, people would accuse me of exaggerating. You were talking to that canary,' said Loiseau. 'You were *talking* to it.'

'I try out all my jokes on Joe,' I said. 'But don't stand on ceremony, carry on ripping the place apart. What are you looking for this time?'

'I've said I'm sorry. What more can I do?'

'You could get out of my decrepit but very expensive apartment and stay out of my life. And you could stop putting your stubby peasant finger into my supply of coffee beans.'

'I was hoping you'd offer me some. You have this very light roast that is very rare in France.'

'I have a lot of things that are very rare in France.'

'Like the freedom to tell a policeman to "scram"?'

133

'Like that.'

'Well, don't exercise that freedom until we have had coffee together, even if you let me buy some downstairs.'

'Oh boy! Now I know you are on the tap. A cop is really on the make when he wants to pick up the bill for a cup of coffee.'

'I've had good news this morning.'

'They are restoring public executions.'

'On the contrary,' said Loiseau, letting my remark roll off him. 'There has been a small power struggle among the people from whom I take my orders and at present Datt's friends are on the losing side. I have been authorized to find Datt and his film collection by any means I think fit.'

'When does the armoured column leave? What's the plan – helicopters and flame-throwers and the one that burns brightest must have been carrying the tin of film?'

'You are too hard on the police methods in France. You think we could work with bobbies in pointed helmets carrying a wooden stick, but let me tell you, my friend, we wouldn't last two minutes with such methods. I remember the gangs when I was just a child – my father was a policeman – and most of all I remember Corsica. There were bandits; organized, armed and almost in control of the island. They murdered gendarmes with impunity. They killed policemen and boasted of it openly in the bars. Finally we had to get rough; we sent in a few platoons of the Republican Guard and waged a minor war. Rough, perhaps, but there was no other way. The entire income from all the Paris brothels was at stake. They fought and used every dirty trick they knew. It was war.'

'But you won the war.'

'It was the very last war we won,' Loiseau said bitterly. 'Since then we've fought in Lebanon, Syria, Indo-China,

Madagascar, Tunisia, Morocco, Suez and Algeria. Yes, that war in Corsica was the last one we won.'

'Okay. So much for your problems; how do I fit into your plans?'

'Just as I told you before; you are a foreigner and no one would think you were a policeman, you speak excellent French and you can look after yourself. What's more you would not be the sort of man who would reveal where your instructions came from, not even under pressure.'

'It sounds as though you think Datt still has a kick or two left in him.'

'They have a kick or two left in them even when they are suspended in space with a rope around the neck. I never underestimate the people I'm dealing with, because they are usually killers when it comes to the finale. Any time I overlook that, it will be one of my policemen who takes the bullet in the head, not me. So I don't overlook it, which means I have a tough, loyal, confident body of men under my command.'

'Okay,' I said. 'So I locate Datt. What then?'

'We can't have another fiasco like last time. Now Datt will be more than ever prepared. I want all his records. I want them because they are a constant threat to a lot of people, including stupid people in the Government of my country. I want that film because I loathe blackmail and I loathe blackmailers – they are the filthiest section of the criminal cesspit.'

'But so far there's been no blackmail, has there?'

'I'm not standing around waiting for the obvious to happen. I want that stuff destroyed. I don't want to hear that it was destroyed. I want to destroy it myself.'

'Suppose I don't want anything to do with it?'

Loiseau splayed out his hands. 'One,' he said, grabbing one pudgy finger, 'you are already involved. Two,' he grabbed the next finger, 'you are employed by some sort of British government department from what I can

135

understand. They will be very angry if you turn down this chance of seeing the outcome of this affair.'

I suppose my expression changed.

'Oh, it's my business to know these things,' said Loiseau. 'Three. Maria has decided that you are trustworthy and in spite of her occasional lapses I have great regard for her judgement. She is, after all, an employee of the Sûreté.'

Loiseau grabbed his fourth digit but said nothing. He smiled. In most people a smile or a laugh can be a sign of embarrassment, a plea to break the tension. Loiseau's smile was a calm, deliberate smile. 'You are waiting for me to threaten you with what will happen if you don't help me.' He shrugged and smiled again. 'Then you would turn my previous words about blackmail upon me and feel at ease in declining to help. But I won't. You are free to do as you wish in this matter. I am a very unthreatening type.'

'For a cop,' I said.

'Yes,' agreed Loiseau, 'a very unthreatening type for a cop.' It was true.

'Okay,' I said after a long pause. 'But don't mistake my motives. Just to keep the record straight, I'm very fond of Maria.'

'Can you really believe that would annoy me? You are so incredibly Victorian in these matters: so determined to play the game and keep a stiff upper lip aand have the record straight. We do not do things that way in France; another man's wife is fair game for all. Smoothness of tongue and nimbleness of foot are the trump cards; nobleness of mind is the joker.'

'I prefer my way.'

Loiseau looked at me and smiled his slow, nerveless smile. 'So do I,' he said.

'Loiseau,' I said, watching him carefully, 'this clinic of Datt's: is it run by your Ministry?'

'Don't *you* start that too. He's got half Paris thinking he's running that place for us.' The coffee was still hot. Loiseau got a bowl out of the cupboard and poured himself some. 'He's not connected with us,' said Loiseau. 'He's a criminal, a criminal with good connections but still just a criminal.'

'Loiseau,' I said, 'you can't hold Byrd for the murder of the girl.'

'Why not?'

'Because he didn't do it, that's why not. I was at the clinic that day. I stood in the hall and watched the girl run through and die. I heard Datt say, "Get Byrd here." It was a frame-up.'

Loiseau reached for his hat. 'Good coffee,' he said.

'It was a frame-up. Byrd is innocent.'

'So you say. But suppose Byrd had done the murder and Datt said that just for you to overhear? Suppose I told you that we know that Byrd was there? That would put this fellow Kuang in the clear, eh?'

'It might,' I said, 'if I heard Byrd admit it. Will you arrange for me to see Byrd? That's my condition for helping you.' I expected Loiseau to protest but he nodded. 'Agreed,' he said. 'I don't know why you worry about him. He's a criminal type if ever I saw one.' I didn't answer because I had a nasty idea that Loiseau was right.

'Very well,' said Loiseau. 'The bird market at eleven A.M. tomorrow.'

'It's Sunday tomorrow,' I said.

'All the better, the Palais de Justice is quieter on Sunday.' He smiled again. 'Good coffee.'

'That's what they all say,' I said.

# 22

A considerable portion of that large island in the Seine is
occupied by the law in one shape or another. There's the
Prefecture and the courts, Municipal and Judicial police
offices, cells for remand prisoners and a police canteen.
On a weekday the stairs are crammed with black-gowned
lawyers clutching plastic briefcases and scurrying like
disturbed cockroaches. But on Sunday the Palais de
Justice is silent. The prisoners sleep late and the offices
are empty. The only movement is the thin stream of
tourists who respectfully peer at the high vaulting of the
Sainte Chapelle, clicking and wondering at its unparal-
leled beauty. Outside in the Place Louis Lépine a few
hundred caged birds twitter in the sunshine and in the
trees are wild birds attracted by the spilled seed and
commotion. There are sprigs of millet, cuttlebone and
bright new wooden cages, bells to ring, swings to swing
on and mirrors to peck at. Old men run their shrivelled
hands through the seeds, sniff them, discuss them and
hold them up to the light as though they were fine vintage
Burgundies.

The bird market was busy by the time I got there to
meet Loiseau. I parked the car opposite the gates of the
Palais de Justice and strolled through the market. The
clock was striking eleven with a dull dented sound.
Loiseau was standing in front of some cages marked
'*Caille reproductrice*'. He waved as he saw me. 'Just a
moment,' he said. He picked up a box marked 'vitamine
phospate'. He read the label: '*Biscuits pour oiseaux*'. 'I'll
have that too,' said Loiseau.

The woman behind the table said, 'The *mélange saxon* is very good, it's the most expensive, but it's the best.'

'Just half a litre,' said Loiseau.

She weighed the seed, wrapped it carefully and tied the package. Loiseau said, 'I didn't see him.'

'Why?' I walked with him through the market.

'He's been moved. I can't find out who authorized the move or where he's gone to. The clerk in the records office said Lyon but that can't be true.' Loiseau stopped in front of an old pram full of green millet.

'Why?'

Loiseau didn't answer immediately. He picked up a sprig of millet and sniffed at it. 'He's been moved. Some top-level instructions. Perhaps they intend to bring him before some *juge d'instruction* who will do as he's told. Or maybe they'll keep him out of the way while they finish the *enquêtes officieuses*.'[1]

'You don't think they've moved him away to get him quietly sentenced?'

Loiseau waved to the old woman behind the stall. She shuffled slowly towards us.

'I talk to you like an adult,' Loiseau said. 'You don't really expect me to answer that, do you? A sprig.' He turned and stared at me. 'Better make it two sprigs,' he

---

[1] Under French Law the Prefect of Paris Police can arrest, interrogate, inquire, search, confiscate letters in the post, without any other authority than his own. His only obligation is to inform the Public Prosecutor and bring the prisoner before a magistrate within twenty-four hours. Note that the magistrate is part of the law machine and not a separate functionary as he is in Britain.

When he is brought before the magistrate – *juge d'instruction* – the police explain that the man is *suspected* and the magistrate directs the building up of evidence. (In Britain, of course, the man is not brought before a magistrate until after the police have built up their case.)

Inquiries prior to the appearance before a *juge d'instruction* are called *enquêtes officieuses* (informal inquiries). In law the latter give no power to search or demand statements but in practice few citizens argue about this technicality when faced with the police.

said to the woman. 'My friend's canary wasn't looking so healthy last time I saw it.'

'Joe's all right,' I said. 'You leave him alone.'

'Suit yourself,' said Loiseau. 'But if he gets much thinner he'll be climbing out between the bars of that cage.'

I let him have the last word. He paid for the millet and walked between the cliffs of new empty cages, trying the bars and tapping the wooden panels. There were caged birds of all kinds in the market. They were given seed, millet, water and cuttlefish bone for their beaks. Their claws were kept trimmed and they were safe from all birds of prey. But it was the birds in the trees that were singing.

# 23

I got back to my apartment about twelve o'clock. At twelve thirty-five the phone rang. It was Monique, Annie's neighbour. 'You'd better come quickly,' she said.

'Why?'

'I'm not allowed to say on the phone. There's a fellow sitting here. He won't tell me anything much. He was asking for Annie, he won't tell me anything. Will you come now?'

'Okay,' I said.

# 24

It was lunchtime. Monique was wearing an ostrich-feather-trimmed négligé when she opened the door. 'The English have got off the boat,' she said and giggled. 'You'd better come in, the old girl will be straining her earholes to hear, if we stand here talking.' She opened the door and showed me into the cramped room. There was bamboo furniture and tables, a plastic-topped dressing-table with four swivel mirrors and lots of perfume and cosmetic garnishes. The bed was unmade and a candlewick bedspread had been rolled up under the pillows. A copy of *Salut les Copains* was in sections and arranged around the deep warm indentation. She went across to the windows and pushed the shutters. They opened with a loud clatter. The sunlight streamed into the room and made everything look dusty. On the table there was a piece of pink wrapping paper; she took a hard-boiled egg from it, rapped open the shell and bit into it.

'I hate summer,' she said. 'Pimples and parks and open cars that make your hair tangled and rotten cold food that looks like left-overs. And the sun trying to make you feel guilty about being indoors. I like being indoors. I like being in bed; it's no sin, is it, being in bed?'

'Just give me the chance to find out. Where is he?'

'I hate summer.'

'So shake hands with Père Noël,' I offered. 'Where is he?'

'I'm taking a shower. You sit down and wait. You are all questions.'

'Yes,' I said. 'Questions.'

'I don't know how you think of all these questions. You must be clever.'

'I am,' I said.

'Honestly, I wouldn't know where to start. The only questions I ever ask are "Are you married?" and "What will you do if I get pregnant?" Even then I never get told the truth.'

'That's the trouble with questions. You'd better stick to answers.'

'Oh, I know all the answers.'

'Then you must have been asked all the questions.'

'I have,' she agreed.

She slipped out of the négligé and stood naked for one millionth of a second before disappearing into the bathroom. The look in her eyes was mocking and not a little cruel.

There was a lot of splashing and ohh-ing from the bathroom until she finally reappeared in a cotton dress and canvas tennis shoes, no stockings.

'Water was cold,' she said briefly. She walked right through the room and opened her front door. I watched her lean over the balustrade.

'The water's stone cold, you stupid cow,' she shrieked down the stair-well. From somewhere below the voice of the old harridan said, 'It's not supposed to supply ten people for each apartment, you filthy little whore.'

'I have something men want, not like you, you old hag.'

'And you give it to them,' the harridan cackled back. 'The more the merrier.'

'Poof!' shouted Monique, and narrowing her eyes and aiming carefully she spat over the stair-well. The harridan must have anticipated it, for I heard her cackle triumphantly.

Monique returned to me. 'How am I expected to keep clean when the water is cold? Always cold.'

'Did Annie complain about the water?'

'Ceaselessly, but she didn't have the manner that brings results. I get angry. If she doesn't give me hot water I shall drive her into her grave, the dried-up old bitch. I'm leaving here anyway,' she said.

'Where are you going?' I asked.

'I'm moving in with my regular. Montmartre. It's an awful district, but it's larger than this, and anyway he wants me.'

'What's he do for a living?'

'He does the clubs, he's – don't laugh – he's a conjurer. It's a clever trick he does: he takes a singing canary in a large cage and makes it disappear. It looks fantastic. Do you know how he does it?'

'No.'

'The cage folds up. That's easy, it's a trick cage. But the bird gets crushed. Then when he makes it reappear it's just another canary that looks the same. It's an easy trick really, it's just that no one in the audience suspects that he would kill the bird each time in order to do the trick.'

'But you guessed.'

'Yes. I guessed the first time I saw it done. He thought I was clever to guess but as I said, "How much does a canary cost? Three francs, four at the very most." It's clever though, isn't it, you've got to admit it's clever.'

'It's clever,' I said, 'but I like canaries better than I like conjurers.'

'Silly.' Monique laughed disbelievingly. ' "The incredible Count Szell" he calls himself.'

'So you'll be a countess?'

'It's his stage name, silly.' She picked up a pot of face cream. 'I'll just be another stupid woman who lives with a married man.'

She rubbed cream into her face.

'Where is he?' I finally asked. 'Where's this fellow that

you said was sitting here?' I was prepared to hear that she'd invented the whole thing.

'In the café on the corner. He'll be all right there. He's reading his American newspapers. He's all right.'

'I'll go and talk to him.'

'Wait for me.' She wiped the cream away with a tissue and turned and smiled. 'Am I all right?'

'You're all right,' I told her.

# 25

The café was on the Boul. Mich., the very heart of the left bank. Outside in the bright sun sat the students; hirsute and earnest, they have come from Munich and Los Angeles sure that Hemingway and Lautrec are still alive and that some day in some left bank café they will find them. But all they ever find are other young men who look exactly like themselves, and it's with this sad discovery that they finally return to Bavaria or California and become salesmen or executives. Meanwhile here they sat in the hot seat of culture, where businessmen became poets, poets became alcoholics, alcoholics became philosophers and philosophers realized how much better it was to be businessmen.

Hudson. I've got a good memory for faces. I saw Hudson as soon as we turned the corner. He was sitting alone at a café table holding his paper in front of his face while studying the patrons with interest. I called to him.

'Jack Percival,' I called. 'What a great surprise.'

The American hydrogen research man looked surprised, but he played along very well for an amateur. We sat down with him. My back hurt from the rough-house in the discothèque. It took a long time to get served because the rear of the café was full of men with tightly wadded newspapers trying to pick themselves a winner instead of eating. Finally I got the waiter's attention. 'Three grands crèmes,' I said. Hudson said nothing else until the coffees arrived.

'What about this young lady?' Hudson asked. He dropped sugar cubes into his coffee as though he was suffering from shock. 'Can I talk?'

'Sure,' I said. 'There are no secrets between Monique and me.' I leaned across to her and lowered my voice. 'This is very confidential, Monique,' I said. She nodded and looked pleased. 'There is a small plastic bead company with its offices in Grenoble. Some of the holders of ordinary shares have sold their holdings out to a company that this gentleman and I more or less control. Now at the next shareholders' meeting we shall . . .'

'Give over,' said Monique. 'I can't stand business talk.'

'Well run along then,' I said, granting her her freedom with an understanding smile.

'Could you buy me some cigarettes?' she asked.

I got two packets from the waiter and wrapped a hundred-franc note round them. She trotted off down the street with them like a dog with a nice juicy bone.

'It's not about your bead factory,' he said.

'There is no bead factory,' I explained.

'Oh!' He laughed nervously. 'I was supposed to have contacted Annie Couzins,' he said.

'She's dead.'

'I found that out for myself.'

'From Monique?'

'You are T. Davis?' he asked suddenly.

'With bells on,' I said and passed my resident's card to him.

An untidy man with a constantly smiling face walked from table to table winding up toys and putting them on the tables. He put them down everywhere until each table had its twitching mechanical figures bouncing through the knives, table mats and ashtrays. Hudson picked up the convulsive little violin player. 'What's this for?'

'It's on sale,' I said.

He nodded and put it down. 'Everything is,' he said.

He returned my resident's card to me.

'It looks all right,' he agreed. 'Anyway I can't go back to the Embassy, they told me that most expressly, so I'll

147

have to put myself in your hands. I'm out of my depth to tell you the truth.'

'Go ahead.'

'I'm an authority on hydrogen bombs and I know quite a bit about all the work on the nuclear programme. My instructions are to put certain information about fall-out dangers at the disposal of a Monsieur Datt. I understand he is connected with the Red Chinese Government.'

'And why are you to do this?'

'I thought you'd know. It's such a mess. That poor girl being dead. Such a tragedy. I did meet her once. So young, such a tragic business. I thought they would have told you all about it. You were the only other name they gave me, apart from her I mean. I'm acting on US Government orders, of course.'

'Why would the US Government want you to give away fall-out data?' I asked him. He sat back in the cane chair till it creaked like elderly arthritic joints. He pulled an ashtray near him.

'It all began with the Bikini Atoll nuclear tests,' he began. 'The Atomic Energy Commission were taking a lot of criticism about the dangers of fall-out, the biological result upon wildlife and plants. The AEC needed those tests and did a lot of follow-through testing on the sites, trying to prove that the dangers were not anything like as great as many alarmists were saying. I have to tell you that those alarmists were damn nearly right. A dirty bomb of about twenty-five megatons would put down about 15,000 square miles of lethal radio-activity. To survive that, you would have to stay underground for months, some say even a year or more.

'Now if we were involved in a war with Red China, and I dread the thought of such a thing, then we would have to use the nuclear fall-out as a weapon, because only ten per cent of the Chinese population live in large – quarter-million size – towns. In the USA more than half the population live in the large towns. China with its dispersed population can only be knocked out by fall-out . . .' He paused. 'But knocked out it can be. Our experts say that about half a billion people live on one-fifth of China's land area. The prevailing wind is westerly. Four hundred bombs would kill fifty million by direct heat-blast effect, one hundred million would be seriously injured though they wouldn't need hospitalization, but three hundred and fifty million would die by windborne fall-out.

'The AEC minimized the fall-out effects in their follow-through reports on the tests (Bikini, etc.). Now the more militant of the Chinese soldier-scientists are using the US reports to prove that China can survive a nuclear war. We couldn't withdraw those reports, or say that they were untrue – not even slightly untrue – so I'm here to leak the correct information to the Chinese scientists. The whole operation began nearly eight months ago. It took a long time getting this girl Annie Couzins into position.'

'In the clinic near to Datt.'

'Exactly. The original plan was that she should introduce me to this man Datt and say I was an American scientist with a conscience.'

'That's a piece of CIA thinking if ever I heard one?'

'You think it's an extinct species?'

'It doesn't matter what I think, but it's not a line that Datt will buy easily.'

'If you are going to start changing the plan now . . .'

'The plan changed when the girl was killed. It's a mess; the only way I can handle it is my way.'

'Very well,' said Hudson. He sat silent for a moment.

Behind me a man with a rucksack said, 'Florence. We hated Florence.'

'We hated Trieste,' said a girl.

149

'Yes,' said the man with the rucksack, 'my friend hated Trieste last year.'

'My contact here doesn't know why you are in Paris,' I said suddenly. I tried to throw Hudson, but he took it calmly.

'I hope he doesn't,' said Hudson. 'It's all supposed to be top secret. I hated to come to you about it but I've no other contact here.'

'You're at the Lotti Hotel.'

'How did you know?'

'It's stamped across your *Tribune* in big blue letters.'

He nodded. I said, 'You'll go to the Hotel Ministère right away. Don't get your baggage from the Lotti. Buy a toothbrush or whatever you want on the way back now.' I expected to encounter opposition to this idea but Hudson welcomed the game.

'I get you,' he said. 'What name shall I use?'

'Let's make it Potter,' I said. He nodded. 'Be ready to move out at a moment's notice. And Hudson, don't telephone or write any letters; you know what I mean. Because I could become awfully suspicious of you.'

'Yes,' he said.

'I'll put you in a cab,' I said, getting up to leave.

'Do that, their Métro drives me crazy.'

I walked up the street with him towards the cab-rank. Suddenly he dived into an optician's. I followed.

'Ask him if I can look at some spectacles,' he said.

'Show him some spectacles,' I told the optician. He put a case full of tortoiseshell frames on the counter.

'He'll need a test,' said the optician. 'Unless he has his prescription he'll need a test.'

'You'll need a test or a prescription,' I told Hudson.

He had sorted out a frame he liked. 'Plain glass,' he demanded.

'What would I keep plain glass around for?' said the optician.

'What would he keep plain glass for?' I said to Hudson.

'The weakest possible, then,' said Hudson.

'The weakest possible,' I said to the optician. He fixed the lenses in in a moment or so. Hudson put the glasses on and we resumed our walk towards the taxi. He peered around him myopically and was a little unsteady.

'Disguise,' said Hudson.

'I thought perhaps it was,' I said.

'I would have made a good spy,' said Hudson. 'I've often thought that.'

'Yes,' I said. 'Well, there's your cab. I'll be in touch. Check out of the Lotti into the Ministère. I've written the name down on my card, they know me there. Try not to attract attention. Stay inside.'

'Where's the cab?' said Hudson.

'If you'll take off those bloody glasses,' I said, 'you might be able to see.'

# 26

I went round to Maria's in a hurry. When she opened the door she was wearing riding breeches and a roll-neck pullover. 'I was about to go out,' she said.

'I need to see Datt,' I said.

'Why do you tell me that?'

I pushed past her and closed the door behind us. 'Where is he?'

She gave me a twitchy little ironical smile while she thought of something crushing to say. I grabbed her arm and let my fingertips bite. 'Don't fool with me, Maria. I'm not in the mood. Believe me I would hit you.'

'I've no doubt about it.'

'You told Datt about Loiseau's raid on the place in the Avenue Foch. You have no loyalties, no allegiance, none to the Sûreté, none to Loiseau. You just give away information as though it was toys out of a bran tub.'

'I thought you were going to say I gave it away as I did my sexual favours,' she smiled again.

'Perhaps I was.'

'Did you remember that I kept your secret without giving it away? No one knows what you truly said when Datt gave you the injection.'

'No one knows yet. I suspect that you are saving it up for something special.'

She swung her hand at me but I moved out of range. She stood for a moment, her face twitching with fury.

'You ungrateful bastard,' she said. 'You're the first real bastard I've ever met.'

I nodded. 'There's not many of us around. Ungrateful

for what?' I asked her. 'Ungrateful for your loyalty? Was that what your motive was: loyalty?'

'Perhaps you're right,' she admitted quietly. 'I have no loyalty to anyone. A woman on her own becomes awfully hard. Datt is the only one who understands that. Somehow I didn't want Loiseau to arrest him.' She looked up. 'For that and many reasons.'

'Tell me one of the other reasons.'

'Datt is a senior man in the SDECE, and that's one reason. If Loiseau clashed with him, Loiseau could only lose.'

'Why do you think Datt is an SDECE man?'

'Many people know. Loiseau won't believe it but it's true.'

'Loiseau won't believe it because he has got too much sense. I've checked up on Datt. He's never had anything to do with any French intelligence unit. But he knew how useful it was to let people think so.'

She shrugged. 'I know it's true,' she said. 'Datt works for the SDECE.'

I took her shoulders. 'Look, Maria. Can't you get it through your head that he's a phoney? He has no psychiatry diploma, has never been anything to do with the French Government except that he pulls strings among his friends and persuades even people like you who work for the Sûreté that he's a highly placed agent of SDECE.'

'And what do you want?' she asked.

'I want you to help me find Datt.'

'Help,' she said. 'That's a new attitude. You come bursting in here making your demands. If you'd come in here asking for help I might have been more sympathetic. What is it you want with Datt?'

'I want Kuang; he killed the girl at the clinic that day. I want to find him.'

'It's not your job to find him.'

'You are right. It's Loiseau's job, but he is holding Byrd for it and he'll keep on holding him.'

'Loiseau wouldn't hold an innocent man. Poof, you don't know what a fuss he makes about the sanctity of the law and that sort of thing.'

'I am a British agent,' I said. 'You know that already so I'm not telling you anything new. Byrd is too.'

'Are you sure?'

'No, I'm not. I'd be the last person to be told anyway. He's not someone whom I would contact officially. It's just my guess. I think Loiseau has been instructed to hold Byrd for the murder – with or without evidence – so Byrd is doomed unless I push Kuang right into Loiseau's arms.'

Maria nodded.

'Your mother lives in Flanders. Datt will be at his house near by, right?' Maria nodded. 'I want you to take an American out to your mother's house and wait there till I phone.'

'She hasn't got a phone.'

'Now, now, Maria,' I said. 'I checked up on your mother: she has a phone. Also I phoned my people here in Paris. They will be bringing some papers to your mother's house. They'll be needed for crossing the border. No matter what I say don't come over to Datt's without them.'

Maria nodded. 'I'll help. I'll help you pin that awful Kuang. I hate him.'

'And Datt, do you hate him too?'

She looked at me searchingly. 'Sometimes, but in a different way,' she said. 'You see, I'm his illegitimate daughter. Perhaps you checked up on that too?'

## 27

The road was straight. It cared nothing for geography, geology or history. The oil-slicked highway dared children and divided neighbours. It speared small villages through their hearts and laid them open. It was logical that it should be so straight, and yet it was obsessive too. Carefully lettered signs – the names of villages and the times of Holy Mass – and then the dusty clutter of houses flicked past with seldom any sign of life. At Le Chateau I turned off the main road and picked my way through the small country roads. I saw the sign Plaisir ahead and slowed. This was the place I wanted.

The main street of the village was like something out of Zane Grey, heavy with the dust of passing vehicles. None of them stopped. The street was wide enough for four lanes of cars, but there was very little traffic. Plaisir was on the main road to nowhere. Perhaps a traveller who had taken the wrong road at St Quentin might pass through Plaisir trying to get back on the Paris–Brussels road. Some years back when they were building the autoroute, heavy lorries had passed through, but none of them had stopped at Plaisir.

Today it was hot; scorching hot. Four mangy dogs had scavenged enough food and now were asleep in the centre of the roadway. Every house was shuttered tight, grey and dusty in the cruel biting midday light that gave them only a narrow rim of shadow.

I stopped the car near to a petrol pump, an ancient, handle-operated instrument bolted uncertainly on to a concrete pillar. I got out and thumped upon the garage doors, but there was no response. The only other vehicle in sight was an old tractor parked a few yards ahead. On the other side of the street a horse stood, tethered to a piece of rusty farm machinery, flicking its tail against the flies. I touched the engine of the tractor: it was still warm. I hammered the garage doors again, but the only movement was the horse's tail. I walked down the silent street, the stones hot against my shoes. One of the dogs, its left ear missing, scratched itself awake and crawled into the shade of the tractor. It growled dutifully at me as I passed, then subsided into sleep. A cat's eyes peered through a window full of aspidistra plants. Above the window, faintly discernible in the weathered woodwork, I read the word 'café'. The door was stiff and opened noisily. I went in.

There were half a dozen people standing at the bar. They weren't talking and I had the feeling that they had been watching me since I left the car. They stared at me.

'A red wine,' I said. The old woman behind the bar looked at me without blinking. She didn't move.

'And a cheese sandwich,' I added. She gave it another minute before slowly reaching for a wine bottle, rinsing a glass and pouring me a drink, all without moving her feet. I turned around to face the room. The men were mostly farm workers, their boots heavy with soil and their faces engraved with ancient dirt. In the corner a table was occupied by three men in suits and white shirts. Although it was long past lunchtime they had napkins tucked into their collars and were putting forkfuls of cheese into their mouths, honing their knives across the bread chunks and pouring draughts of red wine into their throats after it. They continued to eat. They were the only people in the room not looking at me except for a muscular man seated at the back of the room, his feet propped upon a chair, placing the cards of his patience game with quiet confidence. I watched him peel each card loose from the pack, stare at it with the superior impartiality of a computer and place it face up on the marble table-top. I watched him play for a minute or so, but he didn't look up.

It was a dark room; the only light entering it filtered through the jungle of plants in the window. On the marble-topped tables there were drip-mats advertising aperitifs; the mats had been used many times. The bar was brown with varnish and above the rows of bottles was an old clock that had ticked its last at 3.37 on some long-forgotten day. There were old calendars on the walls, a broken chair had been piled neatly under the window and the floor-boards squealed with each change of weight. In spite of the heat of the day three men had drawn their chairs close to a dead stove in the centre of the room. The body of the stove had cracked, and from it cold ash had spilled on to the floor. One of the men tapped his pipe against the stove. More ash poured out like the sands of time.

'I'm looking for Monsieur Datt,' I said to the whole room. 'Which is his house?'

There was not even a change of expression. Outside I heard the sudden yelp of a frightened dog. From the corner came the regular click of playing cards striking the marble. There was no other sound.

I said, 'I have important news for him. I know he lives somewhere in the village.' I moved my eyes from face to face searching for a flicker of comprehension; there was none. Outside the dogs began to fight. It was a ragged, vicious sound: low growls and sudden shrieks of pain.

'This is Plaisir?' I asked. There was no answer. I turned to the woman behind the bar. 'Is this the village of Plaisir?' She half smiled.

'Another carafe of red,' called one of the men in white shirts.

The woman behind the bar reached for a litre bottle of wine, poured a carafe of it and pushed it down the counter. The man who had asked for it walked across to the counter, his napkin stuck in his collar, a fork still in his hand. He seized the carafe by the neck and returned to his seat. He poured a glass of wine for himself and took a large gulp. With the wine still in his mouth he leaned back in his chair, raised his eyes to mine and let the wine trickle into his throat. The dogs began fighting again.

'They are getting vicious,' said the man. 'Perhaps we should do away with one of them.'

'Do away with them all,' I said. He nodded.

I finished my drink. 'Three francs,' said the woman.

'What about a cheese sandwich?'

'We sell only wine.'

I put three new francs on the counter-top. The man finished his patience game and collected the dog-eared cards together. He drank his glass of red wine and carried the empty glass and the greasy pack of cards to the counter. He put them both down and laid two twenty-old-franc pieces on top, then he wiped his hands on the front of his work jacket and stared at me for a moment. His eyes were quick and alert. He turned towards the door.

'Are you going to tell me how to get to Monsieur Datt's house?' I asked the woman again.

'We only sell wine,' she said, scooping up the coins. I walked out into the hot midday sun. The man who had been playing patience walked slowly across to the tractor. He was a tall man, better nourished and more alert than the local inhabitants, perhaps thirty years old, walking like a horseman. When he reached the petrol pump, he whistled softly. The door opened immediately and an attendant came out.

'Ten litres.'

The attendant nodded. He inserted the nozzle of the pump into the tank of the tractor, unlocked the handle and then rocked it to pump the spirit out. I watched them close to, but neither looked round. When the needle read ten litres, he stopped pumping and replaced the nozzle. 'See you tomorrow,' said the tall man. He did not pay. He threw a leg over the tractor seat and started the motor. There was an ear-splitting racket as it started. He let in the clutch too quickly and the big wheels slid in the dust for an instant before biting into the *pavé* and roaring away, leaving a trail of blue smoke. The one-eared dog awoke again as the sound and the hot sun hit it and went bounding up the road barking and snapping at the tractor wheels. That awoke the other dogs and they, too, began to bark. The tall man leaned over his saddle like an apache scout and caught the dog under its only ear with a wooden stick. It sang a descant of pain and retired from the chase. The other dogs too lost heart, their energy sapped by the heat. The barking ended raggedly.

'I'm thinking of driving to the Datt house,' I said to the pump attendant. He stared after the tractor. 'He'll never learn,' he said. The dog limped back into the shade of the petrol pump. The attendant turned to face me. 'Some dogs are like that,' he said. 'They never learn.'

'If I drive to the Datt house I'll need twenty litres of the best.'

'Only one kind,' said the man.

'I'll need twenty litres *if* you'll be kind enough to direct me to the Datt place.'

'You'd better fill her up,' said the man. He raised his eyes to mine for the first time. 'You're going to need to come back, aren't you?'

'Right,' I said. 'And check the oil and water.' I took a ten-franc note from my pocket. 'That's for you,' I said. 'For your trouble.'

'I'll look at the battery too,' he said.

'I'll commend you to the tourist board,' I said. He nodded. He took the pump nozzle and filled the tank, he

159

opened up the rad cap with a cloth and then rubbed the
battery. 'Everything's okay,' he said. I paid him for the
petrol.

'Are you going to check the tyres?'

He kicked one of them. 'They'll do you. It's only down
the road. Last house before the church. They are waiting
for you.'

'Thanks,' I said, trying not to look surprised. Down
the long straight road I watched the bus come, trailed by
a cloud of dust. It stopped in the street outside the café.
The customers came out to watch. The driver climbed on
to the roof of the bus and got some boxes and cases
down. One woman had a live chicken, another a birdcage.
They straightened their clothes and stretched their limbs.

'More visitors,' I said.

He stared at me and we both looked towards the bus.
The passengers finished stretching themselves and got
back aboard again. The bus drove away, leaving just four
boxes and a birdcage in the street. I glanced towards the
café and there was a movement of eyes. It may have
been the cat watching the fluttering of the caged bird; it
was that sort of cat.

## 28

The house was the last one in the street, if you call endless railings and walls a street. I stopped outside the gates; there was no name or bell pull. Beyond the house a small child attending two tethered goats stared at me for a moment and ran away. Near to the house was a copse and half concealed in it a large grey square concrete block: one of the Wehrmacht's indestructible contributions to European architecture.

A nimble little woman rushed to the gates and tugged them open. The house was tall and narrow and not particularly beautiful, but it was artfully placed in about twenty acres of ground. To the right, the kitchen garden sloped down to two large glasshouses. Beyond the house there was a tiny park where statues hid behind trees like grey stone children playing tag, and in between, there were orderly rows of fruit trees and an enclosure where laundry could just be glimpsed flapping in the breeze.

I drove slowly past a grimy swimming pool where a beach ball and some ice-cream wrappers floated. Tiny flies flickered close to the surface of the water. Around the rim of the pool there was some garden furniture: armchairs, stools and a table with a torn parasol. The woman puffed along with me. I recognized her now as the woman who had injected me. I parked in a paved yard, and she opened the side door of the house and ushered me through a large airy kitchen. She snapped a gas tap *en passant*, flipped open a drawer, dragged out a white apron and tied it around her without slowing her walk. The floor of the main hall was stone flags, the walls were white-washed and upon them were a few swords, shields and ancient banners. There was little furniture: an oak chest, some forbidding chairs, and tables bearing large vases full of freshly-cut flowers. Opening off the hall there was a billiard room. The lights were on and the brightly coloured balls lay transfixed upon the green baize like a pop-art tableau.

The little woman hurried ahead of me opening doors, waving me through, sorting amongst a bundle of large keys, locking each door and then darting around me and hurrying on ahead. Finally, she showed me into the lounge. It was soft and florid after the stark austerity of the rest of the house. There were four sofas with huge floral patterns, plants, knick-knacks, antique cases full of antique plates. Silver-framed photos, a couple of bizarre modern paintings in primary colours and a kidney-shaped bar trimmed in golden tin and plastic. Behind the bar were bottles of drink and arranged along the bar-top some bar-tender's implements: strainers, shakers and ice-buckets.

'I'm delighted to see you,' said Monsieur Datt.

'That's good.'

He smiled engagingly. 'How did you find me?'

'A little bird told me.'

'Damn those birds,' said Datt, still smiling. 'But no matter, the shooting season begins soon, doesn't it?'

'You could be right.'

'Why not sit down and let me get you a drink. It's damned hot, I've never known such weather.'

'Don't get ideas,' I said. 'My boys will come on in if I disappear for too long.'

'Such crude ideas you have. And yet I suppose the very vulgarity of your mind is its dynamic. But have no fear, you'll not have drugged food or any of that nonsense. On the contrary, I hope to prove to you how very wrong your whole notion of me is.' He reached towards a bevy of cut-glass decanters. 'What about Scotch whisky?'

'Nothing,' I said. 'Nothing at all.'

'You're right.' He walked across to the window. I followed him.

'Nothing,' he said. 'Nothing at all. We are both ascetics.'

'Speak for yourself,' I said. 'I like a bit of self-indulgence now and again.'

The windows overlooked a courtyard, its ivy-covered walls punctuated by the strict geometry of white shutters. There was a dovecote and white doves marched and counter-marched across the cobbles.

There was a hoot at the gate, then into the courtyard drove a large Citroën ambulance. 'Clinique de Paradis' it said along the side under the big red cross. It was very dusty as though it had made a long journey. Out of the driver's seat climbed Jean-Paul; he tooted the horn.

'It's my ambulance,' said Datt.

'Yes,' I said, 'Jean-Paul driving.'

'He's a good boy,' said Datt.

'Let me tell you what I want,' I said hurriedly.

Datt made a movement with his hand. 'I know why you are here. There is no need to explain anything.' He eased himself back into his armchair.

'How do you know I've not come to kill you?' I asked.

'My dear man. There is no question of violence, for many reasons.'

'For instance?'

'Firstly you are not a man to use gratuitous violence. You would only employ violent means when you could see the course of action that the violence made available to you. Secondly, we are evenly matched, you and I. Weight for weight we are evenly matched.'

'So are a swordfish and an angler, but one is sitting strapped into an armchair and the other is being dragged through the ocean with a hook in his mouth.'

'Which am I?'

163

'That's what I am here to discover.'

'Then begin, sir.'

'Get Kuang.'

'What do you mean?'

'I mean get Kuang. K.U.A.N.G. Get him here.'

Datt changed his mind about the drink; he poured himself a glass of wine and sipped it. 'I won't deny he's here,' he said finally.

'Then why not get him?'

He pressed a buzzer and the maid came in. 'Get Monsieur Kuang,' he said.

The old woman went away quietly and came back with Kuang. He was wearing grey flannel trousers, open-neck shirt and a pair of dirty white tennis shoes. He poured himself a large Perrier water from the bar and sat down in an armchair with his feet sprawled sideways over the arm. 'Well?' he said to me.

'I'm bringing you an American hydrogen expert to talk to.'

Kuang seemed unsurprised. 'Petty, Barnes, Bertram or Hudson?'

'Hudson.'

'Excellent, he's a top man.'

'I don't like it,' said Datt.

'You don't have to like it,' I said. 'If Kuang and Hudson want to talk a little it's nothing to do with you.' I turned to Kuang. 'How long will you want with him?'

'Two hours,' said Kuang. 'Three at the most, less if he has written stuff with him.'

'I believe he will have,' I said. 'He's all prepared.'

'I don't like it,' Datt complained.

'Be quiet,' said Kuang. He turned to me. 'Are you working for the Americans?'

'No,' I said. 'I'm acting for them, just this one operation.'

Kuang nodded. 'That makes sense; they wouldn't want to expose one of their regular men.'

I bit my lip in anger. Hudson had, of course, been acting on American instructions, not on his own initiative. It was a plan to expose me so that the CIA could keep their own men covered. Clever bastards. Well, I'd grin and bear it and try to get something out of it.

'That's right,' I agreed.

'So you are not bargaining?'

'I'm not getting paid,' I said, 'if that's what you mean.'

'How much do you want?' asked Kuang wearily. 'But don't get big ideas.'

'We'll sort it out after you've seen Hudson.'

'A most remarkable display of faith,' said Kuang. 'Did Datt pay you for the incomplete set of documents you let us have?'

'No,' I said.

'Now that our cards are on the table I take it you don't really want payment.'

'That's right,' I said.

'Good,' said Kuang. He hooked his legs off the arm of the chair and reached for some ice from the silver bucket. Before pouring himself a whisky he pushed the telephone across to me.

Maria was waiting near the phone when I called her. 'Bring Hudson here,' I said. 'You know the way.'

'Yes,' said Maria. 'I know the way.'

# 29

Kuang went out to get ready for Hudson. I sat down again in a hard chair. Datt noticed me wince.

'You have a pain in the spine?'

'Yes,' I said. 'I did it in a discothèque.'

'Those modern dances are too strenuous for me,' said Datt.

'This one was too strenuous for me,' I said. 'My partner had brass knuckles.'

Datt knelt down at my feet, took off my shoe and probed at my heel with his powerful fingers. He felt my ankle bone and tut-tutted as though it had been designed all wrong. Suddenly he plunged his fingers hard into my heel. 'Ahh,' he said, but the word was drowned by my shout of pain. Kuang opened the door and looked at us.

'Are you all right?' Kuang asked.

'He's got a muscular contraction,' said Datt. 'It's acupuncture,' he explained to me. 'I'll soon get rid of that pain in your back.'

'Ouch,' I said. 'Don't do it if it's going to make me lame for life.'

Kuang retreated back to his room. Datt inspected my foot again and pronounced it ready.

'It should get rid of your pain,' he said. 'Rest for half an hour in the chair.'

'It is a bit better,' I admitted.

'Don't be surprised,' said Datt, 'the Chinese have practised these arts for centuries; it is a simple matter, a muscular pain.'

'You practise acupuncture?' I asked.

'Not really, but I have always been interested,' said

166

Datt. 'The body and the mind. The interaction of two opposing forces: body and mind, emotion and reason, the duality of nature. My ambition has always been to discover something new about man himself.' He settled back into his chair. 'You are *simple*. I do not say that as a criticism but rather in admiration. Simplicity is the most sought-after quality in both art and nature, but your simplicity encourages you to see the world around you in black-and-white terms. You do not approve of my inquiry into human thoughts and actions. Your puritan origin, your Anglo-Saxon breeding make it sinful to inquire too deeply into ourselves.'

'But you don't inquire into yourself, you inquire into other people.'

He leaned back and smiled. 'My dear man, the reason I collect information, compile dossiers and films and recordings and probe the personal secrets of a wide range of important men, is twofold. Primarily because important men control the fate of the world and I like to feel that in my small way I influence such men. Secondly, I have devoted my life to the study of mankind. I love people; I have no illusions about them, it's true, but that makes it much easier to love them. I am ceaselessly amazed and devoted to the strange convoluted workings of their devious minds, their rationalizations and the predictability of their weaknesses and failings. That's why I became so interested in the sexual aspect of my studies. At one time I thought I understood my friends best when I watched them gambling: their avarice, kindness, and fear were so much in evidence when they gambled. I was a young man at the time. I lived in Hanoi and I saw the same men every day in the same clubs. I liked them enormously. It's important that you believe that.' He looked up at me.

I shrugged. 'I believe it.'

'I liked them very much and I wished to understand them better. For me, gambling could never hold any fascination: dull, repetitive and trivial. But it did unleash the deepest emotions. I got more from seeing their reactions to the game than from playing. So I began to keep dossiers on all my friends. There was no malign intent; on the contrary, it was expressly in order to understand and like them better that I did it.'

'And did you like them better?'

'In some ways. There were disillusions, of course, but a man's failings are so much more attractive than his successes – any woman will tell you that. Soon it occurred to me that alcohol was providing more information to the dossiers than gambling. Gambling showed me the hostilities and fears, but drink showed me the weaknesses. It was when a man felt sorry for himself that one saw the gaps in the armour. See how a man gets drunk and you will know him – I have told so many young girls that: see your man getting drunk and you will know him. Does he want to pull the blankets over his head or go out into the street and start a riot? Does he want to be caressed or to commit rape? Does he find everything humorous, or threatening? Does he feel the world is secretly mocking him, or does he throw his arms around a stranger's shoulders and shout that he loves everyone?'

'Yes. It's a good indication.'

'But there were even better ways to reach deep into the subconscious, and now I wanted not only to understand people but also to try planting ideas into their heads. If only I could have a man with the frailty and vulnerability of drunkenness but without the blurriness and loss of memory that drink brought, then I would have a chance of really improving my dossiers. How I envied the women who had access to my friends in their most vulnerable – post-coital *triste* – condition. Sex, I decided, was the key to man's drives and post-sex was his most vulnerable state. That's how my methods evolved.'

I relaxed now that Datt had become totally involved in

his story. I suppose he had been sitting out here in this house, inactive and musing about his life and what had led to this moment of supreme power that he was now enjoying so much. He was unstoppable, as so many reserved men are once explanations start burbling out of them.

'Eight hundred dossiers I have now, and many of them are analyses that a psychiatrist would be proud of.'

'Are you qualified to practise psychiatry?' I asked.

'Is anyone qualified to practise it?'

'No,' I said.

'Precisely,' said Datt. 'Well, I am a little better able than most men. I know what can be done, because I have done it. Done it eight hundred times. Without a staff it would never have developed at the same rate. Perhaps the quality would have been higher had I done it all myself, but the girls were a vital part of the operation.'

'The girls actually compiled the dossiers?'

'Maria might have been able to if she'd worked with me longer. The girl that died – Annie Couzins – was intelligent enough, but she was not temperamentally suited to the work. At one time I would work only with girls with qualifications in law or engineering or accountancy, but to find girls thus qualified and also sexually alluring is difficult. I wanted girls who would understand. With the more stupid girls I had to use recording machines, but the girls who understood produced the real results.'

'The girls didn't hide the fact that they understood?'

'At first. I thought – as you do now – that men would be afraid and suspicious of a woman who was clever, but they aren't, you see. On the contrary, men like clever women. Why does a husband complain "my wife doesn't understand me" when he goes running off with another woman? Why, because what he needs isn't sex, it's someone to talk to.'

169

'Can't he talk to the people he works with?'

'He can, but he's frightened of them. The people he works with are after his job, on the watch for weakness.'

'Just as your girls are.'

'Exactly, but he does not understand that.'

'Eventually he does, surely?'

'By then he no longer cares – the therapeutic aspect of the relationship is clear to him.'

'You blackmail him into co-operating?'

Datt shrugged. 'I might have done had it ever proved necessary, but it never has. By the time a man has been studied by me and the girls for six months he needs us.'

'I don't understand.'

'You don't understand,' said Datt patiently, 'because you persist in regarding me as some malign monster feeding on the blood of my victims.' Datt held up his hands. 'What I did for these men was helpful to them. I worked day and night, endless sessions to help them understand themselves: their motives, their aspirations, their weaknesses and strengths. The girls too were intelligent enough to be helpful, and reassuring. All the people that I have studied become better personalities.'

'Will become,' I corrected. 'That's the promise you hold out to them.'

'In some cases, not all.'

'But you have tried to increase their dependency upon you. You have used your skills to make these people *think* they need you.'

'You are splitting hairs. All psychiatrists must do that. That's what the word "transference" means.'

'But you have a hold over them. These films and records: they demonstrate the type of power you want.'

'They demonstrate nothing. The films, etc. are nothing to me. I am a scientist, not a blackmailer. I have merely used the sexual activities of my patients as a short cut to understanding the sort of disorders they are likely to

170

have. A man reveals so much when he is in bed with a woman; it's this important element of *release*. It's common to all the activities of the subject. He finds release in talking to me, which gives him freedom in his sexual appetites. Greater and more varied sexual activity releases in turn a need to talk at greater length.'

'So he talks to you.'

'Of course he does. He grows more and more free, and more and more confident.'

'But you are the only person he can boast to.'

'Not boast exactly, talk. He wishes to share this new, stronger, better life that he has created.'

'That you have created for him.'

'Some subjects have been kind enough to say that they lived at only ten per cent of their potential until they came to my clinic.' M. Datt smiled complacently. 'It's vital and important work showing men the power they have within their own minds if they merely take courage enough to use it.'

'You sound like one of those small ads from the back pages of skin magazines. The sort that's sandwiched between acne cream and peeping-tom binoculars.'

'*Honi soit qui mal y pense*. I know what I am doing.'

I said, 'I really believe you do, but I don't *like* it.'

'Mind you,' he said urgently, 'don't think for one moment I'm a Freudian. I'm not. Everyone thinks I'm a Freudian because of this emphasis on sex. I'm not.'

'You'll publish your results?' I asked.

'The conclusions possibly, but not the case histories.'

'It's the case histories that are the important factor,' I said.

'To some people,' said Datt. 'That's why I have to guard them so carefully!'

'Loiseau tried to get them.'

'But he was a few minutes too late.' Datt poured himself another small glass of wine, measured its clarity

171

and drank a little. 'Many men covet my dossiers but I guard them carefully. This whole neighbourhood is under surveillance. I knew about you as soon as you stopped for fuel in the village.'

The old woman knocked discreetly and entered. 'A car with Paris plates – it sounds like Madame Loiseau – coming through the village.'

Datt nodded. 'Tell Robert I want the Belgian plates on the ambulance and the documents must be ready. Jean-Paul can help him. No, on second thoughts don't tell Jean-Paul to help him. I believe they don't get along too well.' The old woman said nothing. 'Yes, well that's all.'

Datt walked across to the window and as he did so there was the sound of tyres crunching on the gravel.

'It's Maria's car,' said Datt.

'And your backyard Mafia didn't stop it?'

'They are not there to stop people,' explained Datt. 'They are not collecting entrance money, they are there for my protection.'

'Did Kuang tell you that?' I said. 'Perhaps those guards are there to stop you getting out.'

'Poof,' said Datt, but I knew I had planted a seed in his mind. 'I wish she'd brought the boy with her.'

I said, 'It's Kuang who's in charge. He didn't ask you before agreeing to my bringing Hudson here.'

'We have our areas of authority,' said Datt. 'Everything concerning data of a technical kind – of the kind that Hudson can provide – is Kuang's province.' Suddenly he flushed with anger. 'Why should I explain such things to you?'

'I thought you were explaining them to yourself,' I said.

Datt changed the subject abruptly. 'Do you think Maria told Loiseau where I am?'

'I'm sure she didn't,' I said. 'She has a lot of explaining

172

to do the next time she sees Loiseau. She has to explain why she warned you about his raid on the clinic.'

'That's true,' said Datt. 'A clever man, Loiseau. At one time I thought you were his assistant.'

'And now?'

'Now I think you are his victim, or soon will be.'

I said nothing. Datt said, 'Whoever you work for, you run alone. Loiseau has no reason to like you. He's jealous of your success with Maria – she adores you, of course. Loiseau pretends he's after me, but you are his real enemy. Loiseau is in trouble with his department, he might have decided that you could be the scapegoat. He visited me a couple of weeks ago, wanted me to sign a document concerning you. A tissue of lies, but cleverly riddled with half-truths that could prove bad for you. It needed only my signature. I refused.'

'Why didn't you sign?'

M. Datt sat down opposite me and looked me straight in the eye. 'Not because I like you particularly. I hardly know you. It was because I had given you that injection when I first suspected that you were an *agent provocateur* sent by Loiseau. If I treat a person he becomes my patient. I become responsible for him. It is my proud boast that if one of my patients committed even a murder he could come to me and tell me; in confidence. That's my relationship with Kuang. I must have that sort of relationship with my patients – Loiseau refuses to understand that. I must have it.' He stood up suddenly and said, 'A drink – and now I insist. What shall it be?'

The door opened and Maria came in, followed by Hudson and Jean-Paul. Maria was smiling, but her eyes were narrow and tense. Her old roll-neck pullover and riding breeches were stained with mud and wine. She looked tough and elegant and rich. She came into the room quietly and aware, like a cat sniffing, and moving stealthily, on the watch for the slightest sign of things

173

hostile or alien. She handed me the packet of documents: three passports, one for me, one for Hudson, one for Kuang. There were some other papers inside, money and some cards and envelopes that would prove I was someone else. I put them in my pocket without looking at them.

'I wish you'd brought the boy,' said M. Datt to Maria. She didn't answer. 'What will you drink, my good friends? An aperitif perhaps?' He called to the woman in the white apron, 'We shall be seven to dinner but Mr Hudson and Mr Kuang will dine separately in the library. And take Mr Hudson into the library now,' he added. 'Mr Kuang is waiting there.'

'And leave the door ajar,' I said affably.

'And leave the door ajar,' said M. Datt.

Hudson smiled and gripped his briefcase tight under his arm. He looked at Maria and Jean-Paul, nodded and withdrew without answering. I got up and walked across to the window, wondering if the woman in the white apron was sitting in at dinner with us, but then I saw the dented tractor parked close behind Maria's car. The tractor driver was here. With all that room to spare the tractor needn't have boxed both cars tight against the wall.

# 30

'Read the greatest thinkers of the eighteenth century,'
M. Datt was saying, 'and you'll understand what the
Frenchman still thinks about women.' The soup course
was finished and the little woman – dressed now in a
maid's formal uniform – collected the dishes. 'Don't stack
them,' M. Datt whispered loudly to her. 'That's how they
get broken. Make two journeys; a well-trained maid
never stacks plates.' He poured a glass of white wine for
each of us. 'Diderot thought they were merely courtesans,
Montesquieu said they were pretty children. For Rousseau they existed only as an adjunct to man's pleasure
and for Voltaire they didn't exist at all.' He pulled the
side of smoked salmon towards him and sharpened the
long knife.

Jean-Paul smiled knowingly. He was more nervous
than usual. He patted the white starched cuff that artfully
revealed the Cartier watch and fingered the small disc of
adhesive plaster that covered a razor nick on his chin.

Maria said, 'France is a land where men command and
women obey. "Elle me plaît" is the greatest compliment
a woman can expect from men; they mean she obeys.
How can anyone call Paris a woman's city? Only a
prostitute can have a serious career there. It took two
world wars to give Frenchwomen the vote.'

Datt nodded. He removed the bones and the salmon's
smoke-hard surface with two long sweeps of the knife.
He brushed oil over the fish and began to slice it, serving
Maria first. Maria smiled at him.

Just as an expensive suit wrinkles in a different way
from a cheap one, so did the wrinkles in Maria's face add

175

to her beauty rather than detract from it. I stared at her, trying to understand her better. Was she treacherous, or was she exploited, or was she, like most of us, both?

'It's all very well for you, Maria,' said Jean-Paul. 'You are a woman with wealth, position, intelligence,' he pause, 'and beauty . . .'

'I'm glad you added beauty,' she said, still smiling.

Jean-Paul looked towards M. Datt and me. 'That illustrates my point. Even Maria would sooner have beauty than brains. When I was eighteen – ten years ago – I wanted to give the women I loved the things I wanted for myself: respect, admiration, good food, conversation, wit and even knowledge. But women despise those things. Passion is what they want, intensity of emotion. The same trite words of admiration repeated over and over again. They don't want good food – women have poor palates – and witty conversation worries them. What's worse it diverts attention away from them. Women want men who are masterful enough to give them confidence, but not cunning enough to outwit them. They want men with plenty of faults so that they can forgive them. They want men who have trouble with the little things in life; women excel at little things. They remember little things too; there is no occasion in their lives, from confirmation to eightieth birthday, when they can't recall every stitch they wore.' He looked accusingly at Maria.

Maria laughed. 'That part of your tirade at least is true.'

M. Datt said, 'What did you wear at your confirmation?'

'White silk, high-waisted dress, plain-front white silk shoes and cotton gloves that I hated.' She reeled it off.

'Very good,' said M. Datt and laughed. 'Although I must say, Jean-Paul, you are far too hard on women. Take that girl Annie who worked for me. Her academic standards were tremendous . . .'

'Of course,' said Maria, 'women leaving university have such trouble getting a job that anyone enlightened enough to employ them is able to demand very high qualifications.'

'Exactly,' said M. Datt. 'Most of the girls I've ever used in my research were brilliant. What's more they were deeply involved in the research tasks. Just imagine that the situation had required men employees to involve themselves sexually with patients. In spite of paying lip-service to promiscuity men would have given me all sorts of puritanical reasons why they couldn't do it. These girls understood that it was a vital part of their relationship with patients. One girl was a mathematical genius and yet such beauty. Truly remarkable.'

Jean-Paul said, 'Where is this mathematical genius now? I would dearly appreciate her advice. Perhaps I could improve my technique with women.'

'You couldn't,' said Maria. She spoke clinically, with no emotion showing. 'Your technique is all too perfect. You flatter women to saturation point when you first meet them. Then, when you decide the time is right, you begin to undermine their confidence in themselves. You point out their shortcomings rather cleverly and sympathetically until they think that you must be the only man who would deign to be with them. You destroy women by erosion because you hate them.'

'No,' Jean-Paul said. 'I love women. I love all women too much to reject so many by marrying one.' He laughed.

'Jean-Paul feels it is his duty to make himself available to every girl from fifteen to fifty,' said Maria quietly.

'Then you'll soon be outside my range of activity,' said Jean-Paul.

The candles had burned low and now their light came through the straw-coloured wine and shone golden on face and ceiling.

Maria sipped at her wine. No one spoke. She placed

177

the glass on the table and then brought her eyes up to Jean-Paul's. 'I'm sorry for you, Jean-Paul,' she said.

The maid brought the fish course to the table and served it: *sole Dieppoise,* the sauce dense with shrimps and speckled with parsley and mushroom, the bland smell of the fish echoed by the hot butter. The maid retired, conscious that her presence had interrupted the conversation. Maria drank a little more wine and as she put the glass down she looked at Jean-Paul.

He didn't smile. When she spoke her voice was mellow and any trace of bitterness had been removed by the pause.

'When I say I'm sorry for you, Jean-Paul, with your endless succession of lovers, you may laugh at me. But let me tell you this: the shortness of your relationships with women is due to a lack of flexibility in you. You are not able to adapt, change, improve, enjoy new things each day. Your demands are constant and growing narrower. Everyone else must adapt to you, never the other way about.

'Marriages break up for this same reason – my marriage did and it was at least half my fault: two people become so set in their ways that they become vegetables. The antithesis of this feeling is to be in love. I fell in love with you, Jean-Paul. Being in love is to drink in new ideas, new feelings, smells, tastes, new dances – even the air seems to be different in flavour. That's why infidelity is such a shock. A wife set in the dull, lifeless pattern of marriage is suddenly liberated by love, and her husband is terrified to see the change take place, for just as I felt ten years younger, so I saw my husband as ten years older.'

Jean-Paul said, 'And that's how you now see me?'

'Exactly. It's laughable how I once worried that you were younger than me. You're not younger than me at all. You are an old fogey. Now I no longer love you I can

178

see that. You are an old fogey of twenty-eight and I am a young girl of thiry-two.'

'You bitch.'

'My poor little one. Don't be angry. Think of what I tell you. Open your mind. Open your mind and you will discover what you want so much: how to be eternally a young man.'

Jean-Paul looked at her. He wasn't as angry as I would have expected. 'Perhaps I am a shallow and vain fool,' he said. 'But when I met you, Maria, I truly loved you. It didn't last more than a week, but for me it was real. It was the only time in my life that I truly believed myself capable of something worthwhile. You were older than me but I liked that. I wanted you to show me the way out of the stupid labyrinth life I led. You are highly intelligent and you, I thought, could show me the solid good reasons for living. But you failed me, Maria. Like all women you are weak-willed and indecisive. You can be loyal only for a moment to whoever is near to you. You have never made one objective decision in your life. You have never really wanted to be strong and free. You have never done one decisive thing that you truly believed in. You are a puppet, Maria, with many puppeteers, and they quarrel over who shall operate you.' His final words were sharp and bitter and he stared hard at Datt.

'Children,' Datt admonished. 'Just as we were all getting along so well together.'

Jean-Paul smiled a tight, film-star smile. 'Turn off your charm,' he said to Datt. 'You always patronize me.'

'If I've done something to give offence . . .' said Datt. He didn't finish the sentence but looked around at his guests, raising his eyebrows to show how difficult it was to even imagine such a possibility.

'You think you can switch me on and off as you please,' said Jean-Paul. 'You think you can treat me like a child; well you can't. Without me you would be in big trouble now. If I had not brought you the information about Loiseau's raid upon your clinic you would be in prison now.'

'Perhaps,' said Datt, 'and perhaps not.'

'Oh I know what you want people to believe,' said Jean-Paul. 'I know you like people to think you are mixed up with the SDECE and secret departments of the Government, but we know better. I saved you. Twice. Once with Annie, once with Maria.'

'Maria saved me,' said Datt, 'if anyone did.'

'Your precious daughter,' said Jean-Paul, 'is good for only one thing.' He smiled. 'And what's more she hates you. She said you were foul and evil; that's how much she wanted to save you before I persuaded her to help.'

'Did you say that about me?' Datt asked Maria, and even as she was about to reply he held up his hand. 'No, don't answer. I have no right to ask you such a question. We all say things in anger that later we regret.' He smiled at Jean-Paul. 'Relax, my good friend, and have another glass of wine.'

Datt filled Jean-Paul's glass but Jean-Paul didn't pick it up. Datt pointed the neck of the bottle at it. 'Drink.' He picked up the glass and held it to Jean-Paul. 'Drink and say that these black thoughts are not your truly considered opinion of old Datt who has done so much for you.'

Jean-Paul brought the flat of his hand round in an angry sweeping gesture. Perhaps he didn't like to be told that he owed Datt anything. He sent the full glass flying across the room and swept the bottle out of Datt's hands. It slid across the table, felling the glasses like ninepins and flooding the cold blond liquid across the linen and cutlery. Datt stood up, awkwardly dabbing at his waist-coat with a table napkin. Jean-Paul stood up too. The only sound was of the wine, still chug-chugging out of the bottle.

'*Salaud!*' said Datt. 'You attack me in my own home!

You *casse-pieds*! You insult me in front of my guests and assault me when I offer you wine!' He dabbed at himself and threw the wet napkin across the table as a sign that the meal would not continue. The cutlery jangled mournfully. 'You will learn,' said Datt. 'You will learn here and now.'

Jean-Paul finally understood the hornet's nest he had aroused in Datt's brain. His face was set and defiant, but you didn't have to be an amateur psychologist to know that if he could set the clock back ten minutes he'd rewrite his script.

'Don't touch me,' Jean-Paul said. 'I have villainous friends just as you do, and my friends and I can destroy you, Datt. I know all about you, the girl Annie Couzins and why she had to be killed. There are a few things you don't know about that story. There are a few more things that the police would like to know too. Touch me, you fat old swine, and you'll die as surely as the girl did.' He looked around at us all. His forehead was moist with exertion and anxiety. He managed a grim smile. 'Just touch me, just you try . . . !'

Datt said nothing, nor did any one of us. Jean-Paul gabbled on until his steam ran out. 'You need me,' he finally said to Datt, but Datt didn't need him any more and there was no one in the room who didn't know it.

'Robert!' shouted Datt. I don't know if Robert was standing in the sideboard or in a crack in the floor, but he certainly came in fast. Robert was the tractor driver who had slapped the one-eared dog. He was as tall and broad as Jean-Paul but there the resemblance ended: Robert was teak against Jean-Paul's papier-mâché.

Right behind Robert was the woman in the white apron. Now that they were standing side by side you could see a family resemblance: Robert was clearly the woman's son. He walked forward and stood before Datt like a man waiting to be given a medal. The old woman stood in the doorway with a 12-bore shotgun held steady in her fists. It was a battered old relic, the butt was scorched and stained and there was a patch of rust around the muzzle as though it had been propped in a puddle. It was just the sort of thing that might be kept around the hall of a country house for dealing with rats and rabbits: an ill-finished mass-production job without styling or finish. It wasn't at all the sort of gun I'd want to be shot with. That's why I remained very, very still.

Datt nodded towards me, and Robert moved in and brushed me lightly but efficiently. 'Nothing,' he said. Robert walked over to Jean-Paul. In Jean-Paul's suit he found a 6.35 Mauser automatic. He sniffed it and opened it, spilled the bullets out into his hand and passed the gun, magazine and bullets to Datt. Datt handled them as though they were some kind of virus. He reluctantly dropped them into his pocket.

'Take him away, Robert,' said Datt. 'He makes too much noise in here. I can't bear people shouting.' Robert nodded and turned upon Jean-Paul. He made a movement of his chin and a clicking noise of the sort that encourages horses. Jean-Paul buttoned his jacket carefully and walked to the door.

'We'll have the meat course now,' Datt said to the woman.

She smiled with more deference than humour and withdrew backwards, muzzle last.

'Take him out, Robert,' repeated Datt.

'Maybe you think you don't,' said Jean-Paul earnestly, 'but you'll find . . .' His words were lost as Robert pulled him gently through the door and closed it.

'What are you going to do to him?' asked Maria.

'Nothing, my dear,' said Datt. 'But he's become more and more tiresome. He must be taught a lesson. We must frighten him, it's for the good of all of us.'

'You're going to kill him,' said Maria.

'No, my dear.' He stood near the fireplace, and smiled reassuringly.

'You are, I can feel it in the atmosphere.'

Datt turned his back on us. He toyed with the clock on the mantelpiece. He found the key for it and began to wind it up. It was a noisy ratchet.

Maria turned to me. 'Are they going to kill him?' she asked.

'I think they are,' I said.

She went across to Datt and grabbed his arm. 'You mustn't,' she said. 'It's too horrible. Please don't. Please father, please don't, if you love me.' Datt put his arm around her paternally but said nothing.

'He's a wonderful person,' Maria said. She was speaking of Jean-Paul. 'He would never betray you. Tell him,' she asked me, 'he must not kill Jean-Paul.'

'You mustn't kill him,' I said.

'You must make it more convincing than that,' said Datt. He patted Maria. 'If our friend here can tell us a way to guarantee his silence, some other way, then perhaps I'll agree.'

He waited but I said nothing. 'Exactly,' said Datt.

'But I love him,' said Maria.

'That can make no difference,' said Datt. 'I'm not a plenipotentiary from God, I've got no halos or citations to distribute. He stands in the way – not of me but of what I believe in: he stands in the way because he is spiteful and stupid. I do believe, Maria, that even if it were you I'd still do the same.'

Maria stopped being a suppliant. She had that icy calm that women take on just before using their nails.

'I love him,' said Maria. That meant that he should never be punished for anything except infidelity. She looked at me. 'It's your fault for bringing me here.'

Datt heaved a sigh and left the room.

'And your fault that he's in danger,' she said.

'Okay,' I said, 'blame me if you want to. On my colour soul the stains don't show.'

'Can't you stop them?' she said.

'No,' I told her, 'it's not that sort of film.'

Her face contorted as though cigar smoke was getting in her eyes. It went squashy and she began to sob. She didn't cry. She didn't do that mascara-respecting display of grief that winkles tear-drops out of the eyes with the corner of a tiny lace handkerchief while watching the whole thing in a well-placed mirror. She sobbed and her face collapsed. The mouth sagged, and the flesh puckered and wrinkled like blow-torched paintwork. Ugly sight, and ugly sound.

'He'll die,' she said in a strange little voice.

I don't know what happened next. I don't know whether Maria began to move before the sound of the shot or after. Just as I don't know whether Jean-Paul had really lunged at Robert, as Robert later told us. But I was right behind Maria as she opened the door. A. 45 is a big pistol. The first shot had hit the dresser, ripping a hole in the carpentry and smashing half a dozen plates. They were still falling as the second shot fired. I heard Datt shouting about his plates and saw Jean-Paul spinning drunkenly like an exhausted whipping top. He fell against the dresser, supporting himself on his hand, and stared at me pop-eyed with hate and grimacing with pain, his cheeks bulging as though he was looking for a place to vomit. He grabbed at his white shirt and tugged it out of his trousers. He wrenched it so hard that the buttons popped and pinged away across the room. He had a great bundle of shirt in his hand now and he stuffed it into his mouth like a conjurer doing a trick called 'how to swallow my white shirt'. Or how to swallow my pink-dotted shirt. How to swallow my pink shirt, my red, and finally dark-red shirt. But he never did the trick. The cloth fell away from his mouth and his blood poured over his chin, painting his teeth pink and dribbling down his neck and ruining his shirt. He knelt upon the ground as if to pray but his face sank to the floor and he died without a word, his ear flat against the ground, as if listening for hoof-beats pursuing him to another world.

He was dead. It's difficult to wound a man with a .45. You either miss them or blow them in half.

The legacy the dead leave us are life-size effigies that only slightly resemble their former owners. Jean-Paul's bloody body only slightly resembled him: its thin lips pressed together and the small circular plaster just visible on the chin.

Robert was stupefied. He was staring at the gun in horror. I stepped over to him and grabbed the gun away from him. I said 'You should be ashamed,' and Datt repeated that.

The door opened suddenly and Hudson and Kuang stepped into the kitchen. They looked down at the body of Jean-Paul. He was a mess of blood and guts. No one spoke, they were waiting for me. I remembered that I was the one holding the gun. 'I'm taking Kuang and Hudson and I'm leaving,' I said. Through the open door to the hall I could see into the library, its table covered with their scientific documents: photos, maps and withered plants with large labels on them.

'Oh no you don't,' said Datt.

'I have to return Hudson intact because that's part of the deal. The information he's given Kuang has to be got back to the Chinese Government or else it wasn't much good delivering it. So I must take Kuang too.'

'I think he's right,' said Kuang. 'It makes sense, what he says.'

'How do you know what makes sense?' said Datt. 'I'm arranging your movements, not this fool; how can we trust him? He admits this task is for the Americans.'

'It makes sense,' said Kuang again. 'Hudson's information is genuine. I can tell: it fills out what I learnt from that incomplete set of papers you passed to me last week. If the Americans want me to have the information, then they must want it to be taken back home.'

'Can't you see that they might want to capture you for interrogation?' said Datt.

'Rubbish!' I interrupted. 'I could have arranged that at any time in Paris without risking Hudson out here in the middle of nowhere.'

'They are probably waiting down the road,' said Datt. 'You could be dead and buried in five minutes. Out here in the middle of the country no one would hear, no one would see the diggings.'

'I'll take that chance,' said Kuang. 'If he can get Hudson into France on false papers, he can get me out.'

I watched Hudson, fearful that he would say I'd done no such thing for him, but he nodded sagely and Kuang seemed reassured.

'Come with us,' said Hudson, and Kuang nodded agreement. The two scientists seemed to be the only ones in the room with any mutual trust.

I was reluctant to leave Maria but she just waved her hand and said she'd be all right. She couldn't take her eyes off Jean-Paul's body.

'Cover him, Robert,' said Datt.

Robert took a table-cloth from a drawer and covered the body. 'Go,' Maria called again to me, and then she began to sob. Datt put his arm around her and pulled her close. Hudson and Kuang collected their data together and then, still waving the gun around, I showed them out and followed.

As we went across the hall the old woman emerged carrying a heavily laden tray. She said, 'There's still the *poulet sauté chasseur*.'

'Vive le sport,' I said.

# 31

From the garage we took the camionette – a tiny grey corrugated-metal van – because the roads of France are full of them. I had to change gear constantly for the small motor, and the tiny headlights did no more than probe the hedgerows. It was a cold night and I envied the warm grim-faced occupants of the big Mercs and Citroëns that roared past us with just a tiny peep of the horn, to tell us they had done so.

Kuang seemed perfectly content to rely upon my skill to get him out of France. He leaned well back in the hard upright seat, folded his arms and closed his eyes as though performing some oriental contemplative ritual. Now and again he spoke. Usually it was a request for a cigarette.

The frontier was little more than a formality. The Paris office had done us proud: three good British passports – although the photo of Hudson was a bit dodgy – over twenty-five pounds in small notes (Belgian and French), and some bills and receipts to correspond to each passport. I breathed more easily after we were through. I'd done a deal with Loiseau so he'd guaranteed no trouble, but I still breathed more easily after we'd gone through.

Hudson lay flat upon some old blankets in the rear. Soon he began to snore. Kuang spoke.

'Are we going to an hotel or are you going to blow one of your agents to shelter me?'

'This is Belgium,' I said. 'Going to an hotel is like going to a police station.'

'What will happen to him?'

'The agent?' I hesitated. 'He'll be pensioned off. It's bad luck but he was the next due to be blown.'

'Age?'

'Yes,' I said.

'And you have someone better in the area?'

'You know we can't talk about that,' I said.

'I'm not interested professionally,' said Kuang. 'I'm a scientist. What the British do in France or Belgium is nothing to do with me, but if we are blowing this man I owe him his job.'

'You owe him nothing,' I said. 'What the hell do you think this is? He'll be blown because it's his job. Just as I'm conducting you because that's my job. I'm doing it as a favour. You owe no one anything, so forget it. As far as I'm concerned you are a parcel.'

Kuang inhaled deeply on his cigarette, then removed it from his mouth with his long delicate fingers and stubbed it into the ashtray. I imagined him killing Annie Couzins. Passion or politics? He rubbed the tobacco shreds from his fingertips like a pianist practising trills.

As we passed through the tightly shuttered villages the rough *pavé* hammered the suspension and bright-eyed cats glared into our lights and fled. One a little slower than the others had been squashed as flat as an ink blot. Each successive set of wheels contributed a new pattern to the little tragedy that morning would reveal.

I had the camionette going at its top speed. The needles were still and the loud noise of the motor held a constant note. Everything was unchanging except a brief fusillade of loose gravel or the sudden smell of tar or the beep of a faster car.

'We are near to Ypres,' said Kuang.

'This was the Ypres salient,' I said. Hudson asked for a cigarette. He must have been awake for some time. 'Ypres,' said Hudson as he lit the cigarette, 'was that the site of a World War One battle?'

'One of the biggest,' I said. 'There's scarcely an Englishman that didn't have a relative die here. Perhaps a piece of Britain died here too.'

Hudson looked out of the rear windows of the van. 'It's quite a place to die,' he said.

# 32

Across the Ypres salient the dawn sky was black and getting lower and blacker like a Bulldog Drummond ceiling. It's a grim region, like a vast ill-lit military depot that goes on for miles. Across country go the roads: narrow slabs of concrete not much wider than a garden path, and you have the feeling that to go off the edge is to go into bottomless mud. It's easy to go around in circles and even easier to imagine that you are. Every few yards there are the beady-eyed green-and-white notices that point the way to military cemeteries where regiments of Blanco-white headstones parade. Death pervades the topsoil but untidy little farms go on operating, planting their cabbages right up to 'Private of the West Riding – Known only to God'. The living cows and dead soldiers share the land and there are no quarrels. Now in the hedges evergreen plants were laden with tiny red berries as though the ground was sweating blood. I stopped the car. Ahead was Passchendaele, a gentle upward slope.

'Which way were your soldiers facing?' Kuang said.

'Up the slope,' I said. 'They advanced up the slope, sixty pounds on their backs and machine guns down their throats.'

Kuang opened the window and threw his cigarette butt on to the road. There was an icy gust of wind.

'It's cold,' said Kuang. 'When the wind drops it will rain.'

Hudson leaned close to the window again. 'Oh boy,' he said, 'trench warfare here,' and shook his head when no word came. 'For them it must have seemed like for ever.'

'For a lot of them it was for ever,' I said. 'They are still here.'

'In Hiroshima even more died,' said Kuang.

'I don't measure death by numbers,' I said.

'Then it's a pity you were so careful not to use your atom bomb on the Germans or Italians,' said Kuang.

I started the motor again to get some heat in the car, but Kuang got out and stamped around on the concrete roadway. He did not seem to mind the cold wind and rain. He picked up a chunk of the shiny, clay-heavy soil peculiar to this region, studied it and then broke it up and threw it aimlessly across the field of cabbages.

'Are we expecting to rendezvous with another car?' he asked.

'Yes,' I said.

'You must have been very confident that I would come with you.'

'Yes,' I said. 'I was. It was logical.'

Kuang nodded. 'Can I have another cigarette?' I gave him one.

'We're early,' complained Hudson. 'That's a sure way to attract attention.'

'Hudson fancies his chances as a secret agent,' I said to Kuang.

'I don't take to your sarcasm,' said Hudson.

'Well that's real old-fashioned bad luck, Hudson,' I said, 'because you are stuck with it.'

Grey clouds rushed across the salient. Here and there old windmills – static in spite of the wind – stood across the skyline, like crosses waiting for someone to be nailed upon them. Over the hill came a car with its headlights on.

They were thirty minutes late. Two men in a Renault 16, a man and his son. They didn't introduce themselves, in fact they didn't seem keen to show their faces at all. The older man got out of the car and came across to me. He spat upon the road and cleared his throat.

'You two get into the other car. The American stays in this one. Don't speak to the boy.' He smiled and gave a short, croaky, mirthless laugh. 'In fact don't speak to me even. There's a large-scale map in the dashboard. Make sure that's what you want.' He gripped my arm as he said it. 'The boy will take the camionette and dump it somewhere near the Dutch border. The American stays in this car. Someone will meet them at the other end. It's all arranged.'

Hudson said to me, 'Going with you is one thing, but taking off into the blue with this kid is another. I think I can find my own way . . .'

'Don't think about it,' I told him. 'We just follow the directions on the label. Hold your nose and swallow.' Hudson nodded.

We got out of the car and the boy came across, slowly detouring around us as though his father had told him to keep his face averted. The Renault was nice and warm inside. I felt in the glove compartment and found not only a map but a pistol.

'No prints,' I called to the Fleming. 'Make sure there's nothing else, no sweet wrappers or handkerchiefs.'

'Yes,' said the man. 'And none of those special cigarettes that are made specially for me in one of those exclusive shops in Jermyn Street.' He smiled sarcastically. 'He knows all that.' His accent was so thick as to be almost unintelligible. I guessed that normally he spoke Flemish and the French was not natural to him. The man spat again in the roadway before climbing into the driver's seat alongside us. 'He's a good boy,' the man said. 'He knows what to do.' By the time he got the Renault started the camionette was out of sight.

I'd reached the worrying stage of the journey. 'Did you

take notes?' I asked Kuang suddenly. He looked at me without answering. 'Be sensible,' I said. 'I must know if you are carrying anything that would need to be destroyed. I know there's the box of stuff Hudson gave you.' I drummed upon it. 'Is there anything else?'

'A small notebook taped to my leg. It's a thin book. I could be searched and they would not find it.'

I nodded. It was something more to worry about.

The car moved at high speed over the narrow concrete lanes. Soon we turned on to the wider main road that led north to Ostend. We had left the over-fertilized salient behind us. The fearful names: Tyne Cot, St Julien, Poelcapelle, Westerhoek and Pilckem faded behind us as they had faded from memory, for fifty years had passed and the women who had wept for the countless dead were also dead. Time and TV, frozen food and transistor radios had healed the wounds and filled the places that once seemed unfillable.

'What's happening?' I said to the driver. He was the sort of man who had to be questioned or else he would offer no information.

'His people,' he jerked his head towards Kuang, 'want him in Ostend. Twenty-three hundred hours tonight at the harbour. I'll show you on the city plan.'

'Harbour? What's happening? Is he going aboard a boat tonight?'

'They don't tell me things like that,' said the man. 'I'm just conducting you to my place to see your case officer, then on to Ostend to see his case officer. It's all so bloody boring. My wife thinks I get paid because it's dangerous but I'm always telling her: I get paid because it's so bloody boring. Tired?' I nodded. 'We'll make good time, that's one advantage, there's not much traffic about at this time of morning. There's not much commercial traffic if you avoid the inter-city routes.'

'It's quiet,' I said. Now and again small flocks of birds

193

darted across the sky, their eyes seeking food in the hard morning light, their bodies weakened by the cold night air.

'Very few police,' said the man, 'The cars keep to the main roads. It will rain soon and the cyclists don't move much when it's raining. It'll be the first rain for two weeks.'

'Stop worrying,' I said. 'Your boy will be all right.'

'He knows what to do,' the man agreed.

# 33

The Fleming owned an hotel not far from Ostend. The car turned into a covered alley that led to a cobbled courtyard. A couple of hens squawked as we parked and a dog howled. 'It's difficult,' said the man, 'to do anything clandestine around here.'

He was a small broad man with a sallow skin that would always look dirty no matter what he did to it. The bridge of his nose was large and formed a straight line with his forehead, like the nose metal of a medieval helmet. His mouth was small and he held his lips tight to conceal his bad teeth. Around his mouth were scars of the sort that you get when thrown through a windscreen. He smiled to show me it was a joke rather than an apology, and the scars made a pattern around his mouth like a tightened hairnet.

The door from the side entrance of the hotel opened and a woman in a black dress and white apron stared at us.

'They have come,' said the man.

'So I see,' she said. 'No luggage?'

'No luggage,' said the man. She seemed to need some explanation, as though we were a man and girl trying to book a double room.

'They need to rest, *ma jolie môme*,' said the man. She was no one's pretty child, but the compliment appeased her for a moment.

'Room four,' she said.

'The police have been?'

'Yes,' she said.

'They won't be back until night,' said the man to us.

'Perhaps not then even. They check the book. It's for the taxes more than to find criminals.'

'Don't use all the hot water,' said the woman. We followed her through the yellow peeling side door into the hotel entrance hall. There was a counter made of carelessly painted hardboard and a rack with eight keys hanging from it. The lino had the large square pattern that's supposed to look like inlaid marble; it curled at the edges and something hot had indented a perfect circle near the door.

'Name?' said the woman grimly as though she was about to enter us in the register.

'Don't ask,' said the man. 'And they won't ask our name.' He smiled as though he had made a joke and looked anxiously at his wife, hoping that she would join in. She shrugged and reached behind her for the key. She put it down on the counter very gently so she could not be accused of anger.

'They'll need two keys, Sybil.'

She scowled at him. 'They'll pay for the rooms,' he said.

'We'll pay,' I said. Outside the rain began. It bombarded the window and rattled the door as though anxious to get in.

She slammed the second key down upon the counter. '*You* should have taken it and dumped it,' said the woman angrily. 'Rik could have driven these two back here.'

'This is the important stage,' said the man.

'You lazy pig,' said the woman. 'If the alarm is out for the car and Rik gets stopped driving it, then we'll see which is the important stage.'

The man didn't answer, nor did he look at me. He picked up the keys and led the way up the creaky staircase. 'Mind the handrail,' he said. 'It's not fixed properly yet.'

'Nothing is,' called the woman after us. 'The whole place is only half-built.'

He showed us into our rooms. They were cramped and rather sad, shining with yellow plastic and smelling of quick-drying paint. Through the wall I heard Kuang swish back the curtain, put his jacket on a hanger and hang it up. There was the sudden chug-chug of the water pipe as he filled the wash-basin. The man was still behind me, hanging on as if waiting for something. I put my finger to my eye and then pointed towards Kuang's room; the man nodded. 'I'll have the car ready by twenty-two hundred hours. Ostend isn't far from here.'

'Good,' I said. I hoped he would go but he stayed there.

'We used to live in Ostend,' he said. 'My wife would like to go back there. There was life there. The country is too quiet for her.' He fiddled with the broken bolt on the door. It had been painted over but not repaired. He held the pieces together, then let them swing apart.

I stared out of the window; it faced south-west, the way we had come. The rain continued and there were puddles in the roadway and the fields were muddy and windswept. Sudden gusts had knocked over the pots of flowers under the crucifix and the water running down the gutters was bright red with the soil it carried from somewhere out of sight.

'I couldn't let the boy bring you,' the man said. 'I'm conducting you. I couldn't let someone else do that, not even family.' He rubbed his face hard as if he hoped to stimulate his thought. 'The other was less important to the success of the job. This part is vital.' He looked out of the window. 'We needed this rain,' he said, anxious to have my agreement.

'You did right,' I said.

He nodded obsequiously, as if I'd given him a ten-pound tip, then smiled and backed towards the door. 'I know I did,' he said.

# 34

My case officer arrived about 11 A.M.; there were cooking smells. A large black Humber pulled into the courtyard and stopped. Byrd got out. 'Wait,' he said to the driver. Byrd was wearing a short Harris tweed overcoat and a matching cap. His boots were muddy and his trouser-bottoms tucked up to avoid being soiled. He clumped upstairs to my room, dismissing the Fleming with only a grunt.

'You're my case officer?'

'That's the ticket.' He took off his cap and put it on the bed. His hair stood up in a point. He lit his pipe. 'Damned good to see you,' he said. His eyes were bright and his mouth firm, like a brush salesman sizing up a prospect.

'You've been making a fool of me,' I complained.

'Come, come, trim your yards, old boy. No question of that. No question of that at all. Thought you did well actually. Loiseau said you put in quite a plea for me.' He smiled again briefly, caught sight of himself in the mirror over the wash-basin and pushed his disarranged hair into place.

'I told him you didn't kill the girl, if that's what you mean.'

'Ah well.' He looked embarrassed. 'Damned nice of you.' He took the pipe from his mouth and searched around his teeth with his tongue. 'Damned nice, but to tell you the truth, old boy, I did.'

I must have looked surprised.

'Shocking business of course, but she'd opened us right up. Every damned one of us. They got to her.'

'With money?'

198

'No, not money; a man.' He put the pipe into the ashtray. 'She was vulnerable to men. Jean-Paul had her eating out of his hand. That's why they aren't suited to this sort of work, bless them. Men were deceivers ever, eh? Gels get themselves involved, what? Still, who are we to complain about that, wouldn't want them any other way myself.'

I didn't speak, so Byrd went on.

'At first the whole plan was to frame Kuang as some sort of oriental Jack-the-Ripper. To give us a chance to hold him, talk to him, sentence him if necessary. But the plans changed. Plans often do, that's what gives us so much trouble, eh?'

'Jean-Paul won't give you any more trouble; he's dead.'

'So I hear.'

'Did you arrange that too?' I asked.

'Come, come, don't be bitter. Still, I know just how you feel. I muffed it, I'll admit. I intended it to be quick and clean and painless, but it's too late now to be sentimental or bitter.'

'Bitter,' I said. 'If you really killed the girl, how come you got out of prison?'

'Set-up job. French police. Gave me a chance to disappear, talk to the Belgians. Very co-operative. So they should be, with this damned boat these Chinese chappies have got anchored three miles out. Can't touch them legally, you see. Pirate radio station; think what it could do if the balloon went up. Doesn't bear thinking of.'

'No. I see. What will happen?'

'Government level now, old chap. Out of the hands of blokes like you and me.'

He went to the window and stared across the mud and cabbage stumps. White mist was rolling across the flat ground like a gas attack.

'Look at that light,' said Byrd. 'Look at it. It's positively ethereal and yet you could pick it up and rap it. Doesn't it make you ache to pick up a paintbrush?'

'No,' I said.

'Well it does me. First of all a painter is interested in form, that's all they talk about at first. But everything is the light falling on it – no light and there's no form, as I'm always saying; light's the only thing a painter should worry about. All the great painters knew that: Francesca, El Greco, Van Gogh.' He stopped looking at the mist and turned back towards me glowing with pleasure. 'Or Turner. Turner most of all, take Turner any day . . .' He stopped talking but he didn't stop looking at me. I asked him no question but he heard it just the same. 'Painting is my life,' he said. 'I'd do anything just to have enough money to go on painting. It consumes me. Perhaps you wouldn't understand what art can do to a person.'

'I think I'm just beginning to,' I said.

Byrd stared me out. 'Glad to hear it, old boy.' He took a brown envelope out of his case and put it on the table.

'You want me to take Kuang up to the ship?'

'Yes, stick to the plan. Kuang is here and we'd like him out on the boat. Datt will try to get on the boat, we'd like him here, but that's less important. Get Kuang to Ostend. Rendezvous with his case chappie – Major Chan – hand him over.'

'And the girl, Maria?'

'Datt's daughter – illegitimate – divided loyalties. Obsessed about these films of her and Jean-Paul. Do anything to get them back. Datt will use that factor, mark my words. He'll use her to transport the rest of his stuff.' He ripped open the brown envelope.

'And you'll try to stop her?'

'Not me, old boy. Not my part of the ship those dossiers, not yours either. Kuang to Ostend, forget everything else. Kuang out to the ship, then we'll give you a spot of leave.' He counted out some Belgian money and

200

gave me a Belgian press card, an identity card, a letter of credit and two phone numbers to ring in case of trouble. 'Sign here,' he said. I signed the receipts.

'Loiseau's pigeon, those dossiers,' he said. 'Leave all that to him. Good fellow, Loiseau.'

Byrd kept moving like a flyweight in the first round. He picked up the receipts, blew on them and waved them to dry the ink.

'You used me, Byrd,' I said. 'You sent Hudson to me, complete with prefabricated hard-luck story. You didn't care about blowing a hole in me as long as the overall plan was okay.'

'London decided,' Byrd corrected me gently.

'All eight million of 'em?'

'Our department heads,' he said patiently. 'I personally opposed it.'

'All over the world people are personally opposing things they think are bad, but they do them anyway because a corporate decision can take the blame.'

Byrd had half turned towards the window to see the mist.

I said, 'The Nuremberg trials were held to decide that whether you work for Coca-Cola, Murder Inc. or the Wehrmacht General Staff, you remain responsible for your own actions.'

'I must have missed that part of the Nuremberg trials,' said Byrd unconcernedly. He put the receipts away in his wallet, picked up his hat and pipe and walked past me towards the door.

'Well let me jog your memory,' I said as he came level and I grabbed at his chest and tapped him gently with my right. It didn't hurt him but it spoiled his dignity and he backed away from me, smoothing his coat and pulling at the knot of his tie which had disappeared under his shirt collar.

Byrd had killed, perhaps many times. It leaves a

blemish in the eyeballs and Byrd had it. He passed his right hand round the back of his collar. I expected a throwing knife or a cheese-wire to come out, but he was merely straightening his shirt.

'You were too cynical,' said Byrd. 'I should have expected you to crack.' He stared at me. 'Cynics are disappointed romantics; they keep looking for someone to admire and can never find anyone. You'll grow out of it.'

'I don't want to grow out of it,' I said.

Byrd smiled grimly. He explored the skin where my hand had struck him. When he spoke it was through his fingers. 'Nor did any of us,' he said. He nodded and left.

## 35

I found it difficult to get to sleep after Byrd had gone and yet I was too comfortable to make a move. I listened to the articulated trucks speeding through the village: a crunch of changing gears as they reached the corner, a hiss of brakes at the crossroads, and an ascending note as they saw the road clear and accelerated. Lastly, there was a splash as they hit the puddle near the 'Drive carefully because of our children' sign. Every few minutes another came down the highway, a sinister alien force that never stopped and seemed not friendly towards the inhabitants. I looked at my watch. Five thirty. The hotel was still but the rain hit the window lightly. The wind seemed to have dropped but the fine rain continued relentlessly, like a long-distance runner just getting his second breath. I stayed awake for a long time thinking about them all. Suddenly I heard a soft footstep in the corridor. There was a pause and then I saw the door knob revolve silently. 'Are you asleep?' Kuang called softly. I wondered if my conversation with Byrd had awakened him, the walls were so thin. He came in.

'I would like a cigarette. I can't sleep. I have been downstairs but no one is about. There is no machine either.' I gave him a pack of Players. He opened it and lit one. He seemed in no hurry to go. 'I can't sleep,' he said. He sat down in the plastic-covered easy chair and watched the rain on the window. Across the shiny landscape nothing moved. We sat silent a long time, then I said, 'How did you first meet Datt?'

He seemed glad to talk. 'Vietnam, 1954. Vietnam was a mess in those days. The French *colons* were still there but they'd begun to realize the inevitability of losing. No matter how much practice they get the French are not good at losing. You British are skilled at losing. In India you showed that you knew a thing or two about the realities of compromise that the French will never learn. They knew they were going and they got more and more vicious, more and more demented. They were determined to leave nothing; not a hospital blanket nor a kind word.

'By the early 'fifties Vietnam was China's Spain. The issues were clear, and for us party members it was an honour to go there. It meant that the party thought highly of us. I had grown up in Paris. I speak perfect French. I could move about freely. I was working for an old man named de Bois. He was pure Vietnamese. Most party members had acquired Vietnamese names no matter what their origins, but de Bois couldn't bother with such niceties. That's the sort of man he was. A member since he was a child. Communist party adviser; purely political, nothing to do with the military. I was his secretary – it was something of an honour; he used me as a messenger boy. I'm a scientist, I haven't got the right sort of mind for soldiering, but it was an honour.

'Datt was living in a small town. I was told to contact him. We wanted to make contact with the Buddhists in that region. They were well organized and we were told at that time that they were sympathetic to us. Later the war became more defined (the Vietcong versus the Americans' puppets), but then the whole country was a mess of different factions, and we were trying to organize them. The only thing that they had in common was that they were anti-colonial – anti-French-colonial, that is: the French had done our work for us. Datt was a sort of soft-minded liberal, but he had influence with the Buddhists – he was something of a Buddhist scholar and they respected him for his learning – and more important, as far as we were concerned, he wasn't a Catholic.

'So I took my bicycle and cycled sixty kilometres to see Datt, but in the town it was not good to be seen with a rifle, so two miles from the town where Datt was to be found I stopped in a small village. It was so small, that village, that it had no name. Isn't it extraordinary that a village can be so small as to be without a name? I stopped and deposited my rifle with one of the young men of the village. He was one of us: a Communist, in so far as a man who lives in a village without a name can be a Communist. His sister was with him. A short girl – her skin bronze, almost red – she smiled constantly and hid behind her brother, peering out from behind him to study my features. Han Chinese[1] faces were uncommon around there then. I gave him the rifle – an old one left over from the Japanese invasion; I never did fire a shot from it. They both waved as I cycled away.

'I found Datt.

'He gave me cheroots and brandy and a long lecture on the history of democratic government. Then we found that we used to live near each other in Paris and we talked about that for a while. I wanted him to come back and see de Bois. It had been a long journey for me, but I knew Datt had an old car and that meant that if I could get him to return with me I'd get a ride back too. Besides I was tired of arguing with him, I wanted to let old de Bois have a go, they were more evenly matched. My training had been scientific, I wasn't much good at the sort of arguing that Datt was offering me.

'He came. We put the cycle in the back of his old Packard and drove west. It was a clear moonlit night and soon we came to the village that was too small even to have a name.

---

[1] A Chinese description to differentiate pure Chinese from various minority groups in China or even Vietnamese etc. Ninety-five per cent of China's population are Han Chinese.

'"I know this village," said Datt. "Sometimes I walk out as far as this. There are pheasants."

'I told him that walking this far from the town was dangerous. He smiled and said there could be no danger to a man of goodwill.

'I knew that something was wrong as soon as we stopped, for usually someone will run out and stare, if not smile. There was no sound. There was the usual smell of sour garbage and woodsmoke that all the villages have, but no sound. Even the stream was silent, and beyond the village the rice paddy shone in the moonlight like spilled milk. Not a dog, not a hen. Everyone had gone. There were only men from the Sûreté there. The rifle had been found; an informer, an enemy, the chief – who knows who found it. The smiling girl was there, dead, her nude body covered with the tiny burns that a lighted cigarette end can inflict. Two men beckoned Datt. He got out of the car. They didn't worry very much about me; they knocked me about with a pistol, but they kicked Datt. They kicked him and kicked him and kicked him. Then they rested and smoked Gauloises, and then they kicked him some more. They were both French, neither was more than twenty years old, and even then Datt wasn't young; but they kicked him mercilessly. He was screaming. I don't think they thought that either of us was Viet Minh. They'd waited for a few hours for someone to claim that rifle, and when we stopped near by they grabbed us. They didn't even want to know whether we'd come for the rifle. They kicked him and then they urinated over him and then they laughed and they lit more cigarettes and got into their Citroën car and drove away.

'I wasn't hurt much. I'd lived all my life with the wrong-coloured skin. I knew a few things about how to be kicked without getting hurt, but Datt didn't. I got him back in the car – he'd lost a lot of blood and he was a heavy man, even then he was heavy. "Which way do you want me to drive?" I said. There was a hospital back in the town and I would have taken him to it. Datt said, "Take me to Comrade de Bois." I'd said "comrade" all the time I'd spoken with Datt, but that was perhaps the first time Datt had used the word. A kick in the belly can show a man where his comrades are. Datt was badly hurt.'

'He seems to have recovered now,' I said, 'apart from the limp.'

'He's recovered now, apart from the limp,' said Kuang. 'And apart from the fact that he can have no relationships with women.'

Kuang examined me carefully and waited for me to answer.

'It explains a lot,' I said.

'Does it?' said Kuang said mockingly.

'No,' I said. 'What right does he have to identify thuggery with capitalism?' Kuang didn't answer. The ash was long on his cigarette and he walked across the room to tap it into the wash-basin. I said, 'Why should he feel free to probe and pry into the lives of people and put the results at your disposal?'

'You fool,' said Kuang. He leaned against the wash-basin smiling at me. 'My grandfather was born in 1878. In that year thirteen million Chinese died in the famine. My second brother was born in 1928. In that year five million Chinese people died in the famine. We lost twenty million dead in the Sino–Japanese war and the Long March meant the Nationalists killed two and a half million. But we are well over seven hundred million and increasing at the rate of fourteen or fifteen million a year. We are not a country or a party, we are a whole civilization, unified and moving forward at a speed that has never before been equalled in world history. Compare

our industrial growth with India's. We are unstoppable.'
I waited for him to go on, but he didn't.

'So what?' I said.

'So we don't need to set up clinics to study your foolishness and frailty. We are not interested in your minor psychological failings. Datt's amusing pastime is of no interest to my people.'

'Then why did you encourage him?'

'We have done no such thing. He financed the whole business himself. We have never aided him, or ordered him, nor have we taken from him any of his records. It doesn't interest us. He has been a good friend to us but no European can be very close to our problems.'

'You just used him to make trouble for us.'

'That I will admit. We didn't stop him making trouble. Why should we? Perhaps we have used him rather heartlessly, but a revolution must use everyone so.' He returned my pack of cigarettes.

'Keep the pack,' I said.

'You are very kind,' he said. 'There are ten left in it.'

'They won't go far among seven hundred million of you,' I said.

'That's true,' he said, and lit another.

# 36

I was awakened at nine thirty. It was *la patronne*. 'There is time for a bath and a meal,' she said. 'My husband prefers to leave early, sometimes the policeman calls in for a drink. It would be best if you were not here then.'

I supposed she noticed me look towards the other room. 'Your colleague is awake,' she said. 'The bathroom is at the end of the corridor. I have put soap there and there is plenty of hot water at this time of night.'

'Thanks,' I said. She went out without answering.

We ate most of the meal in silence. There was a plate of smoked ham, trout *meunière* and an open tart filled with rice pudding. The Fleming sat across the table and munched bread and drank a glass of wine to keep us company through the meal.

'I'm conducting tonight.'

'Good,' I said. Kuang nodded.

'You've no objection?' he asked me. He didn't want to show Kuang that I was senior man, so he put it as though it was a choice between friends.

'It will suit me,' I said. 'Me too,' said Kuang.

'I've got a couple of scarves for you, and two heavy woollen sweaters. We are meeting his case officer right on the quayside. You are probably going out by boat.'

'Not me,' I said. 'I'll be coming straight back.'

'No,' said the man. 'Operations were quite clear about that.' He rubbed his face in order to remember more clearly. 'You will come under his case officer, Major Chan, just as he takes orders from me at this moment.'

Kuang stared impassively. The man said, 'I suppose they'll need you if they run into a coastguard or fisheries protection vessel or something unexpected. It's just for territorial waters. You'll soon know if their case officer tries something.'

'That sounds like going into a refrigerator to check that the light goes out,' I said.

'They must have worked something out,' said the man. 'London must . . .' He stopped and rubbed his face again.

'It's okay,' I said. 'He knows we are London.'

'London seemed to think it's okay.'

'That's really put my mind at rest,' I said.

The man chuckled. 'Yes,' he said, 'yes,' and rubbed his face until his eye watered. 'I suppose I'm blown now,' he said.

'I'm afraid so,' I agreed. 'This will be the last job you'll do for us.'

He nodded. 'I'll miss the money,' he said sadly. 'Just when we could most do with it too.'

# 37

Maria kept thinking about Jean-Paul's death. It had thrown her off balance, and now she had to think lop-sidedly, like a man carrying a heavy suitcase; she had to compensate constantly for the distress in her head.

'What a terrible waste,' she said loudly.

Ever since she was a little girl Maria had had the habit of speaking to herself. Many times she had been embarrassed by someone coming close to her and hearing her babbling on about her trivial troubles and wishes. Her mother had never minded. It doesn't matter, she had said, if you speak to yourself, it's what you say that matters. She tried to stand back and see herself in the present dilemma. Ridiculous, she pronounced, all her life had been something of a pantomime but driving a loaded ambulance across northern France was more than she could have bargained for even in her most imaginative moments. An ambulance loaded with eight hundred dos-siers and sex films; it made her want to laugh, almost. Almost.

The road curved and she felt the wheels start to slide and corrected for it, but one of the boxes tumbled and brought another box down with it. She reached behind her and steadied the pile of tins. The metal boxes that were stacked along the neatly made bed jangled gently together, but none of them fell. She enjoyed driving, but there was no fun in thrashing this heavy old blood-wagon over the ill-kept back roads of northern France. She must avoid the main roads; she knew – almost instinctively – which ones would be patrolled. She knew the way the road patrols would obey Loiseau's order to intercept

Datt, Datt's dossiers, tapes and films, Maria, Kuang or the Englishman, or any permutation of those that they might come across. Her fingers groped along the dash-board for the third time. She switched on the wipers, cursed, switched them off, touched the choke and then the lighter. Somewhere there must be a switch that would extinguish that damned orange light that was reflecting the piled-up cases, boxes and tins in her windscreen. It was dangerous to drive with that reflection in the screen but she didn't want to stop. She could spare the time easily but she didn't want to stop. Didn't want to stop until she had completed the whole business. Then she could stop, then she could rest, then perhaps she could be reunited with Loiseau again. She shook her head. She wasn't at all sure she wanted to be reunited with Loiseau again. It was all very well thinking of him now in the abstract like this. Thinking of him surrounded by dirty dishes and with holes in his socks, thinking of him sad and lonely. But if she faced the grim truth he wasn't sad or lonely; he was self-contained, relentless and distressingly complacent about being alone. It was unnatural, but then so was being a policeman unnatural.

She remembered the first time she'd met Loiseau. A village in Périgord. She was wearing a terrible pink cotton dress that a friend had sold her. She went back there again years later. You hope that the ghost of him will accompany you there and that some witchcraft will reach out to him and he will come back to you and you will be madly in love, each with the other, as you were once before. But when you get there you are a stranger; the people, the waitress, the music, the dances, all of them are new and you are unremembered.

Heavy damned car; the suspension and steering were coarse like a lorry's. It had been ill treated, she imagined, the tyres were balding. When she entered the tiny villages the ambulance slid on the *pavé* stones. The villages were old and grey with just one or two brightly painted signs advertising beer or *friture*. In one village there were bright flashes of a welding torch as the village smith worked late into the night. Behind her, Maria heard the toot, toot, toot of a fast car. She pulled over to the right and a blue Land-Rover roared past, flashing its headlights and tooting imperious thanks. The blue rooftop light flashed spookily over the dark landscape, then disappeared. Maria slowed down; she hadn't expected any police patrols on this road and she was suddenly aware of the beating of her heart. She reached for a cigarette in the deep soft pockets of her suede coat, but as she brought the packet up to her face they spilled across her lap. She rescued one and put it in her mouth. She was going slowly now, and only half her attention was on the road. The lighter flared and trembled, and as she doused the flame, more flames grew across the horizon. There were six or seven of them, small flaring pots like something marking an unknown warrior's tomb. The surface of the road was black and shiny like a deep lake, and yet it couldn't be water, for it hadn't rained for a week. She fancied that the water would swallow the ambulance up if she didn't stop. But she didn't stop. Her front wheels splashed. She imagined the black water closing above her, and shivered. It made her feel claustrophobic. She lowered the window and recoiled at the overwhelming smell of *vin rouge*. Beyond the flares there were lamps flaring and a line of headlights. Farther still were men around a small building that had been built across the road. She thought at first that it was a customs control hut, but then she saw that it wasn't a building at all. It was a huge wine tanker tipped on to its side and askew across the road, the wine gushing from the split seams. The front part of the vehicle hung over the ditch. Lights flashed behind shattered glass as men tried to extricate the driver. She slowed up. A policeman beckoned her into the side of the road, nodding frantically.

'You made good time,' the policeman said. 'There's four dead and one injured. He's complaining, but I think he's only scratched.'

Another policeman hurried over. 'Back up against the car and we'll lift him in.'

At first Maria was going to drive off but she managed to calm down a little. She took a drag on the cigarette. 'There'll be another ambulance,' she said. She wanted to get that in before the real ambulance appeared.

'Why's that?' said the policeman. 'How many casualties did they say on the phone?'

'Six,' lied Maria.

'No,' said the policeman. 'Just one injured, four dead. The car driver injured, the four in the tanker died instantly. Two truck-drivers and two hitch-hikers.'

Alongside the road the policemen were placing shoes, a broken radio, maps, clothes and a canvas bag, all in an impeccably straight line.

Maria got out of the car. 'Let me see the hitch-hikers,' she said.

'Dead,' said the policeman. 'I know a dead 'un, believe me.'

'Let me see them,' said Maria. She looked up the dark road, fearful that the lights of an ambulance would appear.

The policeman walked over to a heap in the centre of the road. There from under a tarpaulin that police patrols carry especially for this purpose stuck four sets of feet. He lifted the edge of the tarpaulin. Maria stared down, ready to see the mangled remains of the Englishman and Kuang, but they were youths in beards and denim. One of them had a fixed grin across his face. She drew on the cigarette fiercely. 'I told you,' said the policeman. 'Dead.'

'I'll leave the injured man for the second ambulance,' said Maria.

'And have him ride with four stiffs? Not on your life,' said the policeman. 'You take him.' The red wine was still gurgling into the roadway and there was a sound of tearing metal as the hydraulic jacks tore the cab open to release the driver's body.

'Look,' said Maria desperately. 'It's my early shift. I can get away if I don't have to book a casualty in. The other ambulance won't mind.'

'You're a nice little darling,' said the policeman. 'You don't believe in work at all.'

'Please.' Maria fluttered her eyelids at him.

'No I wouldn't darling and that's a fact,' said the policeman. 'You are taking the injured one with you. The stiffs I won't insist upon and if you say there's another ambulance coming then I'll wait here. But not with the injured one I won't.' He handed her a little bundle. 'His personal effects. His passport's in there, don't lose it now.'

'No, I don't parle,' said a loud English voice. 'And let me down, I can toddle myself, thanks.'

The policeman who had tried to carry the boy released him and watched as he climbed carefully through the ambulance rear doors. The other policeman had entered the ambulance before him and cleared the tins off the bed. 'Full of junk,' said the policeman. He picked up a film tin and looked at it.

'It's hospital records,' said Maria. 'Patients transferred. Documents on film. I'm taking them to the other hospitals in the morning.'

The English tourist – a tall boy in a black woollen shirt and pink linen trousers – stretched full length on the bed. 'That's just the job,' he said appreciatively. The policeman locked the rear doors carefully. Maria heard him say, 'We'll leave the stiffs where they are. The other ambulance will find them. We'll get up to the road blocks. Everything is happening tonight. Accident, road blocks, contraband search and the next thing you know we'll be asked to do a couple of hours' extra duty.'

'Let the ambulance get away,' said the second policeman. 'We don't want her to report us leaving the scene before the second ambulance arrived.'

'That lazy bitch,' said the first policeman. He slammed his fist against the roof of the ambulance and called loudly, 'Right, off you go.'

Maria turned around in her seat and looked for the switch for the interior light. She found it and switched off the orange lamp. The policeman leered in through the window. 'Don't work too hard,' he said.

'Policeman,' said Maria. She said it as if it was a dirty word and the policeman flinched. He was surprised at the depth of her hatred.

He spoke softly and angrily. 'The trouble with you people from hospitals,' he said, 'you think you're the only normal people left alive.'

Maria could think of no answer. She drove forward. From behind her the voice of the Englishman said, 'I'm sorry to be causing you all this trouble.' He said it in English hoping that the tone of his voice would convey his meaning.

'It's all right,' said Maria.

'You speak English!' said the man. 'That's wonderful.'

'Is your leg hurting you?' She tried to make it as professional and clinical as she knew how.

'It's nothing. I did it running down the road to find a telephone. It's hilarious really: those four dead and me unscratched except for a strained knee running down the road.'

'Your car?'

'That's done for. Cheap car, Ford Anglia. Crankcase sticking through the rear axle the last I saw of it. Done for. It wasn't the lorry driver's fault. Poor sod. It wasn't my fault either, except that I was going too fast. I always drive too fast, everyone tells me that. But I couldn't have avoided this lot. He was right in the centre of the road. You do that in a heavy truck on these high camber roads. I don't blame him. I hope he doesn't blame me too much either.'

Maria didn't answer; she hoped he'd go to sleep so she could think about this new situation.

'Can you close the window?' he asked. She rolled it up a little, but kept it a trifle open. The tension of her claustrophobia returned and she knocked the window handle with her elbow, hoping to open it a little more without the boy's noticing.

'You were a bit sharp with the policeman,' said the boy. Maria grunted an affirmative.

'Why?' asked the boy. 'Don't you like policemen?'

'I married one.'

'Go on,' said the boy. He thought about it. 'I never got married. I lived with a girl for a couple of years . . .' He stopped.

'What happened?' said Maria. She didn't care. Her worries were all upon the road ahead. How many road blocks were out tonight? How thoroughly would they examine papers and cargoes?

'She chucked me,' said the boy.

'Chucked?'

'Rejected me. What about you?'

'I suppose mine chucked me,' said Maria.

'And you became an ambulance driver,' said the boy with the terrible simplicity of youth.

'Yes,' said Maria and laughed aloud.

'You all right?' asked the boy anxiously.

'I'm all right,' said Maria. 'But the nearest hospital that's any good is across the border in Belgium. You lie back and groan and behave like an emergency when we get to the frontier. Understand?'

Maria deliberately drove eastward, cutting around the Forêt de St Michel through Watigny and Signy-le-Petit. She'd cross the border at Riezes.

'Suppose they are all closed down at the frontier?' asked the boy.

'Leave it with me,' said Maria. She cut back through a narrow lane, offering thanks that it hadn't begun to rain. In this part of the world the mud could be impassable after half an hour's rain.

'You certainly know your way around,' said the boy. 'Do you live near here?'

'My mother still does.'

'Not your father?'

'Yes, he does too,' said Maria. She laughed.

'Are you all right?' the boy asked again.

'You're the casualty,' said Maria. 'Lie down and sleep.'

'I'm sorry to be a bother,' said the boy.

Pardon me for breathing, thought Maria; the English were always apologizing.

# 38

Already the brief butterfly summer of the big hotels is almost gone. Some of the shutters are locked and the waiters are scanning the ads for winter resort jobs. The road snakes past the golf club and military hospital. Huge white dunes, shining in the moonlight like alabaster temples, lean against the grey Wehrmacht gun emplacements. Between the points of sand and the cubes of concrete nightjars swoop open-mouthed upon the moths and insects. The red glow of Ostend is nearer now and yellow trams rattle alongside the motor road and over the bridge by the Royal Yacht Club where white yachts – sails neatly rolled and tied – sleep bobbing on the grey water like seagulls.

'I'm sorry,' I said. 'I thought they would be earlier than this.'

'A policeman gets used to standing around,' Loiseau answered. He moved back across the cobbles and scrubby grass, stepping carefully over the rusty railway lines and around the shapeless debris and abandoned cables. When I was sure he was out of sight I walked back along the *quai*. Below me the sea made soft noises like a bathful of serpents, and the joints of four ancient fishing boats creaked. I walked over to Kuang. 'He's late,' I said. Kuang said nothing. Behind him, farther along the *quai*, a freighter was being loaded by a huge travelling crane. Light spilled across the waterfront from the spotlights on the cranes. Could their man have caught sight of Loiseau and been frightened away? It was fifteen minutes later than rendezvous. The standard control procedure was to wait only four minutes, then come back twenty-four hours later; but I hung on. Control procedures were invented by diligent men in clean shirts and warm offices. I stayed. Kuang seemed to notice the passage of time – or more accurately perhaps he revelled in it. He stood patiently. He hadn't stamped his feet, breathed into his hands or smoked a cigarette. When I neared him he didn't raise a quizzical eyebrow, remark about the cold or even look at his watch. He stared across the water, glanced at me to be sure I was not about to speak again, and then resumed his pose.

'We'll give him ten more minutes,' I said. Kuang looked at me. I walked back down the quayside.

The yellow headlight turned off the main road a trifle too fast and there was a crunch as the edge of an offside wing touched one of the oil drums piled outside the Fina station. The lights kept coming, main beams. Kuang was illuminated as bright as a snowman and there was only a couple of foot of space between him and the wire fence around the sand heap. Kuang leapt across the path of the car. His coat flapped across the headlight, momentarily eclipsing its beam. There was a scream as the brakes slammed on and the engine stalled. Suddenly it was quiet. The sea splashed greedily against the jetty. Kuang was sucking his thumb as I got down from the oil drum. It was an ambulance that had so nearly run us down.

Out of the ambulance stepped Maria.

'What's going on?' I said.

'I'm Major Chan,' said Maria.

'You are?' Kuang said. He obviously didn't believe her.

'You're Major Chan, case officer for Kuang here?' I said.

'For the purposes that we are all interested in, I am,' she said.

'What sort of answer is that?' I asked.

'Whatever sort of answer it is,' said Maria, 'it's going to have to do.'

'Very well,' I said. 'He's all yours.'

'I won't go with her,' said Kuang. 'She tried to run me down. You saw her.'

'I know her well enough to know that she could have tried a lot harder,' I said.

'You didn't show that sort of confidence a couple of minutes ago,' said Maria. 'Scrambling out of the way when you thought I was going to run *you* down.'

'What's confidence?' I said. 'Smiling as you fall off a cliff to prove that you've jumped?'

'That's what it is,' said Maria and she leaned forward and gave me a tiny kiss, but I refused to be placated. 'Where's your contact?'

'This is it,' said Maria, playing for time. I grabbed her arm and clutched it tight. 'Don't play for time,' I told her. 'You said you're the case officer. So take Kuang and start to run him.' She looked at me blankly. I shook her.

'They should be here,' she said. 'A boat.' She pointed along the jetty. We stared into the darkness. A small boat moved into the pool of light cast by the loading freighter. It turned towards us.

'They will want to load the boxes from the ambulance.'

'Hold it,' I told her. 'Take your payment first.'

'How did you know?'

'It's obvious, isn't it?' I said. 'You bring Datt's dossiers as far as this, using your ingenuity, your knowledge of police methods and routes, and if the worst comes to the worst you use your influence with your ex-husband. For what? In return Datt will give you your own dossier and film, etc. Am I right?'

'Yes,' she said.

'Then let them worry about loading.' The motor boat was closer now. It was a high-speed launch; four men in pea-jackets stood in the stern. They stared towards us

221

but didn't wave or call. As the boat got to the stone steps, one man jumped ashore. He took the rope and made it fast to a jetty ring. 'The boxes,' I called to them. 'Your papers are here.'

'Load first,' said the sailor who had jumped ashore.

'Give me the boxes,' I said. The sailors looked at me and at Kuang. One of the men in the boat made a motion with his hand and the others took two tin boxes, adorned with red seals, from the bottom of the boat and passed them to the first man, who carried them up the steps to us.

'Help me with the boxes,' said Maria to the Chinese sailor.

I still had hold of her arm. 'Get back into the ambulance and lock the doors from inside,' I said.

'You said I should start . . .'

I pushed her roughly towards the driver's door.

I didn't take my eyes off Maria but on the periphery of my vision to the right I could see a man edging along the side of the ambulance towards me. He kept one hand flat against the side of the vehicle, dabbing at the large scarlet cross as if testing to see if the paint was wet. I let him come to within arm's length and still without swivelling my head I flicked out my hands so that my fingertips lashed his face, causing him to blink and pull back. I leaned a few inches towards him while sweeping my hand back the way it had come, slapping him not very hard across the side of the cheek.

'Give over,' he shouted in English. 'What the hell are you on?'

'Get back in the ambulance,' Maria called to him. 'He's harmless,' she said. 'A motor accident on the road. That's how I got through the blocks so easily.'

'You said Ostend hospital,' said the boy.

'Stay out of this, sonny,' I said. 'You are in danger

even if you keep your mouth shut. Open it and you're dead.'

'I'm the case officer,' she insisted.

'You are what?' I said. I smiled one of my reassuring smiles, but I see now that to Maria it must have seemed like mockery. 'You are a child, Maria, you've no idea of what this is all about. Get into the ambulance,' I told her. 'Your ex-husband is waiting down the jetty. If you have this cart-load of documents with you when he arrests you things might go easier for you.'

'Did you hear him?' Maria said to the sailor and Kuang. 'Take the documents, and take me with you – he's betrayed us all to the police.' Her voice was quiet but the note of hysteria was only one modulation away.

The sailor remained impassive and Kuang didn't even look towards her.

'Did you hear him?' she said desperately. No one spoke. A rowboat was moving out around the far side of the Yacht Club. The flutter of dripping blades skidding upon the surface and the gasp of oars biting into the water was a lonely rhythm, like a woman's sobs, each followed by the sharp intake of breath.

I said, 'You don't know what it's all about. This man's job is to bring Kuang back to their ship. He's also instructed to take me. As well as that he'll try to take the documents. But he doesn't change plans because you shout news about Loiseau waiting to arrest you. In fact, that's a good reason for leaving right away because their big command is to stay out of trouble. This business doesn't work like that.'

I signalled Kuang to go down to the motor boat and the sailor steadied him on the slimy metal ladder. I punched Maria lightly on the arm. 'I'll knock you unconscious, Maria, if that's the way you insist I do it.' I smiled but I meant it.

'I can't face Loiseau. Not with that case I can't face

him.' She opened the driver's door and got into the seat. She would rather face Datt than Loiseau. She shivered. The boy said, 'I feel I'm making a lot of trouble for you. I'm sorry.'

'Just don't say you're sorry once again,' I heard Maria say.

'Get in,' I called to the sailor. 'The police will be here any moment. There's no time to load boxes.' He was at the foot of the ladder and I had my heavy shoes on. He shrugged and stepped into the boat. I untied the rope and someone started the motor. There was a bright flurry of water and the boat moved quickly, zigzagging through the water as the helmsman got the feel of the rudder.

At the end of the bridge there was a flashlight moving. I wondered if the whistles were going. I couldn't hear anything above the sound of the outboard motor. The flashlight was reflected suddenly in the driver's door of the ambulance. The boat lurched violently as we left the harbour and entered the open sea. I looked at the Chinese sailor at the helm. He didn't seem frightened, but then how would he look if he did? I looked back. The figures on the quay were tiny and indistinct. I looked at my watch: it was 2.10 A.M. The Incredible Count Szell had just killed another canary, they cost only three francs, four at the most.

# 39

Three miles out from Ostend the water was still and a layer of mist hugged it; a bleak bottomless cauldron of broth cooling in the cold morning air. Out of the mist appeared M. Datt's ship. It was a scruffy vessel of about 10,000 tons, an old cargo boat, its rear derrick broken. One of the bridge wings had been mangled in some long-forgotten mishap and the grey hull, scabby and peeling, had long brown rusty stains dribbling from the hawse pipes down the anchor fleets. It had been at anchor a long time out here in the Straits of Dover. The most unusual feature of the ship was a mainmast about three times taller than usual and the words 'Radio Janine' newly painted in ten-foot-high white letters along the hull.

The engines were silent, the ship still, but the current sucked around the draught figures on the stem and the anchor chain groaned as the ship tugged like a bored child upon its mother's hand. There was no movement on deck, but I saw a flash of glass from the wheelhouse as we came close. Bolted to the hull-side there was an ugly metal accommodation ladder, rather like a fire-escape. At water level the steps ended in a wide platform complete with stanchion and guest warp to which we made fast. M. Datt waved us aboard.

As we went up the metal stairs Datt called to us, 'Where are they?' No one answered, no one even looked up at him. 'Where are the packets of documents – my work? Where is it?'

'There's just me,' I said.

'I told you . . .' Datt shouted to one of the sailors.

225

'It was not possible,' Kuang told him. 'The police were right behind us. We were lucky to get away.'

'The dossiers were the important thing,' said Datt. 'Didn't you even wait for the girl?' No one spoke. 'Well didn't you?'

'The police almost certainly got her,' Kuang said. 'It was a close thing.'

'And my documents?' said Datt.

'These things happen,' said Kuang, showing little or no concern.

'Poor Maria,' said Datt. 'My daughter.'

'You care only about your dossiers,' said Kuang calmly. 'You do not care for the girl.'

'I care for you all,' said Datt. 'I care even for the Englishman here. I care for you all.'

'You are a fool,' said Kuang.

'I will report this when we are in Peking.'

'How can you?' asked Kuang. 'You will tell them that you gave the documents to the girl and put my safety into her hands because you were not brave enough to perform your duties as conducting officer. You let the girl masquerade as Major Chan while you made a quick getaway, alone and unencumbered. You gave her access to the code greeting and I can only guess what other secrets, and then you have the effrontery to complain that your stupid researches are not delivered safely to you aboard the ship here.' Kuang smiled.

Datt turned away from us and walked forward. Inside, the ship was in better condition and well lit. There was the constant hum of the generators and from some far part of the ship came the sound of a metal door slamming. He kicked a vent and smacked a deck light which miraculously lit. A man leaned over the bridge wing and looked down on us, but Datt waved him back to work. He walked up the lower bridge ladder and I followed him, but Kuang remained at the foot of it. 'I am hungry,'

Kuang said. 'I have heard enough. I'm going below to eat.'

'Very well,' said Datt without looking back. He opened the door of what had once been the captain's cabin and waved me to precede him. His cabin was warm and comfortable. The small bed was dented where someone had been lying. On the writing table there were a heap of papers, some envelopes, a tall pile of gramophone records and a vacuum flask. Datt opened a cupboard above the desk and reached down two cups. He poured hot coffee from the flask and then two brandies into tulip glasses. I put two heaps of sugar into my coffee and poured the brandy after it, then I downed the hot mixture and felt it doing wonders for my arteries.

Datt offered me his cigarettes. He said, 'A mistake. A silly mistake. Do you ever make silly mistakes?'

I said, 'It's one of my very few creative activities.' I waved away his cigarettes.

'Droll,' said Datt. 'I felt sure that Loiseau would not act against me. I had influence and a hold on his wife. I felt sure he wouldn't act against me.'

'Was that your sole reason for involving Maria?'

'To tell you the truth: yes.'

'Then I'm sorry you guessed wrong. It would have been better to have left Maria out of this.'

'My work was almost done. These things don't last for ever.' He brightened. 'But within a year we'll do the same operation again.'

I said, 'Another psychological investigation with hidden cameras and recorders, and available women for influential Western men? Another large house with all the trimmings in a fashionable part of Paris?'

Datt nodded. 'Or a fashionable part of Buenos Aires, or Tokyo, or Washington, or London.'

'I don't think you are a true Marxist at all,' I said. 'You merely relish the downfall of the West. A Marxist at least comforts himself with the idea of the proletariat joining hands across national frontiers, but you Chinese Communists relish aggressive nationalism just at a time when the world was becoming mature enough to reject it.'

'I relish nothing. I just record,' said Datt. 'But it could be said that the things of Western Europe that you are most anxious to preserve are better served by supporting the real, uncompromising power of Chinese communism than by allowing the West to splinter into internecine warrior states. France, for example, is travelling very nicely down that path; what will she preserve in the West if her atom bombs are launched? We will conquer, we will preserve. Only we can create a truly world order based upon seven hundred million true believers.'

'That's really 1984,' I said. 'Your whole set-up is Orwellian.'

'Orwell,' said Datt, 'was a naïve simpleton. A middle-class weakling terrified by the realities of social revolution. He was a man of little talent and would have remained unknown had the reactionary press not seen in him a powerful weapon of propaganda. They made him a *guru*, a pundit, a seer. But their efforts will rebound upon them, for Orwell in the long run will be the greatest ally the Communist movement ever had. He warned the bourgeoisie to watch for militancy, organization, fanaticism and thought-planning, while all the time the seeds of their destruction are being sown by their own inadequacy, apathy, aimless violence and trivial titillation. Their destruction is in good hands: their own. The rebuilding will be ours. My own writings will be the basis of our control of Europe and America. Our control will rest upon the satisfaction of their own basest appetites. Eventually a new sort of European man will evolve.'

'History,' I said. 'That's always the alibi.'

'Progress is only possible if we learn from history.'

'Don't believe it. Progress is man's indifference to the lessons of history.'

'You are cynical as well as ignorant,' said Datt as though making a discovery. 'Get to know yourself, that's my advice. Get to know yourself.'

'I know enough awful people already,' I said.

'You feel sorry for the people who came to my clinic. That's because you really feel sorry for yourself. But these people do not deserve your sympathy. Rationalization is their destruction. Rationalization is the aspirin of mental health and, as with aspirin, an overdose can be fatal.

'They enslave themselves by dipping deeper and deeper into the tube of taboos. And yet each stage of their journey is described as greater freedom.' He laughed grimly. 'Permissiveness is slavery. But so has history always been. Your jaded, overfed section of the world is comparable to the ancient city states of the Middle East. Outside the gates the hard nomads waited their chance to plunder the rich, decadent city-dwellers. And in their turn the nomads would conquer, settle into the newly-conquered city and grow soft, and new hard eyes watched from the barren stony desert until their time was ripe. So the hard, strong, ambitious, idealistic peoples of China see the over-ripe conditions of Europe and the USA. They sniff the air and upon it floats the aroma of garbage cans overfilled, idle hands and warped minds seeking diversions bizarre and perverted, they smell violence, stemming not from hunger, but from boredom, they smell the corruption of government and the acrid flash of fascism. They sniff, my friend: you!'

I said nothing, and waited while Datt sipped at his coffee and brandy. He looked up. 'Take off your coat.'

'I'm not staying.'

'Not staying?' He chuckled. 'Where are you going?'

'Back to Ostend,' I said. 'And you are going with me.'

'More violence?' He raised his hands in mock surrender.

I shook my head. 'You know you've got to go back,' I said. 'Or are you going to leave all your dossiers back there on the quayside less than four miles away?'

'You'll give them to me?'

'I'm promising nothing,' I told him, 'but I know that you have to go back there. There is no alternative.' I poured myself more coffee and gestured to him with the pot. 'Yes,' he said absent-mindedly. 'More.'

'You are not the sort of man that leaves a part of himself behind. I know you, Monsieur Datt. You could bear to have your documents on the way to China and yourself in the hands of Loiseau, but the converse you cannot bear.'

'You expect me to go back there and give myself up to Loiseau?'

'I know you will,' I said. 'Or live the rest of your life regretting it. You will recall all your work and records and you will relive this moment a million times. Of course you must return with me. Loiseau is a human being and human activities are your speciality. You have friends in high places, it will be hard to convict you of any crime on the statute book . . .'

'That is very little protection in France.'

'Ostend is in Belgium,' I said. 'Belgium doesn't recognize Peking, Loiseau operates there only on sufferance. Loiseau too will be amenable to any debating skill you can muster. Loiseau fears a political scandal that would involve taking a man forcibly from a foreign country . . .'

'You are glib. Too glib,' said Datt. 'The risk remains too great.'

'Just as you wish,' I said. I drank the rest of my coffee and turned away from him.

'I'd be a fool to go back for the documents. Loiseau

230

can't touch me here.' He walked across to the barometer and tapped it. 'It's going up.' I said nothing.

He said, 'It was my idea to make my control centre a pirate radio boat. We are not open to inspection nor even under the jurisdiction of any government in the world. We are, in effect, a nation unto ourselves on this boat, just as all the other pirate radio ships are.'

'That's right,' I said. 'You're safe here.' I stood up. 'I should have said nothing,' I said. 'It is not my concern. My job is done.' I buttoned my coat tight and blessed the man from Ostend for providing the thick extra sweater.

'You despise me?' said Datt. There was an angry note in his voice.

I stepped towards him and took his hand in mine. 'I don't,' I said anxiously. 'Your judgement is as valid as mine. Better, for only you are in a position to evaluate your work and your freedom.' I gripped his hand tight in a stereotyped gesture of reassurance.

He said, 'My work is of immense value. A break-through you might almost say. Some of the studies seemed to have . . .' Now he was anxious to convince me of the importance of his work.

But I released his hand carefully. I nodded, smiled and turned away. 'I must go. I have brought Kuang here, my job is done. Perhaps one of your sailors would take me back to Ostend.'

Datt nodded. I turned away, tired of my game and wondering whether I really wanted to take this sick old man and deliver him to the mercies of the French Government. They say a man's resolution shows in the set of his shoulders. Perhaps Datt saw my indifference in mine. 'Wait,' he called. 'I will take you.'

'Good,' I said. 'It will give you time to think.'

Datt looked around the cabin feverishly. He wet his lips and smoothed his hair with the flat of his hand. He flicked through a bundle of papers, stuffed two of them in his pocket, and gathered up a few possessions.

They were strange things that Datt took with him: an engraved paperweight, a half-bottle of brandy, a cheap notebook and finally an old fountain pen which he inspected, wiped and carefully capped before pushing it into his waistcoat pocket. 'I'll take you back,' he said. 'Do you think Loiseau will let me just look through my stuff?'

'I can't answer for Loiseau,' I said. 'But I know he fought for months to get permission to raid your house on the Avenue Foch. He submitted report after report proving beyond all normal need that you were a threat to the security of France. Do you know what answer he got? They told him that you were an X., an *ancien X*. You were a Polytechnic man, one of the ruling class, the elite of France. You could *tutoyer* his Minister, call half the Cabinet *cher camarade*. You were a privileged person, inviolate and arrogant with him and his men. But he persisted, he showed them finally what you were, Monsieur Datt. And now perhaps he'll want them to pay their bill. I'd say Loiseau might see the advantage in letting a little of your poison into their bloodstream. He might decide to give them something to remember the next time they are about to obstruct him and lecture him, and ask him for the fiftieth time if he isn't mistaken. Permit you to retain the dossiers and tapes?' I smiled. 'He might well insist upon it.'

Datt nodded, cranked the handle of an ancient wall phone and spoke some rapid Chinese dialect into it. I noticed his large white fingers, like the roots of some plant that had never been exposed to sunlight.

He said, 'You are right, no doubt about it. I must be where my research is. I should never have parted company from it.'

He pottered about absent-mindedly. He picked up his

Monopoly board. 'You must reassure me on one thing,' he said. He put the board down again. 'The girl. You'll see that the girl's all right?'

'She'll be all right.'

'You'll attend to it? I've treated her badly.'

'Yes,' I said.

'I threatened her, you know. I threatened her about her file. About her pictures. I shouldn't have done that really but I cared for my work. It's not a crime, is it, caring about your work?'

'Depends upon the work.'

'Mind you,' said Datt, 'I have given her money. I gave her the car too.'

'It's easy to give away things you don't need,' I said. 'And rich people who give away money need to be quite sure they're not trying to buy something.'

'I've treated her badly.' He nodded to himself. 'And there's the boy, my grandson.'

I hurried down the iron steps. I wanted to get away from the boat before Kuang saw what was happening, and yet I doubt if Kuang would have stopped us; with Datt out of the way the only report going back would be Kuang's.

'You've done me a favour,' Datt pronounced as he started up the outboard motor.

'That's right,' I said.

# 40

The Englishman had told her to lock the ambulance door. She tried to, but as her finger hovered over the catch, the nausea of fear broke over her. She imagined just for a moment the agony of being imprisoned. She shuddered and pushed the thought aside. She tried again, but it was no use, and while she was still trying to push the lock the English boy with the injured knee leaned across her and locked the door. She wound the window down, urgently trying to still the claustrophobia. She leaned forward with her eyes closed and pressed her head against the cold windscreen. What had she done? It had seemed so right when Datt had put it to her: if she took the main bulk of the documents and tapes up to the rendezvous for him, then he would be waiting there with her own film and dossier. A fair exchange, he had said. She touched the locks of the case that had come from the boat. She supposed that her documents were inside, but suddenly she didn't care. Fine rain beaded the windscreen with little lenses. The motor boat was repeated a thousand times upside down.

'Are you all right?' the boy asked. 'You don't look well.'

She didn't answer.

'Look here,' he said, 'I wish you'd tell me what all this is about. I know I've given you a lot of trouble and all that, you see . . .'

'Stay here in the car,' Maria said. 'Don't touch anything and don't let anyone else touch anything. Promise?'

'Very well. I promise.'

She unlocked the door with a sigh of relief and got out

into the cold salty air. The car was on the very brink of the waterside and she stepped carefully across the worn stones. Along the whole quayside men were appearing out of doorways and warehouse entrances. Not ordinary men but men in berets and anklets. They moved quietly and most of them were carrying automatic rifles. A group of them near to her stepped under the wharfside lights and she saw the glitter of the paratroop badges. Maria was frightened of the men. She stopped near the rear doors of the ambulance and looked back; the boy stared at her across the metal boxes and film tins. He smiled and nodded to reassure her that he wouldn't touch anything. Why did she care whether he touched anything? One man broke away from the group of paratroops near her. He was in civilian clothes, a thigh-length black leather coat and an old-fashioned trilby hat. He had taken only one step when she recognized Loiseau.

'Maria, is it you?'

'Yes, it's me.'

He hurried towards her, but when he was a pace away stopped. She had expected him to embrace her. She wanted to hang on to him and feel his hand slapping her awkwardly on the back, which was his inadequate attempt to staunch miseries of various kinds.

'There are a lot of people here,' she said. '*Bif?*'

'Yes, the army,' said Loiseau. 'A paratroop battalion. The Belgians gave me full co-operation.'

Maria resented that. It was his way of saying that she had never given him full co-operation. 'Just to take me into custody,' she said, 'a whole battalion of Belgian paratroops? You must have exaggerated.'

'There is a ship out there. There is no telling how many men are aboard. Datt might have decided to take the documents by force.'

He was anxious to justify himself, like a little boy

235

seeking an advance on his pocket money. She smiled and repeated, 'You must have exaggerated.'

'I did,' said Loiseau. He did not smile, for distorting truth was nothing to be proud of. But in this case he was anxious that there should be no mistakes. He would rather look a fool for over-preparation than be found inadequate. They stood there staring at each other for several minutes.

'The documents are in the ambulance?' Loiseau asked.

'Yes,' she said. 'The film of me is there too.'

'What about the tape of the Englishman? The questioning that you translated when he was drugged?'

'That's there too, it's a green tin; number B fourteen.' She touched his arm. 'What will you do with the Englishman's tape?' She could not ask about her own.

'Destroy it,' said Loiseau. 'Nothing has come of it, and I've no reason to harm him.'

'And that's part of your agreement with him,' she accused.

Loiseau nodded.

'And my tape?'

'I will destroy that too.'

'Doesn't that go against your principles? Isn't destruction of evidence the cardinal sin for a policeman?'

'There is no rule book that can be consulted in these matters whatever the Church and the politicians and the lawyers tell us. Police forces, governments and armies are just groups of men. Each man must do as his conscience dictates. A man doesn't obey without question or he's not a man any more.'

Maria gripped his arm with both hands, and pretended just for a moment that she would never have to let go.

'Lieutenant,' Loiseau called along the wharf. One of the paratroops slammed to attention and doubled along the waterfront. 'I'll have to take you into custody,' Loiseau said quietly to Maria.

236

'My documents are on the front seat of the ambulance,' she told him hurriedly before the lieutenant reached them.

'Lieutenant,' Loiseau said, 'I want you to take the boxes out of the ambulance and bring them along to the shed. By the way, you had better take an inventory of the tins and boxes; mark them with chalk. Keep an armed guard on the whole operation. There might be an attempt to recover them.'

The lieutenant saluted Loiseau warmly and gave Maria a passing glance of curiosity.

'Come along, Maria,' said Loiseau. He turned and walked towards the shed.

Maria patted her hair and followed him.

It was a wooden hut that had been put up for the duration of World War Two. A long, badly lit corridor ran the whole length of the hut, and the rest was divided into four small, uncomfortable offices. Maria repaired her make-up for the third time. She decided to do one eye at a time and get them really right.

'How much longer?' she asked. Her voice was distorted as she held her face taut to paint the line over her right eye.

'Another hour,' said Loiseau. There was a knock at the door and the paratroop lieutenant came in. He looked briefly at Maria and then saluted Loiseau.

'We're having a little trouble, sir, getting the boxes out of the ambulance.'

'Trouble?' said Loiseau.

'There's some madman with an injured leg. He's roaring and raging and punching the soldiers who are trying to unload the vehicle.'

'Can't you deal with it?'

'Of course I can deal with it,' said the paratroop officer.

Loiseau detected a note of irritation in his voice. 'It's just that I don't know who the little squirt is.'

'I picked him up on the road,' said Maria. 'He was injured in a road crash. I told him to look after the documents when I got out of the car. I didn't mean . . . he's nothing to do with . . . he's just a casualty.'

'Just a casualty,' Loiseau repeated to the lieutenant. The lieutenant smiled. 'Get him along to the hospital,' said Loiseau.

'The hospital,' repeated Maria. 'Everything in its proper place.'

'Very good sir,' said the lieutenant. He saluted with an extra display of energy to show that he disregarded the sarcasm of the woman. He gave the woman a disapproving look as he turned about and left.

'You have another convert,' said Maria. She chuckled as she surveyed her painted eye, twisting her face slightly so that the unpainted eye was not visible in the mirror. She tilted her head high to keep her chin line. She heard the soldiers piling the boxes in the corridor. 'I'm hungry,' she said after a while.

'I can send out,' said Loiseau. 'The soldiers have a lorry full of coffee and sausages and some awful fried things.'

'Coffee and sausage.'

'Go and get two sweet coffees and some sausage sandwiches,' Loiseau said to the young sentry.

'The corporal has gone for his coffee,' said the soldier.

'That's all right,' said Loiseau. 'I'll look after the boxes.'

'He'll look after the boxes,' Maria said flatly to the mirror.

The soldier looked at her, but Loiseau nodded and the soldier turned to get the coffee. 'You can leave your gun with me,' Loiseau said. 'You'll not be able to carry the coffee with that slung round your neck and I don't want guns left lying around in the corridor.'

'I'll manage the coffee and the gun,' said the soldier. He said it defiantly, then he slung the strap of the gun around his neck to prove it was possible. 'You're a good soldier,' said Loiseau.

'It won't take a moment,' said the soldier.

Loiseau swung around in the swivel chair, drummed his fingers on the rickety desk and then swivelled back the other way. He leaned close to the window. The condensation was heavy on it and he wiped a peephole clear so that he could see the waterfront. He had promised the Englishman that he would wait. He wished he hadn't: it spoiled his schedule and also it gave this awkward time of hanging about here with Maria. He couldn't have her held in the local police station, obviously she had to wait here with him; it was unavoidable, and yet it was a bad situation. He had been in no position to argue with the Englishman. The Englishman had offered him all the documents as well as the Red Chinese conducting officer. What's more he had said that if Loiseau would wait here he would bring Datt off the ship and deliver him to the quayside. Loiseau snorted. There was no good reason for Datt to leave the pirate radio ship. He was safe out there beyond the three-mile limit and he knew it. All the other pirate radio ships were out there and safe. Datt had only to tune in to other ships to confirm it.

'Have you got a cold?' Maria asked him, still inspecting her painted eye.

'No.'

'It sounds like it. Your nose is stuffed up. You know that's always the first sign with those colds you get. It's having the bedroom window open, I've told you about that hundreds of times.'

'And I wish you'd stop telling me.'

'Just as you like.' She scrubbed around in the tin of eye

239

black and spat into it. She had smudged the left eye and now she wiped it clean so that she looked curiously lopsided: one eye dramatically painted and the other white and naked. 'I'm sorry,' she said. 'Really sorry.'

'It will be all right,' said Loiseau. 'Somehow I will find a way.'

'I love you,' she said.

'Perhaps.' His face was grey and his eyes deep sunk the way they always were when he had missed a lot of sleep.

They had occupied the same place in her mind, Loiseau and her father, but now she suddenly saw Loiseau as he really was. He was no superman, he was middle-aged and fallible and unrelaxingly hard upon himself. Maria put the eye-black tin down and walked across to the window near Loiseau.

'I love you,' she said again.

'I know you do,' said Loiseau. 'And I am a lucky man.'

'Please help me,' said Maria, and Loiseau was amazed, for he could never have imagined her asking for help, and Maria was amazed, for she could not imagine herself asking for help.

Loiseau put his nose close to the window. It was hard to see through it because of the reflections and condensation. Again he rubbed a clear place to look through.

'I will help you,' said Loiseau.

She cleared her own little portion of glass and peered along the waterfront. 'He's a damn long time with that coffee,' said Loiseau.

'There's the Englishman,' said Maria, 'and Datt.'

'Well I'm damned,' said Loiseau. 'He's brought him.'

Datt's voice echoed down the corridor as the hut door swung open. 'This is it,' he said excitedly. 'All my documents. Colour seals denote year, index letters code names.' He tapped the boxes proudly. 'Where is Loiseau?' he asked the Englishman as he walked slowly down the rank of stacked tins and boxes, stroking them as he read the code letters.

'The second door,' said the Englishman, easing his way past the boxes.

Maria knew exactly what she had to do. Jean-Paul said she'd never made one real decision in her life. It was not hysteria, nor heightened emotion. Her father stood in the doorway, tins of documents in his arms, nursing them as though they were a newly-born child. He smiled the smile she remembered from her childhood. His body was poised like that of a tightrope walker about to step off the platform. This time his powers of persuasion and manipulation were about to be tried to the utmost, but she had no doubt that he would succeed. Not even Loiseau was proof against the smooth cool method of Datt, her puppet-master. She knew Datt's mind and could predict the weapons he would use: he would use the fact that he was her father and the grandfather of Loiseau's child. He would use the hold he had over so many important people. He would use everything he had and he would win.

Datt smiled and extended a hand. 'Chief Inspector Loiseau,' he said. 'I think I can be of immeasurable help to you – and to France.'

She had her handbag open now. No one looked at her. Loiseau motioned towards a chair. The Englishman moved aside and glanced quickly around the room. Her hand was around the butt by now, the safety catch slid down noiselessly. She let go of her handbag and it sat upon the gun like a tea cosy.

'The ship's position,' said Datt, 'is clearly marked upon this chart. It seemed my duty to pretend to help them.'

'Just a moment,' said Loiseau wearily.

The Englishman saw what was happening. He punched towards the handbag. And then Datt realized, just as the pistol went off. She pulled the trigger again as fast as

241

she could. Loiseau grabbed her by the neck and the Englishman punched her arm. She dropped the bag. Datt was through the door fumbling with the lock to prevent them from chasing him. He couldn't operate the lock and ran down the corridor. There was the sound of the outer door opening. Maria wrenched herself free and ran after Datt, the gun still in her hand. Everyone was shouting. Behind her she heard Loiseau call, 'Lieutenant, stop that man.'

The soldier with the tray of coffee may have heard Loiseau's shout or he may have seen Maria or the Englishman brandishing a pistol. Whatever it was that prompted him, he threw the tray of coffee aside. He swung the rifle around his neck like a hula-hoop. The stock slammed into his hand and a burst of fire echoed across the waterfront almost simultaneously with the sound of the coffee cups smashing. From all over the waterfront shots were fired; Maria's bullets must have made very little difference.

You can recognize a head shot by a high-velocity weapon; a cloud of blood particles appeared like vapour in the air above him as Datt and his armful of tapes, film and papers was punched off the waterfront like a golf ball.

'There,' called Loiseau. The high-power lamps operated by the soldiers probed the spreading tangle of recording tapes and films that covered the water like a Sargasso Sea. A great bubble of air rose to the surface and a cluster of pornographic photos slid apart and drifted away. Datt was in there amongst it and for a moment it looked as though he was still alive as he turned in the water very slowly and laboriously, his stiff arm clawing out through the air like a swimmer doing the crawl. For a moment it seemed as if he stared at us. The tapes caught in his fingers and the soldiers flinched. 'He's turning over, that's all,' said Loiseau. 'Men float face down, women

242

face up. Get the hook under his collar. He's not a ghost man, just a corpse, a criminal corpse.'

A soldier tried to reach him with a fixed bayonet, but the lieutenant stopped him. 'They'll say we did it, if the body is full of bayonet wounds. They'll say we tortured him.' Loiseau turned to me and passed me a small reel of tape in a tin. 'This is yours,' he said. 'Your confession, I believe, although I haven't played it.'

'Thanks,' I said.

'That was the agreement,' said Loiseau.

'Yes,' I said, 'that was the agreement.'

Datt's body floated deeper now, even more entangled in the endless tape and film.

Maria had hidden the gun, or perhaps she'd thrown it away. Loiseau didn't look at her. He was concerned with the body of Datt – too concerned with it, in fact, to be convincing.

I said, 'Is that your ambulance, Maria?' She nodded; Loiseau was listening but he didn't turn round.

'That's a silly place to leave it. It's a terrible obstruction; you'll have to move it.' I turned to the Belgian para officer. 'Let her move it,' I said.

Loiseau nodded.

'How far?' said the officer. He had a mind like Loiseau's. Perhaps Loiseau read my thoughts. He grinned.

'It's all right,' said Loiseau. 'The woman can go.' The lieutenant was relieved to get a direct order. 'Yes sir,' he said and saluted Loiseau gravely. He walked towards the ambulance.

Maria touched Loiseau's arm. 'I'll go to my mother's. I'll go to the boy,' she said. He nodded. Her face looked strange, for only one eye was made up. She smiled and followed the officer.

'Why did you do that?' Loiseau asked.

'I couldn't risk you doing it,' I said. 'You'd never forgive yourself.'

It was light now. The sea had taken on a dawn-fresh sparkle and the birds began to think about food. Along the shore herring gulls probed for tiny shellfish left by the tide. They carried them high above the dunes and dropped them upon the concrete blockhouses. Some fell to safety in the sand, some hit the ancient gun emplacements and cracked open, some fell on to the concrete but did not crack; these last were retrieved by the herring gulls and then dropped again and again. The tops of the blockhouses were covered in tiny fragments of shell, for eventually each shell cracked. Very high, one bird flew purposefully and alone on a course as straight as a light beam. Farther along the shore, in and out of the dunes, a hedgehog wandered aimlessly sniffing and scratching at the colourless grass and watching the gulls at their game. The hedgehog would fly higher and stronger than any of the birds, if only he knew how.

# The Ipcress File
## Len Deighton

'The poet of the spy story' *Sunday Times*

*The Ipcress File* was Len Deighton's first novel, his first huge bestseller and the book that broke the mould of thriller writing.

For the working-class narrator, an apparently straight-forward mission to find a missing biochemist becomes a journey to the heart of a dark and deadly conspiracy.

The film of *The Ipcress File* gave Michael Caine one of his first and still most celebrated starring roles, while the novel has become a classic.

'Something entirely new in spy fiction: never before has a secret agent's work been described in such convincing detail'                                    *The Standard*

'A spy story with a difference'                                    *Observer*

'A master of fictional espionage'                                    *Daily Mail*

ISBN 0 586 02619 3

# Funeral in Berlin
## Len Deighton

'Brilliant, bright and wicked' *Vogue*

Len Deighton's third novel has become a classic, as compelling and suspenseful now as when it first exploded on to the bestseller lists.

In Berlin, where neither side of the wall is safe, Colonel Stok of Red Army Security is prepared to sell an important Russian scientist to the West – for a price. British intelligence are willing to pay, providing their own top secret agent is in Berlin to act as go-between. But it soon becomes apparent that behind the facade of an elaborate mock funeral lies a game of deadly manoeuvres and ruthless tactics. A game in which the blood-stained legacy of Nazi Germany is enmeshed in the intricate moves of cold war espionage . . .

'A ferociously cool fable, even better than *The Spy Who Came in from the Cold*' *New York Times*

'*Funeral in Berlin* . . . is splendid' *Daily Telegraph*

'A most impressive book in which the tension, more like a chronic ache than a sharp stab of pain, never lets go' *The Standard*

ISBN 0 586 04580 5

# Winter
## Len Deighton

'A monumental work . . . brilliantly executed'
*Daily Telegraph*

A portrait of a Berlin family during the turbulent years of
the first half of this century, *Winter* is also a compelling
study of the rise of Nazi Germany.

At the heart of the story are two brothers: one who
advances to a senior administrative role in the Gestapo,
the other who opposes the spread of Nazism and chooses
exile in America.

With its meticulous research, rich detail and brilliantly
drawn cast of characters, *Winter* is a superb achievement.

'Deighton's research and plotting are as sure-footed as
ever while the pace and tension leave one almost breath-
less. A frightening yet compelling novel' *Sunday Telegraph*

'Deighton's most ambitious and subtle book to date, an
epic fiction' *Evening Standard*

'Deighton brilliantly depicts the evolution of Hitler's
regime through telling detail' *Today*

ISBN  0 586 06895 3

# Faith
## Len Deighton

Bernard Samson returns to Berlin in the first novel
in the new spy trilogy, *Faith, Hope and Charity*

Bernard has known that he is not getting the full picture
from London Central ever since discovering that his wife
Fiona was a double agent.

Werner Volkmann has been cast out by London Central as
untrustworthy. Yet Werner still seems able to pick up
information that Bernard should have been told . . .

'A string of brilliantly mounted set-pieces . . . superbly
laconic wisecracks'
*The Times*

'Like lying back in a hot bath with a large malt whisky –
absolute bliss . . . superbly combines violent action with a
strong emotional undertow. The plotting in *Faith* is
masterly, the atmospheric descriptions superb . . .'
*Sunday Telegraph*

ISBN 0 00 647898 0

## Bestselling novels by Len Deighton

| | | | |
|---|---|---|---|
| ☐ | THE IPCRESS FILE | 0 586 02619 3 | £4.99 |
| ☐ | FUNERAL IN BERLIN | 0 586 04580 5 | £4.99 |
| ☐ | BOMBER | 0 586 04544 9 | £5.99 |
| ☐ | BERLIN GAME | 0 586 05820 6 | £4.99 |
| ☐ | MEXICO SET | 0 586 05821 4 | £4.99 |
| ☐ | LONDON MATCH | 0 586 06635 7 | £4.99 |
| ☐ | WINTER | 0 586 06895 3 | £5.99 |
| ☐ | SPY HOOK | 0 586 06896 1 | £3.99 |
| ☐ | SPY LINE | 0 586 06898 8 | £4.99 |
| ☐ | SPY SINKER | 0 586 06899 6 | £4.99 |
| ☐ | FAITH | 0 00 647898 0 | £4.99 |

All these books are available from your local bookseller or can be ordered direct from the publishers.

To order direct just tick the titles you want and fill in the form below:

Name: _____

Address: _____

_____

Postcode: _____

Send to HarperCollins Paperbacks Mail Order, Dept 8, HarperCollins *Publishers*, Westerhill Road, Bishopbriggs, Glasgow G64 2QT.

Please enclose a cheque or postal order or your authority to debit your Visa/Access account –

Credit card no: _____

Expiry date: _____

Signature: _____

to the value of the cover price plus:

UK & BFPO: Add £1.00 for the first book and 25p for each additional book ordered.

Overseas orders including Eire: Please add £2.95 service charge. Books will be sent by surface mail but quotes for airmail despatches will be given on request.

**24 HOUR TELEPHONE ORDERING SERVICE FOR ACCESS/VISA CARDHOLDERS –**
**TEL: GLASGOW 0141 772 2281 or LONDON 0181 307 4052**

# Political Change in Southeast Asia

In the West industrialisation and new-found wealth catalysed political enlightenment and participatory democracy. The experience of Southeast Asia has been rather different. Rapid economic growth has not resulted in an even distribution of wealth, and progress towards participatory democracy has been slow. Strong governments hold sway over free markets supported by middle classes seemingly content to sacrifice gratification for collective stability. Some now argue that the Western model of political change is not applicable in the Southeast Asian context.

Michael R.J. Vatikiotis examines the contrast between the assumptions about political change based on the Western experience and the Southeast Asian reality. He argues that traditional concepts of power, which stress authoritarian values and paternalism, have not simply survived but have thrived during the post-colonial period despite pressures to Westernise. He points out that while the desire to preserve power has prompted local ruling elites to make exaggerated claims about 'Asian' values, the societies they govern are also finding ways of resisting tyranny.

**Michael R.J. Vatikiotis** is currently Bangkok bureau chief of the *Far Eastern Economic Review*.

# Political Change in Southeast Asia

Trimming the banyan tree

Michael R.J. Vatikiotis

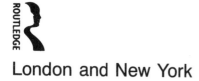

London and New York

First published 1996
by Routledge
11 New Fetter Lane, London EC4P 4EE

Simultaneously published in the USA and Canada
by Routledge
29 West 35th Street, New York, NY 10001

*Routledge is an International Thomson Publishing Company*

Phototypeset in Times by Intype London Ltd
Printed and bound in Great Britain by
TJ Press (Padstow) Ltd, Padstow, Cornwall

*British Library Cataloguing in Publication Data*
A catalogue record for this book is available from the British Library

*Library of Congress Cataloguing in Publication Data*
A catalogue record for this book has been requested

ISBN 0–415–11348–2 (hbk)
ISBN 0–415–13484–6 (pbk)

*For Chloe and Stefan*

# Contents

# Series editor's preface

The countries of Southeast Asia have undergone radical and remarkable changes in the decades since the end of the Pacific War in 1945. As their governments and people confront the uncertain future of the twenty-first century, the nature of impending political change is very much at issue driven as it will be by underlying economic and social change. Very much uncertain is the likely nature of that change. Will text-book democracy in its accepted Western sense become the new political reference point in place of a general authoritarianism justified in the name of social order and economic development? Or will an evident demand for greater participation by a proto-middle class be tempered and controlled in an acceptable manner by paternalistic leaderships espousing the virtues of good and strong government? These are the general questions which Michael Vatikiotis poses in this stimulating analysis of political change in Southeast Asia in which a number of conventional wisdoms about the road to democracy are vigorously contested.

Drawing on his considerable personal experience of living in and writing about Southeast Asia, Michael Vatikiotis asks 'What kind of political culture will prevail at the dawn of a new century?' He takes as his imaginative sub-title and theme the notion of 'Trimming the banyan tree'. That tree, which is sacred to many within the region and beyond, is described as an apt metaphor for the process of political change in Southeast Asia. It is a common aphorism that nothing can grow under the banyan tree. At issue is governmental commitment to its trimming in a political sense and, if so, the extent to which a limited loosening of collective bonds which envelop society serves as a practical proposition compatible with the rising aspirations of succeeding generations with more than growing material appetites. Michael Vatikiotis has not set out to defend the political status quo; nor some of the unwholesome practices of some regional governments. Rather, he is concerned in this volume to address realistically the complex subject of the likely pace and direction of political change drawing in particular, but not exclusively, on the experiences of Indonesia, Malaysia, Singapore and Thailand, the most developed of the Southeast Asian states. He argues that the gradual rather than revolutionary pace of democracy is allowing political elites to adapt to the needs of a more demanding society but not to abdicate power entirely. Indeed, he concludes that for some years to come only token rather than substantive political change will prevail. This book and its conclusion will make a powerful and even controversial contribution to the continuing debate about the relationship between economic and political change in a part of the world which the World Bank has included within its depiction of the East Asian miracle.

Michael Leifer

# Foreword

The germ of the idea for this book came to me in 1991, on a rainy day in Bangkok riding in the back of a taxi. I was passing a trendy cluster of jazz and blues bars frequented by young, middle-class Thai professionals on Sarasin road. One of the bars was called 'Zest Zone'. It struck me how evocative the name of this bar, etched out in purple neon, was of contemporary Thailand – as well as so much of the more developed portion of Southeast Asia. 'Zest Zone' resonated as an emblem of the region's dynamism and prosperity; the creativity of its youthful business community. It was clear to me that money was not just breeding prosperity; it was generating a mood of optimism and confidence that was changing the way Thais and other Southeast Asians were dealing with the outside world.

Fourteen years ago, when I arrived in Thailand as a young graduate student, the country defined itself as a developing country. I was treated as a prosperous visitor from a far away developed country where everything was so much 'better'. Times have changed. Today, cohorts of job-hungry Europeans and Americans are streaming to Southeast Asia, where things are so much 'better' job-wise. The new rich of Southeast Asia are buying up companies and property in European and North American cities. A Thai company recently saved a grand old hotel in London from demolition; a Singaporean conglomerate has bought the Plaza Hotel in New York. An Indonesian businessman bought the famous Italian sports car company 'Lambhorgini'.

I consider myself fortunate to have witnessed for much of the past decade the material transformation of Southeast Asia. It's a transition that could be seen, in global terms, as one of the hallmarks of the postwar era. The successful economies of

Southeast Asia are already making projections for when the size of their GDPs will exceed those of countries in Western Europe. In all the countries I have covered as a journalist – principally Indonesia, Malaysia and Thailand – I have seen people prosper and succeed. Success has bred confidence. How will this confidence be channelled? To what end?

The more I thought about this, the more my optimism for the region's future became tempered by the issue of political change. There are winners and losers in these dynamic economies. Disparities in wealth and social status are growing. These pressures from below sharpen the paradox of dynamic societies largely governed by strong forms of government. The region's political culture does not seem, from a classical Western perspective, to be in step with the advancing dynamism of society – or the demands for equality. That led me to consider what it was about these political cultures, and the societies in which they thrive, that tolerates the paradox – or indeed whether a paradox exists. Contemporary Southeast Asia is not the crucible of social and political ferment that Cold War warriors once worried it might become. Yet there are clearly political and social tensions. What explains the region's comparative stability in a period of rapid economic growth? I was further goaded by the debate that began in the early 1990s over the so-called clash of political values: was there an Asian way of governance, or was the region destined for parity with the Western liberal democratic model of government? Stripping away the rhetoric, I was struck by the strong vein of nationalism which runs through the debate over political culture in the region.

It also struck me that analysing political cultures – what constitutes the basis of the relationships between rulers and the ruled – was a better way to understand the region's political dynamics. With the end of the Cold War, a conflict between political ideologies rooted in recent European history, it has become easier to identify political behaviour driven by more indigenous impulses. The role of history, culture and religion can be more clearly discerned now that we are no longer obsessed with the emotive political labels of the Cold War.

On the other hand, so much of the political debate in Southeast Asia has become entangled in the reordering of global geopolitics. Westerners are prone to claiming an ideological victory now that communism is defeated. Partly in reaction to this, Asians in general, and Southeast Asians in particular, have allowed economic success to blind them to flaws in their own political cultures. As an impartial observer, my objective has not been to award merit, nor allow conscience to govern my analysis. This book tries to distil the realities of the region's political cultures, generalising where possible, so that a more realistic picture of the region's political future can be projected. In this sense I am offering more of a Chinese brush-stroke painting rather than a Balinese painting, which is characteristically full of minute details.

In that vein, it is possible, I think, to suggest that a basic tension informs political culture in Southeast Asia. On the one hand, strong government and popular support for legitimate leadership is a common characteristic of contemporary Southeast Asian political cultures, one that helps distinguish the region's politics from the West. On the other hand, there is also a deeply rooted popular aversion to tyranny and bad government, and a long tradition of challenge to the political status quo when it proves unacceptable. The pace and manner of political change may seem at odds with Western norms, but it would be wrong to assume that people anywhere are naturally disposed to enduring tyranny and oppression. The form of freedom and democracy they crave is not necessarily identical with that practised in the West, but there is a growing desire to be treated as subjects and not objects of political life. (I use the term 'West' throughout the book, and this begs some explanation. I use it to refer to the major European powers, and North America, extending beyond that to the general geographical boundaries of what is generally termed 'Western' culture.)

Many people have shared their views with me on the subject of political culture and change. The preparation of this book spanned a period during which I was based in Jakarta, Kuala Lumpur, and most recently Bangkok as a reporter with the *Far Eastern Economic Review*. It would be hard to mention everybody who has contributed to this book. However, I would like to record a debt of appreciation to some people with whom I have had a running debate, or asked specifically to contribute their views to this book over the past three years. In Indonesia: Mochtar Kusumaatmadja, General (retd) L.B. Moerdani, Abdurrahman Wahid, Marzuki Darusman, Nurcholis Madjid, Nasir Tamara, Jusuf Wanandi, Goenawan Mohammad, Nono Makarim, Fikri Jufri, Marsillam Simanjuntak, and Dewi Fortuna Anwar. In Malaysia: Datuk Seri Anwar Ibrahim, Khalid Jaafar,

Rustam Sani, Rehman Rashid, K.S. Jomo, Karim Raslan, and Chandran Jeshurun. In Thailand: Surin Pitsuwan, Sukhumbhand Paribatra, Kavi Chongkittavorn, Supapohn Kanwerayotin, Trasvin Jittidejarak, Christopher Bruton, and Chaiwat Satha-Anand. Rodolfo Severino and Jose Almonte from the Philippines, and M. Rajaretnam from Singapore have also shared their thoughts with me. Not everyone has agreed with me, but as true Southeast Asians they have all been tolerant of my views and stimulating discussants.

I am especially grateful to Professor Michael Leifer, Dr Chandran Jeshurun, Dr Dewi Fortuna Anwar and Trasvin Jittidejarak who kindly agreed to comment on all or parts of the manuscript.

Without the understanding and support of my wife Janick, and my two children Chloe and Stefan, long evenings and weekends chained to the lap-top computer would have been unthinkable. I am also grateful for the support and encouragement I have received on the publishing side from Victoria Smith, Asia editor at Routledge in London, and Ian Pringle of APD in Singapore. Of course, any errors and shortcomings in this work are entirely my own.

Michael Vatikiotis
Bangkok, September 1995

# Prologue

In May 1992, students, office workers and a sprinkling of young urban professionals took to the streets of Bangkok to demonstrate against the military-led government of General Suchinda Kraprayoon. They were angered by General Suchinda's self-appointment as prime minister after the failure of his National Peacekeeping Council to appoint a civilian elected prime minister. In an apparently calculated response, the army fired on the demonstrators, leaving 52 confirmed dead and over 160 missing. It was the worst political violence the country had seen since the mid-1970s.

But Thailand has changed since then. Set against the affluence of modern Bangkok, the burning cars and overturned buses littering Rajdamnoen Avenue, the angry speeches and the army's violent attempt to restore order looked like turning points in the country's political development. Here at last, the middle class, considered the torchbearers of democracy in the region, was apparently asserting itself and demanding a say in government. Media reports portrayed the army confronted by the urban bourgeoisie wearing designer labels and toting mobile phones. To the surprise of the mostly young, bandanna and t-shirt-clad demonstrators the army caved in and the military-led government fell.

The outcome of the May 1992 disturbances in Bangkok appeared to offer concrete proof of Southeast Asia's changing political culture: of a society now willing to question authority, resist authoritarian power politics and pave the way for broader participation in government. May 1992 in Bangkok was framed alongside the 1986 popular overthrow of the Marcos regime in the Philippines and the pro-democracy demonstrations in Beijing's

Tiananmen Square in 1989; a votive triptych on the altar of democracy.

Strip away the media hype, however, and the middle-class connection becomes less clear. More sober appraisals by leading Thai academics at the time say the middle-class composition of the mob was greatly exaggerated,[1] and that their ability to influence the direction of political change has been somewhat overstated. In fact, at the height of the disturbances King Bhumibol Adulyadej, the world's longest reigning monarch, discretely acted to restore order. Behind the scenes, his privy councillors brokered a settlement with the recalcitrant generals and played a decisive role in forming a civilian government. For many Thais the end of the biggest political upheaval since the mid-1970s was summed up by a televised image of General Suchinda alongside his pro-democracy adversary General Chamlong Srimuang; both men summoned to the palace on 21 May and supplicating the monarch while crouching at his feet. Three days later Suchinda resigned.

A year later, as Thailand's elected civilian prime minister Chuan Leekpai struggled to cement the legacy of those few bloody days in the streets of Bangkok, another political culture was supposedly being recast in neighbouring Cambodia. The fragile peace accord between Cambodia's warring factions struck after 13 years of civil war was only just holding up after UN-sponsored multiparty elections in May 1993. Instead of solidifying that peace with the pluralistic properties of a modern democracy, Cambodia went back in time to become, once again, a monarchy with Prince Norodom Sihanouk's reaccession to the throne he gave up in 1955. The restored Cambodian monarchy is not nearly as influential – or politically effective – as the Thai throne, but King Sihanouk is credited with holding together a frail peace between competing political factions in the country.

Although not obviously connected, the two situations share a common thread; a link with the traditional past. In both Thailand and Cambodia, the end result of these political crises was not a revolutionary change of the political system. Neither the mass protests of 1992 directed against the military in Bangkok nor the UN-sponsored elections in Cambodia a year later, offered a complete solution to the political situations they addressed. Instead, society seemed to fall back on traditional forms of paternalistic leadership through the legitimising role of the monarchy. That a popular challenge to authority could be resolved in the 1990s through the mediation of an ancient rather than modern political institution begs intriguing questions about the political cultures of Southeast Asia. What makes them so enduring and resistant to change? Why do ordinary people prefer firm leadership to participatory politics? For arguably the real issue was not what sort of new political system emerged from the chaos on the streets of Bangkok, or in the tattered villages of postwar Cambodia. What the ordinary citizen seemed to want was security, order, stability and a source of responsible leadership and authority.

As if to drive home the point, less than three years later popular opinion in Bangkok turned against the civilian elected government of 'angels' born of the May 1992 violence. By mid-1995, to cite a prominent Thai politician, people seemed 'less interested in democracy and more interested in leadership'.[2] Writing about Chuan Leekpai, whose government fell in May 1995, an editorial writer commented that 'while there has been no doubt about Chuan's clean lifestyle and honest principles, the public became dissatisfied with his hands-off management style and his lack of courage to tackle problems head on'.[3] Chuan was defeated by a coalition of old-style politicians, many of whom had sided with the military in 1992. But then traditionally it has mattered little to the Thai or Cambodian merchant or farmer whether a government calls itself democratic so long as he or she feels its weight as little as possible and benefits from its security as much as possible – a pragmatic immunity to ideology often lost on outside observers.

Those bent on detecting the emergence of Western-style civic values in Southeast Asia might question this interpretation of two recent milestones in Southeast Asian political history. To those imbued with the prevailing universalistic notions of Western social science monarchy is associated with feudalism and the trappings of aristocracy (never mind the fact that Europe's oldest democracies developed, and continue to thrive, under monarchies – in Britain, the Netherlands and Sweden). Few indeed would credit the ancient indigenous institution of semi-divine monarchy, albeit recast in a constitutional mould, with either the desire or capacity to protect the freedom of ordinary citizens. Surely the solution lies in erecting representative institutions more accountable to society? Will this be the case? Is Southeast Asia's political development on a convergent course, ultimately destined to become a haven of Western-style liberal democratic values? If not, what kind of political culture will prevail at the dawn of the new century? This seems to be the most relevant question about the region's future beyond the period of remarkable economic growth of the 1990s.

The ten countries of Southeast Asia will embark on the new century with more wealth and confidence than many areas of the post-Cold War world. Their economies have enjoyed growth rates of between 6 per cent and 8 per cent a year for over a decade. They mostly enjoy enviable political stability. And, with the exception of China's assertion of sovereignty in the South China Sea, there is no sign of regional conflict on the horizon. There seems to be no question of the region's potential measured in these terms. Where questions are raised, however, they concern the complex relationship between state and society.

Western observers feel most comfortable addressing this issue from a theoretical viewpoint. In theory free trade and an open market are considered the two keystones of sustained growth. The economic momentum created by the thumb and forefinger of Adam Smith's 'invisible hand' is credited with stimulating varying degrees of pressure for political change in almost all the ten countries in Southeast Asia over the past decade. This has given rise to the notion that without changes to the prevailing political culture further economic growth could be stunted. In practice, the theory is supposed to work like this:

> as national wealth accumulates, citizens start to recognise their options, and see less reason for delayed gratification. Clearly they will want more material consumption, and as they start to conceive a better life they are also likely to want more civil liberty and political freedom.[4]

By this reasoning, the expansion of the middle class is expected to fuel demands for more popular sovereignty. The assumption is that a nascent bourgeoisie wants the freedom to influence decisions in the marketplace for themselves because as individuals they now have more of a stake in the economy, either through enterprise or property ownership. It is commonly expected that these middle-class political urges run up against established ruling elites in no hurry to surrender their power. In response to demands for more popular sovereignty these elites set about reinforcing the ideological and economic buttresses of state power by claiming distinct indigenous values have fostered economic progress. The theory predicts that they won't succeed:

the very economic growth which the authoritarians have used to justify their rule is rapidly creating an educated Asian middle class whose members do care about such supposedly western notions as individual rights and press freedoms, and who are prepared to protest publicly against government corruption, incompetence and authoritarianism.[5]

The problem with this well-worn conceptual framework is that it is based on a simplistic and even subjective interpretation of actual events. Southeast Asia has not been kind to the neat predictions of Western social science. Half a century ago, anthropologists found that the highly structured dynamics of ethnic relations, which pioneering fathers of the discipline established working among tribal societies in Africa, became blurred and transient in the more fluid plural complexity of upland Burma and Thailand.[6] The Nuer of North Africa were and remain the Nuer. But a Shan from Burma can become a Thai, and then become Shan again.

Much later, social scientists came in search of the capitalist middle-class affluent, predicting the abandonment of primordial attachments to paternalism and religion. But like the mercurial Shan, the Southeast Asian capitalist has many faces. The middle-class affluence he or she is supposed to represent may be susceptible to liberal impulses, and therefore prone to confrontation with the state. Equally though, affluence can help reinforce primordial traditions of patronage and hierarchy on which the authoritarian state thrives. The middle classes of Thailand or Indonesia may have acquired a level of wealth that implies they have a bigger stake in the national future, but they have not shown much inclination to stand up to the established ruling elite. Political reality in Southeast Asia is amorphous and often defies categorisation. As the Australian academic Richard Robison suggests, there is a complex ambiguity about the middle classes encountered in the region: 'The middle class has neither been internally consistent in its political stance nor unambiguously democratic in its actions.'[7]

The free market promoters say that wealth comes from people, not governments. What they miss in Southeast Asia is a traditional belief that good leadership and strong government is necessary to protect people so they can produce the wealth. How else do you explain the fact that in affluent Bangkok opinion polls consistently ranked former caretaker prime minister Anand Panyarachun as the people's first choice? Anand, a former bureaucrat turned businessman, was neither an elected member of parliament, nor the leader of a political party. Unencumbered by either precondition to holding office, Anand served as interim prime minister on two occasions during 1991–2. In that time he initiated economic reforms which helped boost Thailand's growth rate in the mid-1990s.

If preferring unelected to elected leaders sounds like a paradox, take the following apparently contradictory remarks from three of the wealthiest and most successful businessmen in Southeast Asia: when asked what it was about China that ensured its future stability, Dhanin Chearavanont, the chairman of Thailand's Charoen Pokphand Group cited strong government and the ability of the government to leave businessmen to their own devices.[8] Another successful Chinese businessman, Gordon Wu from Hong Kong, described the legacy of US colonialism in the Philippines as the most egregious because it saddled the country with American-style democracy.[9] Tun Daim Zainuddin was finance minister of Malaysia, presiding over the sweeping liberalisation of the economy in the late 1980s. In early 1993, he said that 'suitable interventionist measures' were required at varying levels 'to ensure that the capitalistic system can still operate successfully'. Daim concluded that 'it is highly improbable that a purely free market mechanism will fulfil the development objectives aspired to by the developing nations of Asia'.[10] Finally, in its 1994 annual report, the Asian Development Bank concluded that the growth of the middle class is likely to have a tremendous effect on economic and social patterns of consumption but that:

> Perhaps the only thing that is sure is that as incomes rise, the pattern of Asian development is unlikely to follow that of the west in any simple way; and where convergence does occur the paths followed in getting there may be different.[11]

Theories claiming that economic growth is the harbinger of political change generally assume that some form of representative democracy is the ultimate political destination. There may well be a linkage between advancing prosperity and political transformation. But will the changes necessarily produce text-book democracies? That tends to be the assumption which lurks behind questions most frequently asked about the region's political future: When will Burma's military junta be replaced by a civilian democratic government? When will Vietnam's Communist Party give up power? When, for that matter, will Indonesia's military disengage from politics? These are all relevant questions in the prevailing Western theoretical context, and the answer is commonly assumed to be soon – or not soon enough. But what if reality is more fuzzy?

What if Burma's generals meet the democratic opposition half way: go into civilian politics and prolong their grip on power, encouraging the spread of material prosperity, but putting full democracy on hold? That is what Indonesia's generals did after 1966, and is one possible interpretation of why Burma's military rulers suddenly released pro-democracy leader Aung San Suu Kyi from 6 years under house arrest in July 1995. 'I have always felt I could work with the army', she told *Time* magazine soon after her release. What if Vietnam's communist cadres yield power to the military and not to more participatory democracy? The Indonesian army's dual political and civilian role may be changing, but shows no sign of breaking up. The army draws strength from visceral fears of divisive social and religious threats to stability. Current realities and realistic projections for the future suggest a pattern of political change that is far from definitive. But change there will be, and it would be wrong to deny that aspects of it will foster freedom and democracy. The form and degree of these ideals may, however, vary greatly.

In social and cultural terms, Southeast Asian states have demonstrated the capacity for as much inertia as change over the centuries. Eras, dynasties, intruders came and went. Each left their mark but failed to effect a radical transformation of society. Even the arrival of modern universal religions such as Hinduism, Theravada Buddhism and Islam failed to eradicate traditional beliefs, which instead were absorbed and accommodated in a way which diluted their orthodoxy, and – as a useful by-product – promoted tolerance. Such a generalisation risks being taken as a denial of progress, when in fact it demonstrates one of the key sources of the region's resilience and stability. The high degree of elasticity involved in maintaining the cultural status quo allows elements of tradition and renewal to blend and interact, but rarely to clash. For most of the region, non-confrontational, gradual change has helped make Southeast Asia a stable platform on which prosperity can flourish, even if it makes the task of charting social and political change rather like watching grass grow.

Yet the focus for the 1990s and beyond, will be on the region's social and political environment. Not just because human rights and democracy are firmly on the agendas of the region's economic partners in the West. If anything there is a growing perception in the region that Western influence is set to decline. Charting political change is important because the risks affecting the region's future seem to lie in this area. Economic prophets of doom predicting the loss of economic momentum in Southeast Asia sound like Philistines these days. Asia as a whole kept on growing through the recession that hit the developed world in the early 1990s. But history has conspired to make the end of the millennium a period of potential political flux for Southeast Asia.

There will be the uncertainty of succession after long periods of unquestionably harsh leadership in Burma under General Ne Win and his subordinate successors in the State Law and Order Restoration Council; Indonesia under President Suharto; Malaysia under Prime Minister Mahathir Mohamad, and Thailand, where succession to the throne is considered a far bigger issue than which political party is in power. Singapore also faces the same challenge, if one takes a broader view of former Prime Minister Lee Kuan Yew's role as 'Senior Minister'. Being very much the father of Singapore as well as one of the region's senior generation leaders, his passing will close a political chapter in the island republic's history. Vietnam's communist party, at some point, will reach an ideological crossroads once the current generation of nationalist leaders fade away.

Once these succession problems are resolved – smoothly or otherwise – there will be other challenges. Nearly two decades of sustained economic growth has left a host of moral and social issues for the new generation of leaders in the region to deal with. Local non-governmental organisations are urging governments not to ignore the impact of growth on the environment, community and human rights. Increasingly, the concerns of local, non-governmental organisations (NGOs) are finding a regional voice through a growing web of transnational organisations. Living standards may have improved overall, but the fruits of growth have not always been distributed equitably. In Indonesia, for instance, the World Bank notes that absolute poverty has fallen from about 60 per cent of the population to around 14 per cent in the past three decades. But the Bank adds that 'instead of generalised poverty, poverty in Indonesia is now increasingly localised by geographical location, occupation, household size, age, gender and other characteristics'. In most countries of the region, the rich have grown richer while the poor have become in relative terms poorer.

As well as the social polarisation accompanying growth, the social and material changes accompanying rapid urbanisation have provoked spiritual and cultural alienation. This spiritual loss is harder to gauge because it doesn't stare at you like a roadside beggar outside a shiny glass skyscraper. But if you look more closely at the snooker bars and shopping malls, the question marks haunting the lives of the urban youth are palpable: who are we?; where do we come from?; and where are we going? The cultural alienation bred by rapid growth crops up commonly as a literary theme. In Thai novelist Khammaan Khonkhai's *The Teachers of Mad Dog Swamp* the central character, the teacher Piya, confronts the alienation of the countryside from Bangkok society. In Malaysian novelist K.S. Maniam's *In a Far Country* a village son goes to the big city and becomes convinced that 'Progress was another name for loneliness, for coldness between people.'[12]

Urban growth has been one of the more remarkable phenomena in modern Southeast Asia, helping to turn once predominantly rural, agrarian cultures into mainly urbanised ones in a matter of two or three decades. But for all the material improvements in standards of living, it is often easy to forget the impact on societies that are traditionally tightly-knit and community oriented. Instead of relying on predictable networks of relatives and neighbours, the city dweller struggles to build more impersonal networks based on the workplace. In some ways, the adjustment involved may be less a matter of how society is governed, than how it thinks of itself in religious and cultural terms. Not all religions consider that consumer driven materialism is the ultimate goal of development, nor are some indigenous cultures so easily tailored to fit concepts like meritocracy and individual enterprise without wrenching them apart.

If there is to be a social reaction to the rapid growth of the last few years, some comfort can be drawn from the fact that most governments are only too aware of the potential cultural and spiritual backlash material progress has invited. Under pressure to face up to these challenges, conservative ruling elites have not retreated behind the ramparts. In some cases they are slowly coming to terms with the need to share power and grant more personal freedom to their more prosperous, better travelled, and better educated people. Aspirations are vastly expanding for people who just a generation ago would have been lucky enough to be clothed, fed and given a basic education. Yet the infrastructure of social well-being has not grown at the same pace as overall economic growth. Schools and universities are becoming overcrowded and standards are not improving greatly, as indicated by the continuing flow of students abroad. Governments not accustomed to spending much on welfare beyond the provision of basic needs must now think about how to satisfy the more complex demands of a more developed society. By adopting a gradual approach to these challenges, governments help prevent violent social upheavals and maintain the conditions for economic growth. Of course, they also perpetuate their existence.

From a political perspective, this acceptance of the need for gradual socio-economic and political change undoubtedly helps camouflage and sustain authoritarian regimes. Typically, a leader with no intention of relinquishing power makes speeches acknowledging the need for political reform and social justice – but works quietly behind the scenes to ensure that reforms are either stalled or tailored to suit the ends of retaining power. Compromises and half-measures prevail in the field of political reform. Thus 'openness' became an official by-word in Indonesia in the late 1980s, even if there was no sign of any fundamental change to a political system which frowns upon dissent. Even this limited official tolerance of openness shrank considerably in the mid-1990s, as the government closed down three popular news magazines and prosecuted journalists who formed an independent journalists union. In Malaysia, some elements in the government acknowledge that a law which permits the detention of individuals for up to two years without trial is anachronistic, yet the state clings to stringent internal security laws that were introduced under colonial rule. In Singapore's intensely controlled political microclimate, a younger generation of politicians have been brought on, but it is no easier for opposition parties to thrive.

Those who advocate a gradual pace of change appear to have

time on their side. Even without the weight of state control over the media, popular awareness about modern forms of democratic government, though growing, would still seem to be limited to a narrow spectrum of urban intellectuals. Indonesia's middle class may only comprise less than 10 per cent of the population – rising as high as 15 per cent in urban areas. Of this limited cohort, an even smaller percentage is actively engaged in political activities, or has been exposed to alternative political systems. The middle class in Indonesia is also a privileged class. In any one year, there might be as many as 10,000 Indonesians studying abroad – not all of whom will become convinced that their political rights are being abused after they return and find prime opportunities in the private or state sectors. In Thailand, intellectuals speak about a rural–urban divide in politics. A small minority of city people want political parties to present concrete policies and political leadership; but the majority of votes are cast in rural areas where traditional patronage means that personality means more than policy and votes are still bought for cash.

Popular participation in the debate about political change has yet to achieve a critical mass in Southeast Asia. Ironically, the more politically enlightened among the middle classes of the region are the Western educated sons and daughters of the narrow elite which hold the reins of political and economic power. Many of them are easily won over by the establishment to which they ultimately belong. Galloping rates of literacy and education, which should go some way towards spreading new political ideas, have not succeeded in eroding ingrained cultural acceptance of strong leadership and control – especially when it offers common security and a measure of wealth and prosperity the people have only just begun to enjoy. 'Here, people don't talk about civil liberties, they talk about creature comforts', complains a Malaysian opposition MP.[13]

## THE REGION AND ITS COUNTRIES

Of course, to generalise about ten countries in a region as diverse as Southeast Asia is fraught with difficulty. To attempt a composite polaroid snapshot of political development would seem to be even more hazardous. We might begin by defining the framework for generalisation, and identifying some anomalies.

The region defined here as Southeast Asia comprises ten

countries stretching from the borders of India and Bangladesh to the borders of China. Burma, Thailand, Laos, Cambodia and Vietnam are commonly described as the states of mainland Southeast Asia; Brunei, Malaysia, Singapore, and Indonesia straddle the islands to the South. The Philippines sits out on the margins, remote from the rest of the region in more ways than one. As a whole, the region has a population of some 470 million people, growing in aggregate at a rate of between 2 per cent and 4 per cent a year.

Much of the material in this book is drawn from what could be described as the four core countries of more developed Southeast Asia. They are Indonesia, Malaysia, Singapore and Thailand. These four countries have the highest growth rates, the highest rate of domestic savings and have been the recipients of most of the region's foreign investment for the past two decades. These countries will double their level of per capita GNP by the year 2005, putting Singapore almost on a par with Japan.

*Table 1.1* Per capita GNP in selected Southeast Asian Countries, 1970–2005 (US$)

| Country | Years | | | |
|---|---|---|---|---|
| | *1970–5* | *1980–5* | *1988–93* | *2005 (projected)* |
| Thailand | 390 | 810 | 2,110 | 4,800 |
| Singapore | 2,770 | 7,300 | 19,850 | 40,000 |
| Philippines | 370 | 520 | 820 | 1,600 |
| Malaysia | 890 | 1,910 | 3,140 | 8,000 |
| Indonesia | 220 | 520 | 740 | 1,400 |

*Sources:* World Bank, 1995 and Asia Pacific Profiles, Australian National University

It is here, in these four countries, that the pace of economic growth has invited the most speculation about the pace of political change. But what of the rest of the region?

The Philippines celebrates 100 years of independence from Spain and latterly the United States in 1998, an historical benchmark that should remind the rest of the region how long that country has called itself a republic and a democracy. For despite a long period of American tutelage (1898–1946), a brutal Japanese occupation, the authoritarian excesses of the Marcoses and flirtation with military rule their overthrow involved, the Philippines has kept faith with its inherited hybridised Spanish-American culture. Unlike the rest of Southeast Asia, the Philippines knew effective European rule for longer, and more importantly before any form of indigenous concept of statehood had fully evolved. Filipino statehood therefore draws heavily on the 400 year colonial experience which created its territorial frame.

Jose Almonte, who is President Fidel Ramos' national security adviser, argues that in a region of strong states, the Philippine state is uniquely weak. Although many Filipinos would proudly point to the strong institutions of democratic rule inherited from their former American rulers, Almonte offers another explanation: 'Our economic system is more Latin American than East Asian in the way it has concentrated power in a few families.'[14] In the modern Philippines, the top 5.5 per cent of all landowning families own 44 per cent of arable land, and as little as 100 families control all elective positions at the national level.

But for all the pride Filipinos have in their democracy with all its imperfections, the price they have paid has been their marginalisation from the region's cultural mainstream of politics. Recent attempts to remedy the situation have only etched out the differences more clearly. When foreign secretary Raul Manglapus tried to entice Burma out of its shell to talk about human rights and democracy in 1992, he was politely told to mind his own business. When Lee Kuan Yew tried to tell Filipinos that their democracy was bad for business, the venerable former prime minister was, somewhat less politely, told that no level of prosperity would tempt Filipinos to trade their freedom – however imperfectly it is shared. The difference in attitude has brought the Philippines into low intensity diplomatic conflict with its regional neighbours. In May 1994, Indonesia protested against the holding of a human rights conference in Manila on the disputed territory of East Timor. Almost a year later, the government of the Philippines came close to severing diplomatic ties with Singapore over the island republic's hanging of a Filipina maid convicted of murder.

The tiny oil-rich sultanate of Brunei Darulsalam is considered another anomaly for the purposes of this study. Granted independence by the British in 1984, Brunei is the only modern Southeast Asian state which claims to follow the social and political precepts of medieval Malay society. Sultan Hassanal Bolkiah rules his 280,000 subjects in every sense of the term. He is head of the religion, military commander in chief and prime minister – in that order. The only semblance of political ideology is a creed promoting the interlocking roles of the Malay race, Islamic religion and the monarchy. Perhaps more of an anomaly than the feudal character of the Sultan's rule is the sheer wealth of the state. Brunei's hydrocarbon wealth, and the careful management of the revenues, notionally gives each of the Sultanate's subjects an average per capita income of US$ 19,000, one of the highest in the world. There are calls for political change, muted demands for an elected assembly and more freedom of speech from a small group of intellectuals and dissidents linked to an attempted revolt against the monarchy in the 1960s. But with such a sustainable basis of wealth, Brunei is unlikely to experience popular pressure for change.

This leaves those states (Burma, Cambodia, Indonesia, Malaysia, Laos, Singapore and Vietnam) whose political evolution has been influenced by long periods of precolonial sovereignty, as well as subjugation to European rule (except Thailand). The political cultures of these states are harder to fathom. Most have experienced political upheavals in the past five decades registering intense pressures for political change, yet ultimately very little has changed. In actual fact, despite the rhetoric of democratic reform in Thailand, or public commitment to a more open system by Indonesia's leadership, their political cultures remain largely unchanged.

Thailand's elected civilian government supports the greater application of the rule of law, but it has yet to free itself from a powerful blend of paternalistic bureaucratic, military and business elite interests. Whereas once it was the army which drew criticism, now people are becoming disenchanted with the money-backed bossism of provincial politicians and their business cronies. Instead of looking to the army, which has retreated from the political field since 1992, more politically conscious urban voters are turning to successful businessmen, viewing their corporate and technical expertise as valid credentials for national leadership. Some fear the trend will see the abuse of political power in the interests of big business and, eventually, the army's return to politics to clean up the mess. 'One day, someone will get up in parliament and call for the army to intervene', sighed a retired general.

In the 1990s, Indonesians wait out the long rule of a president who has blended Javanese traditional culture with military might to fashion a monolithic power-base. Most intellectuals expect his successor to be cut from the same military as well as cultural cloth. For ordinary Indonesians, the image of their smiling paternalistic president is tarred by the stories they hear about the extensive business activities of his family. Yet even the wealth of his children is mitigated by popular respect for a leader who saved Indonesia from a bloody period of internecine feuding and national bankruptcy at the end of founding president Sukarno's rule.

Singapore has been governed by a single political party since independence. Under the People's Action Party, order and stability are given a higher priority than political freedom. In the words of Singapore's former prime minister, now senior minister, Lee Kuan Yew the system he has helped shape envisages: 'society as No.1, and the individual, as part of society, as No.2'.[15] Political opposition is criticised in the government-controlled media for not serving the public interest, and therefore makes a minimal showing at the polls – even though the popular vote for the PAP has fallen in recent years. Despite tacit acknowledgment by the establishment of the need to encourage more popular participation in government, Singapore's leaders make it clear that they won't be changing the system overnight. By being vocal about the merits of a collective society where the rights of the individual are subjugated to obligations to the state, Singapore has placed itself at the forefront of the debate over universal human and political values. Yet here and in neighbouring Malaysia, where a strong-willed Prime Minister Mahathir Mohamad shares a similar view, well organised and, by many standards, reasonably fair elections are held on a regular basis under the semblance of the rule of law; and the government wins a convincing two-thirds majority.

For states like Vietnam and Burma, which are only now emerging from long periods of internal turmoil, the pace of political change could be that much slower. Both countries are eager to catch up with their more developed neighbours in economic terms. On the political side of the equation their governments are less enthusiastic about what this spells for the future of strong, centralised state control. It's a tough balancing act, one that Vietnam's communist party General secretary Do Muoi suggested in July 1994 involved industrialising and modernising within 'the framework of a modern economy', while at the same time avoiding 'individualism, disorder and violation of state law and order'.[16]

## CONTINUITY AND CHANGE

What explains the persistence of these seemingly dichotomous situations lies very much at the heart of this study. Why is it that states considered potential powder kegs, like Indonesia and more recently Burma, fizzle rather than explode? Political systems which seem threatened by apparently anachronistic systems of authority preside over economies which look increasingly robust. People expected not to tolerate much more state control, bend like the proverbial bamboo. What does this resistance to political change tell us about the region? Perhaps that continuity and resistance to change are innate characteristics of the political culture not easily pushed aside by the theoretical notions of a global village.

It would be wrong, however, to deduce from this observation that today's Southeast Asian states are hidebound and unchanging. In fact, the cultures they harbour are highly adaptable, constantly absorbing and reshaping external influences to suit their own conditions. This is perhaps where the region has suffered too much from comparison with what is commonly termed 'East' or 'Northeast Asia'. It is fashionable these days to talk about the 'Asia–Pacific region', or simply 'Asia'. Drawing out Southeast Asia's distinctive characteristics has not been easy. Many Southeast Asian scholars in the West are reluctant to define common themes in the region because of its awesome ethnic and cultural diversity. Yet by this same argument Europe should be, and perhaps is becoming, impossible to envisage as a borderless union.

There are marked differences between East Asia and Southeast Asia. In China and Japan, Western cultural influence collided with monolithic and largely homogeneous imperial traditions which embraced value systems predating concepts which Westerners consider universal. If the Chinese today refer to English as a 'minor' language, what must they make of Adam Smith? China has been slow to adapt, and continues to experience a painful process of integration with the rest of the world. One day China may be strong enough to claim that the rest of the world should adapt to its own standards. Japan, an island state with a continental mindset, went for an awkward grafting of Western ideas on to a rigid indigenous cultural framework, leaving the Japanese and those who deal with them equally confused about what they are trying to be. Japan's influence in the region is also constrained by memories of the Pacific War; memories that die hard despite the passage of half a century, numerous official expressions of remorse, and lately an apology of sorts.

Southeast Asia's cultural evolution has always been eclectic, reflecting the diverse origins of its people and the plethora of external influences exerted on the region through the medium of trade. Indigenous languages are shot through with foreign loan-words. In the middle ages, Malay and Portuguese were lingua francas: today, the English language is recognised as an important medium for business; tomorrow Chinese may take its place. Modern politics has drawn on an even broader cultural field. Indonesia's Sukarno cited Thomas Jefferson and Karl Marx to prop up rhetoric aimed at impressing the world and suppressing his people. Malaysia's Prime Minister Mahathir Mohamad is at home with Naisbitt and Drucker, yet he co-authored (with maverick Japanese Diet member Shintaro Ishihara) a book calling on Asians to reject Western values. Perhaps this eccentrically eclectic approach reflects a diplomatic tradition of playing one external influence off against another in a bid to preserve political and cultural sovereignty. Thailand, for example, spent much of its history embracing foreign ideas simply to keep foreigners at arms length. Nevertheless, it is important not to underestimate the strong impulse in South East Asian cultures to claim an indigenous path to development.

**Economic and political change**

Sustained economic growth is breeding self-confidence and a desire to become less dependent on the West for capital and technology. While the volume of exports to major Western markets remains important, the volume of intraregional trade is also increasing. Exports from Indonesia, Malaysia, Thailand and the Philippines to the Asia–Pacific region increased by over 30 per cent in the period 1990 to 1992.[17] By the end of the decade over half the region's trade will be concentrated in the Asia–Pacific region. The reality may still be that traditional Western markets and investment remain vital to the region's economic health; but the prospect of reduced dependency on traditional markets is beginning to have an impact on policy. Thailand's trade relationship with the United States looked very one-sided when Thailand relied on quotas and trade privileges granted by the US government. But as the volume of Thailand's exports to its fellow ASEAN countries reached the same level as its exports to the US in the mid-1990s, Thai officials began to talk about putting the relationship on a more equal footing.

At the same time, the growing prosperity of the regional market has fast begun to erode the bargaining positions of Western multinationals, many of which started looking at the region less as a place to dabble, and more as an absolutely vital place to be. The buoyancy of regional markets in the 1990s and the liquidity of its corporations have Western investors queuing up for a slice of the pie. This is no longer a market for pioneers and risk-takers; it is a market everybody has to be in. Even though the governments of more advanced states like Malaysia, Thailand and Singapore started to worry about rising costs of production, and the consequent erosion of their competitive advantage to foreign investors, this concern was balanced by the low-cost promise of emerging markets in Indochina and Burma. Overall, Southeast Asia remained the brightest spot in the global economic firmament in the mid-1990s.

The confidence bred of economic success has had a profound impact on perceptions of political change, at least in the minds of political elites in the region. For if the systems they preside over can sustain high levels of growth for so long, it is but a short step to claiming a set of unique values and questioning whether the West has the sole patent for political rectitude. If there is a defining tone about the last decade of the twentieth century in this region, it is a desire to stand on its own two feet; a final exorcism of the ghosts of the colonial past.

Prime Minister Vo Van Kiet of Vietnam declared that the country aimed to 'learn but not copy' from outside how to open up its economy. Vietnam, together with fellow economic laggard Burma, are more inclined to learn from their Asian neighbours rather than from the West. Two years after the UN-sponsored election in Cambodia, co-prime minister Norodom Rannaridh declared that Western-style democratic governance was an inappropriate model for the country to adopt at its present stage of development. Shunning purely democratic models of government, the ruling elites of these emerging economies looked to their neighbours for guidance on how to modernise society without losing control over it. Hence Burma's interest in the Indonesian army's dual civilian and military role.

The subtle blending of acquired ideas with tradition, sometimes makes it hard to distinguish one from the other, or can be mistaken for unprogressive inertia. Hence the reason why Southeast Asia has long been characterised as a cauldron of diversity defying a common identity. The legacy of this over-stressed divarication has unfortunately helped breed the contemporary perception of the region as either immutable, or dependent on external stimuli for change. From here it is but a short step to asserting moral superiority, something which most people of Southeast Asia experienced under colonial rule. With questions that sound like 'now that you have a developed economy, when will you develop a mature political system', some may be wondering if colonial attitudes have really been expunged.

This study tries to approach the issue of political change with a more open mind. It argues that the gradual rather than revolutionary pace of democratisation in the region is allowing political elites to adapt to the needs of a more demanding society – but not to abdicate power entirely. This suggests that for some years to come only token rather than substantive change will prevail. A Singaporean official once described this measured, cautious approach to political change as 'trimming the banyan tree'. The banyan is a sturdy tree with long hanging branches offering ample shade. In many parts of Southeast Asia the tree is considered sacred, often planted in the grounds of Hindu or Buddhist temples. Its political significance stems from the ancient practice of using its protective shade as a place of teaching or supplication. In Thailand, monks still teach beneath venerable banyan trees. In the Javanese tradition, petitioners with a grievance would sit under the banyan to signal a desire for an audience with the ruler. In modern Indonesia, the banyan tree is the symbol of the government-backed Golkar party. The banyan tree is perhaps an apt metaphor for the process of political change in the region and its impact on society – it is said that nothing can grow under the banyan tree. For not only are ruling elites unwilling to yield their grip on power but also they are only prepared to see a limited loosening of the collective bonds which envelop society like the many overhanging branches of the banyan tree. In Southeast Asia there is a fine balance between what some may consider the keystone of social order, and others as a hindrance to the assertion of individual rights.

Finding the correct level is no easy task as conflicting arguments are loading up on both sides of the scales. Some argue that strong government in Southeast Asia has been conspicuously successful. Take away liberal concerns for intellectual freedom and the rights of the individual, and you have a form of benign dictatorship in many countries which has undisputedly elevated living standards beyond expectations. Stability and prosperity have bred confidence and a conviction that the system works. Some countries are even selling their brand of strong government. Singapore has tried for some years to convince its neighbours that firm control over the media is best for everyone. Malaysian media entrepreneurs are trading their knowledge of how to run a pro-government newspaper in the emerging media markets of Indochina. Singapore is advising Vietnam and Burma on how to reform their economies and promote trade; Thailand wants to help mediate between Rangoon and Burma's ethnic minorities. Again, confidence is breeding self-assurance, and a conviction about the way things are done in the region.

Some of this salesmanship is bearing fruit. When the leaders of Burma's junta visited Indonesia in late 1993 they came away impressed by the military's dual civil political and military roles. A senior Indonesian military officer observed that what impressed the Burmese was the way the 'dual function' kept a cork on popular pressures for change while fostering economic development. Sure enough, when the Burmese junta sat down in late 1994 to deliberate how to change its spots, one of the proposals was for an Indonesian-style legislature in which the military retains a quarter of the seats. 'The SLORC [State Law and Order Restoration Council – the name of the 21-member military junta] appears to be looking toward an Indonesian future', suggests Burma specialist David Steinberg, 'a military dominated regime that appears externally to be civilian but in which power is clearly in the hands of the military establishment'.[18]

Strong government in the region has arguably become more entrenched: shored up on one side by well-oiled state machinery, and on the other by the acquiescence bred by increasing wealth and social well-being. In the ranks of the middle class there is a tendency to accept strong government and leadership as a means of preserving their new found wealth and security. There are precious few signs of dissent in the luxurious leafy housing developments springing up on the outskirts of Jakarta. Although some theorists have predicted that the middle classes will shoulder the burden of pressing for political reform, the principal source of discontent seems to be the dispossessed under classes. Poor farmers and slum-dwellers are incensed by the wealth they see accumulating in the hands of the middle classes. To protect themselves from the anger of the less-privileged, the middle classes seem happy to see that government remains strong, and above all provides the leadership needed to preserve social and economic stability.

There are varying degrees of social discontent, but as we shall see later on, this is not always directed against the concept of strong government so much as at the way it is abused. On the whole, capitalism in the Southeast Asian context is breeding passive contentment faster than classical sociological theory predicts. And since the more developed Southeast Asian states no longer have to rely on foreign, usually Western aid, they can afford to thumb their noses at their critics.

Generally speaking, the Cold War and a corporate thirst for lucrative overseas contracts allowed these states to flaunt their democratic imperfections with impunity for 20 years. But this changed when the West won the Cold War. Freedom of the individual is not a debatable matter in the eyes of Western governments which once considered the non-communist states of the region a model of capitalist values when they confronted the 'Red' threat. With communism possibly consigned to history's waste pile, the West, and in particular the United States under President Bill Clinton, began to look for a new global role. Insisting on conformity to its own standards of political freedom as a fundamental basis for relations in the post-Cold War world was a logical follow-up. This view has brought Southeast Asia into what amounts to an ideological conflict with the West, as arguments over what constitutes freedom dwell on the difference between Eastern and Western values and traditions.

## Social and cultural forces

It may be dangerously deterministic to draw too fine a distinction between East and West. But equally it would be naïve to think that Western political philosophy is alone in promoting notions of freedom and popular sovereignty. There are other social and cultural forces moulding the political landscape of Southeast Asia. They may not be those commonly associated with the development of modern states, but they are familiar agents of change in the regional context. Religion has always played a dual role in the societies under consideration here. Religion has helped to legitimise ruling elites and define national identity on the one hand, but also offered an outlet for protest against the burden of tyranny and oppression. After almost half a century of modernisation and nation-building, during which governments did their best to bottle up or co-opt the popular appeal of religious belief, the side-effects of sustained growth – the widening gap between rich and poor, alienation in the urban environment, and overall moral decline – are generating social tensions. More importantly, in the absence of effective mass-based political organisations, these popular grievances are finding expression through a revival of populist as opposed to state-backed religion.

Reacting to the assault on their legitimacy, both from Western derived and indigenous sources of protest, the region's ruling elites have resorted to claiming distinctive moral and social values to shore up their authority. The formulation of core values with the help of corporatist state ideologies has exaggerated the collective, disciplined nature of Southeast Asian societies to help preserve strong government and defend the system against its critics. In the process there is a danger that the constructive balance between individual freedom and collective compliance inherent in the traditional political culture could be lost. By forcing normative aspects of morality, religion and political culture into strictly-defined areas of behaviour, there is a danger that some of the tolerance and flexibility of Southeast Asian society may also be lost.

The wider geopolitical context is going to be an important factor in shaping the post-modern political landscape of Southeast Asia. Some analysts consider that the greatly feared, but unspoken threat of a hegemonistic China is accelerating moves towards regional integration in Southeast Asia. It would certainly be optimistic to assume that efforts to forge a free trade area, closer security ties and an ambitious communion of all ten Southeast Asian states, stems from the conviction that shared commercial interests and a European-style union is around the corner. The existing grouping of seven states under the Association of

Southeast Asian Nations (ASEAN) has spent the past quarter of a century crafting a thin veneer of common interest and cooperation, mainly in the interests of avoiding conflict with one another. Now there are important external stimuli to enhanced cooperation: the perceived threat of a regional superpower in the neighbourhood; declining confidence in the countervailing balance of power offered by the United States; and the pressures to conform to a global system of political and economic behaviour.

Whatever the motives, the fact that these states will be thrown closer together must have an impact on the social, economic and political shape of the region. It will tease out common, shared beliefs but also allow them to scrutinise each other more closely, and comment on each other's affairs. The seven ASEAN states (Brunei, Indonesia, Malaysia, Singapore, Thailand, Vietnam and the Philippines) have long cherished a principle of non-interference in one another's affairs, and expect solidarity from one member state when another is criticised by an outside power. But in a more transparent regional environment, there are bound to be conformist pressures. All the more so when all the former communist states of Indochina and long-isolated Burma eventually join the ASEAN club.

## Ethnicity

Ethnicity is also a very important component of the region's economic and commercial tradition. The premodern states of Southeast Asia were far from isolated, and played host to a bewildering mix of wandering merchants and adventurers. One of the earliest accounts of a Southeast Asia state was recorded by Chou Ta Kuan, a Chinese visitor to the Khmer Kingdom in the eighth century. There he noted the presence of foreign artisans and merchants. Over a millennium later the foreigners are still there, for the most part happily integrated within their host societies. By far the most visible are the 23 million overseas Chinese. There are also Indians, and large communities of immigrants or historical refugees who have crossed borders and made their homes in one another's countries. The overseas Chinese stand out because of their high economic profile. In almost every country of the region, their dominance of commerce far outweighs their numerical strength. How long will they maintain their distinctive ethnic networks, business-practices and cultural traditions? What impact will a dynamic mainland China, with closer commercial and political links to Southeast Asia, have on indigenous attitudes to the overseas Chinese? In some countries there are already concerns that overseas Chinese investment in China could siphon capital and investment away from Southeast Asia. Although this is probably an exaggerated fear, less considered is the impact on politics and business in Southeast Asia if China were to adopt, for the first time since the Mongol era, a forward policy in the region.

The political landscape of Southeast Asia is changing; the problem is that common assumptions about the nature and direction of this change may not match the eventual reality. Western and even some educated Asian perceptions about the nature of political change rest on a body of economic and political philosophy to which the region's political elites are proving remarkably resistant. Economies grow at rates three times that of the Western economies without the state fully disengaging itself from the market; politicians respond to people's needs even though the people are poorly represented; kings play the role of democrats. What does this tell us about the political culture of Southeast Asia? Some of the dinosaurs in Stephen Spielberg's popular celluloid fantasy 'Jurassic Park' adapted to biological conditions when they were genetically recreated in the modern post-Jurassic era – demonstrating the adaptive power of evolution. Are Southeast Asia's strong governments, considered the political dinosaurs of the New World Order, really on their last legs? Or are they merely in the process of adapting to new conditions?

# Chapter 1

# Recovering tradition

*We do not live by universal ideals alone. We have specific cultures and traditions inherited from the past, some representing the collective wisdom of ages, which need to be revitalised and harnessed in our progress towards the future.*
*Anwar Ibrahim addressing the Fifth Southeast Asia Forum,*
*4 October 1993*

The years 1853 to 1966 spanned the lives of two of the most influential political figures in modern Southeast Asia. King Chulalongkorn the Great of Thailand was born in 1853. In the course of his long reign from 1868–1910, King Chulalongkorn is credited with transforming Thailand from a 'traditional Southeast Asian Kingdom into a modern nation state'.[1] Just a year before Chulalongkorn died, a 'native' prosecutor from West Sumatra in the employ of the Dutch Indies government fathered a son by one of his wives. His mother named him Sutan Sjahrir. A bright student, Sjahrir was given the best education a 'native' could expect to have under Dutch rule in Indonesia. He spent three years in metropolitan Holland and returned to become one of the leading intellectual figures of the Indonesian nationalist struggle. He served his country briefly as prime minister in 1945–6, but died sad and disillusioned while receiving medical treatment in Switzerland in 1966.

Although Chulalongkorn was a king and Sutan Sjahrir only briefly prime minister, both men are credited with contributing to the modernisation of political thinking in their respective countries, and both are often cast as having rejected traditional ways in favour of ideas from the West. Unfortunately, this rather simplistic view misrepresents their endeavours. For while both men drew on Western thinking to rationalise their programmes for modernisation and change, arguably they remained loyal to their own cultures and traditions. They were, in fact, quintessential Southeast Asian nationalists, blending renewal and tradition in a way that fostered progress, but at the same time preserved tradition. They shared a remarkable talent for synthesis.

Chulalongkorn modernised the bureaucracy and made primary education accessible to ordinary people, setting society on the road to political reform and enlightenment. However, he stopped short of granting full sovereignty to the people and allowing the monarchy's role to be diluted in any way. He was presented with the idea of a constitutional monarchy, but rejected it. He wrote:

> The use of Western ideas as a basis for reform in Siam is mistaken. The prevailing conditions are completely different. It is as if one could take European methods of growing wheat and apply them to rice growing in this country.[2]

Yet, in his view, there existed 'no incompatibility between such acquisition of European modern science and the maintenance of our individuality as an independent Asiatic nation'. King Chulalongkorn's approach to modernisation, considers the modern Thai scholar Thongchai Winichakul, typified the essence of Thai nationalist discourse which 'presumes that great leaders [in this case monarchs] selectively adopted only good things from the West for the country while preserving the traditional values at their best'.[3] Sjahrir is similarly credited with conceiving independent Indonesia as a modern constitutional democracy. But scholars now doubt whether he envisaged totally abandoning the country's traditional political culture; that in fact he was searching for a middle ground in which Indonesians could be proud of their modernity without losing sight of their past.[4]

Both men are considered model nationalists. Importantly, though, they were not radicals – even if that is how much of what they said at the time was perceived. In fact, neither man envisaged a complete departure from the past. If they could survey the modern political landscape of Southeast Asia, what would they think? King Chulalongkorn might well be satsified with the degree of political continuity; to the extent that the principal pillars of Thai identity – Nation, Religion and King – have been preserved. The political reforms he initiated have enfranchised a broader spectrum of Thais. Yet progress towards popular empowerment has not been made at the expense of strong centralised rule and the institution of the monarchy. Thai society remains for the most part intrinsically hierarchical and status conscious, fostering a state of semi-democracy which preserves the interests of a narrow elite. While most observers felt sure that the events of May 1992 marked the end of the Thai army's involvement in politics, there is no indication that the traditional tensions between bureaucratic and military factions in government have been fully resolved. Political parties are weak and fractious; politicians are mistrusted by the public and prone to corruption. Perhaps to his relief as a monarch, Chulalongkorn would see few signs that Thailand could do without the mediating role of the King.

Sjahrir died in 1966, just as Indonesia was embarking on a new era of political leadership under a relatively unknown general called Suharto. From his later writings in the early 1960s though, it was plain that Sjahrir was deeply disillusioned with the country's political course. Despite his socialist sympathies, he saw no future for the communist party. Betraying an old political emnity, he viewed Sukarno as the embodiment of the feudal tradition he so vehemently rejected. It was plain to Sjahrir that the army harboured political pretensions. Yet to him the army seemed like a 'traveller who has lost his compass'.[5] If he were alive in Indonesia today, the venerable nationalist might be struck the same way. He would detect no appreciable popular support for political ideals or ideology, and note that the middle classes generally supported strong, authoritarian rule. He would be appalled by the survival of a feudal culture of leadership and power and find an army that was still struggling to reconcile its political and security roles. Sjahrir was also an optimist. Close to the end of his life he wrote that he felt the Indonesian people did have a chance of exercising their sovereignty, so long as 'the government truly behaves like a father of its people'.[6]

Both men would take some comfort from the elements of continuity; the survival of strong leadership acting as a cohesive, bonding agent of state and society – although they would probably recoil from the way it has been abused. They might be pleased to recognise elements of tradition that have survived the upheaval of the colonial era; less happy, though, to see tyranny and injustice justified in the name of tradition – in reality little different from methods used by the colonial powers. What they might look for, as they did in their own era, was a means to knit the best, most desirable elements of tradition with the most desirable aspects of change. In the best tradition of Southeast Asian nationalism they would seek to blend and synthesise tradition with modernity.

It is ironic indeed that King Chulalongkorn is remembered as a moderniser, yet his image is worshipped by modern Thais to help keep them in touch with their spiritual past (See Chapter 5). For here in Southeast Asia, the tendency to assume uniformity and conformity in global political development runs foul of the apparent tenacity of culture and tradition, particularly in the arena of power and politics. What explains the tenacity of tradition? After all, these states have managed to modernise their economies largely along non-traditional lines. The region's economic infrastructure is becoming one of the most advanced in the world. Yet these countries harbour political cultures which draw on primordial, pre-modern customs and often reject imported 'modern' ideas. Political leaders in Southeast Asia are often heard praising the virtues of modernisation, yet they demand respect for traditional values of authority and leadership. The blending of tradition and modernity can lead to confusion. Perhaps this is because, as we shall see, pioneering nationalists of Southeast Asia adopted superficial forms of Western government to legitimise their states in the eyes of the victorious allies in the post-Pacific War era. In much the same way, finding it hard to dissent from the prevailing world view of political legitimacy, today's political elites are learning to assume the cloak of liberalism while having no illusions about their distinctiveness. Arguably this is part of a longer tradition in the region of dealing with intrusive change.

One of the most enduring facets of Southeast Asia is the tenacity of tradition. Tradition, not in an archaic or stagnant sense, but more as a dynamic, adaptable component of identity and culture. Scholars have tended to view the role of tradition in a political context as a strawman; something that can be invented, revived and salvaged to serve the ends of power.[7] They see politicians invoking tradition to justify or sanctify power. In his ground-breaking study of nationalism, Benedict Anderson described the 'imagined communities' that constituted new states, pointing out that even erstwhile revolutionary regimes, like those in Vietnam and Cambodia, could still wrap themselves in the feudal trappings of the past; why 'revolutionary leaderships, consciously or unconsciously, come to play lord of the manor'.[8] Certainly, tradition in the broader Asian context can be moulded and forged into active creeds, and should not be mistaken for quaint near-forgotten custom. Archaic tradition can also be deployed as a barrier to change. As foreign investors flocked to exploit Vietnam's rapidly liberalising economy, state officials warned that capital and skills were not the only determinants of a successful bid to invest – an understanding of Vietnamese culture and tradition would also be required.

The central, legitimising role of indigenous tradition and culture is perhaps the most important point to grasp about the process of political change in Southeast Asia. It helps us to understand how and perhaps why political evolution has been kind to strong government in the region. Far from failing, the concept and practice of strong, centralised power is adapting and mutating. It may ultimately be doomed (who can predict the course of any of the world's political systems?), but it has a long way to run. There are no signs in any of the ten Southeast Asian nations that radically different political systems are about to supplant existing ones. Political change is proceeding at a gradual, in places, almost glacial pace. And everywhere the changes seem to protect ruling elites and their interests far more than altering their relations with society.

All the modern political ideologies espoused by contemporary Southeast Asian states draw on tradition but present themselves as modern, forward-thinking creeds. Indonesia's *Pancasila* state ideology, Singapore's 'Core Principles', and Malaysia's *Rukun Negara*, all espouse Western civil society principles such as freedom, justice and human dignity. They also emphasise the traditional, and for the most part collective, foundations of society: the need for tolerance, a strong sense of community, collective discipline, respect for leadership, and spirituality. This common approach to defining the state in ideological terms underlines the fact that for most countries in Southeast Asia, the challenge presented by Western influence was not how to *assimilate*, but how to *adapt or synthesise* the old, the traditional, with the new. For as the Australian academic Clive Kessler aptly puts it: 'It is in culture that people fashion power as well as acceptance of it.'[9] Thus, any study of political culture in Asia must grasp the importance attached to indigenous tradition in the formulation of contemporary political ideas.

This is not an easy argument to sell. Contemporary Southeast Asia is, in economic terms, the fastest growing region in the world. The universalism colouring so much Western social science dictates that it must jettison the baggage of the past in order to catch up with the rest of the modern world. This assumes that modernity, like Pepsi-Cola, comes in a single, universal form – a view that comes naturally to Americans and Europeans, but not to Southeast Asians. They are more eclectic about definitions, tending to shun concrete definitions. Flexibility, more a reluctance to define matters in a strict, definitive sense, acts as a useful means of avoiding conflict. Beliefs are coloured by transience and often determined by circumstance, thus presenting a sterile environment for dialectic and dogma. Take this description of the Javanese epistemology described by a perceptive Japanese observer:

> In the Javanese world of ideas, diverse ideologies do not exist as mutually separate entities where interrelationships are those of hostility, compromise, or mechanical eclecticism. They are rather fluid liquids which can easily mix together under certain conditions.[10]

That is not to rule out the role of ideology altogether. Ideology is an important tool for legitimising authority and maintaining a cohesive society in the region. A key feature of state creeds adopted by Southeast Asian states is their blending of imported and indigenous principles – principles of freedom, justice, and human dignity juxtaposed, often in seemingly contradictory ways, with more collective, cultural and religious definitions of society.

Of course, traditionalism helps preserve and concentrate rather than diffuse power. Traditional forms of democracy in Southeast Asia like the *balai* (a place where rulers heard audiences) in the Malay tradition, are built into shining examples of how freedom can and should be controlled – or, as Indonesian officials are fond of saying 'expressed politely'. Ruling elites in the region commonly invoke history and tradition to legitimate the structure of power they preside over. In Singapore this takes the form of Confucianism conveyed as a set of ideal family values all Singaporeans should aspire to. In Indonesia, the traditions of gratitude and respect for those in authority inherent in the Javanese culture of the Solo-Jogyakarta area are cited as values all Indonesians should cherish – even if these values clash with other, more egalitarian cultures. Burma's military rulers have revived traditional forms of corvée labour to press civilians into service to build roads and railways the cash-starved regime can ill-afford to pay wages for. In Thailand, the process of democratisation has greatly liberalised political debate in the media, but strict sanctions remain in force when it comes to discussion of the monarchy. Nightly news broadcasts carry laudatory coverage of the Royal household, and Thai civil servants working up-country still stand to attention when they hear the royal anthem.

These living examples of the strength of traditional power and authority often seem at odds with what is touted as the prevailing global trend. The common assumption is that having been exposed to the West since the colonial period, the subsequent history of these states has been the gradual evolution of Western-style society. Francis Fukuyama hailed this impending outbreak of Western-style liberal democracy as the 'end of the evolution of human thought' and hence 'the end of history'.[11] The romantic notion that liberal democracy is the 'final form of human government' appears to rule out the possibility that the evolution of thought might be less universal, or that it is influenced by differential economic realities and ethnic, cultural or religious differences; indeed by a very different historical *weltanschauung*. Not enough thought is given either to the possibility that for Southeast Asians the intrusion of Western (principally European) influence in the colonial era *was* the end of *their* history. And, more importantly, that the end of colonial rule allowed the start of a *recovery* of that history.

Fukuyama considers that in a 'post-historical' world 'the chief axis of interaction between states would be economic, and the old rules of power politics would have decreasing relevance . . . '.[12] But doesn't this also neatly capture Southeast Asia at the height of colonial power in the late nineteenth century? At that time, colonial trading interests governed interaction between states. Ancient rivalries between states – the old rules from an indigenous perspective – were interrupted by depriving them of sovereignty. Since then, these states have recovered (and in some cases invented) independence, become economically successful and affluent, and are therefore in a position to reassert the 'old rules' of power politics for the region. In the process they have rediscovered traditional forms of political expression. Recognising the enduring role of tradition in modern Asian political culture, Fukuyama has since taken a new tack by suggesting that instead of non-Western traditions conforming with those of the West, there may be 'fewer points of incompatibility' between Asian and Western traditions – King Chulalongkorn's rice and wheat. All the same, he insists that democracy will be the ultimate product of political development.[13]

After the Pacific War it was almost unimaginable that Southeast Asian states could draw on their indigenous cultural roots for the basis of statehood. Somehow the assumption, or perhaps the hope, was that as independent states they would emulate the political systems of the departing colonial powers. The colonial powers liked to think they left a civilising legacy. What they forgot was the strength of the civilisation and cultures they had sat upon for so long. The noted anthropologist Stanley Tambiah considers that one of the most important features of the Theravada Buddhist polities (Sri Lanka, Burma, Thailand) is 'their active consciousness of historical continuity'.[14]

Today, there is a common assumption that because Southeast Asian states are engaged in the broader global context and exposed to the communications revolution, they are in the process of subsuming their own traditions and culture in favour of Western fashions, music and television. That may be true of society in the region if culture is considered in an ephemeral sense. Culture is all too often defined by what one wears, or the car one drives. But consider this: Western broadcasting companies involved in the scramble to dominate Asia's massive satellite market have discovered that even without censorship, unadulterated Western fare does not guarantee an audience. Inevitably, programming has begun to shape itself to local culture and tastes, featuring more Asian faces and Asian music.[15] In 1994 Asians spent almost US$ 2 billion on music recordings. More importantly, the region's profitable media market is giving birth to indigenous media enterprise with less parochial aspirations. Regional newspapers owned by Southeast Asians and a number of satellite television networks beaming locally-made programmes to the region are already on the starting blocks. In Thailand alone, two daily newspapers, *Business Day* and *Asia Times*, are targeting a regional market. Thailand's Shinawatra Communications and TelecomAsia plan satellite television services for the region with more homegrown programming.

Either through the power of the state, or the power of the market, Southeast Asian societies are finding ways to resist the onslaught of foreign values, and in the process preserve a measure of their tradition and history. This process points to the essence of a common Southeast Asian nationalism: pragmatism and synthesis. You absorb external influences to preserve sovereignty; you take the best elements of those influences and blend them with indigenous values to enhance your identity. The point is that the process of change involves the adaptation and preservation of tradition.

The resistant properties of culture and tradition, whether the product of genuine historical continuity or modern manipulation, constitute an important contextual backdrop to any analysis of political change in the region. It is too easy to assume that economic growth and modernisation that draw on Western models and material culture necessarily guarantee political change along the same lines. Was that the outcome of Latin America's economic development in the 1930s? This brief survey of Southeast Asia's political landscape assumes that history (in the broad evolutionary sense which embraces the experience of a people through time) is more resilient than the globalists would have us believe. What's more it can be recovered and manipulated.

In Southeast Asia, societies and cultures buffeted by intrusive external influences for around a century and a half are in the process of restoring a sense of indigenous identity. With the increasing prosperity of the region people now have the means and collective confidence to do so; and the end result will not be the cloning of Western norms and values but at best an adaptation – or mutation. History is not ending in Southeast Asia but was restarted at the end of the colonial era. (The process actually began with the nationalist movements founded in the twilight of European colonial rule.) Since then, slowly but steadily, ruling elites have recovered and reconstructed traditional models of power and authority. These models may not be wholly swept away by the dynamics of global trade and free market economics commonly believed to be creating a borderless world. Instead, as frameworks of political behaviour, they are learning how to cohabit.

Conceptually, the revival of tradition in this way may be difficult to grasp. From a Western perspective the colonial period of
exploitation was succeeded by an era of development which
happily maintained the primacy of European culture beyond the
period of European colonial domination. Perhaps because it was
economically imperative for former colonial powers to trade with
their former colonies, or perhaps out of a sense of guilt, helping to
define the shape and course of these countries after independence
became an extension of the old colonial *mission civiliatrice*. There
was no going back to 'pre-modern', 'old world' or even 'primitive'
traditions. In Western eyes these new nations became instead
fledgling democracies and newly-developing economies. In the
crude economic jargon of the immediate postwar period, developing countries would at some stage achieve 'take-off' and become
fully-fledged industrial societies: chips off the old block.

As fledgling industrial societies these 'new nations' were
expected to develop in a prescribed fashion. Industrial society,
Ernest Gellner contends in his 1983 study of nationalism, lives
by and relies on 'sustained and perpetual growth, on an expected
and continuous improvement'.[16] Naturally, those Westerners
observing the industrialisation process in Southeast Asia
measured 'improvement' against a Western yardstick. Since
modern mankind is irreversibly committed to industrial society,
Gellner argues, a high degree of universality has been introduced
to societies wherever they are. 'Modern man is not loyal to a
monarch, or a land, or a faith, whatever he may say, but to
a culture', Gellner asserts. The fundamental elements of this universal culture of industrial society are, he suggests, education,
science, technology and so on.

No one can dispute the march of progress, or man's universal
attraction to higher planes of knowledge. The problem is that
the term 'universal' is so often construed as meaning anything
'Western'; the implication being that non-Western traditions are
backward or parochial. Andre Malraux, the idealistic French
writer who lived in French Indochina in the 1930s, characterised
the arrogance of Western civilisation as 'Every man dreams of
being God.' Malraux was vexed by the arrogance of French
'colon' culture with its claim of cultural superiority. Not much
has changed, except perhaps that non-Western cultures are beginning to challenge that primacy. Samuel Huntingdon's controversial survey of the post-Cold War world bravely forecasts a new

pattern of global conflict. One in which 'the principal conflicts of global politics will occur between nations and groups of different civilisations'. In the politics of civilisations, he claims, 'the peoples and governments of non-Western civilisations no longer remain the objects of history as targets of Western colonialism but join the West as movers and shapers of history'.[17] Huntingdon's projection of conflict may be contentious, perhaps even well short of reality. But his call for a new definition of what constitutes a civilisation is an important step towards recognising that industrialisation and other aspects of modernity are not necessarily generating uniform societies and political systems. More importantly, he points to the trend among non-Western elites towards 'indigenisation':

> A de-Westernisation and indigenisation of elites is occurring in many non-Western countries at the same time that Western, usually American, cultures, styles and habits become more popular among the mass of the people.[18]

Huntingdon's generalisation may sound alarming, but in a more benign sense it captures in essence what is happening in contemporary Southeast Asia. Traditional models of power and authority have been recovered or reinvented to support strong forms of government authority and leadership. Thus the region's political culture is evolving in a direction which may diverge from trends that are apparent in society.

## STAGES OF POLITICAL DEVELOPMENT SINCE 1945

We might consider the political development of modern Southeast Asia as proceeding through three distinct stages. Stage one was initiated by the growth of nationalist movements prior to the Pacific War, and their eventual triumph over colonial rule after the Japanese defeat in 1945. The principal characteristic of stage one was its imitation of Western ideological and institutional political norms. These brave new independent states were conceived by the departing colonial powers as fledgling liberal democracies. Exceptionally, Vietnamese nationalists secured independence for the country north of the seventeenth parallel in 1954, with communist party rule. But it is possible that Ho Chi Minh, who was more of a pragmatist than an ideologue, was forced to rely on Moscow after failing to gain support from

Washington. For mainly Western-educated nationalists the democratic system seemed like the best way to legitimise the state in the eyes of the international community as well as to provide an arena for the mediation of local political demands. Political parties proliferated, and parliaments were elected – or at least the intention to do so was declared in liberal constitutions. Indeed, these states took the first few steps after independence along the path of democracy. They soon strayed off it.

In the course of stage two, which roughly coincides with the mid-1950s, we see democracy on the decline. Implementing liberal democracy proved to be harder than at first envisaged. Local demands proved overwhelming: there were problems of national unity, diverse groups and territories in need of integration. There was a gaping void between the political background and aspirations of the new ruling elite and the capacity of the mass of the population to understand them. Much like colonial reformers who began implementing liberal reforms towards the end of their rule, the indigenous ruling elite talked in terms of an interim stage before a fully fledged democracy could work. The rhetoric spoke of closing the gap between elite and masses through education and economic growth, arguing that as the populace became ready for constructive participation, it would be allowed a greater voice in the running of its affairs.

With real democracy on hold, those who put growth and unity before representation began to dominate the political scene. From the mid-1950s onward, a decade or so after independence in Burma, Cambodia, Laos, Indonesia, the Philippines and Thailand, progressive democratic regimes were replaced by uncompromising autocratic ones. As Ruth McVey, a noted scholar of Southeast Asian affairs eloquently wrote:

> the degree but not the direction has varied, from the reduction to marginalities of the permitted area of political discourse through the symbolic concentration of power and popular will in a charismatic leader, to a bare reliance on command from above.[19]

But more importantly, the kind of political power wielded during this stage represented a recovery of indigenous political tradition. The situation may not have looked quite this way. After all, the autocrats who swept to power wore modern (Western) military uniforms and drove tanks. Attention focused on the new role being played by the military, which was mistakenly considered a modern institution. The pre-modern and inward-looking perceptions of the officer corps was largely overlooked.

There seems little doubt that Southeast Asian ruling elites were, consciously or otherwise, in a position to select differing models of power in the first decade after independence. Intellectually grounded in a Western political framework by their colonial masters, some of them opted to accept the Western model of constitutional democracy as the only viable way to run a state. These were the 'lonely, bilingual intelligentsias unattached to sturdy local bourgeoisies' described by Benedict Anderson.[20] In the competition for power which ensued others preferred to fall back on traditional patterns of power and authority, seeking support from the conservative local bourgeoisie. At a time when the bulk of society was not fully exposed to outside influences, the return to a paternalistic tradition of authority may have seemed like the most appropriate route. It was certainly very effective.

Post-colonial society in countries like Indonesia and Burma was ill-equipped to understand the significance of the right of individuals to vote for leaders. Herb Feith points out in his arresting analysis of the decline of democracy in Sukarno's Indonesia that the choices made by voters in the 1955 elections were 'meaningful – not as assessments of the performance of particular governments, but as quasi-ideological identifications by villagers'. Successful parties, in his words, were those who 'succeeded in linking themselves with major social groupings'.[21] The Indonesian elections of 1955 are generally considered the fairest the country has ever held; but the result suggested that people were more concerned about religious and ideological affiliation than matters of policy. The elections therefore alerted the establishment to the destabilising religious and ethnic strife which could be provoked by democracy.

Before the colonial intruders either erased or modified indigenous patterns of government, most Southeast Asian societies were accustomed to the imposition of leadership – although whether leaders were accepted or obeyed often depended on a public consensus of their performance. After independence the urge to modernise political institutions ran up against the inability of most segments of the population to comprehend modern principles of government. Ignorance encouraged abuse of the modern systems introduced. For example, rural voters in Thailand's north-eastern region in the 1980s were enticed to vote for candidates by the manipulation of auspicious numbers and lucky colours on posters and ballot sheets. Rampant vote buying for sums as little as US$ 2 per vote continues to plague elections in rural areas, and in a survey of rural and urban voters up and down the country in 1995, a Thai sociologist found that 17 per cent openly admitted that they sold their vote.[22] In Malaysia, the government party warns rural voters that support for the opposition could deny them development; the opposition Islamic Party of Malaysia warns villagers that voting for the government could deny them a place in the afterworld.[23] In June 1992 a farmer in Central Java, when pressed to consider his political rights ahead of a general election, responded by saying things were better because he now owned three shirts instead of one.

Ironically, development – the very instrument of Western-inspired social and economic change – became a powerful political placebo in post-colonial Southeast Asia. Industrialisation, self-sufficiency in food production and a supporting cast of prestige projects persuaded people that they were better off without having to demand the right to choose their governments. Indonesians have been showered with economic development and told that political development will follow. In Malaysia, the government attacks its critics for hindering development. The thinking is that if a government delivers development why criticise it. Besides, the collective discipline, social harmony and political acquiescence which supported strong government also helped foster growth and productivity in the early stages of Southeast Asia's economic development. Who could argue with that?

In more recent times, the balance has swung the other way. Stage three of the region's political development has seen more affluent educated sections of societies exposed to the outside world who are in a better position to judge for themselves how they want to be ruled. The materialistic values revered in Western societies have proven attractive to some. Traditional Asian collective values are criticised in liberal intellectual quarters for stifling freedom and hindering creativity. Liberal intellectuals argue that respect for the individual and the celebration of personal achievement may be essential if the region wants to maintain its economic edge – an argument considered more fully later on. But the spread of Western values in Asian societies has also reinforced the belief among ruling elites in their own traditional models of power. They fear what a more Westernised future holds for their societies; drug addiction, soaring crime rates, and the breakdown of the nuclear family. They see *extreme* tendencies in Western society which they don't want emulated in their own countries. As Singapore's Minister of Information and the Arts recently put it:

> In the spectrum between extreme communitarianism at one end and extreme individualism at the other, Eastern societies have moved towards the centre while many Western societies are veering off to the other extreme.[24]

Individuals and their capacity to influence society with ideas: the very thought that an individual could think differently from the rest of the community and then affect that community's thinking frightens those who conceive the societies they govern as fragile and constantly in need of guidance from above. A Singaporean minister has compared ideas with the motor car: 'Just as cars can knock down people, ideas can also be dangerous.... Ideas can kill.'[25] The 'cult' of the individual, small group advocacy and the breakdown of family values all seem to threaten the harmony of society. Of course, they also imply a greater sharing of power and a threat to the political status quo.

The tension between harmony conscious political elites and the changing societies they govern is central to the contemporary political analysis of modern Southeast Asia, and is the hallmark of the third and latest stage of political development there. Basically, the state in Southeast Asia is entering a period of relative strength. It has survived the ideological conflict of the Cold War, and achieved legitimacy by endowing society with a substantial but differential measure of prosperity. Stable and conservative, the modern state in Southeast Asia is slow to change its fundamental character, but quick to adopt the superficial characteristics of progressive modernity as defined in Western terms. Many observers have termed this the era of 'semi-democracies'.[26]

These hybridised systems are prone to tension. As long as there are elements in society challenging the authority of the state, the state feels it must preserve the boundaries of its power. The challenge for the observer is to steer the analysis clear of subjective value judgements about how this tension is going to be resolved. No one is predicting social revolution any time soon in a region where the tinder for social discontent is dampened by opportunities for wealth creation, social mobility and the fulfilment of basic needs. Governments which maintain harsh laws restricting the freedom of expression of their subjects also make sure that enough of these same subjects can buy shares in lucrative privatisation schemes or invest money overseas.

For a more plausible assessment of the region's future political development, the trend must be projected along a more conservative path – one that recognises the role of traditional political culture as much as modern external influences. But that is not to say that Southeast Asian societies must be cast in the 'orientalist's' conceptual strait jacket. We should not consider that the way Southeast Asian polities develop will be any less dynamic, or conceptually less advanced than those of modern Europe. The political systems they fashion might even one day be considered more advanced and less intrinsically unstable than models hallowed in the West. As Henry Luce, the Chinese-born American publisher predicted over half a century ago:

> The future of Mankind depends on Asia's response to the West. And that depends on whether the West knows what it has to say. We'll end up learning from Asia, learning how our assumptions need to be corrected in order that we may more surely make our way toward the goals of universal truth and concord.

Yet for now, Southeast Asia is still considered by many in the West to be politically underdeveloped. Prevailing paternalistic models of power and authority have allowed economic and material development to proceed at an astonishing pace. But the authoritarian nature of these models has not impressed advocates of Western-style democracy. Before assessing whether or not these advocates have a case for global political uniformity, it is important to understand the expression of Southeast Asian political culture in the contemporary context, how it has evolved, and where it is heading.

## ASSERTING AUTHORITY IN THE POST-COLONIAL ERA: THE DECLINE OF CONSTITUTIONAL DEMOCRACY IN INDONESIA

For most of the colonised countries of Southeast Asia, the most pervasive contact with the West occurred in the last decades of the nineteenth century and the first four decades of the twentieth century. It was only by then, after 300 hundred years or more of contact with Europeans, that all resistance to colonial rule was overcome, administrative systems installed, and communications beyond the colonial chief cities effectively established. Besides, concern about forms of government and the administration of justice were low on the list of priorities for the early merchant-colonisers. It was only by the nineteenth century that liberal and humanitarian concerns – newly established in Europe – began to have any impact on colonial administration. The physical impact of the European presence is easy to exaggerate in the early colonial period. In the late-seventeenth century the number of Europeans living on Java probably numbered no more than 2,500, most of them huddled behind the walls of Batavia, the head-quarters of the Dutch East India Company. By the first decade of the twentieth century, a provincial city like Bandung boasted over 15,000 Europeans, while Batavia was described as a 'suburb of the Hague', 'too much influenced by the manners and opinions of the mother country to be accounted a colonial town'.[27]

During this relatively brief period, urban centres in Southeast Asia were exposed to the full weight of European metropolitan culture. Not everyone was affected, however. The cultural impact of Western colonialism never penetrated large areas of rural Southeast Asia, especially at the village level. The most pervasive impact was on those the colonial rulers groomed as servants of the colonial state. Liberal education was offered to the privileged few. The rest of the population was intermittently exposed to 'liberal' notions of administration and justice. In the process, the last vestiges of precolonial power and authority were reduced to purely symbolic forms. While this development is usually considered a liberating experience, one which prepared elites to govern their newly-independent countries in an enlightened way, the more recent political history of the region has demonstrated that these precolonial traditions were not altogether lost.

Wherever one looks in modern Southeast Asia, the process of recovering tradition can be observed. The newly-formed Republic of Indonesia initially adopted a liberal constitutional model of democracy after independence in 1949. As Herb Feith points out, the fact that a Western model of constitutional democracy was adopted at the outset could be explained in part by the lack of practical alternatives, and partly to seek approval from the

Western powers. Only a few individual leaders like Mohammad Hatta and Mohamad Natsir were attached to the values of constitutional democracy. This was not necessarily a democracy recognisable in a Western context:

> it was not seen as having representative functions, nor as necessarily linked with majority rule or with institutionalized opposition. There was in fact, little support in the prevailing body of political ideas for the characteristic principles and mechanisms of constitutional democracy.[28]

As approval from the West became less important, and the factionalism bred of a multiparty system made actual government of the country difficult, so the appeal of radical nationalist ideas favoured by president Sukarno weakened Hatta and his band of Western-educated liberals (including Sjahrir). Political parties struggled to balance the demands of their constituencies to provide money and jobs against the technical and economic realities of participating in government. Their ideological differences sharpened primordial communal tensions in Indonesian society. Muslims demanded a greater say in running the state. The numerous coalition governments of this 1949–56 period were considered democratic, but they did little to implement urgently-needed economic and social policies.

Sukarno's solution to the weakness of constitutional democracy was to fall back on tradition. Instead of finding new ways to order democratic life, he imposed top-down control. In what was to become a common excuse for resorting to traditional patterns of authority in the region, Sukarno sought to forge a consensus (citing the traditional practice of *gotong royong*, or 'mutual cooperation') among key elements in society. That this consensus drew all the contending factions and parties into the government did not necessarily contravene the ethics of democracy. However, Sukarno's insistence on the need for 'guidance' from above effectively meant the abandonment of Constitutional Democracy. Guidance was provided by a 'National Council', a body composed of various functional groups in society appointed by the President which shunned voting and made decisions by reaching a consensus. The Constituent Assembly was dissolved and government was conducted in the National Council in tandem with the military, which by this time had emerged as an important focus of political power. 'Guided Democracy' was born in collusion with the army in July 1959 and Sukarno announced that 'free-fight liberalism' and 'Western-style democracy' had failed.

In its place, a traditional model of authority based on manipulating patron–client relations was substituted. Sukarno projected himself as the *bapak* or 'father' who knew best how to run the country. The late Indonesian philosopher S. Takdir Alisjahbana noted that 'a salient point in the structure of Sukarno's Guided Democracy is the pre-condition that he is the only and absolute leader, not to be disturbed by councils, parties, nor by other personalities'.[29] In subsequent speeches Sukarno maintained this stress on leadership. 'The time has now arrived to declare clearly and unequivocally the Leadership of the Revolution', he thundered on 17 August 1961. Sukarno enshrined the position of leadership in a new political trinity, the so-called 'Re-So-Pim' which stood for Revolution, Socialism and Leadership, as an inseparable trinity. By becoming the Great Leader of the Revolution, Sukarno also insinuated his leadership of the querulous military. In the wake of Guided Democracy, Sukarno acquired other grand titles like 'Great Leader of the Workers', 'Father of the Proletariat', and so on.

In the process, the concept of leadership as absolute and unquestioned was reinjected into the Indonesian political context, from which it has yet to be removed. 'We have been independent for 50 years', remarked Islamic intellectual Nurcholis Madjid, 'but so far we have only experienced leadership under fathers of the nation'.[30] Sukarno was the father of independence. Suharto since the early 1980s has been dubbed the father of development.

Under Sukarno's paternal brand of leadership disagreement or opposition was frowned upon as not in keeping with the spirit of the 'family principle' of statehood. The system bore no relation to the Western-style constitutional democracy of the 1950s. Only the physical institutions of democracy were retained as empty symbols of representative government. In the end the system failed him, not so much because he could not wield power effectively, but because the direction in which he channelled this power – tilting at the major powers, inviting outside interference, attacking neighbouring countries, and running down the economy – eventually stirred the army to move against him. Yet because by this stage Sukarno had become president for life, the military's only recourse was to the traditional palace coup.

Sukarno's successor was Major General Suharto, a staff officer who had been a soldier since the 1940s and fought in the revolution against the Dutch. He rose to the presidency in the wake of a still not completely explained coup attempt launched on 30 September 1965 when elements of Sukarno's palace guard, among others, kidnapped and murdered six army generals in central Jakarta. The military stepped in to restore order, blaming the Indonesian Communist Party with its links to Sukarno. Sukarno was eased out of power, and the army replaced the civilian government, with Suharto at the helm.

Suharto further refined traditional elements of power and authority after becoming president in 1968. There was no return to Constitutional Democracy under President Suharto's New Order. Instead, the original 1945 Constitution was used. With 37 articles, the charter has been described as 'one of the shortest written constitutions in the world'.[31] Drawn up under the supervision of Dr Supomo, a traditionally-minded Javanese lawyer, the charter contains short clauses prescribing religious freedom and equality before the law. But unlike the longer, more detailed, 'Provisional' constitution that replaced it in 1950, the legal underpinning of these rights was not clearly spelled out.[32] Sukarno had reintroduced the 1945 constitution along with Guided Democracy in 1959. Suharto saw no reason to go back to the more democratic 1950 document, and the 1945 Constitution has remained in force ever since.

The uncertain and chaotic state of Indonesia in 1966 generated tremendous anxiety among minority groups. Indonesian Chinese and Christians (the two groups overlapped considerably) feared a Muslim backlash against them. The 30 September coup attempt appeared to unlock centrifugal forces inherent in Indonesia's ethnic and religious diversity, which could explain why Suharto was virtually given a mandate by the middle classes and the business community to trim political freedoms and focus on restoring economic and social stability. Riding a wave of elite support for making economic growth a priority over political development, political parties were further emasculated and eventually consolidated into three 'functional groups' which were not permitted to differ from the government over matters of policy and state ideology. Decree Number 6, 1968, vested the President with extraordinary powers to use whatever means necessary to secure the stability of the state – effectively empowering him to go beyond the limits of constitutional rule. This decree was only revoked in 1992.

Why has Suharto been able to legally hold unlimited power for so long? Unlike Sukarno, Suharto managed to innoculate society against destabilising political mobilisation and concentrate on constructive economic growth. Suharto's brand of leadership was fuelled by development and stability, rather than confrontation and revolution. Ultimately, this meant he could serve the ends of modernisation and progress yet at the same time wield power with impunity.

The cultural roots of how Suharto conceived the relationship between ruler and the ruled are not hard to trace. Suharto grew up in the shadow of the old Javanese kingdom of Martaram, steeped in the medieval palace culture of Jogyakarta. He spoke the Javanese language which still today is characterised by complex levels of speech determined by the status of who is being addressed. The Javanese language has no word which allows someone of high status to address someone of lower status. The word for 'thank you' can only be used when addressing someone of higher status. Thus gratitude flows from the lower levels of society upward – never down. Little wonder, perhaps, that early Indonesian nationalism, as reflected in the writing of Pramoedya Ananta Toer, was as preoccupied with how to dilute the stubborn aloofness of the traditional Javanese aristocracy, as it was with shaking off Dutch rule.[33]

Suharto has nurtured a political culture that represents the distillation of indigenous Javanese political instincts, or as some would have it 'neo-Javanism', where the emphasis is on the strict observance of hierarchy reinforced by patronage to maintain the harmony of society.[34] It is important to stress, however, that this aspect of the Javanese culture is specific to the court cities of Jogyakarta and Solo, nor does it bear much similiarity to other, more egalitarian cultures in Indonesia, like that of the Bataks of North Sumatra, or the Minangkabau of West Sumatra. Indonesia's immediate post-colonial elite, men like Hatta and Shajrir, tried but failed to match the liberal ideas they learned from Europe to the broader reality of Indonesian society. In the ensuing chaos of Sukarno's fall, establishing order became a priority. To do so, Suharto and his military partners fell back on their instincts and their rather parochial origins. Not coming from the Western-educated aristocratic elite groomed by the Dutch, these instincts were rooted more in traditional Javanese society, or at least how they perceived that society to be.

## FINESSING FEUDALISM: THE CONTEST FOR ABSOLUTE POWER IN MALAYSIA

In the neighbouring Malay peninsular, traditional forms of power and authority were preserved but modified by the colonial regime. The British in Malaya reduced the nine traditional Malay rulers of the peninsular states to pale eccentric shadows of their former feudal stature. British officials fully exploited the influence of the rulers over Malay society by preserving the institution of the Malay monarchy, embellishing it with the trappings of symbolic sovereignty, but actually reducing its political power. The new administrators made sure that the ruler was progressively isolated from his people. Ancient forms of popular access to the ruler through the chiefs and the *balai*, or public audience hall were restricted or done away with altogether:

> There might occasionally be a gathering in the *balai* to confer a title on the successor to a chieftanship or court office but the interplay, formal as it may have been, between ruler and royal court had lost its significance. Even the most impotent of rulers had been the apex, the 'organising principle', of Malay aristocratic life and also the symbol of the state to the general body of his subjects.[35]

Replacing the *balai* with garden parties in London helped erode traditional forms of representation and government built into the Malay monarchy. The monarchy was effectively fossilised which enhanced its feudal trappings, but at the same time allowed the more pluralistic social and political functions governing the relationship between ruler and subject to decay. Modified in this way the traditional Malay monarchy was left to be revived once the colonial intruders departed.

In 1946, the founders of Malaysia's United Malays National Organisation (UMNO – still the dominant political party) enlisted the monarchy as a symbol to promote Malay nationalism. This helped the Malays to recover their rulers with independence. But the traditional role the rulers played as the organising principle of Malay aristocratic life was lost. The British encouraged the sultans to acquire a taste for Earl Grey tea and tennis, which at once made them identify with the cultural trappings of British aristocracy remote from ordinary Malays. Moreover, the new organising principle for Malaysian society was a form of administration and justice left behind by the departing British which, following the British constitutional model, eschewed royal involvement in politics. Constitutionally detached from the political process, the Malay monarchy initially served as a useful symbol of Malay nationalism, tying Malay identity firmly to Islam and Malay culture as enshrined by the sultans. Ironically, the identification of Malays with their sultans to achieve modern nationalistic ends, allowed aspects of the sultan's feudal tradition to seep down into the Malay political arena. Decorations or *pingkat* awarded by royalty have become important symbols of status for the Malay political elite. Prime Minister Mahathir Mohamad is one of the most decorated of them all. And even though he sometimes publicly eschews being referred to by his honorific title *Datuk Seri*, few ordinary Malaysians have the temerity to refer to him by the more familiar 'Doc'.

For all his royal decorations, Mahathir himself increasingly felt bridled by the residual power and status of the sultans. Royal protocol always seats him, the ambitious leader of one of the region's successful nations, behind the sultans at public functions; the federal system left the rulers with annoying residual powers that included land, religion and matters of customary law, as well as complete legal immunity. The more confident the Malay political establishment was of its powers of patronage, the more uncomfortable it seemed to become with the social and economic status of the country's nine reigning sultans. The government's push for Malays to modernise their outlook on life – to become more technologically and economically oriented – sat awkwardly with the blind respect traditional Malay culture accorded the sultans. So did UMNO's quest for legitimacy as the pre-eminent guardian of Malay culture and interests. An initial attempt to cut the sultans down to size by amending the constitution in the early 1980s, failed because public sentiment was against Mahathir. But when Sultan Mahmood Iskandar ibni al-Marhum Sultan Ismail of Johor, a former King of Malaysia, allegedly flayed a school hockey coach in late 1992 the stage was set for a new round of confrontation between politicians and rulers.

Even a decade later, moving to curtail the power of the sultans was considered risky. But as it turned out, stripping the sultans of

their legal immunity by an act of parliament in 1993 had a cathartic effect on the Malay political elite. Their confidence stemmed
from the fact that the general public, though not totally in accord
with the move, were growing uncomfortable with the extent of
privilege enjoyed by the rulers. The public therefore stood by
while the last vestige of the sultans' power was removed. What
many feared, though, was that instead of erasing feudalism for
good, the changes merely transferred supreme power to Malay
politicians.

Mahathir and his brash young political deputies resented the
divided loyalty between state and the centre implied by the sultans' titular role in the federal system. Sultan Mahmood of Johor,
for example, presided over a notionally independent constitution
and a small private army. Now that the rulers had lost their legal
immunity, the fear was that the ground was prepared for the
greater concentration of power in the hands of Mahathir's United
Malays National Organisation.[36] And in the Malay political culture, where effective power must be absolute, the emasculation
of the rulers also cleared the way for commoners to take their
place as distributors of patronage. In the old days, one former
UMNO stalwart mused, there was accountability, a degree of
modesty among politicians, as well as concern about corruption.
'Look at them now', he said. 'They no longer worry about the
size of their houses, or number of their cars. Their attitude is so
what? who cares?'[37] Mirroring the days when the sultans used to
shop at Harrods and buy their baubles at the crown jewellers, a
local fashion designer in Kuala Lumpur told of how he was
welcomed at fashionable boutiques in Paris and Rome with champagne and limousine rides once he introduced himself as a Malaysian. When he was invited to sign their guest books, they read
like a roll call of the Malaysian political and business elite.[38]

To outsiders Malaysia's political system looks more pluralistic
and democratic; look closely and a carefully constructed system
of social and political control becomes evident. The Australian
academic Harold Crouch argues that the country's 'essentially
democratic political system' has been modfied by an 'entrenched
elite that took whatever steps were considered necessary to
ensure its continued control of the government'.[39] In addition
to the maintenance of a stringent internal security act allowing
detention without trial for a period of up to two years, there is
a constitutional provision enabling the government to declare a

state of emergency 'if the security or economic life of the Federation or any part thereof is threatened'.[40]

While few Malaysians would argue with the need for safeguards against incitement of racial hatred in Malaysia's plural society, the government has used these measures to deal with political opposition. In 1977, a Proclamation of Emergency was used to overthrow an opposition state government in the north-eastern state of Kelantan. In 1992, Jeffery Kittingan, the younger brother of Sabah's then chief minister, was detained without trial for two years on suspicion that he was plotting to take Sabah out of the Federation. Jeffery's brother, Pairin, led the United Sabah Party, which left the ruling coalition on the eve of the 1990 elections, and almost precipitated a defeat for Mahathir. The government takes care to invoke democracy and the rule of law whenever it deploys these legal mechanisms of state control. 'They confuse rule of law with rule *by* law', is how a Malaysian lawyer puts it.[41] A prominent Malaysian human rights lawyer argues that periodic amendments to the constitution and existing statutes 'have gradually curtailed the freedom of speech and information'.[42]

## INVENTING THE STRONG STATE: THE CASE OF SINGAPORE

Singapore had to invent a political culture. Ejected from the Malaysian Federation in 1965, this prosperous entrepôt mainly populated by overseas Chinese merchants found itself washed up in a sea of Malay and Muslim nationalism. The sources of Singapore's invention were colourfully eclectic. It all began with a group of British-educated, mostly Chinese, professionals who were caught up by the tide of nationalism sweeping Asia after the Pacific War. Led by a charismatic and intensely bright British-educated barrister by the name of Lee Kuan Yew, they helped win self-government for the island after 123 years of British colonial rule in 1959. Afterwards, there was an immediate demand for popular support, which this group did not have. Initially Lee and his People's Action Party turned to the communists with their mass appeal. The communists helped the PAP win power in the island's first elections, after which Lee realised that Marxism was not going to feed mouths and set up businesses. So he turned to neighbouring Malaya for inclusion in the planned multiracial Federation of Malaysia to ensure that Singapore could have access to a hinterland market. When the merger failed in 1965, Lee turned his back on democratic socialism. He opted instead for a strict and uncompromising style of government that prompted a US official in the 1970s to describe Singapore as 'the best run country in the world'.

Lee Kuan Yew is undoubtedly one of Southeast Asia's most successful leaders. A character of some complexity, he defies accurate interpretation. To most observers his pragmatic, flexible shepherding of Singapore through one economic phase to the next – always willing to adapt and change according to prevailing circumstances – presents a record rivalled by few other regional leaders. More recently Lee has apparently developed the firm conviction that Confucian Chinese values and a close but balanced relationship with modern China are crucial to Singapore's survival. The balance is provided by Singapore's close economic and security ties with the United States.

While it is easy to define Singapore's strategic position, it is less easy to find a genus for its politics. In the course of leading Singapore first to independence and then on to a meteoric economic ascent, Lee seemed to select social and political models as casually as a browser in a Sunday market. At each stage Lee defended the principles of the hour with a passion few could match. In the 1950s democratic socialism was needed to garner popular support. When the authorities were locking up anti-colonial strikers, Lee defended democratic society as one 'which allows the free play of ideas, which avoids revolution by violence because revolution by peaceful methods is allowed'. Later he condemned liberal politics as an unworkable formula for newly-developing Asian countries.[43]

What has ultimately emerged is a curious cross between the Leninist secret cell system and the Confucian Chinese Mandarinate. Opposition is muted, if not altogether muffled. Much like the Communist Parties of China and Vietnam, the PAP is led by a central executive committee elected by a few hundred selected party cadres. These few hundred cadres are recruited from the party's regular membership which is not widely known as the membership rolls are kept secret. Party proceedings are shrouded in secrecy. It was hard for Lee, as party secretary general, to be unseated. There are no open elections for the post and he alone selected the cadres and the central executive committee – who in turn elect the secretary general. The pope chooses the cardinals, and the cardinals elect the next pope.

Having said that, Singapore also does a very good impression of a modern civic society. It is almost a cliché to say that modern Singapore is run efficiently. Its educational and health standards are among the highest in the region, and perhaps exceed those in the United States. The republic's legal system is based on a British model – although political dissidents, like former Solicitor General Francis Seow would argue that it is administered less fairly.[44] Singapore boasts well-run public services, and an orderly urban administration. These are features which have attracted foreign multinationals to go beyond manufacturing and locate their regional corporate headquarters in the city state. In this respect Singapore has transformed a poor and unruly immigrant Chinese population into one that respects authority or pays for transgression through seemingly minor yet culturally humilating acts of penance. Hence convicted felons find their crimes published in the daily newspapers to shame them. Litterbugs are tasked to clear up public places wearing yellow suits so they can be clearly identified. Video-cameras installed in lifts detect spitters and urinators, and errant motorists are identified using hidden cameras. Edicts in the shape of by-laws or ordinances and humiliating punishment in the guise of community service; these faintly amusing Singaporean phenomena nevertheless betray the establishment's abiding faith in methods for imposing collective order and discipline by exploiting the cultural importance of face.

## DEMOCRACY THAI-STYLE

Thailand was never subject to colonial rule, but was constantly threatened by external powers. Thailand has therefore been forced to adapt its political culture to changing regional and international circumstances. The Thais of course have been shaping their culture in response to external influence ever since Chinese attempts to subjugate them in their ancestral hearth of Yunnan forced them to migrate southward into mainland Southeast Asia. The historian D.G.E Hall described the Thais 'as remarkable as assimilators as the Normans in Europe'.[45] They took elements of Chinese civilisation with which they were familiar, came into contact with Hinduism through the Khmers, and probably adopted Buddhism through trade. Despite its eclectic beginnings, Thai civilisation has proved to be enduring. A key factor was the assiduous cultivation of good ties with China. Foreshadowing Thailand's later diplomatic prowess, early Thai kings rarely neglected sending tribute to the Chinese emperor, and therefore fended off the traumatic invasion neighbouring Burma suffered. Recurring conflict with the neighbouring Burmese kingdom saw cities rise and fall, populations come and go. But the early system of administration established in the mid-fifteenth century survived more or less intact until the mid-nineteenth century.

Thailand's response to the arrival of the European was to play one ambitious trading power off against another. The strategy cleaved neatly with the intense commercial competition between English, Dutch and French trading interests in the seventeenth century and probably saved the country from colonial subjugation. But it also meant that along the way Thailand was forced to accept dealing with foreigners and their ways. At one stage in the reign of King Narai (1657–88), this meant coming close to accepting Christianity from the French. The lessons learnt proved useful when, in the modern period, Thailand fended off the full weight of Japanese imperial rule by capitulating. Postwar reprisals from the victorious allies were forestalled, though, by never having presented a formal declaration of war to the United States.

Throughout its history Thailand has preserved the monarchy which for over 700 years has been the apex of power and authority. The absolute monarchy was abolished in 1932, when reforming bureaucrats and soldiers forced a weak King to retreat behind a constitutional screen. But if the monarchy initially withdrew from the political arena, political circumstances in the late 1950s allowed a comeback when Field Marshal Sarit Thanarat, one of Thailand's more colourful military dictators, harnessed the royal family to support his regime. Sarit well knew that despite the events of 1932, ordinary Thai people never really stopped revering their King as a near deity. In the spiritual sense, the King continued to be the real source of legitimate power.

The painful separation of church and state experienced in Europe, makes it hard for Western observers to comprehend the unquestioned legitimacy of Asian royalty – which placed divine and worthy kings and their more secular constitutional successors above the political fray and therefore in the best position to determine the outcome of political conflict. The 1932 coup notionally deprived the monarchy of its absolute powers, but once political power was conferred on the bureaucracy it was not long before the formal compartments into which traditional Thai administration had been divided since the fifteenth century began competing for pre-eminence. In the ensuing struggle between the civil and military arms of government, the king emerged as the power-broker – a role so astutely played by the current monarch, King Bhumibol Adulyadej (who ascended the throne in 1946), that many contemporary observers fail to notice the direct parallel with the Thai monarchy's traditional role as the sole source of legitimate power.

The King's influence was first effectively brought to bear when students in Bangkok mounted mass demonstrations against military rule, demanding more democracy in October 1973. In a move foreshadowing his intervention almost two decades later, the King sided with the people, forcing the termination of the Thanom/ Phrapas regime and ushering in a civilian prime minister, Sanya Dharmasakti. The power-broking role played by the King has not always promoted democracy. In 1976, the King sided with the military when democracy tested the cohesion of the state. Addressing his people at the time, King Bhumibol rationalised his stand by asserting that the threat of communist insurgency called for support from the military: 'The Thai military has the most important role in the defence of our country at all time, ready always to carry out its duty to protect our country.'[46]

Over the last 25 years of coup and counter coup, the King became astute at playing one military faction off against another. Take the abortive coup of April 1981. The coup was instigated by a group of some fifty young officers who resented the power politics of their elders – which fostered favouritism and therefore hindered promotion. Typical of a 'young turk' military faction, they projected their frustration in idealised terms of a return to professional military principles to recover the army's *esprit de corps*. But when they launched a coup on 1 April, the King and Queen were able to evacuate the capital to the north-eastern provincial capital of Korat (also known as Nakhorn Ratchasima). From there, the incumbent Prime Minister, and former assistant army commander, General Prem Tinsulanond was able to supervise the military operation against the coup-makers. At the time, many Thais saw Prem's close palace connections and the King's move up to Korat – a traditional royal manoeuvre to combat insurrection – as the decisive factor crushing the coup. Professor Likhit Dhiravegin observed that these coup attempts failed, not only because of the lack of unity within the armed forces, but:

> also because of the fact that the most important power centre [meaning the throne] did not want to see the country torn apart by a violent power struggle ... and wanted instead to see a healthy development of the democratic process.[47]

Thailand's 'most important power centre' demonstrated this resolve once again in May 1992, when the world's attention was focused on the show of 'people's power' on the streets of Bangkok. It was the King's public castigation of army leaders in a televised audience on 20–1 May, which actually brought the army to a grinding halt and sent the soldiers back to their barracks. More recently, the King has deployed his knowledge and experience of political affairs to castigate politicians and criticise society for selfish material desires. King Bhumibol's astute but discrete political role in the latter part of his 50 year reign is perhaps best seen as a constant effort to balance the forces within the Thai political elite.

The role of the monarchy in the past three decades demonstrates how much of its former power has been recovered since 1932. With the demise of the absolute monarchy in 1932 this has effectively involved playing civilian bureaucrats off against military cliques. The precise ordering and composition of that elite may be what is changing rather than the political culture *per se*. Military influence in the political arena has waned since the Army's February 1991 intervention and its bloody aftermath. Younger officers leave the service early because of the perceived lack of opportunities for social and financial advancement, or they stay on for professional reasons only. Regional political and business interests find themselves in the ascendant and are trying to fashion a constitution which suits their specific interests – and more importantly wards off future military intervention. Now, they are running up against a Bangkok-centred business elite that boasts a less parochial brand of leadership.

Yet however more democratic Thailand becomes, it seems unlikely that the monarchy will not be called upon again to legitimise political coalitions and sanctify the government of the day. Indeed, the monarchy's sway cuts both ways, as the newly installed government of Prime Minister Banharn Silpa-archa found during its first month in office in mid-1995. In what Thai observers regarded as unprecedented comments from the throne on a sitting elected government, the King spoke his mind to remind the government of its frail legitimacy. 'The country's image is not particularly good', said the King, adding that instead of tackling the critical problem of Bangkok's traffic, 'They [the government] only talk, talk, and argue argue, argue.'[48]

These are occasions when the King appears to be speaking his mind. In August, when he criticised the Banharn government's handling of the traffic problem, he invoked his constitutional rights as a citizen; but few Thais take his words as anything less than a command – 'a heavenly blessing' as one of the chastised ministers put it. Oustiders may consider it inappropriate for a constitutional monarch to assert his influence over the political process. But for most Thais, the King's actions are far from anachronistic. In a society where the gulf between elite interests at the centre and the mass of rural people remains wide, it is seen as the moral duty of a good monarch to ensure good governance.

From the examples given above we can see that the political development of modern states in Southeast Asia has drawn, in an active sense, as much on pre-colonial tradition as it has on imported Western models. Ironically, the tendency of some colonial regimes to preserve those elements of indigenous political culture which enhanced control over their subjects, left intact the more rigid, authoritarian aspects of that culture for independent indigenous elites to recover. Why is this point so important to grasp? First because it helps us to understand the region in an indigenous context. But more importantly, perhaps, because this context offers a better guide to the future shape of these states.

Modernisation is a two-way street. While it is safe to say that the region's astonishing economic growth has followed many of the precepts of Western industrial development – and benefited from a considerable amount of Western capital and expertise – the full spectrum of social and political change is far too complex to ascribe solely to imported norms and values. One of the major factors overlooked in the analysis of how Southeast Asia has coped with the structural changes accompanying this growth, is the remarkable degree of cultural continuity. One aspect of this continuity most overlooked is the relationship between political leaders and society in Southeast Asia.

# Chapter 2

# *Deus ex impera*

*The emperor's speeches were remarkably kind, gentle, and comforting to the people, who had never heard his mouth form a harsh or angry word. And yet you cannot rule an empire with kindness.*

Ryszard Kapuscinski, The Emperor

Rarely has any journalist got close enough to Indonesia's President Suharto to question him. However, one intrepid foreign reporter managed to throw a question about Indonesia's democracy to the septuagenarian president as he was casting his vote in the June 1992 parliamentary elections. The fearless questioner asked whether the country's two opposition parties would be given a role in government if they won sufficient proportions of the popular vote. 'No sir', the president firmly replied, 'We have a different system here.'

In neighbouring Malaysia, the bicameral parliament is modelled closely on the British parliament at Westminster, right down to the silver mace that nestles in front of the be-gowned speaker. The country holds elections without fail every four or five years that are, by regional standards, considered free and fair. Given these similarities with the British system, this author asked the speaker of the Malaysian parliament, Tan Sri Zahir Ismail, why the Prime Minister only rarely attended parliamentary question time. One conspicuous difference between the House of Commons at Westminster and Malaysia's 192 seat *Dewan Rakyat* is the infrequent appearance of the majority leader. Government ministers generally leave their parliamentary replies to parliamentary secretaries and there are times that the government benches are almost deserted. Sometimes there is barely a quorum in the chamber because politicians find it more congenial to discuss politics in the member's tea room. The speaker's rationale for this casual approach to parliamentary democracy was that government leaders are far too busy running the country to attend parliament. And besides, he said, why should the Prime Minister, Mahathir Mohamad, answer questions from the opposition since the two-thirds majority he commands is proof enough of the confidence he enjoys among the people.

One of the striking features about the politics of modern Southeast Asia is how openly political leaders flaunt its democratic shortcomings. Their self-assurance, and the longevity of their regimes fly in the face of those who argue that economic success begets political change. These strong leaders may once have relied upon constitutional support for legitimacy. But now, basking in the reflection of their achievements, they merely observe the protocols and go through the motions of democracy. They no longer act as if the paraphernalia of democratic government are really needed. They preside over systems which, in the words of a retired Indonesian general 'look like democracies on the outside, but function differently within'.[1]

Yet, the longer men like Suharto and Mahathir stay in power, the more secure their position seems. Local popular perceptions measure their success in terms of stability and material progress which cloud memories of how they may have abused their power. In the mid-1990s, Indonesians tended to think of Suharto as the leader who has raised per capita incomes from a meager $75 in 1966 to around $1,000, rather than as a general who incarcerated thousands of political prisoners on a remote island in the 1970s, or who may have ordered the extrajudicial killings of criminals in the mid-1980s. Mahathir's sweep of 162 out of 192 parliamentary seats in the April 1995 elections suggested that voters were unperturbed by the detention without trial of key opposition figures in 1987. 'Make no mistake, this can only be interpreted as a thundering endorsement of Mahathir and no one else. He's got the mandate to lead the country into the twenty-first century', observed a Malaysian university lecturer inclined towards the opposition after the election.[2]

Political parties, elections, parliament and the cabinet all seem to be treated as casually as theatre props by Suharto. In his 1988 autobiography, Suharto dwelt at length on the first elections of his rule in 1971 as a symbol of democracy. Barely a sentence was devoted to the actual results. Mahathir Mohamad appears to have a constricted view of political freedom. According to Mahathir, the opposition's role is one of 'constructive criticism and engagement, not shouting your head off'.[3] What defines 'shouting your head off' in a notionally free society is, of course, hard to construe. (Malaysians still require a permit to hold legal political gatherings of more than five people.)

Malaysia's Prime Minister Mahathir Mohamad has periodically detained his opponents, including the leader of the opposition in parliament, Lim Kit Siang, in 1987 and stands accused of eroding freedom of speech and the independence of the judiciary. Yet only a small minority of Malaysians have questioned these actions. In the 1990 elections, Chinese voters did register a token opposition to Mahathir's ruling coalition in voting for the opposition Democratic Action Party at the federal level. Their strategy was apparently to ensure that government could be questioned in parliament to check corruption in high places, rather than to question Mahathir's leadership. The same voters made sure of their security closer to home by returning government candidates in the state assemblies.[4] In the April 1995 general election, Mahathir's National Front coalition won 64 per cent of the popular vote in a crushing defeat for the opposition. Apparently, voters felt there wasn't much need even for an effective token opposition in parliament, as the DAP saw the number of its seats halved from twenty to nine.

Of all Southeast Asians, Malaysians are perhaps the most accustomed to the notional pluralism of democratic institutions. People are represented by elected representatives in parliament and elections are held regularly. Yet, Malaysians are also among the most collectively oriented when it comes to politics – preferring to vote along communal lines, consciously preserving a system that confers more economic and political power on the Malay community and its small clique of political bosses. This appears to be part of a racial bargain that puts communal harmony and mutual prosperity above competitive or democratic urges. Many Malaysians consider that the harmony of their fragile plural society hinges on strong, uncompromising leadership. When asked if he ever envisaged a Chinese party coming to power, the Chinese leader of a small pro-government party in Malaysia explained: 'We prefer strong leadership. A strong leader won't succumb to racial sentiment or religious dogma.'[5]

In Thailand, popular perceptions of how best the interests of the majority are served by the political leadership tend to vary. A period of strong, uncompromising leadership, demonstrated by a succession of military strongmen from the 1950s through to the 1970s, generated calls for more democracy. It was also a time of economic hardship. Thais have experienced a gentler, more democratic form of government under two elected prime ministers since the late 1980s, and enjoyed the fruits of rapid economic growth. But remarkably, by the mid 1990s with the infrastructure of Bangkok coming apart at the seams, Thais were clamouring for the return of firm, decisive leadership.

Opinion polls ahead of the July 1995 elections in Bangkok consistently showed that people looked back fondly on the two short governments of non-elected prime minister Anand Panyarachun. 'To business people and professionals like myself, Anand showed leadership and took initiatives', commented a middle class university lecturer in Bangkok.[6] Anand was appointed prime minister in the wake of a military coup in 1991, without a popular mandate. However, the former diplomat and bureaucrat turned businessman combined two qualities Thais admire: ability and integrity. Gathering a group of technocrats around him, he introduced economic reforms and set about proscribing the military's role in politics. His elected successor, Chuan Leekpai, a lawyer from southern Thailand, rode a wave of popularity because of his pledge to institutionalise democracy and the rule of law. Two and a half years later Chuan's government fell before an opposition censure vote, backed by popular opinion, which perceived his government as weak and indecisive.

Anand showed leadership. His critics say that he has an authoritarian streak. Yet, his administration is fondly remembered, and even yearned for again. Endless bickering among the fragile elected coalitions that succeeded Anand has made for a lively and pluralistic parliament, but has not solved Bangkok's traffic woes. Urban gridlock is now beginning to threaten prosperity. The Thai Farmers Bank now estimates that Bangkok's traffic chaos shaves off 2.7 per cent in potential GDP growth annually. Bangkok people have grown weary of politicians who bicker in parliament and talk about the problems of their rural constituencies, while no decisions are taken to alleviate the problems in the capital. Speaking ahead of July 1995 elections, a political party leader suggested that: 'In the next election, people will vote for the quality of leadership rather than the quality of democracy.'[7] Apparently, Thais had forgotten what excessively strong leadership can do to a democracy not yet firmly anchored in institutional terms. The election brought to power a conservative coalition led by the Chart Thai Party. Many members of the new government had been accused of corruption, or sided with the military junta brought down in May 1992.

What explains this acquiescence to power, specifically the power of leadership? Manipulation of the electoral system through vote buying tells part of the story, at least in the Thai context. The cost of the July 1995 elections, in terms of money spent on vote buying, is thought by Thai Farmers Bank to have exceeded US$ 8 million. Image-building around the symbolism of strong leadership also plays a role. For, as we shall see, respect for strong leadership inherent in Southeast Asian societies has more to do with paternalistic traditions of authority than with any modern concepts of popular sovereignty. For in Southeast Asia it is not always easy to detect 'the endless and elusive process of calling power into account'.[8]

Leadership is of course indispensable in any political system. In Western liberal democracies, strong leadership is regarded more ambivalently, both as the *sine qua non* of effective government, and an invitation to tyranny. Italy's fascist dictator Benito Mussolini made the trains run on time but persecuted his people. Ultimately the Italian people preferred late trains. In Southeast Asia strong leaders like Indonesia's President Suharto have jailed political opponents and sanctioned the extrajudicial killings of alleged criminals. According to Amnesty International as many as 350 political detainees were still held in prisons throughout Indonesia in 1994. In his ghost-written autobiography, Suharto described the extrajudicial killings of alleged criminals as 'shock therapy' that was necessary 'so that the general public would understand that there was still someone capable of taking action . . . '.[9] In neighbouring Malaysia, successive prime ministers have enhanced their executive powers while curbing the independence of the judiciary and the freedom of the press.[10] Yet even considering these curbs on freedom, the brand of strong leadership exercised by men like Suharto and Mahathir apparently enjoys forbearance for the time being.

Strong leadership has been a key factor undergirding Southeast Asia's remarkable political stability. But untrammelled executive authority is also blamed for the widespread prevalence of corruption and woeful lack of initiative in these societies. Experienced foreign business executives in the region reflect this ambivalent view: complaining about the lack of political freedom that stifles creativity and breeds corruption, but agreeing that without strong leadership nothing would ever get done. Strong leadership is considered both an asset and a liability to states in the region and as such is one of the most intriguing aspects of indigenous political culture.

In this chapter we will ask why this seems to be the case, by looking principally at Indonesia's President Suharto and Malaysia's Prime Minister Mahathir Mohamad. Suharto, who became President in 1968, and Mahathir who succeeded Prime Minister Hussein Onn in 1981, are the longest ruling leaders in the region. In different ways both men have combined harsh and uncompromising attitudes towards political freedom with remarkably liberal economic policies. They are good examples of strong leaders who have modernised their countries while wielding power through a blend of modern and traditional ways. In the terminology of the Indonesian and Malay culture, they are *Bapak*, an honorific title which connotes a wise but powerful father figure. Mahathir has yet to formally acquire the title of *Bapak* earned by Malaysia's founding Prime Minister, Tunku Abdul Rahman, but in 1983 Suharto was formally proclaimed *Bapak pembangunan*, the father of development. The mid-1980s also marked the beginning of a long period of minimal challenge to the style of his rule. Becoming a *Bapak* means acquiring an aura of respect and legitimacy which says much about the culture of leadership. What are the historical antecedents of this culture of leadership, and what if anything do they tell us about the style of contemporary leaders in Southeast Asia?

## THE HIDDEN LINK: TRADITIONAL MONARCHY AND MODERN LEADERSHIP

Southeast Asia did not acquire a model of leadership from the West in the same way it inherited parliaments and constitutions. The culture of strong leadership in Southeast Asia evolved out of indigenous models of kingship. Most polities in the region were kingdoms at one time or another. Indeed, Southeast Asia remains one of the last bastions of monarchy. Brunei, Cambodia, Malaysia and Thailand constitute a good portion of the world's remaining kingdoms. Perhaps more importantly, all these monarchs wield considerably more influence than their constitutional cousins in Europe and Japan. In Brunei, the Sultan is also Prime Minister and actually rules the tiny oil-rich sultanate. Until 1994, the Malaysian King could still withhold assent from a government bill and prevent it from becoming law. In Thailand, as we have seen, the King is the single most important unifying factor in the political firmament. He has discreetly helped resolve political conflicts, and has more recently directly chided a sitting elected government.

The ideal of the leader as a 'father of the people', the exemplary centre of the realm and source of all moral authority and the well-being of the state, has its origins in traditional Southeast Asian kingship. The central feature of the monarchy in premodern Southeast Asia was its sacral power. 'In older Southeast Asian belief', writes Anthony Reid, 'all power was spiritual. The powerful chief or ruler was the one who best controlled the cosmic forces.'[11] The notion of the divine king in Southeast Asia possibly developed as a means of expressing the abstraction of religion. The crude stone symbols of early God cults inspired rituals which conferred tangible form on these early religions. From here it was a short step to the conferment of divine status on the community leader, as the mediator, or communicator, between divine and profane worlds. In the Javanese language the words meaning God and Lord (*pengirran* and *gusti*) in the religious domain, are also applied to the royal courts where they mean prince and princely lord.

With the growth of state power which, fuelled by trade and commerce, reached its apogee in the fifteenth and sixteenth centuries, came the elevation of the monarch as the symbolic embodiment of the state. As the central focus of the state, the monarch was both the spiritual and temporal source of harmony. Without his spiritual powers, chaos and darkness threatened. Without his power to organise corvée labour – by demanding the services of all able bodied men for a specific period – the hydraulic agricultural regime would suffer and armies could not be raised. In modern Southeast Asian societies this moral interpretation of legitimate leadership has arguably been passed on, surviving in a cultural context, and has bred an innate acceptance of being subject to legitimate leadership without questioning its strength or accountability.

In the temporal context, the monarch was also the chief merchant of the state, a monopolist *par excellence*. In Thailand, state control over trade was established as far back as the fifteenth century and was formally enforced until the middle of the nineteenth century. As the state's principal trader, the Thai king amassed huge profits from the sale of imports. He also made huge sums on goods secured as tribute from outlying vassal states which were consigned to merchants for sale and export. This synergy between the spiritual and real world functions of the ruler meant that once ordained, it not only became difficult to question the leader's wisdom or right to rule on spiritual grounds, but also pretty hard to match his command of resources.

The role played by strong leaders has perhaps had the greatest impact on socio-cultural attitudes towards power and authority. What is often taken as a submission to leadership bred by the weight of authority, may stem from a popular conception of how leaders should be regarded. Revolting against the king in precolonial times meant violating religious as well as political sanctions and therefore interfering with the harmony of the state. It is a theme that runs through one of the most influential literary works of the Asian world, the *Bhagwad Gita*:

> It is indeed here on the battlefield, Arjuna, that you are faced with the most crucial and difficult decision a *ksatria* knight must make. Is it right to take drastic measures to oppose tyranny and despotism, which frequently appear in the guise of the more noble values so dear to your heart? Or, on the other hand, should a true knight hesitate to combat tyranny simply because he is bewitched by their guise of nobility and kinship?[12]

Ambivalent attitudes towards those who question legitimate authority are a marked feature of the region's political culture. In Malaysia, intellectuals still debate whether the actions of a fifteenth-century Malay prince, Hang Jebat, who rebelled against the authority of the Sultan of Malacca were justified. In Indonesia, rebellion or usurping power in any way carries a negative connotation, associated either with banditry or religious fanaticism. In the official accounts of the 30 September 1965 coup attempt which brought down the country's first president,

Sukarno, there is no suggestion that the army's moves to restore order were aimed at overthrowing Sukarno. In fact, Suharto and his clique waited almost three years before effecting a formal transfer of power. Even in the contemporary Indonesian political context, an individual who questions authority is usually described as 'mentally unstable'. Confronted by one or two Indonesian demonstrators in a crowd outside the Indonesian embassy while on a visit to Germany in early 1995, Suharto's angry response was to consider them 'insane'.

However, it would be wrong to assume that the semi-divine monarchs of pre-colonial Southeast Asia enjoyed untrammelled power. In fact, the extent of their writ may have been rather more circumscribed than early European observers of 'oriental despotism' presumed. Often the strength and power of a monarch depended as much on the strength and virtue of his personality, as on the mechanism for wielding power at his disposal. A good modern example would be Thailand's King Bhumibol Adulyadej, who celebrates 50 years on the throne in 1996. The throne he ascended in 1946 was still in the throes of recovering from the constitutional revolution of 1932, which abolished the absolute monarchy. It is not easy to discuss the politics of monarchy in contemporary Thailand. However, many Thais would privately agree that set against the legacy of 1932, the strength and popularity of the current monarch is very much a reflection of his energetic dedication to duty. The King's popularity, constantly reinforced by his tireless dedication to the country's development, has allowed him to intervene in times of crisis and not draw criticism or any suggestion that he has stepped beyond the bounds of his constitutional role.

The limits to the power of traditional authority allude to important ways in which modern authoritarian successors are also limited in the exercise of their power. In one of the earliest records of Thai monarchy, the late thirteenth century 'Ramkham-haeng' inscription, the King of the early Thai Kingdom of Sukho-thai was reported to be accessible to his subjects in the following manner:

> He has hung a bell in the opening of the gate over there: if any commoner in the land has a grievance which sickens his belly and gripes his heart, and which he wants to make known to his ruler and lord, it is easy; he goes and strikes the bell

which the king has hung there; King Ramkhamhaeng ... hears the call; he goes and questions the man, examines the case, and decides it justly for him.[13]

Was this merely an early example of political doublespeak? Would a revered and powerful leader like Ramkhamhaeng, who claimed vassal states as far south as the Malay peninsular, really 'go' and question his supplicants? Was he really that powerful?

The historian David Wyatt speculates that early Thai society was much more horizontally stratified than in later epochs when a strict hierarchy evolved around the court and its attendant bureaucracy.[14] The Japanese scholar Yoneo Ishii speculates that Thai kings enjoyed only partial control over their subjects. From his intriguing study of rice-cultivation in medieval Thailand, he discovered that the scope for state intervention in agriculture was constrained by the unusually fertile environment of the Thai central flood plain, which gave common people more autonomy over the means of production by not relying on state-sponsored irrigation works. This, he says, was something less than the despotic 'hydraulic societies' described by Karl Witfogel in ancient Mesopotamia. Assured agrarian subsistence enabled communities to escape dependence on the central government.[15] Strong traditions of local autonomy are also found in Vietnam, where the saying went that the emperor's writ stopped at the village gate.

Royal power was also proscribed by the difficulty of enforcing allegiance upon outlying vassal states, which meant that territorial boundaries remained fluid until the improvement of infrastructure and communications in the nineteenth century. Travellers often found that passports issued by the central government in, say, Pagan (the Burmese capital), or Ayudhya and later Bangkok in Thailand, were ineffective unless sanctioned by local warlords. Territorial control and even the measure of authority over individual 'citizens' was rather vaguely defined in the pre-colonial history of these states. In other words, the tradition of despotism ascribed to the early political culture of Southeast Asia was much exaggerated. As the historian Anthony Reid aptly surmised:

> The exalted rhetoric of Southeast Asian rulers was always in tension with the tenuousness of their power base.[16]

So while there was no formal social contract between the ruler and the ruled, no ruler wielded absolute power. It could be that as society became less influenced by Hinduistic notions of the sacral power of monarchs (a development prompted by the arrival of populist religions including Islam and Theravada Buddhism), the monarchs themselves had to rely more on their 'personal ability – military as well as moral prestige – and economic wealth'.[17] What has often confused the outside observer is the sustained importance of symbolic power. Pre-modern rulers maintained their authority using the tools of culture and religion. Power was turned into an aspect of collective morality and identity – enabling rulers to justify their rule in the name of tradition and religion. The traditional ruler's actual power may have been tenuous, but for society it was important for the ruler to uphold an image of power to fulfil his other-worldly role as the focus of moral and cosmic order. Perhaps this helps explain why in contemporary Southeast Asian politics, appearances are everything.

The model of power and authority derived from the monarchy in Southeast Asia possesses one important and enduring asset. Because leadership carries moral weight, society needs less convincing of its legitimacy in a temporal context. Modern leaders in the post-colonial period have translated the moral ingredients of traditional leadership into the contemporary jargon of politics. Following the nationalist struggle, with its vision of freedom from tyranny, they added 'visions' of development and fully-attained social harmony, usually envisaging a prosperous arcadia in a not too immediate future – the implication being that once the vision is sanctified, so also is the leadership that conveys the vision. Indonesia has long-term development plans lasting 25 years, Malaysia's Mahathir launched an ambitious plan for the future in 1992 which he called 'Vision 2020'. Not only do these visions of nationhood strengthen the legitimacy of modern leaders in a temporal sense, they also imply a degree of moral control over the people that is not too distant from the ancient concept of the God-King or *devaraja* as the 'exemplary centre' of the realm.

## IN THE SHADOW OF MODERN *DEVARAJAS*

The survival of traditional Southeast Asian monarchy is most striking in the case of Thailand. King Bhumibol inherited a throne in 1946 that had barely survived the upheaval of 1932 which brought an end to the absolute monarchy. During the brief reign of Bhumibol's elder brother, who was a minor when he was crowned, the throne endured a period of infringed sovereignty under the Japanese during the Pacific War. The weak throne enhanced the power of Thailand's political elite, and the young King's absence from Thailand for the first four years of his reign suggested an insecure position. By the 1970s, however, King Bhumibol had restored much of the Thai throne's former prestige – and power – if not formally, then through popular respect. Some historians attribute this revival of royal influence to the machinations of military politicians who harnessed the monarchy to legitimise their political power. But there can be no doubt that King Bhumibol's own astuteness played a major role. From the start of his reign he deployed the prestige of the monarchy to good effect, impressing foreigners and Thais alike with his dedication to duty and concern for the country's development.

Modern Cambodia has witnessed a similar revival of monarchy with traces of an absolute tradition. In the aftermath of the Cambodian peace settlement and democratic elections in 1993, King Norodom Sihanouk was described as 'the only figure revered by all sides in Cambodia, and the key to peace and stability in a country now enjoying a tenuous peace after 13 years of bloody civil war ... '.[18] Within a year of his reascending the throne in August 1993, King Sihanouk was holding traditional mass audiences with the people (*savanaka cheahmoireastr*). These royal audiences notionally offered ordinary Cambodians the chance to present petitions to their King. Potentially this enabled the King to bypass the squabbling politicians in the governing coalition – something King Sihanouk showed little inclination to do in a serious way. Remarkably enough, a local pro-government newspaper commented that the mass audiences 'served to mark the return of the *Devaraja* as the all-important figure in a Buddhist polity'.[19]

Where royal power and authority has been eroded, or extinguished altogether, there has been no rush to install popularly-elected heads of state as the best expression of democratic government. Executive authority developed in place of the monarchy has often acquired distinctly monarchical characteristics. Thus while it is tempting to consider Indonesia's government as army dominated, it might be more accurate to concur with the Dutch anthropologist Neils Mulder that:

in spite of election rituals, the current president has styled himself more and more after the Javanese sultans of old, initiating a kind of monarchical control that legitimates the claim to constituting the exemplary centre of the realm, which thus also justifies the attempt to exercise moral control of the population.[20]

One significant feature of this kind of leadership is the attempt it makes to fit both modern and ancient models of authority. President Suharto follows the country's constitution to the letter. He appears before an elected national assembly, presents budgets, presides over monthly cabinet meetings, and holds elections once every 5 years. From a distance, the president of the republic is a model constitutional chief executive. Closer scrutiny of these modern political institutions, however, reveals almost no system of checks and balances against the abuse of executive power. The national consultative assembly elected once every 5 years is packed with government nominees, and all candidates have to be carefully screened. Quinquennial elections are stage managed by the government-backed Golkar Party, which ensures that the country's 4 million government civil servants vote for Golkar.[21]

Now take a closer look at President Suharto. Although apparently living in a modest one-storey bungalow in a leafy suburb of downtown Jakarta, the humble facade masks an extensive complex of rooms and courtyards which extends back almost two blocks. A visit to the village of his birth on the outskirts of the royal capital of Jogyakarta reveals a village residence mimicking the layout of an old Javanese 'kraton' or palace. He had a large family mausoleum built near his birthplace in Central Java. Costing around US$ 1 million, the tomb emulated the custom of Javanese royalty who are buried on hill-tops.[22] Also in the tradition of the old sultans, Suharto is rarely seen making policy publicly. His ministers troop out of the president's simple wood-panelled office – austere, but for a curious gold-plated telephone – and reveal what, 'in his wisdom', the president has 'revealed' or 'ordered'. When he talks directly to the people his manner is paternalistic to the point of condescension. He once told a gathering that people were complaining so much they were forgetting the virtue of 'gratitude'.[23]

There is no denying the stultifying intellectual deficit this kind of leadership has imposed on Indonesian officials. No one likes to take initiatives and everything is referred up. The more power Suharto has accumulated, the less willing his ministers are to cross him. It has even become difficult for advisers to advise him: no one wants to be the harbinger of bad news. The fear driving this reticence is not a product of Suharto's repressive powers, but more a function of the remarkable concentration of patronage in his hands. Indonesian officials are haunted by the prospect of losing status. Like courtiers in a medieval court, Suharto's ministers vie for the president's ear; and when they have it, mutter the political equivalent of sweet nothings. In an earlier study of Suharto's power, this author argued that among Suharto's key talents has been his ability to defuse threats to his rule and then mostly co-opt his opponents. Suharto's command of the resources required to buy off political challenges is far greater than anybody else's.

Strong leadership in Indonesia implies power over resources – the power to dispense favours. There is always the fear that dissent will leave the dissenter cut off from the system – out of the resource loop. No one else will help you if the leader has cut you off. There is no recourse through the courts or parliament. When the former youth and sports minister Abdul Ghaffur was inexplicably dropped from the cabinet in 1988, he felt very much out of the loop. The hapless Ghaffur spent the next 5 years in the political wilderness. He even went to the length of writing a sycophantic biography of Suharto. The president rewarded him with a newspaper editorship.

The power of patronage flowing from the leadership can have remarkable effects on people opposed to the leadership. One of Suharto's oldest and most bitter opponents is former armed forces commander General Abdul Haris Nasution. Nasution is credited with being the chief strategist of Indonesia's guerrilla campaign against the Dutch during the 1945–9 revolutionary war. Considered one of the fathers of the Indonesian army, Nasution narrowly missed being rounded up and murdered on the night of 30 September 1965. His survival made him the highest ranking officer in the struggle to restore order. Yet Nasution inexplicably never stepped forward to fill the power vacuum. Possibly this was a tactical reluctance – Suharto was also bashful about assuming power; it took him 3 years before he was proclaimed president in 1968. At any rate, Nasution opposed the way Suharto and his clique seemed bent on brushing aside what little was left of

Indonesia's democracy. They ended up as bitter opponents, with Nasution consigned to quiet retirement.

For opposition figures and senior officers in the army disenchanted with Suharto, Nasution became a beacon of hope as well as a source of ideas. They would quietly visit his modest little house in central Jakarta and talk about politics. Almost a quarter of a century later, Suharto apparently decided the time had come for a reconciliation. The man who had staunchly opposed Suharto from the same modest house where he had almost met his death, was now summoned to a gathering of senior army officers at the Merdeka Palace in central Jakarta in late 1993. At first Nasution was defiant. He came armed with a petition. But just as Nasution was about to produce his list of grievances, Suharto excused himself, and did not return. Nasution left a bitter man, perhaps most of all because he knew the game Suharto had played. He was rehabilitated. He was now shaded by the umbrella of power again. He could never be critical about Suharto in quite the same way, as this would appear unseemly and ungrateful.[24]

For the business community, Suharto's firm leadership represents stability. Strong leadership offers entrepreneurs a stable platform on which to build prosperity. Many of them are Indonesian Chinese who are insecure about their rights and privileges before the law and in society; an element of power that is unaccountable to law ironically offers them more security. Perhaps that is why the Malaysian Chinese are among Mahathir's staunchest allies, and why Thailand's Chinese community traditionally drew close to the monarchy. Anthony Reid points out that traditional rulers in sixteenth-century Southeast Asia, relied extensively on foreigners because they posed no threat to their power as they were excluded from the polity.[25]

The tradition survives in the form of the close ties between overseas Chinese entrepeneurs, always vulnerable to bouts of resentment from the indigenous population, and the leadership in most states of the region. Their inherent insecurity also explains why there was more nervousness than relief in the Indonesian business community when the late 1980s saw political issues debated more openly and the succession question was raised. Talking about succession made the business community nervous. 'People are interested in stage-managing the succession because they are not sure the masses can be controlled', suggested a young liberal politician in late 1990. He saw the middle classes favouring a de-coupling of politics from the masses and less support for the idea of a full democracy. Instead he predicted that what they wanted from the succession was 'a responsive and friendly leadership'.[26] As in the medieval period, absolutism in modern Southeast Asia tends to draw strength from the pluralistic nature of commerce.

In Malaysia, where the Western-style constitution made politics off limits to the traditional Malay sultans, the Malay political elite has adopted the political jargon of absolute monarchy. The term for civil government is *kerajaan* (literally 'of the King'), people are expected to respect its *kedaulatan* (sovereignty) and pay it *setia* (loyalty or homage). Since recovering from a perilous challenge to his power in 1987, Mahathir's leadership has been more or less unquestioned. Not just on the basis of his mandate from the UMNO party, which holds party elections every three years, but more obviously from the popular legitimacy he derives from the economic growth his government has presided over.

Malaysia has experienced growth rates over 8 per cent for over a decade. Growth and prosperity offer the kind of security to people they seem unwilling to gamble with at the ballot box. Despite accusations of gerrymandering and unfair treatment of the opposition in the media, there is no arguing about the margin of victory Mahathir achieved in the 1995 election. Having seen his Democratic Action Party lose 11 of their seats in parliament, Malaysia's opposition leader Lim Kit Siang said that 'he accepted the people's verdict'. Tempting as it is to consider the landslide as a rational verdict, it could also be considered as the recognition of Mahathir's leadership as distinct from the strength of his party – a form of moral legitimacy transcending the electoral process and harking back to the days of the Malay sultanate.

Rather less successfully in Burma, the ruling military junta known as the State Law and Order Restoration Council, is struggling to achieve this traditional form of legitimacy – without resorting to the ballot box. Ignoring a generally free and fair election in 1990 won by a civilian coalition, the Burmese army set up the ruling council of senior officers and promised to draw up a new constitution and political system at a later date. While the army does not lack the tools of repression to keep the populace cowed – Human Rights Watch/Asia, a US based human rights organisation, estimates that 1,000 political prisoners were held in Burmese jails in mid-1995 – the chief concern seems to be to establish legitimacy by promoting prosperity.

For Burma's ruling generals, development and foreign investment are considered more important goals than granting political freedom to the population. In their eyes, a wealthier population will be more interested in accumulating more wealth than in holding political opinions. The priorities are quite strikingly counterpoised. On the one hand the military junta is prepared to allow foreign companies to own 100 per cent of their subsidiaries in Burma and play the black market; yet ordinary Burmese can be jailed for up to 4 years for handling foreign currency and are told that modernisation of the political system must wait. While foreign businessmen generally look upon Burma as a country with significant potential as an emerging market, and tend to downplay the brutality of the regime, ordinary Burmese continue to be questioned by military intelligence officials when they meet with foreigners.

Clearly the SLORC considers that, following the example of Indonesia's military regime, political legitimacy will grow out of economic success rather than the ballot box. In this sense, one of the more significant and effective statements made by Burmese democratic leader Daw Aung San Suu Kyi on her release from house arrest in July 1995 was that foreign investors should not 'rush' into Burma. Yet even the US-based human rights organisation, Human Rights Watch/Asia aired doubts about the effectiveness of her plea. Many commentators saw her release as a measure of the SLORC's confidence and ability to control the country. In a report published shortly after her release in July, the organisation said it was

> difficult . . . to know whether the release of Daw Suu will lead to an improvement or lead only to further entrenchment as the SLORC achieves its main aim of increased international investment and economic aid and, as a result, finds less and less need to heed the calls from the international community.

It has been suggested that the evil genius of totalitarian leadership lies in its profound awareness that human personality cannot tolerate moral isolation, and that offering membership of a community is the key to maintaining absolute power. It was precisely this ability to obviate questioning of the system by convincing individuals to fear existence without the system, which many thought made the Soviet Union under Communist Party rule self-perpetuating. Its downfall, the critics now say, was economics – the inability of that system to turn a profit in the global market-place. In Southeast Asia, authoritarian models of power thrive precisely because they guarantee a profit. Perhaps no better example of this can be found in contemporary Malaysia.

## MAHATHIR MOHAMAD: FINESSING MORAL AUTHORITY

The executive offices of Malaysia's United Malays National Organisation (UMNO) occupy the top two floors of a thirty-six storey tower known as the World Trade Centre in the heart of Kuala Lumpur. Here on the thirty-sixth floor, usually on the first Wednesday of every month, Malaysian Prime Minister Datuk Seri Mahathir Mohamad holds a meeting of his ruling party's supreme council. He presides over the meeting from an oversized swivel chair set at the end of a long hardwood table. Behind the chair hangs a portrait of himself making a speech, flanked on either side by the flags of all nine Malaysian states. Contrasting with the idealised heroic image of Mahathir on the canvas, the real Mahathir slouches, languidly playing with a pen as he allows the chair to swivel left and right. He wears a half-smile that comes across as an expression of contempt for his least favourite pro-fession (after lawyers): the fourth estate. 'So, any questions?', he asks after a making a brief statement. With a reverence verging on the sycophantic, the assembled reporters politely tender their questions. Mahathir's responses are also polite, but terse. The overall effect is to convey a sense of impatience. He wears the expression of a young man in a hurry to get things done, to move on to the next job. His bright, constantly darting eyes are not at all the eyes of a man in his late sixties who has had heart bypass surgery. Of political writers, he recently coined the term *Pelacur tulis*, which translates from the Malay as 'Whore writers'. In the presence of Malaysia's leader for the past 14 years, it is easy to forget that he holds the office of Prime Minister, that he is not the titular head of state, or that he is accountable to his cabinet, parliament and his party.

In a short story entitled 'Piem', Malaysian writer Shahnon Ahmad parodied the national political scene as a long play in which there were many roles, but none of any significance except

for the central figure of 'Piem'. 'There were those', Shahnon
wrote, 'who criticised the play for being a one man show, even
though there were many parts.' Using direct and sometimes
coarse language, the story ends with the ugly demise of 'Piem' at
the hands of the other actors, who finally realise that they –
rather than 'Piem'– have the most important role in the drama.[27]
It isn't hard to detect the object of Shahnon's parody. Mahathir
is popularly known as 'PM', short for Prime Minister. The title
conveys as much power and status in the contemporary Malaysian
context, as 'President' might do in a Republic. Indeed, Mahathir's
actual powers would make many kings and presidents envious.
He is concurrently Prime Minister and Home Minister, which
gives him overall control of the police and the civil service.

Shahnon Ahmad's parody crudely captures the essence of the
culture of power in modern Malaysia. Mahathir's power verges
on the absolute: he commands total control over a political party
that is the most powerful element in a multiparty coalition that
holds a healthy two-thirds majority in parliament. He has been
described as 'a reluctant swing man charting the route to greater
democratic openness. While he valued the legitimation of his rule
through electoral victory, it was not clear that he was so committed to democratic norms that he would accept electoral defeat.'[28]
But it would be unfair to attribute the growth of this power solely
to Mahathir. His three predecessors as prime minister similarly
developed authoritarian habits within the framework of
Malaysia's parliamentary democracy. The prevailing political culture of Malay society has played a key role in allowing them to
do so.

When an opposition motion sneaks past the speaker's inclination not to 'waste parliament's time', assembled government
MPs make speeches attacking it for being 'anti-Malaysian' and
'disrespectful towards PM'. The two are almost synonymous.
Criticising 'PM' often calls for an abject retraction. When one of
his own party officials recently dared to question a Mahathir
decision, he was shouted down and described as 'uncouth'. In the
Malay cultural context, power must be absolute to command
loyalty. In a society which considers direct access to power as a
way of acquiring wealth or protecting interests, it doesn't pay for
a leader to play the humble servant of the people. Because the
people will soon cast around for a figure who exudes more power.
When Mahathir's ambitious and politically astute young

lieutenant Anwar Ibrahim won the deputy presidency of the ruling UMNO party in November 1993 there were already those who perceived Mahathir's power to be waning. Some even replaced the requisite icon-like photographs they had taken of themselves with Mahathir with pictures taken alongside Anwar – a decision they may have regretted after Mahathir's landslide victory at the polls in April 1995.

Mahathir is perhaps the most striking example of a Southeast Asian leader who projects himself as modern and progressive, yet who wields power, consciously or otherwise, in a traditional manner. The same could be said of Lee Kuan Yew of Singapore and Suharto in Indonesia. Lee of course has been quite open about blending Confucian Chinese values with the intellectual acrobatics of the Oxbridge debating society. Lee's culture of power is consciously bifurcated. Suharto's is less so. As described above, his use of traditional Javanese political devices is barely disguised by a thin veil of modern constitutionalism.

Mahathir's style is, however, more complex and perhaps less consciously executed. More importantly, Malaysian society – specifically the dominant Malay culture – has had much to do with the evolution of Mahathir's style of rule. A Malay politician laments the strength of a culture in which 'the liberal element is so weak and the collective element is so strong, creating a society in which no one is prepared to defend the role of the individual'. At worst Mahathir's style of politics represents the way ruling elites dress up authoritarian rule in a constitutional suit of clothes. At best, it reflects Malaysian popular perceptions of how power should be wielded, whatever the intentions of those in power. Ironically, Mahathir himself alluded to this problem in his out-spoken 1970 treatise *The Malay Dilemma*. 'The Prime Minister in particular became so powerful both by virtue of his office and by popular acclaim,' he noted, referring to the long and popular term served by Malaysia's founding Prime Minister Tunku Abdul Rahman, 'that the party became subservient to the person.' 'The general feeling', he wrote, 'was that whether or not the Parliament sat, the Government would carry on.'[29]

Many people see Mahathir as a maverick politician. Trained as a medical doctor in Singapore, he developed a passion for politics in the heady days of anti-colonial sentiment during the Pacific War. Some say his father, a stern school teacher, was an admirer of the pro-Axis Indian nationalist Subash Chandra Bose. This could explain Mahathir's later obsession with drawing away from the West and 'looking East' to Japan. Like others of his generation, the young Mahathir was inspired by Sukarno's passionate anti-colonial rhetoric. At the time, there were not many Malay households in Malaya without a picture of the Indonesian leader. He joined UMNO in his early twenties at its birth in 1946. But this was a time when the Malay elite was dominated by suave, British-educated anglophiles – those the calculating British rulers wanted to see assume the reins of power once they left, so that British economic interests could be preserved.

In this context, Mahathir must indeed have appeared something of a radical. He was ejected from the party in the late 1960s for criticising the leadership, and spent some years in what is now reverently termed the wilderness. Mahathir's view, propounded with brutal frankness in his *Malay Dilemma*, was that the Malays would never dominate their own land if they remained subservient to the immigrant Chinese and Indians brought to Malaya by the British to serve the colony as merchants, clerks and labourers. To this day, academics write regular newspaper columns to disprove the notion that the 'gentle' Malays tilled the land, while the immigrants made their fortunes in trade. In his most recent treatise, *The Asia that can say No*, a book co-written with maverick Japanese legislator and outspoken nationalist Shintara Ishihara, Mahathir demonstrates remarkable continuity of thought:

> It is possible for Asia to create a cultural region of unmatched historical greatness. What is important is that we consciously strive to maintain our value systems. If we do so, we will never come under European domination again.[30]

Mahathir gleans many of these ideas from a wide range of popular reading. 'He reads a lot, but not deeply', reveals an academic who has advised Mahathir in the past. 'Much of it is popular material which doesn't give him the full grasp of the context.'[31] This could explain why the Japan Mahathir knows it is a country pioneering a successful management strategy; not how they achieved it by borrowing from the West.

It would be simple enough to dismiss Mahathir as a demagogue. There are indeed shades of a latter-day Sukarno – blasting away at the forces of imperialism. A former US ambassador in Kuala Lumpur considered that Mahathir had aspirations to play on a bigger stage. 'If you sum it all up, he's looking for a place in the sun and history; looking for a lasting international title to go along with his domestic title.'[32] A more charitable view from one of his own diplomats is that Mahathir 'sincerely believes in his ideas. He is not looking for leadership, but genuinely believes some things need to be said.'[33] But like Sukarno, focusing on the oratory bravado fails to explain Mahathir's political strength and popularity at home. (He has won five general elections in a row.) Perhaps more accurately Mahathir exemplifies the 'good ruler' of Southeast Asian tradition. The ruler whose power becomes magnified by popular acclaim because he delivers wealth and security to his subjects – the absence of which brought Sukarno down.

Apart from the obvious link between political strength and economic welfare, we find in Mahathir's style of leadership a model of power which conveys a curious form of benevolence: one which strikes hard and ruthlessly at enemies of the state, justifying the uncompromising use of power in terms of nationalism and loyalty, but which rewards its faithful servants more than amply. Recent Malaysian history is shot through with expressions of both sides in this culture of power. On one side there was undermining of the country's independent judiciary in the late 1980s because it dared to question the legal propriety of the country's leadership.[34] On the other side of the equation there is a string of millionaires who have built their fortunes on political patronage. One need not look far to find the direct link with the historical Malay tradition. At UMNO party assemblies for the past few years large canvases painted by a local artist have hung in the assembly hall, depicting Mahathir and his party minions as heroes from the glorious Malay past.

## THE POWER OF MONOPOLY

As with the kings of pre-colonial Southeast Asia, the success of modern leaders cannot be interpreted purely on a cultural plane. Modern Southeast Asian leaders may no longer claim semi-divine status but they have retained the propensity to monopolise the means of production. Strong leadership in Southeast Asia relies as much today on economic patronage as it does on culturally-driven respect for authority. David Steinberg suggests, for instance, that Burma's lurch towards socialism under the military rule of General Ne Win (a man whose belief in the traditional culture of leadership rivals that of Indonesia's Suharto; he is said to have changed the denominations of Burma's banknotes and the side of the road people drive, on the advice of soothsayers) can be considered 'both as an effort to create a secular modernis-ation programme, and also a reversion to traditional monarchical practices'.[35] Socialism, Steinberg notes, allowed for heavy state intervention and the state's monopolisation of production.

In the early years of modern statehood economic patronage, concentrated in the hands of the ruling elite, evolved with the help of strict import-substitution regimes by which access to imports was controlled through state-run monopolies. When pres-sure from the private sector and foreign investors forced liberal reforms on the state, governments resorted to cronyism or the use of nominees to ensure that they retained a monopolistic grip on key sectors of the economy. From the mid-1980s President Suharto's family emerged as key players on the Indonesian cor-porate scene. The conglomerates established by Suharto's three sons and eldest daughter grew rapidly on a broad base of activi-ties extending into every conceivable sector of the economy. Sometimes the sector of the economy they played in was intrinsi-cally profitable, like the trading of oil and natural gas; sometimes they made it so by monopolising production, as in the case of the cloves used in Indonesia's popular *kretek* cigarettes, or the production of essential feedstocks for the plastics industry.

Pressure from multilateral lending agencies to shape reforms that reduce the power of monopolies have succeeded in disengag-ing powerful, but inefficient, state enterprises but not the hold of the Suharto family on profitable areas of the economy. In recent interviews with the press, Suharto's eldest daughter, Siti Hardiyanti Rukmana, has defended her business activities by denying she has ever exploited state funds, and insisting that not every project up for grabs goes her way. More recently the Suharto family conglomerates have taken steps to list their hold-ings as public companies – most probably as a hedge against their uncertain future after Suharto has left the scene.

Less well-known are the string of cash-rich social welfare foun-dations which Suharto has set up, and in which he and his children serve as trustees. Here we begin to see how Suharto combines tradition with the pursuit of power more starkly. The foundations, or *yayasan*, are a popular mechanism in Indonesia for marshalling wealth under the guise of philanthropy.[36] Ironically, they became popular among Indonesian nationalists exploiting an old Dutch law which made money collected from donations for social purposes exempt from an audit by the state. Needless to say, the fiscal loophole persists and it is difficult to gauge how much money Suharto and his family has amassed under the *yayasan* umbrella.

One thing is certain, Suharto projects these foundations as proof of his munificence. The people can't afford to provide basic welfare for themselves nor can the government do it all, he claims, in his 1988 ghost-written biography. So the funds must come from outside the government. As President, he requests the donations and decides where they are spent. In fact all civil servants have nominal monthly sums of as much as US$ 0.50c docked from their wage packet to contribute to a foundation dedicated to religious works. As with the Presidential Aid Scheme, or *Inpres*, the money spent on welfare is seen to come directly from Suharto, the father of the nation, to the needy villager. Government agencies and provincial authorities are bypassed, and in the process the people see their president as the font of sustenance. 'If people say I'm rich', Suharto declares in his biography, 'indeed I am rich, but as the head [of these] foundations.'[37] As an afterthought, he adds that 100 per cent of the money is used for social purposes.

In neighbouring Malaysia, political patronage has become more and more important as a factor in Malaysian capitalism. In his ground-breaking analysis of political involvement in Malaysian business, Edmund Gomez traces the role of the state to the implementation of the New Economic Policy in the 1970s, which sought to channel corporate ownership towards the economically weak Malay Community.[38] Under the NEP the government aimed at transferring 30 per cent of the corporate sector to the Malay, or *bumiputera* community by 1990. Public agencies were set up to acquire corporate assets on behalf of *bumiputeras*, and ostensibly to train and protect *bumiputera* entrepreneurs. Large portions of public share issues were reserved for *bumiputeras*. But as Gomez points out, the promotion of communal business interests brought in communal political organisations:

> As ruling ethnic-based political parties involved themselves in what were essentially rentier capitalistic pursuits, they also

became increasingly aware of the influence and power they could exert over their constituents in developing and furthering their business interests.[39]

The chief beneficiary was the United Malays National Organisation, which dominates Malaysia's multiethnic ruling coalition. UMNO's hegemony and the centralised nature of power within the coalition and the party concentrated this wealth. In 1990 it was estimated that UMNO owned four billion Malaysian Ringgit's worth of shares, as well as land and property worth several billion Ringgit.[40] By owning as much as 2 per cent of the market capitalisation of Malaysia's stock market, UMNO's influence in the market was considerable. This means that share prices of UMNO-owned companies could, in theory, be artificially boosted when cash was needed for political campaigns. (UMNO members allege that funds derived from the stock market were deployed to a more limited degree by the opposition UMNO splinter party Semangat 46.) In short, the political leadership of Malaysia had access to a political automatic teller machine.

The more obvious state monopolies may be disappearing as the region's economies liberalise and bring themselves into line with the global economy, but ruling elites are finding new ways to monopolise the nation's wealth. Patronage that was once dished out in the form of monopolies is now distributed in the form of shares and company directorships. Mahathir's sons are becoming tied in to major industrial development projects allied with influential entrepreneurs. A company search done in Kuala Lumpur's registry of companies revealed in late 1993 that Mirzan Mahathir was connected with almost forty companies. In 1992, Mokhzani Mahathir bought a controlling stake in a small company called Tongkah holdings that had posted losses for 8 straight years. In the financial year to June 1994, the holding company made a profit of almost US$ 5 million and was bidding to buy a small private bank.[41]

In fairness, this kind of success and exposure to the business world is just as much a product of the local, notably the Chinese, business community assuming that co-option of the ruling elite is the surest form of business security – which points to a link between the economic buoyancy and the toleration of patronage and favouritism, rather than the other way around. Favourable economic conditions grease the wheels of patronage and keep everyone happy. Periods of economic stress make it more difficult for the leadership to keep the pie evenly divided. Neils Mulder speculates that attacks by the middle classes of Manila's Makati business district on the Marcos regime in the Philippines, in the wake of the August 1983 Aquino assassination, may be explained by the dismal state of the economy in the early 1980s.[42] The overheating of Indonesia's economy in the early 1990s generated more voluble resentment about Suharto's family businesses and the role of conglomerates owned by ethnic Chinese.

Nevertheless, strong ties between leaders and the economic elite in buoyant economic circumstances helps explain why crises of legitimacy are rare in Southeast Asia. More often than not opportunities for political change have arisen from internal factional struggles among the elite. Questioning of the system and the mass mobilisation of popular opinion are the tools one faction deploys against another in the quest for power. But once installed, the elite closes ranks, spurning the social and political sentiment stirred up in the course of the campaign in favour of the status quo. As one senior Indonesian politician warned: 'In a political system that is not fully developed, undercurrents in society can be manipulated, engineered by individuals.'[43]

Western analysts generally consider that the desire for popular sovereignty stems from an innate human desire for recognition and status as individuals. From this philosophical position they argue that the collective norms of Asian societies will eventually be eroded by popular demands for this recognition. From this introductory analysis of Southeast Asian models of power and authority it should be obvious that the post-colonial political development of the region has tended to reinforce rather than sweep away these collective norms. Traditional forms of authority, originating from a basic model of kingship, have by and large been recovered and recast in modern forms. The next question is how well this tradition stands up to scrutiny by those who consider Western forms of democracy as the ultimate form of political development.

# Chapter 3

# Differing on democracy

*Democracy is on the march everywhere in the world. It is a
new day and a great moment for America.*
                          President Bill Clinton, 26 February 1993

*Leave this Europe where they are never done talking of man,
yet murder men everywhere they find them.*
          *Frantz Fanon (1961)* The Wretched of the Earth

In the words of former Japanese prime minister Keiichi
Miyazawa, Southeast Asia is the economic 'prime spot' of the
world. Yet for US lawmakers and Eurocrats from Brussels
the region is something of a black spot for human freedom. In
their eyes, economic success alone does not define regional stature. Political stability, enduring social harmony and prosperity are
not sufficient criteria either. They want to see Southeast Asia
develop more democracy and respect for a universal definition
of human rights in tandem with economic prosperity – a partnership they regard as a defining mark of civilisation.

Rather than bow to a view which defines Western human values
as universal, some Southeast Asian states have demurred, arguing
the case for the diversity of social and political norms. At one
extreme this resistance has assumed the form of a vaguely defined
alternative 'Asian model' of development. This model takes as a
starting point fundamental differences of political culture and
ends up by telling the West: 'We're different, so don't expect us
to conform to your standards.' On a more moderate plane, there
are those Asians who accept that some of those values claimed
by the West play a role in shaping Asian politics and society –
but not as fundamentally as some Westerners believe. In essence,
these people are saying: 'We drink Coca Cola, we can even

make it more cheaply, but don't subscribe to the same corporate philosophy as the Coca Cola company.'

One of the most enduring debates of the 1990s in Southeast Asia has revolved around the relevance of human rights and democracy in the post-Cold War environment of what is commonly called 'open regionalism'. This came about as Western governments cast around for global issues after the end of the Cold War and found the human rights record of some of their former Cold War allies wanting. At the same time in Southeast Asia, once the communist threat receded, the need for foreign aid diminished, and the region's economies became more self-sufficient, a wave of confidence swept through the region. Some politicians began asking whether they needed the West more than the West needed them. Did they need to be told that strong government hindered market forces, or that their people wanted more democracy. And should they be threatened with sanctions of various kinds for not living up to Western standards of political behaviour? In much the same way that the Western powers engaged the former communist bloc with the Helsinki process a decade earlier, the universal issue of human freedom found itself locked in combat with principles of national sovereignty. As a senior Vietnamese official aptly surmised: 'In short, Human Rights has become a matter of international relations.'[1]

To combat this elevation of values to the diplomatic plane, some Asian intellectuals turned to indigenous political philosophy and cultural or religious beliefs to justify rejecting Western values. From the early 1990s it became fashionable for Southeast Asian leaders to speak of a clash of cultures and traditions (before Professor Huntingdon's thesis was published in 1993, though more ardently thereafter). Some political leaders were more strident than others, but the message was essentially the same: 'We are grown-up countries now, and this does not mean we have to resemble the West.' Does this make Southeast Asians any less civilised? Can the region become a sophisticated industrialised society using Western technology, without the wholesale adoption of Western values and attitudes in the social and political sphere? Does a political system which embraces pluralism and democratic principles have to be modelled on Western society? Or is there a cultural middle ground where contrasting approaches to what defines a civil society can be reconciled? Resolving this issue looks like being one of the key challenges of the new world order, one which events have conspired to test in Southeast Asia – though not for the first time.

Western civilisation has been trying to mould the face of Southeast Asia into a likeness of its own ever since the Jesuit missionary St Francis Xavier arrived in the Moluccas in the mid-sixteenth century. At this early stage, however, the clash was more realistically between one set of religious beliefs and another. The scurvy-ridden European ruffians who stumbled up coconut strewn beaches in their rough wool and leather, wielded the sword in one hand and the crucifix in the other. This was no great improvement, perhaps none at all, on the Hindu, Buddhist and Muslim traders who preceded them.

Much later, generations of colonial administrators tried to harness Southeast Asian society to European social norms and political culture. 'As conquerors of Vietnam', wrote the British historian Ralph Smith, 'the French were very much aware of their mission to civilise the Vietnamese: to make their nature as well as their humanity conform to the ideals of the West.'[2] The British in Burma and Malaya salved consciences pricked by their voracious exploitation of resources and labour by passing on to the benighted natives the traditions of British Common Law and the administrative propriety of the colonial civil service. Towards the end of their long rule over the Indonesian archipelago, the Dutch also offered a chosen few 'natives' the opportunity to 'liberate' themselves through education. As the historian V.G. Kiernan mused in his arresting cultural study of British colonialism: 'By thinking the worst of their subjects, they [the colonials] avoided having to think badly of themselves.'[3]

Yet in most cases, this European missionary urge was frustrated by the eclectic tendencies of their host cultures, which neither rejected totally, nor absorbed fully what their colonial masters were trying to cement in place. Pioneer Indonesian nationalist Sutan Sjahrir embraced liberal European philosophy in the 1930s, claiming that the feudal proclivities of the traditional Indonesian elite would inhibit democratic development. Yet, as alluded to earlier, his conception of how democracy should work in the Indonesian context drew on his native West Sumatran traditions of collective decision-making and mutual consent. According to a recent biography, Sjahrir was associated with the view that 'being aristocratic did not mean being individualistic'.[4] Towards the end of his life, imprisoned and ill, Sjahrir seemed to confirm this more catholic approach to Western liberalism, when he wrote in his diary:

> For the time being, in fact, democracy for us cannot mean a technique of governing, and a citizen-like way of life, but mainly a guarantee against tyranny and despotism.[5]

Those civilising Frenchmen fared no better in Vietnam. For as Smith noted: 'The Vietnamese, with their tradition of eclecticism, might wish to borrow from the West; but they would always wish to remain Vietnamese.'[6] Even European Marxism was perhaps interpreted by the Vietnamese with the aim of reinforcing traditional belief in Fate. Through an indigenous lens, Marx's 'dialectic of history' could be regarded by the Vietnamese as the predetermined 'Mandate of Heaven'. 'Just as the Mandate of Heaven could in the old days pass from one dynasty to another, now the Mandate of History is held to be passing from one class to another.'[7] This tendency to harmonise and adapt foreign ideas and principles rather than shun them altogether is evident throughout Southeast Asia's history. To the outsider, the process may look like conversion. In fact, it almost always involved adaptation – leaving plenty of room for rejection. In late 1993, a Vietnamese intellectual who challenged the Hanoi government's adherence to Marxist–Leninist ideology, claimed that Ho Chi Minh only 'borrowed Leninism as a tool' to fight the French colonialists and later the US military.[8]

Though perhaps easily forgotten in the post-colonial era of Western foreign aid and investment Southeast Asians also experienced the darker side of Western civilisation, behaviour which cast doubt on Western claims to be civilised. 'Lofty principles can suddenly disappear the instant the prison door is closed and the joy of the exploitation of others re-emerges', reminds the Indonesian journalist Goenawan Mohamad.[9] Something of the twisted hypocrisy of colonial notions of freedom emerges from the following conversation between the half-caste agent of Dutch imperialism and his Dutch master in Pramoedya Ananta Toer's classic treatment of the rise of Indonesian nationalism, the *House of Glass*:

> 'So, it is your opinion, Meneer, that the more ethnic organisations there are, the more opportunity there will be for people to organise, and the better things will be for the Indies, because

eventually European democratic ways will find their place in the Native world and thereby change the Native's feudal ways?'

'At the very least they will study how to decide things collectively. And so these organisations will also be open and above ground and we will be able to peep in through their doors or windows whenever we like.'[10]

The notion that liberation from the feudal yoke need not diminish the capacity for social control was not lost on colonial regimes, which sought for the most part to organise society to generate wealth for the metropolitan centre, maintain order, and salve their religious consciences at the same time. It should not be forgotten that for many Southeast Asians their first taste of Western civilization was a bitter one.

The intrinsic hypocrisy of colonial rule did not stop early nationalists using Western thought to justify turning on their colonial masters to seize independence. Take the way that Sukarno synthesised Thomas Jefferson and Karl Marx to articulate his Indonesian revolution, even though his own view was that the state should be conceived as a family, with the president as the benevolent father. Ho Chi Minh modelled his revolution against the French in Vietnam along classic communist lines, yet opened his declaration of Vietnam's independence with Jefferson's famous words, 'All men are created free and equal.' Then as now, the West was viewed ambivalently in the region. Ideas and value orientations imported by the colonial powers were accepted where it was felt they furthered nationalism and progress. But there was resistance to aspects of Western culture which contravened social or religious norms. The same way these states had for centuries fended off the threat of a Chinese invasion force by paying lip-service to the universal claims of hegemony from Beijing (and profited from the tributary trade); so the Europeans were led to believe that their civilising mission was working.

In Thailand, which of course successfully resisted colonial rule, the adoption of Western values was selective and deployed as a defence against the erosion of sovereignty by the colonial powers. The 1855 Treaty of Friendship and Commerce with Britain involved the radical restructuring of monopolies controlled by the Siamese aristocracy – favouring the British traders. The British diplomat who concluded the treaty, Sir John Bowring, was struck by how this 'involved a total revolution in all the financial machinery of the Government'.[11] The case of Thailand offers perhaps the finest example of the region's pragmatic adaptability. Facing the threat of colonisation, the Thai opted to modify traditional institutions of the state. But the cost in terms of lost tradition and culture was far less than that which might have been incurred with the loss of sovereignty.

Part of the price the newly independent states of Southeast Asia paid for their freedom was a set of values and institutions governing that freedom which some nationalists sincerely believed was the only way to achieve modern statehood – others did not. Attempts in Burma and Indonesia to implement constitutions modelled on Western democratic principles on gaining independence succeeded initially, but later floundered in a quagmire of factionalism, corruption and economic inefficiency. The first signs of a return to traditional norms of political power and control emerged when the military stepped in to restore order. In Burma, General Ne Win was appointed head of the government in 1958 before seizing power in 1962. In Indonesia, an abortive *coup d'état* brought the army into power after 1965. The generals who seized power in these countries may have worn uniforms tailored in Western styles and wielded weapons purchased from the West, but their political ideas were very much rooted in the Eastern past.

The new constitutions these military regimes enforced enshrined notions of democracy and human rights more in name than in practice. As political power passed from those few nationalists groomed by the colonial elite to those they might have imprisoned, so regard for the advice of their former masters diminished. Traditional paternalistic notions of authority were promoted in the interests of discipline, order and development. Besides, after two world wars and the violent struggle to win independence in some countries, many Southeast Asian intellectuals found no difficulty questioning the validity of Western culture as a universal code of conduct. 'Human rights?', former Vietnamese foreign minister Nguyen Co Thach remarked. 'I learnt about human rights when the French tortured me as a teenager.'[12]

In the postwar era of independence, coinciding with the Cold War, Southeast Asians learnt that human rights and democracy

were functions of which side of the new ideological divide they
opted for. 'While human rights campaigns are portrayed as an
absolute moral good to be implemented without any qualifications, in practice Western governments are prudent and selective', suggests Singaporean diplomat Kishore Mahbubani.[13]
Countless Vietnamese and Cambodians experienced selection of
one method of proving Western moral superiority when their
land and villages were bombed to nothing during the second and
third Indochinese wars. 'It seems also strange somehow to us',
said Tran Quang Co, a veteran Vietnamese Communist Party
leader, later a deputy foreign minister:

> that such a heightened attention and concern can be shown
> from some quarters for a few specific cases of what
> they consider to be human rights violations in our country
> while altogether showing blithe unconcern for the unfortunate
> consequences that hundreds of thousands of Vietnamese whose
> human rights were abridged in many different ways during the
> war still have to suffer today.[14]

Political detainees in Singapore, Malaysia, Thailand, Indonesia
and the Philippines – the non-communist states of Southeast Asia
– experienced another form of selectivity when their plight was
ignored by the West because their governments became strategic
assets in the Cold War era.

Similarly today, the peace dividend claimed by the West after
the Cold War is not so apparent. The Cold War was won in
1989 but capitalism triumphant was overtaken by deep economic
recession and unemployment. The integration of Eastern Europe
with Western Europe, though presented as a triumph of democratic values over Communism, has, from a Southeast Asian perspective, generated more conflict than harmony. Many in the
region would concur with Charles Maier writing in *Foreign
Affairs*[15] that 'in the aftermath of 1989's collapse of communism
... a feeling of anti-climax succeeded initial euphoria'. There is
no evidence that human rights and democracy are being served
by the failure to stop ethnic cleansing in Bosnia-Herzogovina or
ethnic discrimination in France and Germany.

This perception of double standards has become a useful stick
with which Southeast Asian governments can beat their critics in
the West. One of the more strident promoters of this view is
Malaysian Prime Minister Mahathir Mohamad:

When the devotion to democracy results in a stagnant economy, high unemployment and denial of the right to work and
work hard; when democracy protects fascists and neo-Nazis;
when the individual activist takes precedence over the silent
masses then it is time to question whether we have correctly
interpreted democracy.[16]

Mahathir's rhetorical view that the West is distorting democracy
may not sway the urbane Western-educated minority already
sold on the materialistic ephemera of Western culture, but it is
potentially persuasive in less privileged, less worldly-wise strata
of society. Ironically enough, exposure to Western media considered as a measure of openness in Southeast Asia is allowing
ordinary people of the region to witness some of the very problems with Western society their leaders would have them reject.
When Cable News Network brings scenes of ethnic rioting in Los
Angeles into the living rooms of Southeast Asians, they might
think again about the strictures on their own political freedom –
although in some countries governments are not so sure of this,
so they limit access to foreign satellite broadcasts. The end of the
Cold War may have been greeted as a triumph but it unlocked a
whole Pandora's Box of social and moral ills which were subliminally suppressed by the public and the media in the West when
their attention was focused on the bomb and who might use it
first. The mid-1990s was perhaps not the best moment in the
history of Western civilisation to advertise its charms.

It was the moment, though, to cast around for demons. Just as
Western pressure on the regimes of Southeast Asia has generated
criticism of Western society, economic recession in the West has
bred suspicion of Asia's economic success and resilience. The late
former President François Mitterrand of France told a television
interviewer in February 1993 that 'competition from Southeast
Asia, which because of low prices and absence of social protection, sells everything and anything', had caused 'a dramatic crisis
in the Western industrial world'. Sentiments like these, perhaps
motivated by the search for scapegoats, have fuelled mutual suspicions, and etched out even starker differences of approach to
economic and political life. A key question, therefore, is how real
these differences are? Is there a case for a distinctive Asian
alternative to the Western approach to a civil society? If not, is

the region evolving its own pluralistic processes and civil society institutions?

## A NEW IDEOLOGICAL DIVIDE

After the Western powers won the Cold War, attention focused on the politics of the West's Cold War allies. The victory over Communism encouraged a firm belief by Western governments that human rights and democracy as practised in the West should be universally embraced. Anything less is judged to be wrong and ultimately doomed to failure. Thus, undemocratic regimes the West once indulged as allies in the struggle against Communism, now find themselves under scrutiny as foreign policy agendas in Europe and the United States broaden and look for a new global role. Encapsulating this new mood, at least from a Washington perspective, one US commentator wrote in late 1992:

> The demise of communism has not ended assaults on individual rights. In some areas of the world communism's disappearance has only increased the number of actors, governmental and non-governmental, bent on depriving individuals of their rights to free speech, to security from torture, to travel and to all rights enumerated in the 1948 UN Universal Declaration of Human Rights. US support for those rights is the reason that, in benighted countries around the world, pictures of American presidents still hang on the walls of impoverished homes. It is the reason that Chinese students in Tiananmen Square fashioned a Goddess of Liberty like the one in New York's harbour. Clear and consistent support for those rights can provide the foundation of America's role in the post-communist world.[17]

If, as Cullen suggests, US foreign policy is now guided by a 'moral compass', this leaves little scope for the *realpolitik* of the Cold War era. Undemocratic regimes better watch out. The problem for policy-makers in Washington is that for all their cooperation during the Cold War, the countries of Southeast Asia are proving to be reluctant allies in the post-Cold War struggle for democracy. There seems to be no danger of actual conflict over the issue. There is however, the threat of an ideological gulf developing – one similar in scope, if not on the same scale, as that which divided the world over Communism. For by stridently insisting, rightly or wrongly, that human rights and democracy are universal values, the West has forced Southeast Asian countries to adopt a defensive posture – one which ultimately could hinder the propagation of these values.

Rather than simply reject what the West prescribes, some regional regimes have begun formulating alternative definitions of human rights and democracy. Put briefly, these place the collective economic prosperity of society above the rights of individuals thus challenging the atomistic assumptions of Western political philosophy. To some extent, the roots of this particularism lie in the reassertion of traditional concepts of society and political order in the region over the past two decades outlined in Chapter 2. But there is also a sense in which the case for a distinctive approach to what constitutes a civil society in Southeast Asia stems not from any belief in an intrinsically different approach, but rather a reaction to the sermonising of the West.

To those who believe the world is shrinking, the danger lies in these differing views of human development becoming locked in conflict at a time when global trends suggest that peace and the welfare of all are tied even closer than ever before to transnational cooperation and understanding. If, on the other hand, the world is on the verge of a new culturally-driven fragmentation as some have suggested, the challenge to Western thinking should be taken more seriously.

Ideological concerns about human rights and democracy in the West more recently spring from the conviction that free market capitalism and electoral democracy are inseparable, if not indistinguishable. The assumption, of course, is flawed if viewed from the perspective of Western – European and North American – history. The germination of free-market capitalism occurred against a backdrop of the flagrant abuse of human rights – slavery, indentured labour, colonialism and so on. As Andre Gunnar Frank points out: 'Countries in the West have been able to afford the precious luxury of electoral political democracy only where and when the basis of their economy afforded it to them.'[18] The ideological clutter of the Cold War blinded many Westerners to the flawed logic of their argument: it was simply imperative to prove that capitalism was good and socialism was bad. Capitalism thrived in a democracy, it shrivelled under centrally-planned economies. Hence, the issue of human and political freedom became closely identified with economic success.

Of course, to many ordinary Southeast Asians the notion that the freedom to vote enhanced their economic status and security was outlandish. To them, capitalism, as experienced in the colonial period and early years of independence, bred inequality not democracy. After the departure of rent-seeking colonial entrepreneurs, along came corrupt officials and politicians. Initially they looked for popular support, but once in power they preferred to rely on the patronage of rich business cronies to buy them support. In popular terms, therefore, capitalism became associated with corruption and exploitation. Hence the appeal of socialist and communist movements in the region during the first few years of independence. Replacing socialism as the idiom of protest, as we shall see later on, is not so much an appeal to democratic principles, but more traditional forms of moral and religious expression which help people deal with the injustice of social and economic inequality.

Democracy, as practised in contemporary Southeast Asia, is often perceived as a form of government dominated and manipulated by the rich and powerful. In countries like Thailand, Malaysia and the Philippines, where regular elections have assumed more importance in the political process, the chief concern of non-governmental electoral watch-dogs is rampant vote buying. In the July 1995 elections held in Thailand, the Thai Farmers Bank estimated that almost US$ 8 million were spent by political parties. Votes were sold for as much as US$ 60 apiece in urban areas. In state elections held in the Malaysian state of Sabah in February 1994, a regional diplomat observing the polls was told by embarrassed Malaysian election officials that there was little they could do to stop the contesting parties using large sums of money to buy over voters.[19]

People also tend to be aware that Western business interests traditionally support the rich and powerful; not the poor or politically dispossessed in their countries. The association of democracy with free market capitalism does not immediately spring to the minds of the generation of nationalists who battled the colonial powers. Early forms of capitalism rained hardship on the people; it stood for exploitation. Many of these movements flirted with or embraced socialism, because socialism was the liberation ideology of the prewar era. Some of the socialist ideology has been hard to shake off, even in the era of foreign investment. Alongside Indonesia's liberal investment laws, the constitution enshrines cooperatives and the notion of production for the collective good. Even Singapore's seemingly freewheeling entrepôt society is governed by strict notions of forced savings and welfare.

Perhaps it would be more accurate to consider that democracy, seen through the eyes of the pioneer nationalist generation, was more closely identified with the struggle for freedom and not with how to govern. No one paid much heed to the detailed working of a democratic society while they fought to shrug off the imperial yoke. Sukarno's famous declaration of independence on 17 August 1945, went no further than declaring the country free; the details, he said, reading from a small sheet of paper, would be worked out later. Democracy was therefore understood more as a slogan than a working principle. Moreover, the perception of a functioning democracy, with institutionalised checks and balances on executive power, remains complicated by the survival of an indigenous dichotomy with regard to leadership. Virtuous leadership can be strong and blindly obeyed; amoral, tyrannical rulers can and should be opposed. Democracy is still widely treated as a means to an end, rather than an end in itself.

This gulf in perceptions of what democracy means to societies in Southeast Asia has been exploited by a variety of interests and agendas on both sides of the cultural divide, sometimes with less probity than meets the eye. In the West, human rights lobby groups are sometimes hostage to a much broader policy agenda that satisfies Western urges to retain global leadership. In Southeast Asia, the loudest drum-beating about Asian values comes from conservative politicians anxious to perpetuate nationalist virtues and the life of their regimes. Malaysian Prime Minister Dr Mahathir Mohamad's shrill rhetoric about the bullying ways of the West seems to stem as much from a desire to inspire faith in his leadership and a common identity among ethnically diverse Malaysians, as it does from a rational conception of Western intentions.

Even if conflicting interests have helped to generate contrasting definitions which at times obscure the basic issues of individual human freedom and dignity, the conflict of definitions has assumed political dimensions which are affecting relations between the West and Southeast Asia. When the British press made allegations that the Malaysian government accepted bribes from British companies in return for awarding them government contracts, the ever-prickly Mahathir accused the British media of having a 'colonial brain' and slapped an embargo on awarding further contracts to British companies. Although it was tempting to regard Malaysia's response to this perceived affront as an isolated fit of pique, it might be noted that in the same month (March 1994) Thailand told the US to be mindful of accusing the Thai army of lending support to the Khmer Rouge, and Singapore was telling foreigners that it had the right to flog Western teenagers who behaved like hooligans. In all three cases, it was made clear that these were no longer countries which could be pushed around. In an editorial a year later, the Bangkok Post stridently opined:

> as the gap between the standard of living in Thailand and that of the West narrows, so the amount of respect rendered diminishes. It is all too common for some long-staying foreigners to lament the want of courtesy in present-day Thai society. They look back to a golden age of greater, and therefore more picturesque, poverty. . . . Some foreigners are not really able to concede that the impressive advances made in recent years, and those which are to come, are the result of the efforts and ingenuity of ourselves as Asians.[20]

In the war of words which followed the Malaysian embargo on British companies, much of the argument was about whether distinctive Asian values offered valid separate definitions of press freedom, business ethics and face. Valid or not, the aggressive posturing of some Asian politicians, and rather defensive response on the part of the West, has elevated the Asian values debate to a political plane. Politics, therefore, and not the objective consideration of universal ethics, is helping to bifurcate the definition of human values.

The key to understanding this low-intensity ideological divide between Asia and the West is to recognise how the region is developing both economically and politically. The seven countries of the Association of Southeast Asian Nations – the non-communist states of Southeast Asia during the Cold War – constitute a region of some 420 million people, with a combined GDP (excluding Vietnam) of some US$ 293 billion, working out per capita at US$ 888 and growing at an aggregate rate of 7 per cent per year. This is a part of the world only slightly less populous than North America or Europe growing at roughly double their rates. A relatively long period of peace and stability in most cases has also generated a sense of confidence and belief that political maturity has been attained. This means that countries which once hung on every word uttered by their former colonial lords and later paternalistic donors, now feel they can and should make their own choices. At the same time, Western perceptions of the region are also changing.

Southeast Asia was, like Europe, cleaved in two by the Cold War. Vietnam led its political ciphers Laos and later Cambodia down the communist road on one side of this so-called 'bamboo curtain'. The communist tide was halted in Indonesia in the mid-1960s, which together with Malaysia, Singapore, Thailand and the Philippines, formed the Association of Southeast Asian Nations (ASEAN). For over two decades ASEAN offered a beach-head from which the West launched its assault on communism in Asia. Political order and strong economic performance were perhaps more effective as weapons against Communism than the millions of tons of bombs dropped by American bombers on Vietnam and Cambodia.

Unlike Europe, though, not all the non-communist states of Southeast Asia matched their anti-communist fervour with support for Western-style democracy and human rights. Free enterprise and the market were their preferred adopted Western values. Individual rights and political pluralism were deemed destabilising, the more so with 'reds' under the bed. Yet while the non-communist ASEAN countries manned the battlements in the fight against Communism, the West was willing to turn a blind eye to the abuse of human rights – and even defended authoritarian right-wing regimes as the best defence against Communism. Even before the communist tide was turned, however, awkward questions were raised with regard to this uneasy paradox. The dramatic popular overthrow of President Ferdinand Marcos of the Philippines in 1986 heralded a new approach to Western foreign policy in the region; one less willing to tolerate non-communist autocrats. The trend was confirmed when, just two years later, US officials began working a human rights agenda into relations with the Suharto government in Indonesia.

By 1990, human rights and democracy had become a prominent theme at ASEAN 'post-ministerial meetings' that involve ASEAN's dialogue partners from the United States, Canada, Australia, New Zealand and the European Union. The post-ministerial meeting began life as a trade forum; now it became the scene of friction between the two sides over political issues. There were hints that sanctions may be used. The US and European Union (EU) wanted ASEAN to exert pressure on the harsh military regime in Burma after it failed to implement the results of the 1990 general election. The EU wanted to insert a human rights clause in a new bilateral cooperation agreement with ASEAN – making progress on human rights a condition of normal trading relations. Indonesia came under fire for its handling of irredentism in East Timor and Aceh. Some Western governments cut off aid to Indonesia after the 12 November 1991 shooting of demonstrators in East Timor. The US cut off aid to Thailand after a military coup against the democratically elected government of Chatichai Choonhavan in February 1991.

To many ASEAN officials, fresh from labouring to bring about a peace settlement in Cambodia, Western hand-wringing about human rights and democracy seemed unreasonable and inappropriate. ASEAN diplomats employed international law and human rights arguments to condemn Vietnam's invasion of Cambodia at the United Nations. In the 1990s, Muslim communities in Southeast Asia watched the West pulverise Iraq during the 1991 Gulf War, then stand idly by while Orthodox Serbs and Catholic Croats bled Bosnia's Muslims. Mahathir Mohamad went to the United Nations in 1991 and accused the West of 'preaching' and double standards. Singapore's former prime minister Lee Kuan Yew scoffed at Americans as 'great missionaries. They have an irrepressible urge to convert others.'

Angered by the threat of using trade and aid as a lever against them, a collective ASEAN diplomatic counter-offensive got under way in the early 1990s. Some ASEAN governments attacked the West for trying to impose alien values on their tried and stable systems. These, it was said, were deeply rooted in Asian tradition and culture. A culture which, they said, values collective rights more highly than the rights of the individual. 'Asia has never valued the individual over society', Lee Kuan Yew told *Time* magazine in June 1993. 'The society has always been more important than the individual. I think that is what saved Asia from greater misery.' [21] Fragile ethnic equations were put at risk, it was argued, when unbridled freedom was granted to the populace. 'Those of us who have experienced racial riots, as Singapore and Malaysia have, know what effect an inflammatory speech can have', wrote Kishore Mahbubani, a senior Singaporean diplomat.

Above all, Southeast Asian diplomats and politicians said, the region's prosperity was threatened if individual rights were fashioned into a goal more important than development and prosperity for all.

The Bangkok Declaration of April 1993, issued ahead of the United Nations Human Rights Conference in June that year, distilled Asian definitions of human rights in a way which to Western observers eroded their universality. The declaration spoke of the 'imposition of incompatible values', and 'regional particularities'. It diluted the primacy of civil and political rights by insisting that the right to development, social, cultural and economic rights were equally important and interdependent. Many of the region's non-governmental organisations distanced themselves from the declaration on these grounds too. The declaration marked the first attempt to define a set of human values for the region. However, the parameters were set by those in power.

The West was accused of ignoring other rights. A primary human right, it was argued, was the right of survival – the same argument used, incidentally, to counter Western criticism of how Southeast Asian countries exploit their tropical forest resources. 'Developing nations must first secure the economic rights of their people before concentrating on individual rights', said Indonesia's foreign minister Ali Alatas. President Suharto of Indonesia spoke of creating a fair and prosperous society, 'not only for one person, but for the whole of society'. The attitude most governments in the region adopted ahead of the UN human rights conference in Vienna that year was that development should take priority over human rights, and that so-called economic, cultural and social rights are more important than civil and political rights.

The region's pro-active stance on human rights, its active search for an alternative formula rather than a defensive shrug of the shoulders, was a marked departure from earlier diplomatic practice. Apart from anything else, the approach to human rights in the run up to the Vienna conference pulled these countries closer together and made them think harder about what they shared in common. The problem lay in the weakness of the consensus; not all countries were so dogmatic. Reminded of its recent political experience and a century of American influence, the Philippines stoutly defended Western values of human rights and democracy – even to the extent of emphasising contrasts with the rest of the

ASEAN grouping. 'East Asian critics are right about one thing', said the prominent Filipino businessman Jaime Zobel de Ayala:

> Democracy is expensive – but it is not a luxury. It is a necessity for us. But neither has it been a total failure. Among the countries of Asia, we at least have solved the deadly problem of political succession in developing countries without tanks on the streets.[22]

The new generation of civilian politicians in Thailand who owed little or nothing to military patronage, preened their newly-acquired democratic plumage. All the same, with an eye on the interests of regional harmony and a powerful bureaucracy that jealously guards its power, they argued against strident Western advocacy. 'Human rights must emerge primarily from within, and not be imposed from without', insisted Thai Prime Minister Chuan Leekpai in March 1993. Putting this more bluntly, Surin Pitsuwan, a senior minister in Chuan's cabinet, said:

> I tell the Americans: Look, we're developing like you. We're almost a mirror image of you. But you have to understand, that we also have the right to be different from you.[23]

Countering the particularistic stance adopted by core ASEAN countries like Singapore, Malaysia and Indonesia, Western human rights groups scoffed at the suggestion that there was an Asian approach to human rights and democracy. As one Western human rights activist put it: 'There is nothing special about torturing the Asian way. Rape is not something that is done an Asian way. Rape is rape, torture is torture, and human rights are human rights.' Some commentators took exception to the view that strong government made a positive contribution to economic growth, and insisted that 'on the contrary the economic rise of Asia was made possible by precisely the Western liberalism which the Asian model affects to condemn'.[24] The Western academic world lent scholarly weight to this view with the contention that democracy marches just a step behind economic progress. No new-fangled theory this – merely a reworking of classic Weberian thought. Consciously or otherwise, the idea of the universality of industrial society was applied to the region. The empiricists identified Asia's emerging middle classes as the standard bearers of democracy, and pointed to popular expressions of middle-class sentiment in Manila, Beijing, Seoul, Taipei and Bangkok to support their views.

This clash of views is on the verge of distilling a new ideological divide within the boundaries of what, during the Cold War, was considered the 'free world' – something that should worry Western policy-makers as much as it worries liberals in the region. If the US and other Western countries continue to press for progress towards their definition of democracy and human rights, some Asian governments are just as likely to resist and in the process fashion their own definition of these values. A hardening of stands or acknowledgment of differences over issues as fundamental as human rights and democracy would not serve Western interests. In Southeast Asia it would create opportunities for political polarisation similar to that between Left and Right in the 1960s and 1970s. There would be no winners; only losers.

The logic may be flawed, but the impasse is real enough. As pressure from the West on governments in the region to improve their human rights record and promote democracy built up in the early 1990s, however more democratic some of these countries appeared to be, conservative ruling elites worked hard to reinforce traditional models of society and political culture. There were dissonant voices on both sides of the divide, of course. In a deliberately leaked memo about US policy in Asia, Winston Lord, the state department's senior Asian hand complained in May 1994 that the overzealous pursuit of human rights, trade and other concerns was backfiring and driving Asian nations into a united front against the US.[25] In the same month, Malaysia's Deputy Prime Minister Anwar Ibrahim told the author that 'there was too much talk about the excesses of the West and not enough about the excesses of the East'.[26] Before considering the possibility of a middle ground, it may be worth examining more closely why governments which for the most part have been staunchly pro-Western for the past quarter of a century have opted to argue with their former allies over political philosophy.

**Brash new states in a shrinking world**

A primary argument used in the West to promote its human rights and democracy agenda is that the world is shrinking. The shrinking global community and advance of transnationalism brought about by the new information era makes political congruity an inevitability. Gone are the ideological barriers to international discourse and cooperation. Trade is flowing faster over greater distances. Communications technology is shrinking distances. 'Communications and economic activity that leap national borders are homogenising the cultural diversity that heretofore has been one of the main contributions of the nation state system', observed Seyom Brown.[27]

In the Asia Pacific region, this argument has been used by Professor Robert Scalapino to predict that 'nationalism is being undermined by current events'. Yet Scalapino shrewdly recognises the limits of internationalism in Asia. Here after all, Marxist–Leninist regimes survive (in North Korea, Vietnam, and China) and authoritarian systems thrive. Thus, he talks of a 'curious medley of greater global uniformity and diversity'.[28] Nevertheless, encroaching global uniformity is widely considered to herald the triumph of the democratic ideal. While the end of the Cold War has proven this assumption of doubtful validity in a Europe formerly cleaved by immutable ideologies, but now plagued by tribal rivalry, it is arguably even less applicable in Southeast Asia where 'democratic' has its own connotations.

If the relevance of the nation state is diminishing, the problem for Southeast Asian states is that their internal political systems still draw strength from the relatively recent nationalist struggles of the post-colonial era. Most Southeast Asian states only obtained their independence in the late 1940s – Malaysia (then Malaya) as late as 1957, Singapore in 1965, and Brunei only in 1984. Vietnam, it should be remembered, ended three decades of armed struggle as a unified nation state in 1975. As modern nation states, the ten states of Southeast Asia are relatively new and can therefore be acutely sensitive to criticism, often casting outside scrutiny in the role of a threat to sovereignty. Here is how prominent Indonesian newspaper editor Jakob Oetama summed up the position:

> These countries ... are very sensitive towards anything which they perceive as undermining their national sovereignty.... This sensitivity is further strengthened by the fact that in relations between an industrialised country and a developing country, the latter is in a weaker position – in terms of trade, science technology, and now also because of the debt burden.[29]

Few Asian countries experienced the intensity of nationalist sentiment which developed in Indonesia and Vietnam during their struggle for independence. Both countries became independent after bloody revolutions. The Indonesian ruling elite is still dominated by members of that revolutionary generation – Indonesia celebrated half a century of independence in 1995. The transfer of power to a post-revolutionary generation won't be complete until President Suharto leaves the scene – he was elected for a sixth five year term in March 1993 and increasingly has looked as if he would seek another term. While there are hints of diluting the cult built around Ho Chi Minh (who died in 1969) in Vietnam, the ruling elite still draws legitimacy from the nationalist struggle. The fact that Vietnam clings to socialism may have more to do with the legitimacy its leadership draws from over 30 years of nationalist struggle than any commitment to ideology. Their fear is that by suddenly changing the system, their positions – and not just the primacy of Marxism – will be threatened.

Malaysia and Singapore experienced an essentially peaceful transition to independence – Singapore's involving a subsequent ejection from the Malaysian Federation in 1965. For both countries, the earliest years of independence were marked by a threat to their sovereignty from neighbouring states. Sukarno concocted the view that Malaysia (before Singapore left the Malaysian Federation) was a creation of the colonial powers to destabilise Indonesia. Sukarno's ill-fated military response to that perceived threat bred a strategic insecurity in Kuala Lumpur and Singapore which survives to this day. But oddly enough, the very fact that the transition to independence on the Malay peninsula was peaceful also left its mark. Not experiencing the passion of revolution has left Malaysians and Singaporeans quick to take offence, and they are the most prickly when it comes to outside interference. The modern Malay peninsula harbours another paradox, because for all the apparent entrenched Western influence suggested by the widespread use of English and the maintenance of British-style legal and governmental institutions it is the source of some of the most strident anti-Western rhetoric. Whether or not any irony was intended, the *Straits Times* of Singapore described Malaysia as 'possibly the most traditionally-minded country in Southeast Asia'.[30]

Malaysia's strident defence of indigenous tradition is perhaps a reflex born of the need to establish a binding sense of national identity in a fragile multiethnic context, without common indigenous roots. Muslim Malays account for barely half the population of almost 20 million people; Chinese and a small proportion of Indians make up the rest. As part of this effort to instil a national identity, Malaysia's Prime Minister Mahathir Mohamad spent his first years in power after 1981 buying 'British last' and 'looking East'. Faintly echoing Sukarno's tilt away from the developed world at the Bandung Asia–Africa conference in 1955, Mahathir's view of Malaysia was firmly rooted in the Afro-Asian world. More recently, he has led a revival of developing world rhetoric in the 'Group of 15' forum, convened in 1990, which is designed to enhance 'South–South' cooperation. In 1991 he campaigned for an 'East Asian Economic Grouping', later modified to a caucus, to combat the perceived rise of protectionism in the West. When the United States objected to such a caucus, a move which apparently made Japan and Korea reluctant to endorse the idea, a frustrated Mahathir wondered aloud if this was because 'our faces are brown'.

It would be naïve to consider that Mahathir expends so much energy on blasting the West only because of his personal feelings. 'He says what he thinks people want to hear; what he does is something else', commented a close political colleague. 'Mahathir was not and is not a xenophobe', asserts his recent biographer, Khoo Boo Teik. His anti-Western rhetoric, Khoo reasons, represents an attempt to 'depart from … the Malay nationalist's traditional, self-consuming preoccupation with the Malay position vis-à-vis the non-Malay communities'.[31] The need to appeal to conservative Islamic anti-materialism – which associates Western ways with all that is un-Islamic – could explain why Mahathir often attacks the West for its loose moral values, as well as for political double standards. At other times, the official rhetoric seems to be driven by a quest for unity, zeroing in on outside criticism as an assault by forces resentful of the nation's achievements, bent on undermining the country's progress. To some this betrays a sense of insecurity; to others a degree of arrogance born of unquestioned political domination by a small national elite.

Singapore's Prime Minister Lee Kuan Yew stepped down as prime minister in November 1990. Since then, he has frequently criticised the West for trying to impose alien values on Asian society. In June 1995, he blasted the United States for attempting to impose what he called 'cultural domination' on Asia. He amazed many by going to Manila in 1992 and arguing that the liberal democracy practised in the Philippines was an obstacle to economic progress which required collective discipline and firm central control. Both Lee and Mahathir have been outspoken about the dangers of assuming that all societies share the same conception of democracy. More recently, they have attenuated the argument to imply that democracy as such is no guarantee of a stable society – pointing to events in the fragmented former Soviet Union and Eastern Europe. Such views are generally accompanied by justifications of why press freedom and individual rights are more controlled in the region. Neither leader makes any apology for the kind of political system they lead.

The intellectual source of this kind of rhetoric can be traced to the shared backgrounds and political environments from which both these senior regional leaders came. Both men grew up and came of age in the colonial context. The British colonial milieu was more benign and therefore tolerated, or ignored, the incubation of nationalist ideas up to a point. Rhetorical skills took root in the school debating societies encouraged by liberal British teachers. Both men articulated strong anti-colonial views in the course of their political apprenticeship. Later, as leaders they presided over complex plural societies where very often the best defence against internal strife was the fashioning of external threats. However, basic conspiracy theory does not fully explain the stridency of their rhetoric.

To some degree this must betray a shared conviction, if not a measure of grudge, against the West. In Mahathir's case, this may stem from the fact that he did not have an overseas Western education like others of his generation. Mahathir took his medical degree from a colonial university in Singapore. Privately, close associates say he was deeply scarred by the fact that those with a British education initially secured positions in the new Malaysian elite, while he had to work his way up from a humble doctor's practice in a north-eastern provincial town and spent some years in the political wilderness. Publicly Mahathir denies he is anti-Western – in fact he sent two of his children to British public schools. Khoo Boo Teik casts Mahathir's stance as a paradox: 'He would look East to catch up with the West.'[32] Privately, though, he urges Malaysians to strive harder so that one day they can look down on the 'white man' the way the white men once looked down on them.

Lee Kuan Yew's prejudices are harder to fathom because he enjoyed all the privileges of a British education denied to Mahathir. He took a law degree from Cambridge and later qualified as a barrister in London. This equipped him with a convincing intellectual grasp of both Eastern and Western culture. Talking about Democracy at a conference in Tokyo in 1991, for example, Lee drew parallels between Russia and Asia:

> European historians ascribe Russia's lack of a liberal civic society to the fact that she missed the Renaissance and also the Enlightenment. These were the two leavening experiences that lifted Western Europe to a more humane culture. Now, if democracy will not work for the Russians, a white Christian people, can we assume it will naturally work for Asians? [33]

Although it is quite likely that an Asian in postwar England may have encountered some racial prejudice, Lee hardly comes across as an anglophobe. He recently praised the British for not trying to impose their culture on Singapore, as he sees the United States doing today. Both Lee and Mahathir appear to privately enjoy the company of Westerners and appreciate Western culture, almost to the point of craving. Mahathir spends most long holidays in Europe and particularly enjoys the British theatre. Lee enjoys close relationships with a range of Western statesmen, and clearly likes pounding the conference circuit with them. Yet publicly both men reject Western values, harnessing their rhetoric to the search for new expressions of nationalistic fervour. They appear to revel in the notoriety this has won them at no cost to their economic well-being. 'We get investment from the private sector, while thumbing our noses at their governments – and I think they enjoy it', Mahathir once said.[34]

Do either of these two men, who have made deep impacts on the political cultures of their own countries, reflect the views of their countrymen? Perhaps only to the extent that they represent a generation of frustrated nationalists who have yet to pass from the scene. The British colonial system allowed the nurturing of native intellectual skills at the expense of self-esteem. Quite simply, brown or yellow faces were not accepted. The Dutch in Indonesia, the French in Indochina and the Spanish in the Philippines were also racist and treated their colonial subjects less fairly, but they also intermarried with them and cultivated a mestizo race. The Dutch, for example, accepted their 'Indo' offspring into the European circle, even though public places frequented by Europeans were barred to 'dogs and inlanders' (natives). In French colonies, there was greater acceptance of natives or mestizos who opted to embrace the metropolitan culture.

Thus Ho Chi Minh could join the French Communist Party in Paris and become a member of the Party's central committee. Lee Kuan Yew could only have a successful law firm in Singapore, and be patronised later as a leader who might have achieved greater international stature if he had run a bigger country. The British, as George Orwell illustrates in *Burmese Days*, had the club and a set of strict rules barring natives from the long bars they frequented from Rangoon to Singapore. Is it so surprising that when the 'natives' came to power, they felt the urge every so often to debunk their former masters?

The younger generation of Singaporeans and Malaysians thinks differently, but not all that differently. Theirs is a pride born of achievement rather than prejudice. Rather than aspiring to beat the West and somehow make up for the inequities of the colonial past, they yearn for equality. They talk of 'a new history of East–West relations', of 'a new spirit of partnership and shared destiny between East and West'.[35] They are liable to question the actions of their own ruling elites as much as the actions of a Western government. A Malaysian journalist pointedly asked a senior official why the government was criticising the Western powers in Bosnia, and saying nothing about the abuse of human rights in Burma and East Timor.[36] The sentiment of the younger generation was echoed eloquently by Anwar Ibrahim:

> Although we reject the condescending attitude of outsiders in respect of our efforts to deal with these issues, we also deplore at the same time the arrogant elites within our societies, who either condone or seek to perpetuate excesses.[37]

Yet the younger generation's perceptions are finely balanced, and easily swayed by nationalist arguments, for they have been reared on a diet of nationalism born of the colonial struggle. No society entirely discards its past. Indeed, the rapid pace of change in these societies may be helping to preserve rather than erase traditional identities. 'We are all in the midst of very rapid change and at the same time we are all groping towards a destination which we hope will be identifiable with our past', notes Lee Kuan

Yew.[38] To this end, however more liberal the next generation of leaders in Singapore and Malaysia may seem by comparison, they may be tempted to harness nationalism to new definitions of distinctiveness such as religion or culture.

Indonesia faces a nationalist dilemma of another kind when it comes to principles of human rights and democracy. The principal focus of Western criticism has been a small former Portuguese colony of East Timor, which Indonesia unilaterally annexed in 1975. In the following two years, the United Nations General Assembly passed no less than eight resolutions calling for Indonesia to withdraw, affirming the right of the territory's 600,000 people to self-determination and independence. East Timor remains on the UN's decolonisation list, classified as a 'non-self-governing territory'. In March 1993, following two years of renewed trouble in the territory and evidence of an upsurge in separatist activity, the United Nations Human Rights Commission accepted a resolution expressing 'deep concern' at human rights violations in East Timor. Observers saw the move stemming from a hardening of the new US administration's approach to human rights which lent support to the EU's campaign.

For Western observers, the possibility that as many as 100,000 Timorese perished in the process of annexation by Indonesia, has made the issue one of the shining examples of human rights abuse in the region. Yet even the most liberal Indonesians do not question their government's sovereignty over East Timor – even if they do recoil from the methods used to maintain law and order. 'The Indonesian elite sees East Timor as a case of rebellion rather than of rights; even the Indonesian human rights community is not actively concerned', writes American academic John Bresnan.[39] When a university in the Philippines convened a conference on East Timor at the end of May 1994, the Indonesian government put pressure on the government in Manila to stop it. But nationalist hackles were also raised in Indonesia. Only the staunchest Indonesian critics of the government's human rights record felt moved to defend the conference. Indonesia's armed forces take the view that if the government yields to one ethnic or regional group with irredentist claims, then others might raise latent claims, thus threatening the fabric of the unitary state. This reasoning explains why local insurrection is dealt with harshly, with the deliberate motive of setting an example. Clearly their strategy for maintaining order in a unitary state as large and diverse as Indonesia makes few concessions to Western notions of human rights and democracy. For the time being, though, suggestions that Indonesia should define their state by any other means grate with the strong sense of nationalism.

On a broader level, the region's economic confidence also helps explain the rejection of the new Western policy agenda. Despite official harping on 'development' and 'dependency', the region is in fact less dependent than ever before. Having enjoyed growth rates averaging over 8 per cent for the past 5 years or more, most of the region's governments have begun to feel they can afford to shrug off Western pressure. Singapore's minister of arts and information, Brigadier General George Yeo summed up this view when he spoke of the emergence of a Southeast Asian consciousness, a distinct character and identity which is evolving despite the non-homogeneous nature of its population, and the varied sources of its culture.[40] Looking to the future, Yeo hoped that 'Eastern societies' would come into their own and change the present intellectual thinking that Western values should dominate the world.

Old patron–client relations between the West and the new nations of Asia are transforming into economic ties on a more equal footing. Trade between Western countries and Southeast Asia is growing apace – forcing the West on the economic defensive. Asian markets are robust and lucrative and many Western multinationals can no longer afford to lose their footing in them. What is more, some Southeast Asians see themselves as incipient patrons in their own right: Indonesia is chairman of the Non-aligned movement; Malaysia is championing third world causes; and Thailand is fashioning a policy to help put Indochina's economy back on its feet. Ironically, there was even talk in Bangkok of using the events of May 1992 – when pro-democracy forces overcame military might to help install a civilian government – to persuade Burma to adopt a more democratic course. While the West questioned the democratic credentials of ASEAN countries some of those ASEAN countries helped Cambodians learn how to conduct democratic elections, and have since sent peace-keeping troops to the Balkans and Somalia.

This growing sense of economic and political confidence helps explain the negative response to the West's new policy thrust. Here is a part of the world that feels it is now ready to match its economic muscle with a global and regional diplomatic role, and is in no mood to be preached to. As Samuel Huntingdon puts it: 'A West at the peak of its power confronts a non-West that increasingly has the desire, the will, and the resources to shape the world in a non-Western way.'[41] In one sense, therefore, the negative reaction from Southeast Asia to the West's clamouring about human rights and democracy might be driven more by Western preaching rather than a rejection of the principles of human rights and democracy themselves. If this was solely the case, the burden of resolving this impasse falls squarely on Western shoulders. However, there are also those in Southeast Asia who argue that not all societies are the same.

# Chapter 4

# Core values or elitist cores

*Western arrogance is breeding many Lee Kuan Yews in South-
east Asia.*

*A senior Indonesian diplomat
(personal communication to the author)*

One day in October 1993, a group of foreign teenagers attending
an international school in Singapore took an aerosol can of paint
and casually sprayed the sides of a few parked cars. They smeared
some eggs on them, and later engaged in a little adolescent street
vandalism. Little did they know then, that being caught involved
a maximum penalty of flogging, or that one of the boys, called
Michael Fay, would become a test case for the defence of 'Asian
values'.

The caning sentence passed on the miscreant Michael Fay in
early 1994 attracted astonishing international media interest. For
as well as being a teenager, Fay was also an American citizen.
Prescribing corporal punishment for petty vandalism of this kind
in Singapore actually stems from official sensitivity to politically-
induced graffiti — not to the idle boredom of adolescence. The
United States government took the view that the punishment was
too harsh and eventually even the White House appealed for
clemency. Singapore seized on this as proof that the West was
trying to impose its own values on Asia. Ironically, while the *New
York Times* railed against Singapore's 'primitive' laws, opinion
polls taken in crime-racked American cities showed a measure of
support for meting out corporal punishment to convicted vandals.

In the region, opinion was deeply divided. In neighbouring
Malaysia and Indonesia, there was little sympathy for Fay, but
neither are Singapore's stringent laws viewed with much ardour.

Some observers felt that Singapore, already an expensive place to do business, was in danger of driving out the expatriate business community. A European diplomat stationed in Southeast Asia, who lost a son to a drive-by shooting in New York city, thought that caning was too good for people like Fay.

In the end, Fay's sentence was reduced from six to four strokes of the Rotan cane – allegedly in mitigation for his admission of guilt. Michael Fay, his crime and his punishment, may not be the most glamorous of historical benchmarks, but the case marks a point where a Southeast Asian government stoutly defended a set of values it claimed was distinct from those of the West. Francis Fukuyama went so far as to call it 'a challenge being put forth by Asian society to the United States and other Western democracies'.[1]

Western observers have always been struck by the distinctiveness and sophistication of Asian cultures but, with very few exceptions, could not conceive these cultures being supported by a value system of equal merit with that of their own. Although Southeast Asians could hardly be considered primitive when Europeans first gazed at the awesome temples of Angkor Ayudhya or Borobodur, their builders' ignorance of Christianity consigned them to the moral fringe. 'They eat neither milk, cheese, nor butter; and there is nobody who knows how to make it', wrote Portuguese traveller Antonio Galvao of the Moluccan natives on his arrival in Indonesia's eastern islands mid-sixteenth century:

> They do not differ much from each other in bodily make-up facial features, or customs because all of them are addicted to vices, robberies, wars and sorceries.[2]

The overt or mechanical means of asserting this sense of moral superiority may have disappeared with the collapse of colonialism, but traces of it still linger and can be found lurking like a computer virus in much of the ideological debate over political systems in modern Southeast Asia. As one regional newspaper editorial writer put it, 'In the West they have prosperity: We must be content with material consumerism.'[3]

Karl Marx found Asian society unfathomable and difficult to cleave with his revolutionary predictions for the future of mankind. Marx was searching for a universal theory of history based on a unilinear concept of progress. In Asia he found it difficult to apply his thinking because the divisions in society he predicted as a result of progress were not occurring. He therefore dismissed the more populous half of the world with the vaguely explained 'Asiatic mode of production'. Ironically, not long after Marx's proletarian revolution finally floundered in the early 1990s, the idea of an 'Asiatic mode' was resurrected in Southeast Asia. 'Asian values' or the 'Asian way' are the new political buzzwords used by those politicians determined to assert a difference between their political cultures and those of the West. Sometimes the idea is taken seriously; but mostly it is dismissed as a defensive manoeuvre deployed by ruling elites to preserve their power. In the words of one Western diplomat serving in the region and speaking to the author in Bangkok in 1995, 'Perhaps they saw a Human Rights policy coming, and thought that offense was the best form of defense.'

To counter the assumption that Asian society is moving inexorably towards parity with Western values, ruling elites in Southeast Asia have begun to erect fences around what they regard as the core values of their own societies, claiming these as the basis of the region's social harmony and economic success. Collective social norms, respect for authority and suppression of individual interest before that of the community or state, are some of the common denominators claimed by the region's elites – Society as No.1. As we have seen, the rhetoric has been dressed up in terms of a defence of sovereignty and a claim to be masters of their own destiny now that a measure of economic self-sufficiency has been achieved.

Nonsense, say the guardians of the liberal faith. Western commentators, politicians as well as local non-governmental pressure groups argue that differences in norms and value systems, particularly in areas governing the relationship between state and society, are fast being eroded in the new borderless world. In their view, it surely cannot be long before people in the region wake up, abandon anachronistic notions of collective discipline and control, and join the real world. Even those liberals who see merit in the discipline, strong family values and conscientious work-ethic of Asian societies (inasmuch as these diminish the need for costly welfare programmes) assume that the collective tendencies these breed will eventually be tempered by the spirit of individual enterprise.

Truly this is dangerous ground. For if we accept at face value that the relationship between the state and the individual in

Southeast Asia is wholly conditioned by culture, then the need for conservative governments and ruling elites to be accountable flies out of the window. On the other hand, is it right to imagine that political templates forged elsewhere in the world can simply fall into place without adjusting their design? The question is where can the line be drawn in Southeast Asia?

In this chapter it will be argued, with respect to political culture, that the image of a tidal wave of Western-style liberalism washing over sandbags of traditional values is too simplistic. Equally though, it would be wrong to assume that the region can resist changes to prevailing political systems entirely. The fact that governments have been made to think about universal standards of human rights, to set up human rights commissions, and therefore admit that their citizens have individual rights to defend, is in itself a significant shift in attitude – although not a seismically significant one in some cases.

In Indonesia, the National Human Rights Commission, confounding initial scepticism, has in fact shown its independence and promoted the protection of human rights. The trial of soldiers involved in the November 1991 cemetery massacre in East Timor, and the reopening of a case involving the alleged shooting of a labour activist in East Java, were the results of the Commission's investigations. None the less, the Commission's vice-chairman Marzuki Darusman considers 'to be practical in Indonesia, protection and respect of human rights will only be possible if there is cooperation with the Armed Forces of Indonesia'.[4]

Some would argue that this crab-like movement towards parity with liberal norms is the price Southeast Asian societies must pay for social harmony and stability. A younger generation politician with a Western education like Thailand's Surin Pitsuwan agrees:

> It's all a matter of time – a gradual process of change. But the final, mature form of political development won't necessarily exactly replicate Western democracy, but it will approximate democracy none the less.[5]

As we saw earlier with respect to political development in the immediate post-colonial period, a gradual adaptation of imported political institutions to indigenous political culture is underway. Indonesian intellectual Dewi Anwar likens the process to the spread of Islam in the sixteenth century:

The spread of democracy in Southeast Asia will probably follow the pattern of the spread of Islam. It will be evolutionary and it will adapt to local circumstances.... Just as in the case of Islam, the idea of an empowered civil society will initially emerge as a counter-culture, but gradually the ruling elite will become converted, if merely for the sake of maintaining legitimacy.[6]

Realistically speaking, it is a process that is modulating imported values as fast as it is recasting local traditions in distinctive ways. We have seen how the region's governments have reacted to Western preaching on human rights and democracy; now let us hazard a guess at how this will affect the shape of political culture in the region.

First though, a reality check. The more developed countries in the Southeast Asia of the mid-1990s matched enviable political stability with rapid economic growth. Ruling elites in these states argued against rocking the boat from a position of strength. Calling a general election in April 1995, Malaysian Prime Minister Mahathir Mohamad said that 'continuity of development' would be the principal theme of the campaign. 'If you start changing horses in mid-stream, you're likely to drown.' It was a persuasive argument, not merely because of the risk that alternative leaders would tinker with successful policies, but because subliminally the message was that siding with opposition could affect the chances of obtaining funds or contracts.

Although pressure for political change was obvious everywhere, in none of these states was there evidence of an imminent withering of state power or overthrow of the ruling establishment. A kind of dynamic equilibrium existed, in which the forces for change, fuelled by demands for economic justice and political freedom emanating from some sections of society, were balanced by extensive support for the status quo in others. Although such support could be guaranteed by a strong measure of state control, undeniably the material benefits of prosperity also dampened popular enthusiasm for political change. If not, then the spectre of economic decline was brandished by the state in the face of dissenters. Let's call these states – Brunei, Indonesia, Malaysia, Thailand and Singapore – the stable states.

For less economically developed states like Burma, Cambodia, Laos and Vietnam, the prospects of maintaining the political status quo looked less certain. A Vietnamese economist in mid-1994 predicted that his country's medium-term political future would definitely involve changes to the prevailing political system; his only uncertainty was whether the change would be peaceful or involve a violent upheaval.[7] With the free market economy in its early stages of growth, ordinary Vietnamese arguably had less to lose economically by challenging the state.

In Burma, where a military-led regime had not yet adjusted to the ways of the modern world, the chances of a violent upheaval were also deemed to be greater. But in these less stable states too, open door economic policies adopted since the late 1980s were enfranchising potential dissenters faster than their ability to organise dissent. In Burma, the military junta's strategy for consolidating power and political legitimacy appeared to be relying on making people as rich as possible, without too much concern for the inevitable spread of corruption and inefficiency. Pressure for political change in these states fought as hard a battle against the indifference of a population scrambling on to the bandwagon of new economic growth as it did against the intransigence of conservative ruling elites. When Aung San Suu Kyi was arrested and placed under house arrest in July 1989 her popularity among a population starved of economic progress was unmatched. When she gained her freedom in July 1995 her military captors were banking that economic reforms and a measure of growth in urban areas had lent them a modicum of legitimacy. It was a risky assumption.

Generally speaking, the potential political volatility of Southeast Asia has been tempered as much by economic growth, or the prospect of growth, as by strong authoritarian regimes that prevented viable political alternatives from emerging. In the more developed states ruling elites need not fear radical changes to the status quo, so long as there is growth. In emerging economies like that of Burma, where repression is the weapon of choice, even the military junta in Rangoon recognises that ultimately their legitimacy would have to be cemented by spreading wealth.

This was the obverse of thinking in Western countries, where it was assumed that demands for political change naturally accompanied growth. The May 1989 massacre in Beijing's Tiananmen Square was offered as proof that economic reform and growth could not be pursued without accompanying political reform. On the contrary, for Southeast Asian leaders in the 1980s and 1990s economic liberalisation acted as a placebo for political reform. What they feared most was economic decline. Losing the pedals of economic growth meant for them a loss of legitimacy. If members of the ruling elites and their supporters looked upon the future with a degree of anxiety it was because no one could safely predict how long the economic boom would last. By the mid-1990s, as if preparing for this more uncertain future beyond growth, both the challengers and guardians of traditional authority were staking out their positions. In the absence of strong political institutions and a free political dialogue, the debate gravitated towards defining the role of tradition and culture.

## CORE VALUES

In September 1994, aspiring Thai politician Amnuay Viravan told a lunch time gathering of business people, journalists and academics in Bangkok that the region's 'unique cultures' should be considered 'a soil in which the seeds of democracy and civic society must be planted'.[8] While this could be taken as a neat rhetorical resolution of the perceived contradiction between indigenous culture and universal democratic values, the implication was that these values are, like plants, dependent on the environment in which they are planted. Dr Amnuay's metaphor goes right to the heart of the Asian values debate. Across the spectrum of political views there tends to be a consensus on the contribution local traditions and values have made to the region's prosperity and stability. Even proponents of more liberal political values in the region, cannot help crowing with pride about the resilience of regional identity:

> Not long ago, many Westerners saw our societies as bit-players on the wider stage of 'Asian Drama', a dark, endless, all-embracing tragedy, where poverty was the main theme and underdevelopment the central plot. Light years away appeared the *son et lumière* of prosperity and progress, being performed with a flourish and fanfare by the rich nations of the industrialised world.[9]

On a rhetorical level, the economic achievements of the past two decades have bred tremendous confidence in the resilience and dynamism of local cultures and traditions in the more developed countries of Southeast Asia. At the same time, the rapid material changes accompanying growth have bred a desire — not just felt by ruling elites, but in society at large – to assert and reinforce customs and traditions widely perceived as threatened by the onslaught of development.

In Burma, where an unpopular military junta is trying to overcome international opprobrium and the threat of economic sanctions and to drag the country out of three decades of isolation, it is surprising to hear a senior official's concern about the erosion of culture. The junta has implemented a liberal foreign investment law and laid out the welcome mat for foreign businesses. Yet, the line is drawn firmly when it comes to anticipating the impact of the expected growth on cultural values, according to economic planning minister Brigadier General David Abel:

> We were a British colony for over a hundred years, but even then we never changed our cultural outlook. We have maintained a strong hold on culture even when other countries have changed without being colonised. I won't say we'll stay intact – there may be slight changes. But we won't totally lose our cultural values. That won't happen here.[10]

Burma wants to avoid what it perceives has happened to Thailand – hence Abel's veiled reference to countries which have changed 'without being colonised'. The Burmese view Thailand as a country that has abandoned core values in the pursuit of material wealth. Morality and respect for the Buddhist religion have suffered, in their view, from accommodating the foreigner. 'The government would like to emulate the foreign exchange earnings that a Bangkok tourist trade generates, but wants to avoid the tawdry degradation that has accompanied it', notes experienced Burma-watcher David Steinberg.[11]

That is not to say Thais are not concerned about the image their country has acquired as a haven for sex tourists and drug smugglers. Thai artist, Vasan Sitthiket dresses in jack-boots, a military uniform and the ornate head gear of a traditional court dancer to pronounce that 'Thai culture is dead'. His oil painting titled 'modern cock', depicting Thais caressing an American flag in the shape of a penis, was banned from an exhibition at Bangkok's national gallery. In the rapidly-growing urban centres of Southeast Asia everything from suicide to drug abuse is blamed on the undermining of core values. The most common lament focuses on the nuclear family – the family principle being central to the argument used by political elites in favour of collective order and discipline. Development and prosperity do not always destroy culture and tradition, however.

For some sections of society in the more developed countries of the region, modernisation has impacted on tradition but not always replaced it. In some cases traditional behavioural patterns are magnified or distorted. In Thailand, for instance, prosperity has exaggerated the tendency in middle-class Thai society to display status derived from wealth. This helps explain why middle-class Bangkokians cannot be persuaded to abandon their cars for public transport. As a young hotel executive explained: 'There is a strong urge to show off wealth in the shape of a $100,000 luxury automobile. People take their kids to school by car simply to show it off.'[12] Another Bangkokian pressed on why she would not consider taking her child to school on the bus, said that 'only lower-class people use the bus.[13]

Agreement on what constitutes the core values of society is not hard to establish. Where there is divergence is on the extent to which these traditions can and should determine political norms. Some Southeast Asian leaders have argued that the anatomy of their societies is less atomistic than the West perceives it to be and that democracy as it is defined in the West has its own cultural environment. Going further, some have claimed that traditional collective social values which place less emphasis on the rights of the individual, are core values without which anarchy would prevail.

Indonesian officials argue, for example, that allowing the views of a minority to determine the future of the majority is dangerous in a multiethnic, multireligious society. As a senior Indonesian army officer once put it: 'People feel uncomfortable with the notion of less than unanimous support because of the need for harmony, the expression of totality in a cultural and religious context which is highly fractured.'[14] Hence they consider that 50 plus 1 out of 100 constitutes something much less than a majority. In the contemporary political context even one dissenting voice is considered a threat to consensus. When an Indonesian army general stood up at the March 1988 People's Assembly to object to the president's choice of vice-president, he was initially declared mentally unstable. Individual acts of protest are often portrayed in a negative light. A man who threw a bag of excrement at the Thai commerce minister in September 1994 was represented by a local psychiatrist as someone who may have suffered from severe constipation as a child. Something deep in the cultural psyche of the region relates direct, confrontational dissent with dissonant behaviour.

The ethnic complexity of Malaysian society, in which almost half the population are Muslim Malays, a third are either Buddhist or Christian Chinese, and most of the rest are either Hindus or Christians of Indian origin, is used as the principal excuse for the highly modified structure of Malaysian democracy. Malaysia defends a stringent internal security act that allows detention without trial for periods of two years or more on the grounds that without it, there would be no control over racial or religious extremists. The legislation, originally introduced by the British authorities to deal with the communist insurrection of the late 1940s, was never revoked. The country's Printing Presses and Publications Act of 1984 states that parliament may impose restrictions on the freedom of the press 'as it deems necessary or expedient in the interest of security of the Federation, friendly relations with other countries and public order or morality'.[15]

Singapore with its preponderantly ethnic Chinese population rubbing shoulders with smaller numbers of Malays and Indians follows the same logic. In these plural societies racial integration has been slower to occur because the component ethnic groups are large enough to maintain their distinctiveness. At a social level, the importance of ethnic considerations in face-to-face interaction somewhat limits the autonomy of the individual because of the need to be sensitive to the customs of other races. (This ethnic etiquette breaks down in cyberspace, however. On Malaysian and Singaporean 'bulletin boards' ethnic insults are traded freely – and anonymously.) Over time the state has institutionalised these obviously voluntary social mores and turned them into mechanisms of control. For example, it may make sense to restrict freedom of assembly in situations where there is a potential for racial conflict; it becomes something more when a public gathering of more than five people requires a government permit, as in the case of Malaysia.

Behind this sort of thinking lies a strong urge for the imposition of order on society. The prevailing attitude towards popular participation in countries like Indonesia, Thailand, and Burma is that strong government is necessary because the people are too ignorant to help themselves. 'The people are still stupid [masih bodoh].

They must be guided.' The phrase, or something like it, is commonly used by Indonesian officials to explain their overbearing top-down approach to administration and development. The Indonesian government's concept of a cooperative, for instance, is not that of a local-level self-help organisation financed by members' pooled funds. Instead, the idea is that funds are provided by the government to help the cooperative members and relieve poverty.

Even in Thailand, where civilian-led government since the overthrow of military rule in 1992 has made a firm commitment to political openness, there are precious few signs that the state is ready to relinquish its power to the people. Quite the reverse. Calls for bureaucratic decentralisation and provision for elected local officials in Thailand are being resisted at the centre. A senior Thai military officer put it this way:

> We would all like to see the emergence of democracy at some point in the future. But the West should understand that in our culture it is important to secure a sense of unity first.[16]

For countries like Thailand and the Philippines where democracy by Western standards is judged to be more advanced, liberal pressure groups both inside and outside are pushing for what might be called the next stage – downsizing the state still further by empowering those at the grass roots. Although it might be considered naïve to expect states not defined by a federal constitution to grant localities the autonomy enjoyed under a union like the United States of America, many Southeast Asian states are over-centralised. (As we saw earlier, even Malaysia's federal system is becoming more, rather than less, politically centralised.) Yet when elected officials who espouse democracy and human rights for the country as a whole are faced by demands for local freedom, they baulk. More often than not they claim that the country still needs the guidance of the centre, or risks falling apart.

Call it paternalistic or feudalistic, the urge to guide and dictate to society is the centrepiece of bureaucratic culture in Southeast Asia. This top-down urge to guide society has deep roots. Liberal foreign foundations supporting Thailand's fledgling democracy are struck by the reluctance of local non-governmental organisations to be drawn into political action. Representatives of these liberal Western organisations complain that despite being given the right to take public stands on developmental issues many Thai NGOs shy away from politics. Their approach was to work at the grass-roots level with local communities, essentially showing rural people the way to get things done. What worries some Westerners working with NGOs is the convergence of these attitudes and methods with the paternalism of strong centralised government. Instead of teaching people how to govern their own lives, NGOs insist that people have to be constantly guided – as if from above.[17]

Local culture and tradition have provided conservative regimes with the tools needed to impose strict control over society. But the impetus to order society so strictly also stems from the more recent history of nation-building. The painful transition to independence experienced by some states and the urgent desire to develop their economies, bred an instinctive belief that social forces should never be permitted to assert themselves at will otherwise chaos would ensue. Unity is a constant, almost obsessive concern. The immediate post-colonial period saw most of the region's newly independent states embark on a more or less democratic path. In almost every case these democratic beginnings foundered in the wake of internal tensions and threats to the unity of the state.

Indonesia's struggle for independence was marked by a series of internal revolts fuelled by religious, regional, and ideological divisions. Singapore and Malaysia employed harsh legislation restricting personal freedoms in order to bottle up racial tensions in the early years of independence, and continue to justify the limitation of these freedoms on the same grounds. Burma, of course, fell victim to ethnic conflict almost as soon as the idealistic Union of Burma was established in 1948, prompting the military to intervene in the 1950s. Vietnam had to fight a long and bitter war against the French, who were reluctant to abandon their colony after the Pacific War. The Vietnamese Communist Party's obsession with maintaining a monopoly of power – even to the point of restricting membership of the Party itself – though certainly not untypical of communist regimes and echoing the traditional Confucian order, was undoubtedly reinforced by the impact of almost three decades of war.[18]

Strong states became the means by which people could be guided and kept from dividing the polity. In the case of Thailand, the development of centralised state power in the course of the nineteenth century is sometimes explained as a response to the external threat of the colonial powers. To fashion and maintain strong states in the modern context, political elites have reconstructed traditions, albeit in a rather selective fashion. Drawing on traditions of filial piety (in the Confucian or Chinese context) or collective decision-making and consensus (in the Javanese and Malay context), the impression is given that these societies are culturally disposed to obedience and discipline. Society is projected as tightly bound by a sense of solidarity and commitment to the state. Conveniently omitted from the official renderings are traditional forms of popular sovereignty, which included the right of individuals to make petitions to their rulers and have grievances redressed. For it is important to understand that with or without external pressures for change, there are, and always have been, local voices challenging authority.

The cultural roots of political power and legitimacy in Southeast Asia have been greatly misunderstood. The image of the Asian strongman was indelibly etched on the minds of social scientists from the 1960s onwards. They looked at Indonesia's Sukarno, Thailand's Field Marshall prime ministers, Sarit Thanarat and Thanom Kittikachorn, or Ferdinand Marcos in the Philippines and considered them model autocrats (not much more sophisticated than Antonio Galvao's judgement of non-dairy consuming Moluccans.) Some forbearance was given because they governed emerging countries badly in need of growth and development; their leadership produced results and kept communism at bay. Army-led regimes in Thailand and Indonesia were thought to be more purposeful and effective about developing the country – which in reality meant they could be wooed by foreign business interests.

It is dangerous to assume that these strongmen exemplified ideal leaders as judged through the lens of indigenous political culture, however. These ideals can perhaps be found in the purest form at the grass roots level, in the village community. Here there is a definable sense of collective endeavour, a strong stress on family values, and curbs on individual expression. But there is also a strong sense of justice and above all an aversion to tyranny. It is nonsense to assume that Southeast Asian societies are totally cowed by authority. There is respect for legitimate authority and a higher degree of compliance than many Westerners would be accustomed to. But the abuse of authority has always been contested by these societies, and in this sense the definition of social discipline propounded by proponents of Asian values can easily be distorted. Recent political history has been marked by short but effective bursts of popular protest against tyranny.

In 1965, pent-up frustration felt by students and professionals angered by Sukarno's revolutionary hyperbole burst on to the streets of Jakarta after the 30 September coup attempt weakened Sukarno's grip on power. In Thailand, students successfully toppled a military dictatorship in 1973. In 1986 people took to the streets of Manila to force Ferdinand Marcos out of power. Two years later, Burma erupted in mass protests against an inept and creaking regime led by an ageing general. In all these cases there were invisible, manipulative political forces at work, but the strength of public sentiment was real enough. What drives people to rebel against authority, as it does the world over, is the sustained abuse of power and disregard for civil liberties. Effective repression and culturally driven acquiescence does, however, explain why popular unrest can remain suppressed over longer periods. But just because popular grievances do not get aired so openly in Southeast Asian societies does not mean they are not deeply felt.

Not all the cultural ideals embodied by the region's state ideologies should be dismissed. There is a great deal to be said for the formulation of religious and ethnic tolerance included in Indonesia's 'Five principles' or *Pancasila*. Most democratic activists in contemporary Indonesia can find nothing authoritarian about a creed which stipulates equality, social justice and freedom of worship for all. What they argue about is the way *Pancasila* has been implemented. *Pancasila* has been used as a tool for stifling dissent and denying freedom, they say. It has not been utilised as a guide for government and people alike, but rather as a way for the government to impose order on the people. This suggests that *Pancasila* as a set of principles is not the obstacle to expressing popular sovereignty, rather it is the way it has been deployed.

The distortion of core values has taken place at the state level. In fact, modern urban existence and the capitalist system has begun to erode the traditional collective values which the ruling elites claim lie at the core of their cultures. Opportunities for material advancement offered by growth have encouraged the pursuit of individual interests. Urban migration has inevitably disrupted family values and forced individual members of society to fend for themselves. In the process, they are less likely to conceive of themselves as belonging to a certain station in life.

Ironically, and perhaps significantly, this erosion of indigenous collective values has tended not to generate praise for the triumph of the individual over the state. Instead, liberals and conservatives alike are worried about what is happening to the fabric of their society. A Thai newspaper editor, now in academia, reflected thus:

> Thais once lived in a moderately comfortable environment. They were generous. They had good mental health and ethics. But now they behave more like machines. Each day they are programmed to pump out money and increase consumption. They compete ruthlessly, become strenuous and mean. In their violent struggle for power, they choose to embezzle and cheat.

More will be said about the perceived moral malaise in Southeast Asian society in Chapter 5. But it is perhaps worth noting here that the claiming of core values by ruling elites in Southeast Asia is not purely a top-down political process. There is a sense in which some of these societies are also looking for assurance and explanations as to where they are headed in an increasingly materialistic world.

## ELITIST CORES

It is often argued by critics of the harsher regimes in Southeast Asia that claims of cultural distinctiveness, or pleas for time in order to foster more democratic awareness, are less the reflection of fundamental differences, or Asian values, and more the excuses of stubborn political elites unwilling to change their ways. From the conservative core of these elites comes the argument for a set of social and cultural values at odds with Western culture. Are they stalling in the face of external and internal criticism, or are they right? There is no diplomatic answer to this question except to question the parity between official and public perceptions of what constitutes culture.

The arguments are lively, if not always convincing. However, the fact that Southeast Asians are themselves arguing over what constitutes the right model of political freedom is itself a symptom of political pluralism. Take this exchange between two letter writers in the Indonesian news magazine *Tempo*, which was banned in June 1994. Both correspondents were Indonesians living overseas, yet they differed completely in their approach. 'AS' from Germany argued that he saw no reason why Indonesia should mimic Western-style democracy because as an Asian country society was organised differently. A few weeks later, 'MB' from Australia fired back at 'AB' with the argument that the right to free speech and expression was a fundamental human right.

One of the most moderate arguments against the Western human rights agenda can accept the principles but argues that the region's societies will need time to attain either the political maturity or the economic prosperity required to foster an under-standing of democracy and human rights. Progress towards these ideals is something all Asian countries would like to see, some ASEAN officials insist, but it takes time. As one Singaporean official put it:

> The ideal of human rights is compelling because this is an imperfect world and we must strive to make it better. Yet precisely because it is an imperfect world, progress on human rights will be marked by ambiguity, compromise, and at times even contradiction.[19]

Sometimes it is hard to distinguish between compromise and contradiction. Despite the rhetoric of uncompromising leaders like Mahathir Mohamad and Lee Kuan Yew, the orthodoxy of their view is now being questioned. In Singapore, there is a degree of concern that public acceptance of an overbearing state that feels compelled to tell citizens how to run their lives may be waning. The worry is that the next generation of Singaporeans will not accept a state which frowns on individual initiative and insists that their survival is at stake. Demonstrating its character-istic pragmatism – as well as an instinct for preservation – Singa-pore's ruling elite took measured steps to relax and encourage more popular expression in the early 1990s. On a superficial level this meant that adult Singaporeans could watch soft-porn movies and more foreign news broadcasts. But the aim is certainly not a liberal free for all. 'Trimming the banyan tree' was not a licence to saw off whole limbs and branches. The idea is clearly to meet critics of the system half-way; to effect a compromise and pre-serve the system essentially as it is. Hence the tolerance of mildly

questioning voices like this from Leslie Fong, the editor of the
*Straits Times*:

> Where vision of what Singapore should strive to be is con-
> cerned, there is no monopoly of wisdom by anyone. It is for
> every thinking person to contribute his bit on what he judges
> to be not only desirable but achievable.[20]

Significantly, Fong was careful to add a politically-correct rider:
the sense of unease when too much power is invested in one
institution, he wrote, 'is as much a Confucian tradition as it is a
Western liberal one'.

If core values are being manipulated or concocted and imposed
top-down on society to maintain control over society, then how
does society conceive of itself? It is not easy to measure the
contemporary cultural heartbeat in Southeast Asia because of
the eclecticism so endemic to the region. Culture itself can be
defined in many ways. In a recent interview, members of a Malaysian pop group were accused of 'apeing' Western culture. 'We
live in brick houses, wear suits, and drive cars. If that is not
Western, I don't know what is', came back their angry response.
Equally it is too simplistic to assume that all Southeast Asia's
societies are being milled into prefect replicas of 'Middletown'
USA. Another Malaysian pop musician on the same subject said:
'Culture isn't what you wear, it's what you feel inside.'[21]

The most common assumption is that Southeast Asians,
especially the younger generation, are hooked on Western culture. They like the affluence and freedom it imparts. The tendency
to equate the desire for material aspects of Western culture with
a yearning for freedom stems from official control over access to
Western culture which was, and in some countries still is, considered a corrupting influence on local tradition. Just as the
*Economist* has argued that a good way to measure the purchasing
parity of world currencies is to compare the price of a 'Big
Mac', so perceptions of political freedom are often unconsciously
determined by whether teenagers can listen to heavy metal music
legally.

Southeast Asians may have grasped the material aspects of
Western culture, and not fully absorbed the rest, however. Youth
culture in Thailand, Malaysia and Indonesia is not fully Westernised. Young students who enjoy eating at McDonalds and wearing
Reebok or Nike training shoes, may at the same time find moral

refuge in the preaching of an Islamic radical, or a Buddhist ascetic monk. Even more startling examples of this selective acculturation are the Malaysian students sent to American universities to avoid the clutches of Islamic fundamentalism in the Middle East who are attracted to ascetic Islamic teaching in the bosom of their leafy mid-Western campuses. This suggests a bifurcation of youth culture. The material aspects can be Western; the ideology is that of the mosque, the temple, or the charismatic church. In Chapter 5 more will be said about the importance of religion as an ideological catalyst for new political thinking that attempts to distinguish itself from the West.

Economic prosperity and political stability have bred confidence among Southeast Asians, but their eclectic nature has not changed. Walk into any urban bookstore in Kuala Lumpur or Singapore, and the demand for books on how to succeed in business is very evident. But the range of cultures drawn upon to tell people how to make their first million ranges from the art of Chinese geomancy to the wisdom of US auto executive Lee Iacocca. Similarly, the liberal image projected by Western civilisation has great appeal, and there are a growing number of local voices promoting its merits. A survey conducted among young people in Jakarta in May 1993 found a consistently high percentage of awareness on a host of rights including the right to be equal before the law, freedom of conscience, religion, expression and association. On whether or not they were aware of the right to express themselves freely – either verbally or in writing – 82.6 per cent of the 500 respondents surveyed answered in the affirmative. Only 4.6 per cent said that right should be exercised responsibly, and only one respondent said the right of expression was there as long as the opinion expressed was supportive of the government.[22]

Yet this appeal of liberal values competes in a market place of escapist opportunities bred by the failure of governments to provide avenues of expression for the young, especially in urban areas. One way adolescent Thais escape the ennui is to drink and take drugs to excess. Raging Saturday night binges are a common pursuit of teenagers not yet out of high school in the Northern Thai city of Chiangmai. Alchohol and other substance abuse often leads to casual sex and fuels runaway increases in the level of HIV infection among young Thais which are among the highest in the region. Experts are at a loss to explain the root cause of this often fatal escapism, but many point to the pernicious cocktail of lax morality stemming from the break up of the family unit and material aspirations acquired from commercial television.[23] In Malaysia, a government survey of young people aged between 13 and 21 in 1994 found that 71 per cent smoked, 40 per cent watched pornographic videos, 28 per cent gambled, 25 per cent drank alcohol and 14 per cent took hard drugs.[24]

Large numbers of young people are also attracted to religion and indigenous spiritualism as a means of escape. Fatalism and values of life more in tune with age-old traditional values dominate the thoughts of teenagers who risk their lives racing motorcycles on the streets of Kuala Lumpur, Bangkok or Ho Chi Minh City. The flowing green robes and turban worn by members of the Al Arqam movement were a common sight in Malaysia until the movement was banned in mid-1994. The government feared the movement's popularity, especially among young Malays disenchanted with the rigours of city life. Thousands of young people gave up their comfortable materialistic lives to live in communes, following the vague teachings of a former Islamic preacher and Islamic political activist, Sheikh Imam Ashaari Mohamad. Pragmatic asceticism might be a good way of describing the way of life followed by Arqam devotees. Their spiritual leader publicly exhorted them to 'love God and think of the hereafter'. But while life was outwardly simple, and as close to the way they imagined the early Islamic believers lived it in seventh-century Arabia, the organisation ran a number of successful businesses and was not short of funds. What's more, Al Arqam claimed a world-wide membership of around 200,000.

For all the Malaysian government's public moralising about the evils of Western culture, it worried about Arqam's harsh rejection of Western-style materialism. According to a senior Malaysian official with a religious background, 'there is concern that extremist organisations like Arqam have penetrated the urban middle classes'.[25] Mahathir likes to talk about an approach to religion that can be both spiritual and progressive. Ashaari's response was: 'We are progressive. We build schools. The government is not progressive because it is not serving the people's interests, but only those of certain individuals.'[26] The more Ashaari highlighted the corruption and pursuit of personal interests in Malaysian elite circles, the more concerned the authorities became. But people also began to look more closely at the bearded youths behind heavy black eye make-up in their ubiquitous dark green robes; and what they saw was a fresh, moral approach to life, no matter how austere. The potential appeal eventually brought the full force of the law to bear on the movement.[27]

To claim a homogeneous official or common culture against this heterogeneous context clearly misrepresents reality. Seemingly less flimsy than the cultural argument against political change is the plea for time. A common official explanation is that sudden or hastily implemented political change would threaten these countries with instability; that in Indonesia and Malaysia a sudden loosening of strict controls over society might lead to political polarisation – along either ethnic or religious lines. Of course, this kind of fear can be deliberately provoked to encourage people to believe in the constant need for political control and vigilence. In fact, the slow pace of political change may act as a catalyst for unrest because there are no avenues for redressing social and economic grievances.

In Indonesia there were several violent acts committed against Christian churches in Java in the course of 1993 which looked like a worrying by-product of the resentment building up in Islamic circles over the perceived inequalities of wealth between religious communities. In April 1994, a labour protest got out of hand in the North Sumatran capital Medan and an ethnic Chinese businessman was killed. Despite the involvement of some 20,000 workers, and repeated attempts by labour leaders to present their grievances to the provincial authorities, the armed forces publicly took the view that the protest was an illegal riot, bent on provoking violence against Medan's considerable Chinese population.[28]

In elite Indonesian circles there is an allergy to spontaneous popular expression because the focus of popular expression inevitably seizes on ethnic and religious differences, or the gap between rich and poor. It may be in the interests of competing elite interests to *organise* demonstrations to demonstrate popular support, but quite another to allow the populace to express themselves in an unbridled, spontaneous fashion. See what happens when they do. In early 1993 teenage rock fans ran riot through a rich Jakarta suburb after a concert by the Western rock band Metallica. The homes of the rich and their fancy cars were deliberately targeted. Confusing this outburst of youthful frustration with more traditional resentment of the wealthy overseas Chinese, one senior government official came running out of his house shouting that he was a *pribumi*, or native Indonesian. The rioters paid no heed and burnt his car all the same.[29]

Free expression, whether on the campus or by a free trade union on the factory shop floor, is greatly feared by ruling establishments in the region and the business interests close to them. Controlled, channelled and ultimately co-opted, the path trod by those who choose to assert their right to free speech is never smooth. When Indonesian newspaper editor Eros Djarot tried to reopen his popular tabloid *De-Tik* after the government closed it down in June 1994, the successor publication, *Simponi*, was quickly closed on a technicality – its editor was found not to be a member of the state-backed Union of Indonesian Journalists. Being a journalist in Indonesia, suggested Goenawan Mohamad, the editor of *Tempo*, another banned publication; 'is like being a pilot hi-jacked in mid-air'. The editor of a Malaysian Chinese language newspaper explained why he had been trying to resign for the past two years in these terms:

> As a journalist I can never think of playing the watchdog, questioning the actions of those in power. As journalists we have to be compatible with the establishment. We are only running a vehicle. If the government feels comfortable with it, we will survive.[30]

The problem is that the very areas of society Western governments would like to see liberalised are considered by those who hold power as the key to enduring prosperity and stability, and to containing political challenge. Not that there is an easily measured popular consensus of this view. Here perhaps indigenously-driven liberalisation must be separated from the rhetoric of Western policy on human rights and democracy. There is also merit in considering democracy in a conceptual sense, rather than as a precise set of institutions. For with or without Western pressure, social and economic change is influencing local political trends and promoting more individual freedom, if not democracy in the strictest sense.

## TOWARDS A MIDDLE GROUND

Twenty years ago a less educated, less urbanised population was more susceptible to the primordial ethnic or religious tension most governments in the region feared would ensue if democracy was given a free rein. In some countries the pace and structure of economic growth is making it necessary to loosen traditional collective bonds and grant more individuals the space to be creative and innovative. In this sense, an infusion of Western values which have helped promote innovativeness and leadership in industry could be the key to Southeast Asia's economic survival. Traditional regard for collective action and rigorous self-discipline might hinder the absorption of technology on which the region's economic future now depends.

Take the new generation of hi-tech electronics factories being built in Singapore and Malaysia. In the 1970s companies like Motorola, Hewlett Packard and Hitachi gravitated to these locations because labour was cheap and plentiful. Though cost margins remain attractive for this reason, the highly automated manufacturing processes and rigorous quality control standards employed in the industry today also demand a measure of ability and creativity from the workforce. 'Better, faster, cheaper, by working smarter' runs the slogan a new hard-disk manufacturing firm in Penang has introduced to its workforce. 'Not by working harder or longer, but by being creative. We want a thinking workforce, not just a working workforce', stressed the firm's managing director.[31]

Nearly a decade of liberal economic reform and deregulation has generated a robust private sector which makes demands of governments and bureaucracies that not so long ago made all the economic decisions. These economies themselves can no longer rely on exports of primary commodities – simple trading operations that could be monopolised by the bureaucracy. To maintain the momentum, industry must move downstream and diversify into areas which require innovative technological skills. Just as the children of rice farmers or rubber tappers are assembling air-conditioners today, their children will be developing software or refining synthetic fuels. There is already a shortage of skilled management personnel in most ASEAN countries. More alarmingly, the innovative skills of the region's scientific community are poorly developed.

In Malaysia a mobile telephone manufacturing company advertised for over a year for a senior technician in 1993 – and still could not fill the job. Those who fill such jobs are usually so highly valued they jump from job to job, lured by higher salaries. Although the lacunae in Southeast Asia's skilled job market can be blamed on poor educational planning, it has much to do with the core values instilled in the region's schools. Learning by rote and too much collective discipline does little to promote technical skills, which must then be acquired at great expense overseas, and therefore by fewer people.

To accommodate these changes, governments will have to adapt politically – or lose the ability to maintain the economic momentum which sustains their legitimacy. It is one thing for Lee Kuan Yew to insist that Southeast Asians reject the 'American' view that 'out of the clash of different ideas and ideals you get good government'. It is quite another to expect Southeast Asians to compete in the global market place of ideas without the freedom to express their ideas. The initiative to invest offshore and create new areas of economic expansion will not come from a generation bridled by harsh social and political control.

At the same time, the process of wealth creation has created new fissures in these societies. Socio-economic disparities are widening. In Thailand and Indonesia there is an alarming gulf between the very rich and the very poor. If only 3 per cent of Bangkok's population live below a poverty line officially determined as income less than Baht 4,000 a year, this number rises to 37 per cent in the north-eastern region, and over 20 per cent in the North. Poverty in Indonesia may have fallen below 20 per cent of the population, but it is now extremely localised, rising to as much as 40 per cent in some eastern provinces according to World Bank estimates. Even more sensitive in political terms is the disparity in middle-class incomes; civil servants earning barely US$ 500–1,000 can read in the newspaper about the owner of a bank who throws a wedding party for 5,000 guests. A Singaporean official talks about the 'wage gap' between skilled workers commanding 'first world prices' and unskilled workers facing 'third world wages'. 'Politics in the future will be the politics of envy', another Singaporean official suggests. With a much higher percentage of people acquiring secondary and tertiary education, many more Southeast Asians already have the literate ability to express this envy, and they are likely to do so by demanding a much bigger say in how the state is run. These are realities the governments of the region have to face – but the time scale may be rather different from that envisaged in the West.

In the interim, there will be a rather slower process of adaptation – a blend of established political tradition with the needs of a more challenging economic future. Hence the emergence in countries like Indonesia and Malaysia of powerful private sector lobby groups. In Indonesia, Andrew Macintyre detected sections of the business class that have, through 'bargaining and coalition building', begun to influence state decisions.[32] It is too early, perhaps, to see these emerging interest groups as champions of political freedom. Their priority is a profitable business climate, which very often means support for the status quo. In Thailand, the business community initially supported the 1991 military coup. They wanted an end to the perceived corruption prevailing in the late 1980s under the elected government of Chatichai Choonhavan. When they saw the military's lack of popular support, they swung behind an elected civilian government again. Tired of the inaction and indecisive leadership of the elected civilian government they swung back in favour of a firmer, more conservative leadership in 1995. Only this time, some of the corporate actors entered the political arena themselves.

In the Southeast Asian context the business community's commitment to democracy is ambivalent. The corporate sector has learnt to put the interests of its patrons before those of the workforce. Partly, this stems from the residual fears of overseas Chinese, who dominate commerce in most Southeast Asian countries, about their status and security. In the struggle to control the abuse of Vietnam's cheap labour the government found that the worst offenders were Asian companies. Businessmen who are vocal about the need for a freer market, are not necessarily advocates of free trade unions. A senior member of Thailand's Federation of Trade and Industry described labour unions as a 'foreign culture'. In 1995, the Thai textile industry proposed setting up a minimum wage free zone along the Thai–Burmese border so that cheap Burmese labour could be safely exploited. The problem is likely to get worse before it gets better. Some will say that unmitigated exploitation was the key to early industrial development in the West. Meanwhile, in most of the more developed Southeast Asian states, the competitive advantage of cheap labour and low production costs is rapidly being eroded by the spiralling cost of labour and infrastructure. Hence resistance to granting full worker rights can be cast as a nationalist struggle to maintain competitiveness, as it has been in Malaysia.

Some inertia, therefore, needs to be factored in to the political development of Southeast Asia over the next two decades. The prevailing ruling elites and business class are fundamentally conservative. They hide behind a culture of power that demands acceptance of strong leadership and unquestioned loyalty to the state. More liberal elements of the middle class – intellectuals, writers, and non-governmental activists – are a minority without the political or financial means to assert themselves. For now they must rely on the sympathy and support of outside lobbies. The struggle for independence and later against Communism has bred deep suspicion of external influence in the surviving nationalist leaders of the 1940s and 1950s. It also gave them the means of wielding near-absolute power that no politician is so eager to yield. They in turn have passed this political culture on to the generation groomed to succeed them – together with the institutions of control. Their successors may not share the same prejudices but there is no guarantee as yet that they won't savour the same measure of power and authority.

Neither should the possibility of a conservative backlash to the extent of liberalisation achieved so far be ruled out. There are signs of this in Indonesia where prodding by Western donors to open up the economy has not been matched by regulatory controls. With the widening of economic disparities this has brought about, the reaction has been to clamour for state intervention to maintain social harmony. Western pressure does not help. To establish political legitimacy and popularity the new generation of leaders could well tap new sources of nationalist sentiment. They might find perceptions of a clash of values and cultural decoupling useful in the formulation of this new nationalist ideology. There are already faint signs of this in the new Islamic-backed political movement hoping to dislodge the military from power in Indonesia. In Malaysia, the young Islamic idealists planning Anwar Ibrahim's rise to power are searching for a new nationalist ideology which blends Islamic religious values with indigenous cultural norms and entails some distancing from the West.

While education, access to information, and enhanced prosperity have unquestionably bred a degree of popular unease with strict social and political control, broad-based calls for participation in government could easily be offset by fears of instability should political change be introduced too quickly. The middle classes of Asia are fundamentally conservative too. Indonesia's middle class is not sufficiently broad-based or numerous to bridge the gap between rich and poor. They fear the popular backlash against their wealth more political freedom could unleash; they are tied to the system which generated the wealth they now enjoy:

> The Jakarta middle class, like other classes, only struggle for their own practical interests.... They realise that there are a number of unjust practices in their own society, but at the same time they realise that nothing can be done to solve the problems. As a privileged class, they tend to be charitable to the underdog. There is, as such, [something] of the *noblesse oblige* ideology of the European aristocracy.[33]

Indonesian sociologist Benny Subianto concludes that to assume the Indonesian middle class will play a role similar to that of the European *bourgeoisie* of the eighteenth century is misleading. The Indonesian middle class, he believes, is a creation of the state and therefore very much tied to state policy. In much the same way the Malaysian middle class – proportionally a much larger cohort in society – is a prisoner of the state's strict control over interethnic interaction. Malaysians are told that their society comprises of a 'diverse and incompatible ethnic and religious mix'. Strong leadership is required to ensure that the different ethnic groups don't leap at each other's throats. Hence Malaysians of all races and whatever class tend to live in fear of ethnic strife and generally support the government's tough controls on the freedom of expression. 'There is this code of silence, we don't talk about certain things in front of people from other races. This is what I find so stifling', said a Malaysian academic who spent many years overseas. So much for the much vaunted power of the middle class.

The political landscape of Southeast Asia is changing, and it is a pity that the complexity of these changes is being obscured by the obsession with matching the pace and form of political change to Western standards. The key question is not whether political change matches Western standards, but rather whether these changes will satisfy domestic demands and needs. If there is no dispute about the direction of change, there are certainly differences over how it should be defined. Therefore the best approach to preventing a confrontation over the meaning of shared values would be to find a middle ground which limits the scope for semantic argument. In short, while alternative definitions of human rights and democracy must be avoided, there is room for a formula which narrows the gulf of misunderstanding and makes allowances for regional sensitivities.

Democracy in Southeast Asia is likely to be narrowly defined and guided for some time to come. Less adversarial and steering shy of small group advocacy, officially sanctioned forms of political expression will continue to appear underdeveloped in Western eyes. But the governments of Southeast Asia will ignore the need to broaden the popular base of government at their peril. The problem, as seen by former US ambassador Morton Abramowitz, is 'to find a balance between order and personal freedom'.[34]

Finding a compromise formula will seem like a see-saw between increasing popular demand for participation, and co-option of those who the elite permits to participate. Describing this interim stage, observers have coined terms like 'demi-democracy', or 'modified democracy'. The most positive result could be what Malaysian intellectual Syed Farid Alatas calls the triumph of 'elements of democracy'. There will be a greater role for lobbying by pressure groups and NGOs in a controlled fashion, allowing enclaves of Western-style advocacy to thrive under controlled conditions – but for the time being subject to sanction or co-option. The rigidity and tenacity of the strong, anti-democratic state in Southeast Asia seems to ensure its survival, but does not guarantee its effectiveness. Instead of being replaced, Thai academic Chai-anan Samudavanija envisages a 'bypass' process. Helping to limit the relevance and effectiveness of the strong state, he argues is the trend towards globalisation and regionalism:

> Supra nationality and internationalisation, in my view, will lead to new phenomena in state–society relations which I call bypassing the state by grass roots groups and their transnational coalitions.[35]

Something like this process can already be observed in the region. Protectionist lobbies in the business community or the bureaucracy are being overcome by a regional consensus on free trade; human rights concerns are being expressed at a regional level by local NGOs, which makes it harder for governments to blame the interfering West. Professor Chai-anan may have a point, but he is wise enough to add that he feels strong states will not just whither away. Change they will, but it will be a slow process, always subject to adaptation, and possibly even reversal should economic or political insecurity demand the reassertion of strong leadership. Putting it another way, prominent Thai academic Sukhumbhand Paribatra considers that globalisation is certainly forcing governments of the region to become more transparent, 'but that does not make them more democratic'.[36]

History has shown that Southeast Asian societies are successful because of their inherent flexibility, their openness to change. While there is currently broad agreement in Southeast Asia that the rigorous imposition of Western-style democracy runs counter to prevailing social and political traditions, the key to the future is likely to be a balanced, gradual process of change. As Lee Kuan Yew predicts:

> Every country must evolve its own style of representative government. Indeed, a country is not likely to succeed unless it adapts or modifies US or European democratic practices to fit its different circumstances.[37]

If he is right, it seems odd that the clash of values with the West has occurred at all, or has not already dissipated. Perhaps this says more about Western insecurities than Asian shortcomings.

# Chapter 5

# The religious challenge to authority

*After me there will be caliphs; and after the caliphs, amirs; and
after the amirs, kings; and after the kings, tyrants...*
hadith *(tradition) attributed to the Prophet Mohammed*

Every Tuesday and Thursday, crowds of middle-class Thais gather
at the base of an equestrian statue of the late King Rama V in
central Bangkok to make offerings and pray. With mobile phones
strapped to their waists, their BMWs parked nearby, and perhaps
a dinner appointment with clients still to go, Bangkok's yuppies
make time to pay homage to the monarch they consider made
their prosperous lifestyle possible.

Rama V, or King Chulalongkorn, died in 1910 after a long
reign during which he abolished slavery, modernised the fiscal
system, and built the country's first modern schools. Every Thai
student knows Rama V as a reforming King, but only relatively
recently has his memory been revered in a religious rite. On
some nights, thousands of people throng the broad square on
Rajdamnoen Avenue where the bronze equestrian statue stands.
They lay out rush mats on which they erect small altars with
portraits of the King, a kindly-looking man with a fine moustache.
Offerings of brandy, cigars and pink roses are favoured because
it is believed the King was something of a *bon-viveur*. The ritual
bears all the hallmarks of a cult. Young professionals wear gold
and diamond-studded amulets bearing his portrait; his portrait
adorns office walls, the inside of taxi-cabs and buses; and a minor
industry has sprung up reproducing pictures of the late King.
There are even photographers who offer studio portraits where
the subject is dressed in the Edwardian garb fashionable during
his reign.

What draws young professional Thais, with their garlands and offerings of incense, to the statue of Rama V? Why aren't they seeking solace in more modern forms of escapism? Why not take advice from a lawyer or a psychiatrist, rather than a dead king? The answer is that even in a society modernising as rapidly as Thailand's, people turn to traditional symbols and beliefs in search of luck or solace. Chulalongkorn, as we saw earlier, abolished slavery and was the father of modern education in Thailand; but he also showed Thais the way to modernise without losing their sense of identity. For Thais, he was an exemplary nationalist. In this sense, he has become a powerful symbol of Thai identity in the face of the erosive forces of modernity; a protective talisman for those who find that chasing wealth and status in Thailand's high-rolling economy taxes their cultural and spiritual beliefs. Devotion to this ideal image of a past monarch also points to a desire for a tangible faith; something innately spiritual. Despite the modernisation of everything from medicine and management, Thais look for strength in their country's spiritual traditions.

Everywhere one looks in Southeast Asia, religion is an important part of personal and social life. Every year the Governor of the northern Thai city of Chiangmai conducts an elaborate Buddhist ceremony involving a sacred phallic city pillar to ensure the continued safety of the city and its inhabitants. In modern Burma, village children learn to read and write at pagoda schools, and when they attain adulthood will periodically spend a month or so wearing the saffron robes of the monkhood. In the Malaysian capital of Kuala Lumpur, it is *de rigeur* for the Prime Minister and every Muslim member of his cabinet to attend midday Friday prayers at the National Mosque – parliament does not sit on Friday. Every year in Indonesia, the world's largest Muslim country with a per capita GDP of around US$ 700, some 160,000 people each spend the equivalent of nearly US$ 7,000 to make the holy pilgrimage to Mecca. In Singapore, Christian revivalist faiths attract more and more of the island republic's new rich. 'They seem to want to justify their material gains as a heavenly reward', suggests a local writer.[1]

What does the tenacity of religious devotion in the modern context tell us about Southeast Asian society? In general terms, it underlines the fact that, contrary to widely held predictions about the course of modernisation, religious identity in Southeast

Asia is still very much part of the fabric of society. Classical Weberian sociological theory argues that with modernisation, primordial religious beliefs are eventually replaced by secular national and civic values. But this vision of a despiritualised society seems misplaced in Southeast Asia. Indeed, it would be hard for religious beliefs to be eroded in a region where religion continues to play a role in defining statehood. In Thailand, Buddhism is an important pillar of the state, as it is in Burma, Laos and Cambodia. The official motto of the Kingdom of Cambodia is 'Nation, Religion, King'. Islam is not only the official religion of Malaysia and Brunei; Muslim identity also infers a distinct cultural and racial identity. In the case of Brunei, an official ideology has been built around the concept of an indivisible nexus between Malay ethnic identity, Islam and the Monarchy. Indonesia's plural society, where Muslims account for as much as 90 per cent of the population today, carefully avoids regarding Islam as the state religion. Nevertheless the official position is that Indonesia is a religious rather than a secular state.

That is not to say that religion has not been affected by modernity. Materialism has been the principal side-effect of contemporary growth in a region where religious beliefs idealise charity and frugality. As in Western societies, the contest between God and Mammon at first sight appears fairly one-sided. But instead of shrugging off religion in favour of material gain, Southeast Asians have learned to plough their wealth into religious rituals. People in Thailand and Singapore spend increasing sums of money on ever more elaborate religious and spiritual rites – whether it is the multimillion dollar trade in Buddhist amulets, or the opulence of a modern Chinese funeral. Islam too, has become gentrified in this way, with lavish spending on rituals like breaking the fast during the month of Ramadan, or on the annual pilgrimage to Mecca. A young Indonesian professional explains:

> More and more people now go on the haj when they are relatively young, while formerly only older people went on the pilgrimage. Besides, reasons of piety, going on the pilgrimage to Mecca is also a sure sign of economic affluence.[2]

The amount of money people are willing to spend on spiritual salvation only underscores the importance of religion more heavily.

As well as fulfiling spiritual needs, religion in Southeast Asia is more closely associated with politics – at least the boundary between secular and spiritual affairs is not always distinct. Religion is as inherent to the political process in Southeast Asia as the administrative principles inherited from the Western colonial powers, and the fact that religion governs the lives of Southeast Asians with more intensity may also have intriguing implications for the political future of the region. Earlier it was argued that the reassertion of premodern traditions of power and authority has not so far been successfully challenged using the idiom of Western liberal politics. Ruling political elites have instead manipulated indigenous culture to justify strong government and controls over individual freedom. But society has not always been dependent on the thought of Rousseau or Jefferson to combat tyranny and inequality. Traditionally, threats to the established political order in Southeast Asia have in fact been rather commonly articulated from the higher moral ground of the mosque or temple. Rulers of ancient Southeast Asian states co-opted religion and established themselves as the source of moral goodness and focus of cosmic order. Unlike the medieval monarchs of Europe, who were hobbled by the power of Rome, they never allowed the 'clergy' to play an independent role.

Despite the state's co-option of the spiritual domain, religion has played a role in challenging state power. Islamic preachers in the fifteenth century helped transform the Hindu-Buddhist monolithic kingdoms on Java and the Malay peninsular into minor princely states ruled by Muslim sultans. In the nineteenth century, religious teaching inspired the first nationalist movements to challenge European rule in Burma and Indonesia. A Burmese Buddhist monk, U Ottama, influenced by the Congress movement in India, helped initiate agitation against British rule in the 1920s. In Indonesia, Muslim merchants incensed by the lack of fair treatment under Dutch rule and influenced by early Islamic notions of nationalism acquired on pilgrimages to the Middle East, formed *Sarekat Islam*, one of the earliest associations to combat colonial rule. Though seldom played up by present-day governments in Southeast Asia, the fires of nationalism were arguably kindled in the grounds of the temple or mosque.

Modern religions, specifically Islam and Theravada Buddhism, have had a far greater impact on political culture in Southeast Asia than any secular teaching. Arguably, the introduction of Islam to the region complicated the rigidly hierarchical relationship between rulers and the ruled that imported Hinduism had encouraged. In the 1930s, the Indonesian nationalist Sutan Sjahrir asked:

> whether Islam, with regard to Hinduism, does not play the same role in history that Protestantism did against Catholicism in Europe, viz., articulating a bourgeois view of life against a feudal one.[3]

Islam came to Southeast Asia around the fifteenth century, at the apogee of the medieval Islamic world. As A.C. Milner points out, the new religion at first appealed to local rulers; they were attracted to the universal enlightenment imbued by its teaching. Later on, these rulers became vulnerable to reformist trends in the Islamic world that attacked kingship and the lofty and inaccessible mysticism in which it was wrapped.[4] 'There must be no obedience in transgression [against God]', runs a frequently cited traditional saying ascribed to the Prophet Mohammed.

Probably because of the historical potency of religion as a factor in politics, modern Southeast Asian states have emulated their premodern forbears by circumscribing and co-opting religion under the umbrella of the state. In the modern period, the clearest example is in Indonesia, where early attempts by Muslim activists to impose their imprint on the constitution of the new republic after 1945 were rebuffed, and religion was carefully corralled into a constricted space governed by more secular considerations of order. Perhaps the most important function of Indonesia's *Pancasila* state ideology is that it enjoins Islam, the religion of the majority, to tolerate other creeds. Likewise, communist rulers in Vietnam and Cambodia made efforts to erase the populist role played by the Buddhist clergy.[5]

In modern Thailand, political legitimacy can still be derived from association with the Buddhist church. Many a politician assumes the saffron robe to help establish his moral credibility. In the 1990s, urban voters were drawn to the Palang Dharma Party led by Major General Chamlong Srimuang, who consciously drew on the teachings of an ascetic Buddhist sect known as Santi Asoke. 'Although the rulers may cling to the state machinery, the common people must be able to use religion and morality to rule themselves more effectively', asserts Thai social critic Sulak Sivaraksa.[6] This tension between state and society over acceptable moral norms runs deep in Malaysia, where the Muslim–Malay dominated ruling establishment wages an awkward battle against dogmatic Islamic activists struggling to establish an Islamic state – a contest it cannot hope to win outright without losing its own Islamic legitimacy.

In the search for catalysts of political change in Southeast Asia, the tendency has been to assume the primacy of new and modern (i.e. Western) ideas about civic–state relations. While these ideas are important, they are not the exclusive source of political change. An equally potent challenge to established authority could stem from a revival of traditional religious and moral values. There are two separate, but converging reasons why this could happen in Southeast Asia. The first stems from changes in the political idiom which have in fact rendered modern secular ideologies and models less relevant, or morally bankrupt. In short, Communism failed, socialism died, and the ideological fuel of anti-colonial nationalism ran low. While it is fashionable in some quarters to consider that Western liberal political values triumphed after the end of the Cold War, there are other claimants to the emerging New World Order. The perceived moral and economic decline of the West, and its failure to resolve post-Cold War conflicts has inspired alternative visions:

> Islam is emerging as a new patron, offering the City of God alternative to the otherwise secular, capitalist Western model (and/or Eastern Stalinist model) in a world which is expected to continue to be unstable in the coming years.[7]

Reflecting this global trend, two decades of sustained and often rapid economic growth in the region has imposed strains on societies in Southeast Asia. Inequitable distribution of wealth has generated social and moral concerns which a simple diet of order and discipline has proved incapable of resolving. Even the older generation of leaders in the region recognise this:

> We are agricultural societies that have industrialised within one or two generations. What happened in the West over 200 years or more is happening here in about 50 years or less. It is all crammed and crushed into a very tight time frame, so there are bound to be dislocations and malfunctions.[8]

Significantly, Lee Kuan Yew sees these stresses in society being channelled into religious rather than political beliefs. Indeed, some Thai academics suggest that devotion to Rama V among middle-class Thais reflects a yearning for a more benevolent, more accessible, more agreeable state.[9]

That modern, educated Thais seek freedom at the altar rather than at the barricade is perhaps hard to imagine in the contemporary context, where capitalism and material aspirations are deemed to be predominant influences on society. Just as destruction of the environment is considered an inescapable by-product of industrial development, so full engagement with the material world of stock markets and hyper marts is judged to be incompatible with Asian norms of spiritual and moral behaviour. By this material yardstick, Thai investors should not believe that fate governs the stock market, or that a guardian spirit called *Phra Siam Thewathirat* actually decides who the next prime minister should be. In much the same way that we saw earlier with the political process, the conventional, or 'global' view is that tradition makes way for change and transformation – the supplanting of ancient values by modern, usually Western, norms in the interests of economic efficiency and global compatibility. By this reckoning, the affluence of Southeast Asia is setting a course towards a materially-minded society with little time for moral judgement or religious custom.

Here it will be argued that this assumption may be flawed. We shall see in this chapter that religions and their accompanying traditional moral values are experiencing a slow but palpable revival, partly as a response to changing social and economic conditions. More cogently, religion is beginning to play a more conspicuous political role – specifically in the four more developed countries of the region, Indonesia, Malaysia, Singapore and Thailand. Not, as might be expected, in transforming secular states into theocracies; the cultural diversity of most Southeast Asian societies militates against the imposition of a single creed. 'To present yourself on a religious platform smacks of extremism and won't succeed here', explains a prominent Thai politician.[10] There is no foreseeable danger of fundamentalist theocracies evolving in the region. Yet in a more inchoate or benign form, religion can and will be harnessed as a force for moral reform, the assertion of national identity, and perhaps even as a vessel for incubating indigenous forms of democracy. To quote the same Thai politician, a Muslim:

what will succeed is if you take the values from traditional religion and package them to fit the requirements of modern life.[11]

## SOCIAL CHANGE BREEDS RELIGIOUS REVIVAL

A primary factor reinforcing the role of religion stems from prevailing social conditions. Affluent Asia is beginning to feel the side-effects of growth. Gaps are appearing in society between those who have benefited the most from the new prosperity, and those who, despite the cushioning effects of traditional family structures and relatively low unemployment, now feel excluded from the benefits of development. Standards of living have climbed; but so has the cost of living. The fiscal advantage Asian governments gain by not spending huge sums on welfare must increasingly be weighed against the difficulty of offsetting social and economic disparity.

Even for people in the more affluent Southeast Asian countries who have reaped the benefits of growth, the material gains are sometimes offset by non-material losses. The pace of growth has promoted social and cultural dislocation. The transition to prosperity experienced by educated middle-class members of society has been fast, often occurring within a generation. The changes have highlighted contradictions with custom and family values which they find difficult to resolve. 'All of a sudden', says a young Muslim stockbroker in Kuala Lumpur, 'you go from a situation where family and tradition counted for everything, to becoming an urban yuppie with no time for either.'[12] In July 1994, a group of leading Thai business figures met to discuss whether the teachings of the Lord Buddha (*dhamma*) conflict with the pursuit of profits. At the seminar, a local CEO bemoaned the fact that as Thailand modernised, graft greed and vice were swamping traditional Thai Buddhist values.[13] Here is how a prominent Thai artist expressed his view of Thai society:

> The world is spinning out of control. The sickness in the world is coming here to Thailand. Money makes you give up your honesty. We're working hard for what? To be happy in Hell.[14]

In the West, this kind of cynicism born of a sense of marginalisation has often resulted in the breakdown of society – a resort to senseless crime at one extreme; high divorce rates and family abuse at the other. To be sure, there is concern about rising crime rates in major cities like Jakarta and Bangkok. The Indonesian weekly news magazine *Tempo* cited a senior Indonesian police officer who predicted that incidents of violence in the city would increase with the widening of economic disparities.[15] In Singapore the incidence of juvenile crime increased almost 30 per cent between 1992 and 1993. Although stringent policing and controls over personal freedom have generally kept this form of social release within controllable limits, a more interesting phenomenon in urban Southeast Asia is the attraction of the marginalised, or socially insecure, to religion.

Societies which are still bonded by the glue of collective norms and values are likely to fall back on collective action to redress their grievances. In more atomistic Western societies individual action might be considered the best form of escape. Asian societies turn first to the institutions of moral order – to the church, the temple, or mosque – for support. To the socially disenchanted in Buddhist societies the simple contrast between the sacred and the profane is appealing because it sorts out for them what is right and wrong. Submission to faith in Islamic societies can offer relief from the symptoms of social and economic malaise in a similar way because it allows escape into a well-defined moral realm, and an abandonment of this worldly concerns. This need for a moral refuge could help explain why, despite the assumption that religion has been eroded as a force in mainstream politics in the post-independence era, the role of religion as a social force may be growing.

There is some evidence for this. Just as economic exploitation by the British in colonial Burma drove the Buddhist monkhood into political action in the early twentieth century, so the rape of natural resources in contemporary Thailand prompted populist monks like Phra Prajak Kuttajitto to launch an opposition religious movement from his forest temple in north-eastern Thailand's Buri Ram province in 1990. To stop illegal logging and protect Thailand's dwindling forestland, he patrolled the forest by night, and conferred sacred status on individual trees so that no devout Buddhist would dare cut them down.[16]

In Indonesia, the religious component in political discourse has become more important in the 1990s. Filling a political vacuum left by the emasculation of secular political ideology under Indonesia's staunchly anti-communist military regime, Muslim intellectuals were able to marry issues of faith to pressing social and economic problems. Recently, some of these intellectuals have blamed liberal financial reforms urged on Indonesia by the World Bank, and implemented by a coterie of Western-trained technocrats, for what they claim is the economic marginalisation of the Indonesian Muslim majority. They are conscious that non-Muslim Chinese Indonesians dominate large areas of the economy and have prospered from state patronage. To redress the situation, they have criticised the Chinese and demanded more official commitment to establishing a fair and equitable Islamic society.

That ethnic and religious divisions in society have become more pronounced as a result of economic disparities is not a new phenomenon. Historically, religiously inspired political movements in Southeast Asia thrived on social deprivation. Often these movements stemmed from attempts to reconcile traditional religious law or custom to new conditions. The inability to do this, generated the urge to purify and reject all alien influences. What began as a desire to explain social and economic change, ended up as a puritanical movement rejecting the political status quo and the outside world. Hence the belief by some puritanical Indonesian Muslims that the government's family planning programme is a Christian plot to reduce the number of Muslims. Usually, such movements, like the Buddhist Saya San rebellion which erupted in Burma in 1930, found expression in millennial prophecies that periods of disorder would be followed by the appearance of a just leader who would restore harmony to society.

The important nexus here is between religion and nationalism. The dividing line between 'church' and 'state' in Southeast Asia is thin because most of the ruling elites continue to draw a portion of their legitimacy, at least, from the patronage of religion. Among the dominant Muslim Malay elite in Malaysia, there is scarcely any distinction between the secular and religious realm because being a practising Muslim is an important part of Malay ethnic identity. By not fully divorcing religion from the arena of power, religion can, unless continually co-opted, become a powerful weapon against the state. Given the tenacity of religion in contemporary Southeast Asian societies, politicians will find themselves treading a narrow path between identifying with and fending off religious extremism.

The difficulty for politicians is knowing where the danger lies. Some of these religious movements are more benign than aggressive; a product of material success and security reflecting a desire of the middle classes to validate their new, more prosperous way of life using traditional values. The popular Phra Dhammakaya Buddhist sect in Thailand is a good example. It draws middle-class support for a ritual-oriented approach to Buddhism.[17] The more ascetic Santi Asoke sect, however, has made the leap into the political arena by supporting a political party. As much as the politicians have manipulated tradition to justify their power, they must be wary of the way tradition can be turned on them. If radical political movements drawing on external ideologies and non-governmental pressure have failed to address social concerns, indigenous religious movements are stepping into the breach. Their appeal stems from a blend of spiritual and nationalistic sentiments. The progress-oriented appeal of entrenched ruling elites has faded as the economic progress they fostered also bred corruption, greed and inequality. Their pragmatic policies encouraged foreign investment and a liberal trade regime, but to some extent left indigenous interests behind.

In Malaysia, Prime Minister Mahathir Mohamad's idealistic desire (expressed in his twin tracts, *The Malay Dilemma* and the *Challenge*) for the Muslim Malays to spearhead the country's industrial take-off evidently ran into the problem of finding capable, hard-working Malays. So he turned to non-Malay achievers and foreigners who could get things done. Similarly, Indonesia's President Suharto found the path to industrial development much smoother when he relied on a small coterie of cronies (many of them Chinese) who, in return for government protection of their trade monopolies, were glad to pour their capital into showcase industrial schemes. The economy was opened up to foreign investors and exchange controls were lifted. However, by trading nationalism for economic pragmatism, these leaders have generated social resentment or envy and stirred new nationalist forces.

As the fruits of economic growth appeared to become more important to the established elite than its distribution to the people, alternative sources of nationalist appeal framed in a religious context have emerged. In Thailand, Phra Prajak argued that the forest is sacred to Buddhists, and that foreigners were destroying the trees. In Malaysia, conservative religious preachers blame immoral and profane trends in society on 'Western' influence. A recent exposé on profligate wives in a Malaysian tabloid cited a religious teacher as blaming the men for being too busy, but the idea of being unfaithful as 'Western'! The American social scientist Mark Jurgensmeyer considers that in many parts of the Muslim world the rise of religious nationalism has its roots in the rejection of Western secular ideas and institutions because these ideas and institutions are held to be accountable for the moral decline within their own societies.[18] It would be exaggerating to assume that a wholesale moral breakdown afflicts any of the societies under consideration here; but it would be naïve to ignore the signs of moral malaise on the horizon in many countries.

Significantly, the new generation of politicians waiting in the wings to assume power are becoming aware of these trends. Asians may now be basking in the sunshine of economic prosperity and dynamism Surin Pitsuwan, a successful Muslim politician from Thailand, reminds us: but he is concerned about the down-trodden and marginalised:

> The fundamental issue before us, particularly in Southeast Asia today is how to devise a political mechanism, or structure . . . to bring in the minorities, the marginalised, the forgotten and those who are left behind. Failure to do that will render our economic miracle meaningless and our achievement futile, and leave our stability and prosperity undermined.[19]

The rhetoric is consistent with the term 'sustainable development' used by younger generation politicians in Malaysia. Sustainable development essentially means modifying the growth-oriented model employed for the past two decades by factoring in non-economic welfare and social development issues. Looking over the horizon, beyond the period of high growth, means looking beyond economics Malaysia's Anwar Ibrahim argues. In his view, 'the present generation of leaders is obsessed with economics'.[20] To find an ideological basis for a sustainable society, indigenous religious values are being reexamined with a view to harnessing them to the development of a more equitable and, yes, a more democratic society.

If society is turning to religion to address social needs, the politicians are finding ways to exploit the new moral mood to safeguard their power. The need for compassion and spiritual nourishment also dovetails neatly with the broad ideological challenge facing the new generation of political leaders. For strong government and a modified essence of democracy to prevail in

Southeast Asia, political elites need to draw on some form of ideology distinguishable from the West. To sustain a political framework within indigenous cultural parameters, to cope with new social and economic challenges and to resist external pressure for change, something stronger and more relevant than tired appeals to the old rhetoric of neo-colonialism may be needed. One approach has been to invoke woolly definitions of traditional Asian culture. Surin Pitsuwan suggests that the indigenous 'virtues' of 'rationality, tolerance and moderation', are the building blocks of Asian political culture.[21] Anwar Ibrahim talks about tolerance born of 'multiculturism' as the key to the consensus-building tradition of Asian societies.

What these younger generation leaders seem to be searching for is a new vocabulary of political thinking. Their need is twofold. On the one hand they must justify the powerful state mechanism they will shortly inherit from the older generation. On the other they must also address a new set of problems facing society. Of course, whether they are assuming the moral high ground in the search for solutions or simply co-opting the social and political forces mobilised by these problems remains to be seen.

Clearly issues of social justice and morality are fast replacing the old basic concerns of welfare and development in the more developed states of Southeast Asia. In the modern Thai political context it is not enough for a politician to promise factories with jobs, or health clinics to serve the workers: he must also be concerned with conditions in the factory environment; the quality of urban life – principally the traffic woes of urban Bangkok; and stemming corruption. The head of Thailand's narcotics control board is a kindly old police general who is concerned that some form of drug abuse afflicts 40 per cent of Thailand's 70,000 communities. 'What's the point of 8 per cent growth if our society looks like this?', he asks.[22] In Indonesia, people who now have a basic education and jobs and decent healthcare, want a fairer wage and a more equitable distribution of opportunities. And, as a spate of strikes in Indonesia's industrial cities suggests, they are now willing to confront the authorities with their demands. In Malaysia, labour conditions are made more tolerable by the full employment situation. All the same, there is concern in government circles that class differences will replace ethnic cleavages as the new fault lines of social conflict. 'As we progress, our survival must be reflected by our capacity to care for the others', warns Anwar Ibrahim.[23]

Anwar's message carries a moral subtext which suggests that the new politics of Southeast Asia will be coloured by more complex social concerns – which should come as no surprise. Younger generation leaders like Anwar are well-placed to exploit this vein. Anwar is noteworthy in this respect, as he is among the first of his generation to reach a position of power (he was elevated to the position of Deputy Prime Minister in December 1993). Anwar began his political career as leader of Malaysia's Muslim Youth Movement (ABIM). Although initially drawn to the radical anti-establishment thinking of the Muslim Brotherhood in the 1970s, he was later co-opted by the ruling UMNO party, which attracted him to the more benign Islamic activism of the Sudanese Muslim leader Hassan Tourabi.[24]

In 1990, residents of Bangkok elected as their Governor a former army general who eats only one meal a day, is a vegetarian, has taken a vow of celibacy, and donates his salary to charity. Major General Chamlong Srimuang's political party is called the *Palang Dharma* (Moral Force). In some of his writings, he advocates a system of government 'which rests upon an enlightened dictator, a moral leader who follows the *dasarajad-hamma*, or ten Buddhist principles of moral leadership'.[25] According to the Thai scholar Likhit Dhiravegin, Chamlong represents 'a combination of *Dhamma* (morality) and politics, two elements which hardly mix well – but they are substitutes for ideology and politics, the pair which is absent from the Thai political context'.[26] Chamlong later traded his role as Governor for a seat in parliament, where his moralistic approach proved no match for Thailand's machine politics. Facing up to his limitations as a politician, in 1995 Chamlong handed over the party leadership to Thaksin Shinawatra, the telecommunications tycoon. The contrast in personal wealth and lifestyles could not be greater. Thaksin, who expanded his original computer sales contract with government departments into a monopolistic concession on satellite and cellular phone communications, is a billionaire in any currency. Yet Chamlong insists that both he and Thaksin share the same 'moral platform'.[27]

Politicians like Anwar and Chamlong need to reconcile their moralistic message with the corporate interests that are an important facet of patronage politics in Southeast Asia. But by conveying their message using the idiom of religion, they are none the less tapping into a growing constituency. Rather like the unexpected success of the Green movement in Europe at the end of the 1970s, it might not be prudent to dismiss their approach to acquiring and sustaining their power. Chamlong has already served as deputy prime minister, and Anwar is considered the man most likely to succeed Mahathir as prime minister of Malaysia.

Earlier we saw how political development in Southeast Asian states involved the adaptation and reassertion of precolonial or traditional models of leadership and authority – but found that these models accomodated or assimilated more modern influences. If one of the most arresting broader social trends has been the reassertion of traditional religious ritual and belief, does this also mean that society will show the same adaptive flexibility? What happens when neo-traditional models of power combine with reinforced primordial spiritual and religious beliefs? Where does this leave the forces of modernisation? Playing a conspicuous, yet by no means exclusive, role in this development has been Islam, the religion of some 200 million Southeast Asians – about half the region's population.

## ISLAMIC REVIVAL IN INDONESIA

To say that Southeast Asia is experiencing a resurgence of Islam has become almost a cliché. Until recently, few purveyors of this generalisation deviated from the view that the driving force of this Islamic revival was the 1979 Iranian revolution and the consequent diffusion of Islamic militancy. Shortly after the Ayatollah Khomeini of Iran shocked the Western world with his militant resolve the West Indian writer V.S. Naipaul arrived in Malaysia in search of these same religious passions. He wrote of Muslim missionaries spreading militancy among the Malays and of a new Islam which preached 'that the Islamic state will come later – as in Iran, as in Pakistan'.[28] At the time, Naipaul and others were perhaps understandably persuaded that what happened in Iran could spread to other parts of the Islamic world. They had it only fractionally right.

The truth is that Islam is reasserting itself and is becoming a more important social and political force in the Muslim countries of Southeast Asia. But visions of an incipient radical theocracy are misplaced. To begin with, to regard all Islamic movements as theocratic in nature is to overestimate the power and role of the clergy. Even in Iran, since the revolution the tendency has been towards the marginalisation of the radical clergy and towards formulating a more rational Islamic state. In the Southeast Asian context, the political elite has traditionally been allergic to enhancing the role of the religious scholars, or *ulama*, for the simple reason that the ulama's influence on the grass roots of society has always been strong – and thus poses a threat to the authority of the state.

It is also misleading to assume that Islamic thought in the region is wholly nurtured by an invisible umbilical cord stretching westward to the Middle East or the sub-continent. Islam came to Southeast Asia with a universal message which helped it to overcome resistance from existing parochial beliefs. But the religion also has a long and autonomous history in the region. Islam played an important role in the early commercial development of Southeast Asia from the thirteenth century – even before the Europeans arrived. Much later, modernist Islamic thought contributed in no small way to the growth of nationalist movements during the colonial era. In the course of history Islam has adapted to local cultural conditions: so much so that a Muslim Malaysian minister, Anwar Ibrahim, felt he could safely say that his country had more in common with Buddhist Thailand than with Muslim Saudi Arabia. A former Indonesian religious affairs minister, Munawir Sjadzali, went so far as to suggest a reinterpretation of Islamic *shariah* law more suited to the local Asian context. Imported interpretations and dogma are important; but local customs and traditions have also influenced the development of Islam. Today, in the two mainly Islamic countries, Malaysia and Indonesia, Islam is resurgent primarily because of rapid changes in society. It is far more likely that they will become definably Islamic societies, rather than Islamic states.

Islamic revival in Southeast Asia does not fit the misleading popular stereotype of Islamic fundamentalism as a refuge for the rural poor and uneducated. In Indonesia the revival of Islamic devotion in the 1980s and 1990s has been a largely urban and middle-class phenomenon – the segment of society most affected by social and economic change. Partly this phenomenon can be attributed to the increasing number of Muslim devotees who are joining the ranks of the urban middle class. But a more important factor has been the social dislocation which plagues any fast-growing urban society. Many people have strengthened their faith as a reaction to the flagrant disregard for traditional moral values they see around them. In late 1990, the noted Indonesian historian Kuntowidjoyo suggested that the hedonism and immorality spreading through urban society has been mirrored by a move towards moral renewal.[29]

In contemporary Jakarta, neither the roar of rush-hour traffic, which never seems to subside, nor the pounding of construction pile-drivers which never seems to stop, can drown the lyrical call to Muslim prayer. The urban mosque acts as a refuge from the insecurity of urban existence. Indonesia's fairly consistent growth rate, averaging almost 7 per cent in the 1990s, has created a more vertically stratified society. There have been winners and losers. In urban areas, the economic contrasts are more sharply etched, and large numbers of Indonesians feel they have not benefited from the growth in the economy. In the absence of organised welfare programmes and without the family support offered by the extended village clan, those who are less well-off and frustrated have only the mosque to turn to. For the younger generation, the resort to religion is aided by the compulsory religious education they have received since the 1970s. They also have more and more mosques to flock to, thanks to a government-backed drive to build them. The provision of *musholla*, or prayer rooms, in modern office buildings is, for instance, a relatively recent development.

The reassertion of Islamic belief is not entirely a reaction to economic stress. Religiosity in urban Indonesia is also becoming rather chic. 'Formerly, Islam was associated with backwardness and poverty and modern Muslims tended to be a bit ashamed of their Islamic identity', notes Indonesian Muslim intellectual Dewi Anwar. But with economic and career success, she explains: 'Islam is no longer seen as the religion of losers.'[30] Fashion-conscious Indonesians can now shop for up-market Islamic garb, or send their kids to exclusive Islamic kindergarten schools. Islamically influenced popular music, called *dangdut*, is one of the more profitable areas of Indonesia's multifaceted music industry.

Aside from the social conditions inducing more interest in religion, there are also more divisive forces at work in Indonesian society. In 1974 the Dutch scholar W.F. Wertheim wrote:

discontent among the great majority of Muslims is likely to mount. They increasingly resent a military regime which has sold out its riches to foreign capitalists who dominate the Indonesian economy as they did in the colonial period. They also resent the economic advantages enjoyed by Christian communities that receive financial help from the Western world.[31]

A decade later the latent uneasiness between Muslims and the state observed by Wertheim exploded when scores of people fell in a hail of army bullets outside a mosque in the Tanjung Priok area of Jakarta. The army has always said it was forced to fire on the crowd in self-defence. Muslim and human rights activists maintain that the army provoked the incident to justify cracking down on Muslim activists.[32] Another ten years on, Muslim activists were still waiting out the end of the Suharto era and hoping that his successor would foster a more Islamic society in Indonesia. Despite their majority status and all the patronage granted by the state, strong feelings of political discontent exist among Indonesian Muslims, a phenomenon which can be traced to the decision by the Republic's founding fathers not to define the state in Islamic terms.

When Indonesian nationalists were drafting their first constitution in the early months of 1945, Islamic leaders wanted to stipulate that Muslims should adhere to the *shariah* law and that the head of state should always be a Muslim. This would have defined Indonesia as an Islamic state, which seemed logical enough in a country where 90 per cent of the population professed Islam. But the Islamic lobby met with resistance from secular nationalists who were mainly drawn from less devout segments of Indonesian society, and were concerned that predominantly Christian Eastern Indonesia (which also had deeper roots in Dutch colonial society) would opt out of the planned unitary republic. Rightly or wrongly their perception was that Indonesia defined as an Islamic state would breed intolerance. The formula adopted in the final draft, proclaimed in August 1945, fell well short of meeting the Islamic lobby's demands. Yet, by stating that every Indonesian should believe in God (*ketuhanan maha esa*), the drafters established Indonesia as a religious state which tolerated all religions. The compromise ensured religious tolerance and harmony for Indonesian society, but set some Islamic leaders firmly and irrevocably against the government.

The state defused this potential threat to its authority by banning the most effective Muslim political party, Masyumi, and demanding that all religious groups subscribe to the state ideology of *Pancasila*. The move to proscribe Islamic political expression must be set against a rash of regional revolts from the late 1940s until the late 1950s that opposed the central government in the name of Islam. At the 1955 general election, considered one of the freest ever held in Indonesian history, the Muslim parties garnered 45 per cent of the vote. Ironically, political emasculation did not prevent the growth of Islamic consciousness in other ways. In fact, by shutting the door on Islam in the political arena the state helped lay the foundation for the religious revival currently underway in Indonesia. It was once fashionable to talk about the majority of Indonesia's Muslims as 'statistical Muslims' – anthropologists distinguished between *santri* or devout Muslims and *abangan*, mainly Javanese who tended to be Muslim in name only. But today the distinction seems to be fading, as more and more Indonesian Muslims have found their faith relevant to the challenges of survival.

This new-found relevance of faith is the product of new forms of Islamic teaching. Cut off from politics from the 1970s, Muslim intellectuals were forced to dress up religious teaching in a benign form which allayed official suspicions. This meant dropping all references to Islamic statehood and de-emphasising literal adherence to Islamic law. Instead, they focused their energies on making Islam more relevant and appealing to the masses. They applied Islamic ideas to the changing nature of society, addressing the stresses and strains produced by rapid economic growth. By spurning any active role in politics after 1984, and becoming instead a non-governmental organisation addressing mainly the social and economic concerns of its members, Nahdlatul Ulama, Indonesia's largest Muslim organisation with some 30 million members evaded state harassment and built valuable bridges to the armed forces (which offered valuable protection when the organisation's leadership became involved in the democracy movement).

Traditionally opposed to the dogmatic political approach once favoured by Masyumi, NU was regarded as more benign by the government. Rejecting literal interpretations of religious dogma

not only helped foster better relations with the state but broad-
ened the appeal of Islam and appeased an ever nervous non-
Muslim minority. The emphasis placed on moral and ethical
behaviour rather than outward piety offered a model of Islam
that was more acceptable to non-Muslims. This more pluralistic
Islamic thinking also embraced universal concepts of tolerance,
egalitarianism and democracy, which laid the foundations for Islamic thinkers to play a role in the democratisation debate of the
1990s. NU's leader, Abdurrahman Wahid was a co-founder of
the 'Forum Demokrasi' established in 1991.

Being more acceptable to the state allowed the new generation
of Islamic intellectuals to operate moderate Islamic organisations
and educational institutions which attracted government support
and patronage. Being able to work among the urban middle
class and on university campuses, where overt political activity
has been banned since the late 1970s, helped garner support and
foster a wider acceptance of Islam. Thus, Islamic movements
which adapted successfully to the harsher political environment
under Suharto's New Order were in a position to satisfy the
spiritual and ethical needs of the middle class just as those needs
became greater. Today, contemporary Muslim intellectuals, like
Nurcholis Madjid, are satisfied that what looked like a sell-out to
the government in fact allowed the incubation of a more far-
reaching and meaningful Islamic movement:

> We have much greater freedom to interpret our religion
> and equate it to the demands of modernity without being
> apologetic.[33]

There is a danger that this more moderate, cultural expression of
Islam fostered by modernist intellectuals can be hijacked by those
who still harbour political grudges from the past. And there are
signs in Indonesia that religious revival ignited by social and
economic conditions is assuming political significance. There are
more politically minded Muslims who perceive the Suharto
government as a military regime which has relied too heavily
on foreign capitalists and Western aid, and there is simmering
resentment of Chinese and Christian economic dominance. 'The
Islamic community is not poor because it is lazy', remarked a
Muslim intellectual in 1991, 'it is lazy because it is poor.'[34]

Many Muslims are convinced that the economic development
and modernisation of Indonesia has marginalised the Muslim

community, who comprise the majority, and enfranchised a foreign minority, the Chinese. The Chinese comprise only 4 per cent of the population, but by some estimates have cornered a third of the wealth.[35] Some of these activists consider that the New Order regime consciously promoted non-Muslim business interests to weaken any potential Muslim power base. According to Nurcholis Madjid, their view is that: 'The army did not want to cooperate with indigenous entrepreneurs because that would mean drawing close to Masyumi, their political enemies.'[36]

Given the glaring social and economic inequalities of contemporary Indonesia, and the history of official attitudes towards Islam as a political force, many Muslims can be persuaded that the New Order is fundamentally opposed to promoting distinctly Muslim interests. Some elements of the Muslim community feel economically as well as politically alienated. So, while social change has acted as the catalyst to Islamic revival, the politicisation of Islam has fed on the climate of social envy. What worries the government is the congruence of Islamic aspirations with anti-establishment sentiment. This explains why Suharto thought it necessary to bring Muslim activists under his wing with the formation of the Islamic Intellectual Organisation (ICMI) in December 1990.

'Muslim aspirations are secondary in this organisation; the first priority is to ensure the stability of the nation', remarked one of Suharto's aides ahead of ICMI's December 1990 inaugural meeting in the bucolic atmosphere of Malang in East Java.[37] Suharto may have intended ICMI to serve as a political prop, but to the horror of non-Muslims and the dogma-shy army the organisation accelerated the revival of Islamic consciousness and reopened the political arena to Muslim activists. The opportunity Suharto handed them was indeed tempting. After 20 years of banishment to the political periphery, here they were being asked to dine at the head table. More radical activists like Amien Rais, a political scientist from Gaja Madah University in Jogyakarta, saw it as an opportunity to be seized: 'For so long we Muslims have been relatively deprived in economic and political terms; we can't even preach in a mosque without obtaining a licence from the government.' It would not be long, he predicted in 1990, before a Masyumi-style Islamic political party would emerge out of ICMI.[38]

Indeed, by the middle of 1994 it appeared the Muslim factor

in politics was well reentrenched, and might even play a role in the succession process. At 72, Suharto was heading into his sixth and, though difficult to predict, possibly last term in office. An increasingly vocal group of Muslim activists saw the transition period as their best shot at establishing a more powerful role for the majority faith. Yet, as with any political grouping in Indonesia, unity was imperfect and a variety of interests were involved. Describing ICMI as a coalition of interests, a senior military officer distinguished between hard-line fundamentalists, Masyumi remnants, and young opportunists who wanted little more than to replace Suharto. He, like many in the establishment, assumed that Indonesia's very diversity militated against any one of these groups achieving their specific ends. 'The Muslims talk about being the majority. They forget, it is the Javanese who comprise over 100 million Indonesians who are in fact, the majority.'[39]

Yet in the search for a new, more open, more democratic style of politics, the Javanese culture – or the way in which it has been harnessed to politics over the past quarter-century – was coming under increasing fire. Culture and religion, rather than ideology were becoming the intellectual tools of the democratisation debate. Liberally educated Muslim Javanese like Adi Sasono believed that Suharto 'would be the last Javanese to hold power in this country. The new political culture would be tied to the outside world, not the world of feudalism . . . he will be the last King.'[40] Why not? Many educated Indonesians would welcome the modification of a political culture too imbued with paternalistic notions of all powerful patron and humble client.

What would the Javanese feudal culture be replaced with? To many non-Muslims the Javanese culture, for all its feudal ways, also acts as a bulwark against purist notions of Islamic identity: it stands for eclecticism and tolerance. An Indonesia not dominated by Javanese culture, many non-Muslims believed, might also be an Indonesia which defines itself as more Islamic. Suharto may have wanted to co-opt the forces of Islam by patronising ICMI, the new Islamic organisation. There were no signs that he regarded Islam as a replacement for the Javanese culture that allowed him to wield almost absolute power.

## ISLAMIC BRINKMANSHIP IN MALAYSIA

To watch old Shaw Brothers Malaysian movies from the mid-1960s is to step back into another world; a world of mini-skirts and beehive hairdos, where the rich amuse themselves dancing the twist and sipping cocktails. Thirty years on, scratchy prints of these old black and white movies still play on Malaysian TV, but the liberal lifestyle they portray is hard to find in contemporary real life. Today, fashions sported by the younger generation vary markedly between the races. Mini-skirts are still worn – by the Chinese. Muslim Malay girls have traded their beehive hairdos and fashion-boots for more modest body length *baju-kurong* and head coverings to convey the sense of modesty dictated by Islamic custom. There are cocktail bars, but it is an offence for a Muslim to be caught drinking alcohol. A Malaysian Rip Van Winkle who fell asleep in 1964 and awoke in 1994 might think that the country had experienced a religious revolution.

There was no religious revolution. There was an ethnic crisis of confidence, in the course of which Islam was harnessed by the politicians to assert the ethnic dominance of the Malays who comprise about half Malaysia's population. In the process, consciously and sometimes inspite of themselves, Malaysia's ruling elite helped reinforce religious values and Islamic consciousness, and set the stage for the gradual Islamicisation of the country.

The face of Malaysia had changed irrevocably when people woke up on the morning of 14 May 1969. A clumsy show of hubris by a victorious Chinese-led opposition party the day before, sparked off an orgy of ethnic violence which left scores dead and parts of downtown Kuala Lumpur gutted by fire. In those few hours, the old 'clubable Malaya' captured by the British author Anthony Burgess in his *Malayan Trilogy* more or less died. In its place, there emerged a very different Malaysia: less confident of itself, but determined never to allow the centrifugal forces of ethnic conflict out of the bottle again. In his sensitively observed *Malaysian Journey*, the contemporary Malaysian writer Rehman Rashid recalled that the deepest anguish of that time was the 'certain knowledge that the entire nation would be made to pay for the unrestrained furies of a few sections of the population, and there was nothing anyone could do but wait for the axe to fall, and know that nothing would ever be the same again'.[41]

One of the principal changes introduced after May 1969 was an affirmative action programme for the *bumiputeras* (a broad racial classification encompassing Malays and other indigenous groups of Malaysia). The so-called New Economic Policy set out to endow the Malays with the economic means to match the wealth of the Chinese, who at the time comprised almost 40 per cent of the population. As a mechanism for redistributing equity to the mass of under-privileged *bumiputeras* the NEP has not been wholly successful. By 1990 the overall bumiputera share of the economy had risen remarkably from 2.4 per cent to 20.3 per cent, but only 14 per cent was held by individuals – the rest by government-organised trust agencies. The policy worked rather better as a reinforcing agent of ethnic identity. For once the Malays were empowered to dominate, they searched for ways to cement that dominance by shoring up their exclusive identity. As well as amassing corporate wealth, one of the most effective methods has been the assertion of their religious identity as Muslims.

An entire generation of Malays raised in the wake of May 1969 were taught never to compromise on matters of religion and language. One of the conditions for Malays joining the civil service is their ability to recite the Koran. Adherence to religious practices, such as fasting during the holy month of Ramadhan, are legally enforced. Younger generation Malays who remember their parents enjoying a liberal lifestyle, could not think of drinking alchohol in public, or taking their fiancée on a weekend jaunt before marriage. Popular hotel resorts are regularly patrolled by the religious authorities to hunt down unmarried couples committing *khalwat*, or close proximity. In the old Shaw brothers movies the Malay hero might be seen seducing his heroine while bathing in a stream; in contemporary Malaysia, when an actor and actress kiss on stage the morals of society are called into question. As Malaysian Prime Minister Mahathir Mohamad put it: 'The trend here in Malaysia is towards more religiosity.'[42]

Mahathir's public view is that the growth of religious devotion in tandem with the prosperity of Malaysians can save the country from moral decay. 'Affluent people tend to forget God', he says. 'Now that there is more awareness and a desire to adhere to religion . . . we are hopeful that when Malaysians become more affluent they will not forget God.' Privately though, Malaysia's current leaders are concerned about the implications of this assertion of faith. For as well as reinforcing Malay identity and preserving the boundaries of power-sharing in Malaysia's plural society, a more assertive dogmatic Islam since the 1970s has bred rejection of the material values of commerce and consumerism on which the country's economy depends.

Having said this, it would be very difficult for any Malay leader to counter this religious trend with overtly secular policies. Because being a Malay is inseparable from being a Muslim, the Malay ruling elite has to tread a very narrow path between embracing Islamic dogma and rejecting its full implications for governing society. Simple distinctions between what is religious and secular are not as easily worked out as they are in the Indonesian context. A Sudanese Muslim theologian teaching at the International Islamic University in Kuala Lumpur argues that the Malaysian example matches no other in the Muslim world. 'This might be largely due to the interaction between Malayness and religion; more specifically, the profound confusion between Islam and ethnicity in the Malaysian context.'[43]

Religion is a pervasive factor in Malaysian society. This does not mean it is always under control, however. When some of the post-1969 generation of Malays obtained scholarships to study abroad, their sense of separate identity was reinforced by exposure to the revolutionary Islamic ferment of the late 1970s. Rehman Rashid was among them:

> it happened amazingly quickly. Within months of our arrival I was seeing my compatriots only at lectures, watching them don progressively more bizarre attire and steadily lose weight for fear of eating anything tainted by the Unclean.[44]

Radical fringe groups like the Islamic Revolutionary Council that originated in overseas student circles, and Shiite or Messianic movements, found the Malay urban middle class very susceptible to their moral message. The recruiting ground for these fringe groups has been the overseas campus rather than the village mosque. When Malaysian Muslim students arrive at US or British campuses, they are met by representatives of organised Muslim groups and offered what they need most: a cultural refuge. Far from home, and probably overseas for the first time, they find the offer hard to refuse. Over the course of their studies, these impressionable new converts are taught the value of sticking together as a religious community against a backdrop of the decadent morally bankrupt society their teachers want them to reject.

Once home in Malaysia, armed with their degrees, these young Malay graduates join the ranks of the civil service or head into the professions, business or politics. Their exposure to Islamic fundamentalist dogma has traditionally not drawn them to PAS, the mainstream Malaysian Islamic party. PAS is a mainly rural-based party, with large concentrations of traditional support in the Malay heartlands of the northern and eastern peninsular states. From a religious perspective, PAS adheres to the same rigid Sunni orthodoxy followed by the government. 'PAS is not a subversive movement that wants to destroy the country's institutions', said its leader Fadyl Noor in July 1992: 'PAS stands within the political system and only wants to replace the government.'[45] Government sources now acknowledge, however, that PAS has been picking up support in urban middle-class areas. In the April 1995 general election the opposition to Mahathir's National front was generally emasculated at the polls. PAS managed to increase its share of the popular vote from 6 per cent to 7 per cent and maintain the same number of seats in parliament.

It is not inconceivable that if PAS ever came to power in Malaysia they would behave much like the current ruling Malay elite, deploying a moderate Islamic agenda to shore up their legitimacy. The defeated UMNO, might in turn adopt the Islamic struggle to attack PAS. However, the success of Islamic fringe groups in urban middle-class areas over the past two decades cannot be attributed to a competition for power. It appears to feed off a genuine desire for a more Islamic society. Take these extracts from a pamphlet aimed at civil servants and businessmen, which detected public concern about 'the insufficiency of relying mainly on a legal system which separates morality from the law'; or 'the insufficiency of relying on codes of ethics which are mainly derived from and appeal to human reason alone, leaving the seat of conscience and deep spiritual motivations which are connected to accountability to the supreme being'.[46]

From here it is perhaps a short step to asking more fundamental questions. If our government claims to follow an Islamic agenda, how is it that its leaders are so corrupt? What is the answer? A moral cleansing of government? In Indonesia, the question is put somewhat differently: if Muslims constitute a majority, why aren't their aspirations better represented? What is the answer? Mobilise Muslim support for political change? From this brief consideration of religious movements in Indonesia and Malaysia, it should be apparent that religion is becoming more rather than less important – both in society and as a political factor – inspite of the march of modern, capitalist, material progress. Modernisation and progress have not, as some might predict, replaced God with Mammon. Quite the reverse: progress has reinforced, revived and reinvigorated traditional patterns of religious identity and spiritual devotion. Economic disparities and the social upheaval brought about by rapid economic growth laid the foundations of this spiritual revival; political competition and polarisation have helped push it along. Now, apply this phenomenon to the search for alternative sources of political energy with wider social appeal, and religion could conceivably offer an unsullied moral vision – and in some cases a course of political action refreshingly different from existing Western models. But will Southeast Asia's Muslim states follow the examples of Iran, Algeria, or the Sudan? Will religious nationalism become a force for political change?

## ISLAM AND NATIONALISM

Marzuki Darusman, the vice-chairman of Indonesia's Human Rights Commission, is a former MP with considerable political experience in the country's pro-government 'Golkar' party. His establishment background has imbued him with a measure of suspicion when it comes to Muslim activists in politics – even though he is a Muslim himself. 'The transition from striving for an Islamic state to establishing an Islamic society has put a lot of people at ease', he suggests. 'But what's the distinction between state and society? Surely it ends up with the same objective of setting up a Muslim polity?'[47] Marzuki, like many educated Indonesians rejects the notion that the country could become any more Islamic than it already is. Defining the state, even society for that matter, as exclusively Islamic would, in their view, tear the country's multiracial and multireligious society apart.

Talking to some members of the Malaysian establishment elicits a similar response: there is a limit to how far institutionalising Islam can go before it rubs up against other elements in Malaysia's plural society. Thus while Mahathir may publicly welcome the increasing trend towards what he calls 'religiosity', he has harnessed the bureaucracy in an effort to breed a more tolerant strain of Islam. In 1992 the government set up an institution called the Institute of Islamic Understanding (IKIM). IKIM is a fine example of bureaucratic bypass surgery. Originally, the religious affairs department in the Prime Minister's office was tasked with promoting a more open, tolerant, and less conservative brand of Islam. Instead, the officials themselves became more conservative. IKIM holds seminars where Malaysians of all faiths are encouraged to learn just how tolerant Islam really is.

In Indonesia and Malaysia, official propagation of a benign, tolerant Islam comes into direct conflict with scriptural purist interpretations of the faith which rejects the secular or worldly. The frustration for someone like Mahathir in Malaysia is that while he urges his fellow Muslims to consider their faith as receptive to modernity and all sources of knowledge – often harping on the Muslim scientists of the Alhambra in medieval Spain and their influence on the European Renaissance – the religious scholars in their *pondok* (a rural religious school) still treat the non-Islamic world as unpure, and therefore something to be rejected.

In Indonesia, the conflict between open and more closed treatments of Islam highlights the dangers of breeding intolerance. Marzuki Darusman points to the impact that stricter definitions of Muslim identity are already having on Indonesian society. Take the increasing number of urban Muslims using Islamic greetings (which sets them apart from their non-Muslim fellow citizens), a crackdown by the authorities on drinking or an edict from the Indonesian Council of Ulama in 1993 reminding Muslims that it is *haram* to celebrate Christmas with their Christian neighbours. All these changes can be seen as the assertion of Muslim faith. They can also be read by the non-Muslim minority as signs of creeping intolerance in Indonesian society.

At the other extreme, there is the rhetoric of prominent Muslim scholars like Abdurrahman Wahid or Nurcholis Madjid who argue that Islam in its Indonesian context must strive to be an inclusive faith: accepting the ways of non-Muslims as well as trying to broaden the acceptance of Islam. 'It would be beneficial if Islamic values can cater and broaden to apply to non-Muslims, which would contribute to national identity', Abdurrahman Wahid argues.[48] Nurcholis goes so far as to praise the ethics of honesty, thrift and hard work which are characterised as rooted in 'White Anglo-Saxon Protestant' culture. 'These values are not exclusively Christian', he contends: 'If generalised enough, they are shared by people of all faiths.'[49]

But these arguments for tolerance, and even cultural cross-fertilisation, run up against the role of Islam as a driving force of early twentieth-century nationalism in both Indonesia and what was then Malaya. As Harry Benda noted in the case of Indonesia:

> Islam came to serve Indonesians as a rallying point of identity, to symbolise separateness from, and opposition to, foreign, Christian overlords.[50]

Islam could serve as a focus of identity and nationalist aspiration because of three contrasting approaches to the relationship between religion and politics. In secular terms there was the precolonial tradition of the Muslim community ruled by a Muslim King or 'Raja'. In modern terms there was the influence of Islamic modernist movements which, from the early twentieth century, attempted to rationalise the assimilation of modern Western knowledge and Islamic doctrine. Finally there was the more exclusive and dogmatic view that Muslims should live in an Islamic state governed by Islamic customs and laws. For Muslims in Southeast Asia the Islamic state has always been one of the most contentious issues since independence.

Even though an Islamic state would seem to be the most logical product of marrying Islam to politics, neither Indonesia nor Malaysia have become truly Islamic states. Both countries harbour an intriguing historical paradox. Although led by governments claiming to patronise Islam, Islamic opposition movements struggle to establish Islamic states. Given this allergy to theocracy by those in power, it seems unlikely that either Indonesia or Malaysia will fall victim to extreme forms of religious nationalism. The intellectual consensus is that the reality of plural societies and traditions of tolerance will never allow one religious creed to smother another. As Nurcholis Madjid puts it; the nomenclature of Islamic politics is derived from the Arab hearth of Islam, but the social context is purely Asian.

That is not to say that Islam and religion in general won't play a political role. The Islamic revival underway in Indonesia, and to some extent in Malaysia, inevitably rejects the notion that somehow Asian Muslims are less devout than their Arab co-religionists. The new mood of spirituality embraces the view that Asian muslims can be more religious in the spiritual and ethical sense than Muslims in other parts of the world. This suggests that religion has the potential to be an important component of the new politics of Southeast Asia. 'Spirituality will be harnessed as a form of quality control in business and politics', as Malaysian commentator Syed Adam Al Jaffri puts it.[51] What the new generation of Muslim leaders like Anwar Ibrahim say they want to do is work towards an Islamic society that is both morally correct in the doctrinal realm, advanced in the more secular fields of economics and technology, and fully adapted to the region's traditions of pluralism and tolerance.

Whilst drawing intellectually on the Islamic modernism of the earlier twentieth century, this approach falls well short of the more radical ideas of the Muslim brotherhood in Egypt and its related movement in South Asia. Opposed to a dogmatic interpretation of Islamic tradition, the new generation of Islamic activists in Southeast Asia instead would prefer to follow the established practice of *ijtihad* (the right to interpret Islam in the light of modern conditions) so long as the outcome is consistent with the essential message of Islam. Its adherents would see the new Islamic thinking as, above all, indigenously derived. Elements of this new Islamic order would include: the adaptation of Islamic principles of finance and business to the modern context; more interaction between Muslims in the region; and – perhaps most challenging of all – the definition of democracy in an Islamic, and therefore implicitly non-Western context.

The role of religion in the modern nationalist context is more likely to be contextual rather than dogmatic. But this should not diminish the importance of religion as a determining factor in the future shape of political and social institutions. Ironically, perhaps, it is precisely this ambiguous role of religion in the definition of the state that allows religious beliefs to play a core role in the political culture. Unlike Europe, Southeast Asian states never divorced the church from the state – instead they co-opted the church. As Nurcholis Madjid points out: 'In Indonesia, Islam is not the religion of the state, so we have much greater freedom to interpret our religion and equate it to the demands of modernity, without having to be apologetic.'[52]

# Chapter 6

# Coming together

*Wherever one journeys in the region, one comes upon the same towns and villages on plains besides lakes and rivers, surrounded by the same clusters of bamboo, bananas, and other fruit trees.*

*Jose T. Almonte, 'Towards One Southeast Asia'*

Project for Ecological recovery is a Thai non-governmental organisation dedicated to monitoring the impact of development on the environment. Protecting Thailand's environment from the onslaught of commerce has been hard enough for PER's energetic director Witoon Perpongscharoen, as the maps on the wall of his spartan shophouse office in downtown Bangkok testify. In a variety of disarmingly soft colours, they depict the rape of Thailand's forests, the erosion of its watersheds, and the diversion of its natural rivers. The colourful maps also show something else: the spread of ecological damage across Thailand's borders into neighbouring Burma, Laos and Cambodia. Commercial logging has been banned in Thailand since 1989, largely because of persistent campaigning by organisations such as PER.

The success of environmental pressure groups in Thailand has hastened the environmental exploitation of neighbouring countries, however. Unable to log over forests in Thailand, up to 50 private logging firms went to Burma instead. Witoon traces a finger along the red-shaded areas inside the 800 km long Burmese border with Thailand where valuable teak forests are fast disappearing. 'Even though this is Burma', he says, 'we feel we must take some responsibility for what is happening there'.[1]

Witoon's concern about the environment in neighbouring countries points to a new and potentially important factor governing the political landscape of Southeast Asia. What happens when the countries of the region become more concerned about what goes on across their borders? Greater regional integration of the ten countries in Southeast Asia is inevitable. If not by means of institutionalised regionalism, then through enhanced travel and migratory flows, the media and transnational investment by the private sector. There is even an ambitious proposal to foster a regional community bound by common social and cultural ties. A kind of regional council has been suggested to provide a forum for grass roots groups to discuss common concerns for consideration at a state level.[2]

Will such cooperative behaviour, beyond existing diplomatic and economic planes, force authoritarian regimes to relax their grip because the victims of oppression can turn to their neighbours for help? Or will closer contacts between countries with shared or similar political cultures only serve to reinforce the political status quo? The case of Burma suggests that reality cuts both ways. Pro-democracy students fleeing the uprising of May 1988 sought refuge in neighbouring Thailand, where they found a platform for their grievances. Not long afterwards, Burma's military rulers were being offered advice by their military colleagues in Thailand and Indonesia about how best to prolong their grip on power.

One of the least discussed aspects of Southeast Asia's political development is how it will be affected by the fostering of closer regional ties. Contact between Southeast Asian states is forging common endeavours and a striving for common identity in a region once composed of diverse states with conflicting interests. On an official level, contact is being encouraged by the increasing intensity of multilateral cooperation in the region. Everything from security to library science now has its own regional forum. The region's successful entrepreneurs are also casting around for intraregional investment: telecoms companies in Thailand are looking to lucrative untapped markets in Indonesia and the Philippines; Singaporean investors are spreading their wings to Burma and Vietnam; and Malaysians are nurturing a friendly trade relationship with Cambodia. Satellite broadcasting and telecommunications technology means that people in Laos and Cambodia now watch Thai television; Indonesians receive and watch Malaysian television, and even programmes beamed from China.

Personal contacts blossomed in the 1990s as prosperity

increased people's ability to travel. Asians accounted for almost
60 per cent of visitors to other Asia Pacific Countries in 1993.[3]
By the mid-1990s, middle-class professionals from the four more
developed ASEAN countries were so prone to travelling overseas
that their governments started promoting domestic tourism to
entice them back. This rapid development of intraregional contact
not only has implications for established perceptions of security
and nationalism but also lends a new dimension to the study of
political change.

A few years ago a Thai such as Witoon citing concern about a
neighbouring country would have sounded incredible. A decade
or so ago, even talking about a distant town or village invoked
unfamiliar, cool, even alien sentiments. Before advancing prosperity allowed the citizens of Southeast Asia to travel to one
another's countries, the average citizen was hardly worldly-wise.
People were by and large suspicious of their neighbours. In 1982,
poor slum dwellers in the city of Chiangmai told the author that
they were reluctant to take a ten minute bicycle ride to the
central market because it was too far from their 'village'. In spite
of the tropical climate, they felt 'warmer' at home; outside the
bounds of their village, they 'felt cold'. More remarkably, these
psychological feelings of insecurity explained why slum dwellers
endured a 5 or 10 per cent mark-up on goods brought to their
village store by a local merchant.[4] In 1995 a resident of the same
slum area had already made the 500 mile journey to Bangkok in
search of work, and would consider doing so again.

Traditionally, communities in Southeast Asia have been inward
looking. Paradoxically, for a region populated by migrants and
criss-crossed by trade routes, its people have (with a few notable
exceptions like the Buginese, the Minangkabau of West Sumatra,
or the Kelantanese of Malaysia) developed a remarkably sedentary culture. The fostering of close ties with land and place is
rooted in intensive rice cultivation. Rice cultivation is an absorbing form of agriculture, requiring a high input of man-hours and
complex organisation. Both requirements helped develop strong
communal bonds. An individual leaving the village could upset a
family's subsistence regime. Similarly, outsiders coming in would
find water, land and labour scarce commodities. Beyond the rice-
fields lay the untamed forest, a marginal territory perceived as
dark and inhospitable. Local folklore taught that bad spirits lived
in the trees and hills rimming the rice-fields, keeping people in

and discouraging all but the most adventurous to wander far –
as did the need to tend the spirits of deceased kin.

This attachment to place translated on the national plane into
suspicion about the outer world and a particular fear of the
chaotic margins separating one world from another. This does
not mean there was never any contact between these parochial
worlds. Trade was usually in the hands of outsiders, who as a
result became the agents of cultural change as well as commerce.
Reflecting the important conductive power of trade, early
missionaries travelled with merchants. Trade was therefore much
more than a simple medium of commerce: trade was a medium
of cultural change.

At times the threat of invasion and warfare was as pervasive
as that which gripped the continent of Europe in the middle ages.
Often the ravages of war were as drastic: whole towns were
levelled, and rice fields were destroyed. Visit the devastated ruins
of the former Thai capital of Ayudhya, or the sacked Burmese
capital of Ava on the outskirts of Mandalay to judge just how
effectively the victors trod on the vanquished. At the Tat Luang
temple in the centre of the Lao capital of Vientiane, a pile of
broken Buddha images is kept on display to remind Lao people
of the severity of the last Thai invasion in the nineteenth century.

Yet, the cost in human terms was less compared with the
barbarity which prevailed in Europe. The object of warfare in
this region was to capture manpower, not – at least until the rise
of the Khmer Rouge in Cambodia – to extinguish life. Calamity
in one country was considered serendipity by its neighbour – an
opportunity to acquire resources. There was often quite intense
rivalry between one petty state and another. This kind of sentiment lives on. A Thai academic on a visit to Burma watched his
Thai colleagues search for the grave of a long-dead Burmese
King – just so they could gloat over its neglect: the King in
question had been a notorious invader of Thai territory. A party
of Burmese officers on a visit to the ruins of Ayudhya was refused
a ride in a local trishaw: the driver cited Burma's sacking of the
city in 1767. Nationalism, offering citizens an overarching sense
of belonging to a state, may be a relatively new concept, but the
roots of nationalist sentiment are deeply embedded in the historical memories of each society.

Given these parochial traditions, the concept of Southeast
Asia as a unified region has been hard to sell. Academic

conceptualisations of Southeast Asia have tended to dwell on the region's ethnic and environmental diversity, the rivalry between states in the historical period, and the derivative tensions between nation states today. Early studies, like George Coedes' 'Indianised States of Southeast Asia', also stressed the lack of an original unifying culture. Instead, Southeast Asia was conceived as a blend of two great Asian civilising powers, China and India:

> Behind the manifest variations of Asia . . . lies not one civilisation but different root civilisations – the Sinitic, Hindu, Muslim, and Buddhist.[5]

Western scholarship has played up deep and immutable divisions between the cultural components of Southeast Asia, arguing that the notion of Southeast Asia as a coherent geographical region was first derived from the Allied 'Southeast Asia Command' overseeing the campaign against the Japanese imperial army during the Pacific War. The American scholar Lucian Pye admits to the ethnocentricity driving this generalisation when he writes that: 'the conventional wisdom, holding that at times it is appropriate to minimise Europe's diversities and concentrate on its common heritage, judges Asia's differences to be unmanageable'.[6]

Judging how much Southeast Asians have in common with each other is, like any other conception of a region, a subjective exercise. The French eat garlic and cook in olive oil, the British do not. Yet Southeast Asians share a common basic diet of rice, chili and fish. Still, Europeans consider that a common civilisation binds them together and that Southeast Asians, by comparison, have a more diverse cultural heritage. One reason for these mixed perceptions is the contrasting cultural view of diversity.

The region's ethnic and cultural mosaic is undeniably complex. Also irrefutable is the cultural influence of its two great Asian neighbours, China and India. However, the common response to these external influences is often missed. That response might be characterised as a blending process; one that acquired aspects of external culture and religion, while preserving elements of indigenous culture. Thus throughout Southeast Asia, one comes across a spectrum of variation: Islam that retains elements of the pre-existing Hindu tradition in Indonesia; Buddhism that tolerates spirit worship in Thailand and Burma; and Catholicism which never quite suppressed pagan rites associated with ancestor worship in the Philippines. This common response to the waves of external influences that swept over the region through history may not seem like much of a binding principle, but Southeast Asians find that it breeds familiarity:

> You have to understand the moorings of Southeast Asia. Lifeways were shaped by the same environment. The physical environment shapes a kind of behaviour that is homogeneous. True, we all belong to different ethnic groups. But the differences between ethnic groups may not be as intense as between ethnic groups in other regions. The common experience of having been a stamping ground of the great powers is a kind of negative commonality.[7]

Burma, Indonesia and Vietnam were all at some point in history invaded by China. The resistance put up by these states helped define the limits of Chinese imperial control in the period, just as the gates of Vienna marked for a long while the high-tide of Ottoman expansion, and therefore the edge of Europe.

The colonial era helped obscure common features of the region by dividing it up into conflicting spheres of colonial power and influence. Indochina was French, Burma was under the English, and Siam acted as a buffer inbetween. The Netherlands Indies held its own under the Dutch except for a brief period of British rule over Java and Sumatra in the early nineteenth century. The Philippines, which was initially subject to Islamic influence, fell under Spanish Catholic rule in the sixteenth century. European rule infused Southeast Asia with Western culture and ideas, but it also carved up the region erasing areas of overlapping or ambiguous sovereignty that once helped to diffuse cultural identities. Thus Siam was cut off from its vassal states in the Malay archipelago. Sea-trading links between the Indonesian islands and mainland Southeast Asia were supplanted by colonial shipping lines. It is ironic that in the seventeenth and eighteenth centuries, Malay was the lingua franca of trade in much of maritime Southeast Asia. Today, the common language of commerce is English.

Historically, Southeast Asian states were rather more loosely defined, based on sacral centres of power whose radiance diminished with distance from the centre. For centuries Southeast Asian monarchs claimed suzerainty over large swathes of territory based on little more than tenuous personal ties to local rulers and infrequent payment of tithes or tribute. There was also a dimension of sacral space bearing no relation to geographical or social realities. Thus the ancient Mon Kingdom centred in what is today Southern Burma was defined by thirty two sacred shrines or objects. European colonial administrators introduced the notion of physical borders and centralised administration to the region. The Europeans brought with them maps and border-markers. They set up district offices and outposts of central authority. Imperialism not only subjugated Southeast Asian peoples; it also organised them into more strictly defined geographical units most of which later defined modern nation states.

Western colonialism also brought with it the baggage of European prejudice. Most Westerners came from societies that experienced violent schisms over race, religion or ideology. When they observed people of different race or religion living together in an Asian context, their instinct was to assume incompatibility. The social rationality of nineteenth century Weberian thought projects that a secular society is more desirable because non-secular societies are riddled by conflicts of belief. Observing the rise of nationalism in India the British author E.M. Forster saw Hindus, Moslems, Sikhs and others 'trying to like each other more than came natural to them'.[8] Of course, prejudice is not an exclusively European vice, and minorities have faced periodic adversity in Southeast Asia. But intergroup friction that results in violence tends to be the exception in the region, not the rule. It is often the product of abnormal circumstances such as acute economic stress, or the result of ruling elites manipulating prejudice to create a diversion.

Although lack of physical contact, an attachment to land and place and the imposition of concrete borders has maintained Southeast Asia, actually as well as perceptually, as a disembodied region, there are grounds for believing that this is slowly changing. Flying in the face of the tendency to conceive Southeast Asia as too diverse to be considered a region has been the flowering of what is sometimes considered the world's most successful regional association.

## ASEAN: UNITY OUT OF DIVERSITY

Oddly enough it was the Cold War, the greatest political schism of the century, which first drew modern Southeast Asian states together. With Communist China at the door after 1949, the Western powers pushed for the establishment of an ill-conceived

NATO clone, the South East Asian Treaty Organisation (SEATO). Perhaps it bode well for the region that huddling under the wings of a superpower was not to be the vehicle used to foster regionalism. When SEATO was formed in 1955, Indonesia, and later Malaya, refused to join. As Indonesian scholar Dewi Anwar points out, the reluctance with which the allied powers backed the infant Indonesian Republic against their ally the Dutch, bred a deep and lasting suspicion of the West in Indonesian diplomats.[9] This suspicion made Indonesia a natural supporter of the non-aligned movement and led directly to the 1955 Asian–Africa conference, a gathering of many newly independent nations held in the Indonesian town of Bandung under the direction of Indonesia's first president, Sukarno.

The Bandung conference was as much a natural postscript to the region's anti-colonial struggle as it was a natural extension of Sukarno's ego. However, Bandung was an important milestone in regional diplomacy. The conference, convened in the old Dutch hill-resort and university town northwest of Jakarta, bred a sense of pride in the re-emerging states of Asia.[10] For a brief moment, atavistic nationalism and ideology were cast aside in favour of solidarity and brotherhood. At Bandung there was India's Nehru, China's Zhou Enlai, and Egypt's Gamal Abdul Nasser rubbing shoulders and thumbing their noses at the West. Bandung provided a platform for the recently decolonised nations to gloat over the retreat of colonialism. Bandung also put Sukarno and Indonesia firmly in the regional driving seat – a diplomatic opportunity Sukarno was soon to squander with his attack on neighbouring Malaysia. Sukarno's 'Confrontation' of Malaysia from 1963 to 1966 was a pivotal event in regional history.

Initially, the cooperative spirit forged in Bandung was stillborn. The landing of Indonesian forces in West Malaysia in late 1964 dispelled the mesmerising collective euphoria bred by the triumph of nationalism. It focused attention instead on expansionism in the region. Confrontation also brought ideas of a common alliance with the West under the SEATO umbrella down in a hail of rhetoric and military bravado, convincing the Americans that Communism had already crept in through the back door. But ironically, 'Confrontation' provided the real impetus for consociation among Southeast Asian states. They were driven by fear of each other, not the outside world. As Malaysia's Anwar

Ibrahim reminds us: 'traditional statecraft throughout the region has been expansionist and imperialist in tendency'.[11]

If the demise of colonial rule restored the opportunity for states to revive precolonial political traditions, it also allowed them to prey on one another. Thailand marched into the Shan States, the Northern Malay States and parts of Cambodia under Japanese protection in 1941. In the 1920s, Indonesian nationalists tried to persuade their Malay cousins across the Malacca straits that their struggle for independence was one and the same. After the war, Sukarno pressed home these designs on the Malay peninsula and Northern Borneo. The Philippines claimed the old territory of North Borneo, which joined the Malaysian Federation as Sabah, and Malaysia itself had designs on oil-rich Brunei until the mid-1960s.

The formation of the Association of Southeast Asian States (ASEAN) by the Bangkok Declaration on 8 August 1967 was aimed at suppressing these intraregional conflicts. The first sentence of the Bangkok Declaration speaks of 'mutual interests and common problems among countries in Southeast Asia' and calls for a 'firm foundation for common action to promote regional cooperation'. At its birth ASEAN was composed of Indonesia, Malaysia, Thailand, the Philippines, and Singapore. Brunei joined after gaining its independence from the United Kingdom in 1984. Vietnam became ASEAN's newest member in 1995. Cambodia and Laos are not far behind, and Burma is slowly being drawn into the ASEAN diplomatic orbit. Although officially cloaked in the jargon of economic cooperation, ASEAN was actually conceived as a security body. Indonesia, for example, saw the association as a means of erecting a security buffer around the archipelago, shielding it from China and the Soviet Union.[12] Thailand was looking for a bulwark against communist Indochina, and Singapore needed to be considered an equal partner by its two larger neighbours.

However, instead of forging an actual military alliance, ASEAN established a vague, almost symbolic commitment to cooperate across a broad spectrum of endeavours. The senior Malaysian diplomat, who also served as Home Minister, Tan Sri Ghazali Shafie witnessed the founding of ASEAN. He likes to describe the association as resting on the simple principle of togetherness, using the Malay term *sekampung*, the warm feeling of community felt by villagers in a *Kampung*, or village. In fact, ASEAN rests on two important diplomatic principles. The first is that all member states agree to abide by a consensus – meaning that no single state can decide on anything without the full endorsement of all the other members. They also agreed not to interfere in one another's internal affairs. One can quibble about the effectiveness of ASEAN as a vehicle for concrete economic cooperation but it cannot be denied that by using diplomatic rather than military means, as well as a style of diplomacy based on indigenous rather than imported principles, ASEAN has succeeded in fostering a greater sense of regional unity and security. As a Thai diplomat put it: 'In 1967 we were a group of nations who hardly knew each other; two of our members were quarrelling, and we were all developing nations. Yet we agreed on a principle of solidarity, even though this might not be compatible with our own interests.'[13]

Like any other regional association, ASEAN is long on rhetoric and short on substance. Officially the association projects itself as a vehicle for economic cooperation: in fact it is a coalition of strategic and political interests – and perhaps a means of ensuring that these interests remain the same for all the member states. ASEAN does not constitute a perfect union of interests. It was never intended to integrate the region in the same way that Monnet envisaged a united Europe. The concept of regional identity envisaged by ASEAN combines unity with diversity:

> ASEAN as it stands now will not lead to a united Southeast Asia for that was not what it was created to do. On the contrary, ASEAN has contributed to the development of its members into more vigorous and resilient sovereign states.[14]

Preserving sovereignty and 'resilience' has primarily helped preserve the political status quo. Political interests, as we saw earlier, tend to be rooted in a firm conviction in the strength of the state, and the subordination of society to the state. ASEAN has not acted as an organisation to enforce these interests across borders. Rather, it has offered these states the security to defend their political interests against external pressure. ASEAN has served the political interests of ruling elites in Southeast Asia well. It has provided fertile ground for the growth of the banyan tree.

The formula worked well so long as there was no real imperative to enforce uniformity in either political or economic spheres. Global conditions are making it more difficult for ASEAN to

survive as a loose coalition of interests, however. The evolution
of a more interdependent global trading system has made a more
coordinated trade policy essential; the linkage between politics
and trade means that respect for sovereignty has weakened; the
emergence of regional powers raises questions about collective
security. In the face of the changing parameters of international
relations, ASEAN countries have begun to realise that closer
cooperation is not just a remote ideal, but more of a priority.
This may alter the balance between unity and diversity, and ultimately affect the pace of political change.

We are seeing the change occurring first of all in the commercial sphere. Economic cooperation has been slow to take off in
ASEAN. But this should not be surprising, given that member
states compete to sell roughly the same products in the same
markets. Neither have they been really keen to allow their neighbour's products to be sold in their own market. It took almost
25 years to agree on lowering trade barriers. The ASEAN free
trade area (AFTA) launched in 1992 (with the aim of creating a
regional market free of non-tariff barriers and a maximum effective tariff of 5 per cent across the board within 20 years) has run
up against strong protectionist interests in member countries.
Agreement on a timetable of tariff reductions across the board
has been revised twice since then. 'The AFTA agreement only
consists of 12 pages', notes Indonesian regional affairs specialist
Cornelius Luhulima. 'This indicates that ASEAN leaders have
come to an agreement first, instead of thinking, discussing and
planning it first.'[15]

ASEAN may have been ahead of the curve in conceiving itself
as a free trade area, but since the conclusion of the Uruguay
Round, and the formation of the World Trade Organisation in
1994, trade barriers are coming down faster than ever imagined.
ASEAN also faces competition as a regional forum. The Asia–
Pacific Economic Cooperation Process, established at Australia's
initiative in 1989, signalled the desire of states in the wider Asia–
Pacific region to harness themselves to the region's economic
dynamism. Both the WTO and APEC are goading ASEAN into
more action over liberalising trade.

There is, however, a price to be paid for juggling closer cooperation and the congruence of interests with respect for sovereignty.
Inevitably, as the region becomes more integrated, primordial
nationalist sentiment has periodically breached the surface.

Overlapping territorial claims preoccupy diplomats, who hold endless rounds of meetings to argue the finer points of baselines. Indonesia and Malaysia dispute the ownership of Sipadan and Ligitan, two small islands off the coast of Sabah and the Philippines, claim over Sabah remains formally unresolved. The migratory movement of labour across borders is breeding a new set of social problems. Malaysia plays host to over a million Indonesians, Thailand to over half a million Burmese. The presence of large groups of foreigners in the workforce can and has affected bilateral ties. When Singapore hanged the Filipina maid Flor Contemplacion in March 1995, diplomatic relations between Manila and Singapore came close to being severed. On a diplomatic level, ASEAN member states compete with one another over multilateral initiatives. Indonesia's support for the Asia–Pacific Economic Cooperation process is matched by Malaysia's fervour for an East Asian Economic Caucus. Thailand was the progenitor of the AFTA – and so on.

ASEAN addresses these differences by trying to ignore them. The association serves as a valuable institution for dissipating friction and confrontation within the region. The tone of ASEAN statements is always moderate and compromising. There have been no attempts by ASEAN as an association to mediate in unresolved boundary disputes between members. In none of these cases has anyone resorted to asserting their sovereignty by force; the consensus is that it is better to negotiate a legal settlement – 'jaw jaw' instead of 'war war'. Whenever two ASEAN countries squabble, the rest appear to put on blinkers and refuse to comment or intervene – even though quiet mediating efforts may be undertaken to resolve the dispute. More recently, rather than addressing these historical claims to one another's territory directly, ASEAN countries have been exploring joint development. The idea is to dissolve disputed borders using commerce and trade as a solvent. Thailand and Malaysia have formally agreed to jointly develop a disputed area of the Gulf of Thailand. Sub-regional zones of joint economic development and cooperation are helping to dissolve boundaries in areas where they were once either contested or under the threat of contest because of the pressure for command over resources. These are pragmatic solutions to protracted differences – a style of diplomacy the rest of the world could derive some benefit from.

Of course, history teaches us that it never pays to rule out future conflicts. There is a school of thought which sees Southeast Asian states rushing headlong into conflict with one another over land and resources that are becoming less and less abundant with the current pace of growth. Indeed, in late 1993 a Thai defence ministry white paper concluded that the chief threat to the country's security stemmed from unresolved boundary disputes and the competition for resources in the region.[16] But there is also new thinking that sees these potential flash-points becoming less volatile as state and private-sector initiatives dilute the importance of national boundaries through trade and investment.

In the more sensitive field of security many governments still prefer to deal with one another on a bilateral basis. Under the terms of the Treaty of Amity and Cooperation signed by ASEAN leaders in 1976, an ASEAN High Council could technically sit and judge regional squabbles; it has never been called. The ASEAN Regional Forum was established in 1992 to include all the major powers in the region in an informal security dialogue. In one way the ARF sidesteps the whole question of multilateral ASEAN defence cooperation by placing security management in the wider context of the Asia–Pacific region. Quite cleverly, it also brings in the major powers, specifically China and the United States, under a confidence-building umbrella coordinated by the ASEAN states themselves.

After almost three decades, something of an ASEAN bureaucratic culture has evolved. The endless rounds of meetings and bureaucratic paperwork – costing each country in the region of US$ 1 million a year – serves the valuable purpose of putting officials together; forcing them to discuss their problems informally in corridors, over hotel banquet tables, and on the golf course, as well as at the formal conference table. There is no doubt that as a confidence building measure, ASEAN has an astonishing record. When China adopted a more aggressive posture towards its territorial claims in the South China Sea in early 1995, ASEAN responded by issuing a joint statement that was remarkable because it united countries with varying degrees of fear and sympathy for China – against China's actions. Beijing responded, in fact, by withdrawing a claim to the Natuna island chain which Indonesia claims.

Although differences between ASEAN states have often frustrated attempts to knit a common position, regular meetings of officials and ministers have helped to forge, if not a common regional identity, then a fusing of common interests. In some ways, it is almost as if ASEAN has begun to reproduce elements of pre-colonial Southeast Asia; when borders were vaguely defined, the relations between states depended on a web of personal ties, and the actual power of the state was more symbolic than real. On a micro-level this diffusion of central state power can already be seen in the evolution of cross-border economic growth areas agreed upon between Singapore, Malaysia and Indonesia in the South, and Malaysia, Indonesia and Thailand in the North. A third intraregional economic sub-region is being promoted between Northern Thailand, Laos, Burma and Yunnan. Remarkably, a senior Thai military official said he could envisage the day when 'the economic power of regional city-states eclipses the power of the centralised state'.[17] If the future of modern states is diluted sovereignty, Southeast Asia will be protected from any conflict this might lead to by the flexibility and pragmatism of regional diplomacy.

In a broader context, ASEAN has helped put Southeast Asia on the geopolitical map. The association's annual ministerial meetings attract global attention. All the region's major trading partners attend what is called the Post Ministerial Conference. Since 1992, the PMC has been expanded to include all 18 Asia–Pacific nations in a security dialogue dubbed the ASEAN Regional Forum. Attending ASEAN meetings was once a chore for foreign ministers of the major Western powers. Today, they would not miss a single meeting. Their countries are courting ASEAN markets and need a foothold in the region. Now it's the turn of ASEAN diplomats to complain about all the meetings they must have with the major powers.

ASEAN does not entertain plans for a union along European lines. But like the European Union, the association is growing in size as neighbouring states find the post-Cold War environment conducive to establishing a regional identity. ASEAN's non-ideological tradition and respect for diversity made it relatively easy for communist Vietnam to apply for membership. In fact, the main worry for ASEAN has not been whether Vietnam will alter ideological course, but whether it is ready for free trade. Remarkably little is said in ASEAN circles about one another's politics, which means that it is a poor forum in which to lobby for political change. Yet, as we saw in an earlier chapter, ASEAN has helped form a common front against universal notions of human rights and democracy – a move all the more remarkable since ASEAN countries themselves don't share common views on how to define democracy.

The pressure of external influence may, however, be a more powerful impetus for forging a common identity than perceptions of common values. Indeed, as we saw in the earlier discussion about perceptions of democracy, external pressure seems to stimulate the search for common values. In history, the only effective unity Europe ever achieved was against the threat of Islam from the Turkish Empire. It was the belated influence of Islamic civilisation which sowed the seeds of Europe's Renaissance. Similarly, a commonly perceived, but rarely expressed fear of Southeast Asia's near neighbours is also compelling countries in the region to forge closer bonds.

## CHINA KNOCKS: THE STRATEGIC IMPERATIVE FOR A REGIONAL IDENTITY

In 1289, envoys sent by the Mongol Emperor Kublai Khan to exact tribute from the Javanese empire of Majapahit were defiantly sent packing with what the chronicles describe as 'disfigured faces' – generally taken to mean that their ears or noses were cut off.[18] A subsequent Chinese invasion of Majapahit in 1293 met with mixed results and was abandoned. The Chinese never attempted an invasion of Java again. But it is a victory Indonesians have never forgotten. A painting of the disfigured envoys incident hung until recently in the headquarters of the Indonesian intelligence agency (BAKIN). When BAKIN moved to its new office, so the story goes, it left the painting to the Chinese embassy which is now, ironically, temporarily housed in the old BAKIN building. The Imperial army had better luck in Burma, occupying the Burmese capital at Pagan in 1287. After overcoming almost a thousand years of Chinese rule, Vietnam spent much of its early independent history repelling Chinese invasions. A visitor to the National History Museum in Hanoi comes across diorama after technicolour *papier mâché* diorama depicting how and where the Vietnamese threw back the imperial armies. In one particularly striking scene the resourceful Vietnamese use fire boats to defeat an imperial Chinese fleet.

Today, Chinese cultural influence is benignly evident throughout Southeast Asia. The impact of this great northern neighbour is evident from styles of pottery and cuisine to the commercial terms used in many indigenous languages. Much of the region's urban architecture, particularly in provincial towns, follows the same design: the ubiquitous two storey 'Chinese shop house', with retail space on the ground floor and living quarters above. Less often expressed, is the historical memory of China's imperial designs on Southeast Asia. Actual invasion may have failed to subdue the princely states of the region, but the threat of invasion was translated into one of the more successful forms of imperialism ever practised. Few of the precolonial states of Southeast Asia failed at some point in history to pay homage to the celestial kingdom through the payment of tribute.

The tributary system was as benign as it was effective – turning imperial design into commercial gain. In simple terms, far-flung kingdoms undertook to send regular tributary missions bearing goods to Beijing for considerable profit, in return for which Beijing could claim to be the centre of the civilised world – without having to bear the expense and logistical difficulty of actually governing an extended empire. As the British scholar Gerald Segal put it: 'The Chinese empire was able to sustain both the illusion and sometimes the reality of great-power status and self-sufficiency.'[19] In modern times, perhaps only the Ottomans approached the Chinese in the economy of their vassal-state system.

The colonial era and the slow collapse of Imperial China under the Qing dynasty interrupted contact with what the Chinese have always considered their geopolitical bailiwick. From a historical perspective this could be seen as a hiatus – a mere 200 year pause in over 1,000 years of Chinese regional influence. For once China recovered its composure and began to develop economic and military clout, its desire to exercise influence overseas was bound to follow. The new order in China after 1949 may have been a communist one, but it was nothing short of Chinese; it draws on tradition as much for the definition of the state from within, as for its perception of the outside world. There is no evidence that Marxism changed the traditional Chinese world view of what the Thai scholar and diplomat Sarasin Viraphol elegantly characterises as 'national security based on self-imposed semi-isolation and non-equality of foreign intercourse'.[20]

Communist China's adventurism in the region from the 1950s, was a symptom of China's new forward strategy in Southeast

Asia, deploying subversion by local communist parties. Up until the mid-1980s, in places even later, Burma, Thailand, Malaysia and the Philippines battled entrenched local communist insurgencies in rural areas. Communism expired as an international force with the end of the Cold War in 1989, but China was not defeated. The guerrilla-style communist insurgencies backed by Beijing were next to impossible to completely stamp out. Instead, by the early 1980s China itself opted for a change of strategy. Using these local insurgencies as a bargaining chip, Beijing withdrew its backing from local communist parties in favour of a more diplomatic approach to Southeast Asia.

The next phase of China's engagement with Southeast Asia might, to borrow from Mao, be aptly summarised as 'let a thousand capitalists bloom'. The opening of China's economy in the 1980s needed capital which, initially at least, was not forthcoming from the West because of human rights concerns and difficult market conditions. So China tapped the next best source, the ethnic Chinese community. Lee Kuan Yew may be right that as ethnic Chinese 'our stakes are in our home countries, not in China where our ancestors came from'.[21] But for many of the region's more successful ethnic Chinese entrepreneurs there is far more money to be made in a homogeneous market of one billion people than in the diverse, fragmented market of 400 million which defines Southeast Asia. China is regarded as potentially the largest economy on the globe. And for many ethnic Chinese, if not too distant ancestral ties give them a comparative advantage, why not exploit that advantage?

Dhanin Chearavanont, the executive chairman of Charoen Pokphand (CP Group), Thailand's largest conglomerate, laughs when asked about CP's prospects in the ASEAN market. 'ASEAN is a market of 400 million people. China and India together are almost two billion', he says.[22] Dhanin is quick to lay diplomatic stress on the group's core activities in Thailand, but reluctant to say how much CP group has invested in China. (They have joint ventures in virtually every province in China.) Dhanin dismisses the inquiry with a vague reference to the mix of 'private and public concerns' which apparently makes disclosure problematic. Although accurate statistics are hard to come by, Southeast Asia's 23 million ethnic Chinese had probably contributed around US$ 8 billion in foreign direct investment to China by the mid-1990s.[23]

Though small by comparison with the amount of investment in China by Chinese from Hong Kong (around US$ 40 billion) and probably Taiwan as well, the role of Southeast Asia's Chinese in the growth of China's economy has been conspicuous for other reasons. Southeast Asia has by far the largest concentration of ethnic Chinese; they account for about 85 per cent of the region's capital.[24] Concerns about capital flight are growing, both with the threat of ethnic tension at home under conditions of economic stress and because of signs that China is about to enter a period of nationalist fervour. As one regional official put it:

> No longer revolutionary, but still a status quo power, China remains inscrutable. And now regional anxiety is growing that Beijing may be deliberately using Chinese nationalism as the binder of national unity – in place of a bankrupt ideology. This will make China an even more prickly neighbour than it is already.[25]

Latent questions about the dominance of ethnic Chinese enterprise in Southeast Asia are becoming entangled with the elemental strategic issue of China's posture towards the sovereignty of Southeast Asian states.

These two concerns seemed to meet dramatically on 14 April 1994 when a single ethnic Chinese businessmen was killed during a labour protest in the Indonesian city of Medan. Remarkably enough, China responded. A foreign ministry official in Beijing said that China hoped order would be restored as soon as possible in Medan. Though no reference was made to the Indonesian Chinese casualty, Beijing's comments were met by a stern riposte from Jakarta. And, of all places, Singapore, which reminded China that the affairs of overseas Chinese were no longer tied to China.

China has consistently denied any strategic designs on Southeast Asia. Beijing consistently asserts that China's foreign policy is governed by five principles of peaceful coexistence: mutual respect for territorial integrity and sovereignty; mutual non-aggression; non-interference in the internal affairs of other nations; equality and mutual benefit; and peaceful coexistence. However, the following assessment of how China sees the world is perhaps a better guide to China's probable role in the region:

In terms of comprehensive national strength, the US, of course, is still the most powerful country in the Pacific region. But with the relative decline of its economic strength, over-extension of its front, and the limitation of its power, the heyday of US unitary hegemony has gone forever. Japan has become an economic power and is going to be a political power. Without doubt its role in East Asia will be continuously enhanced. But due to fundamental contradictions and conflicts between Japan and the US in the economic area, the domestic constraints within Japan, and the opposition of many countries of the region, it is difficult for Japan to realise the 'Japan Dominating System' or the 'US–Japan Alliance Dominating System' in East Asia.[26]

The author, a prominent academic from Shanghai, goes on to cast doubt on an immediate role for Russia in the region, and concludes by saying that: 'China has become an important political stabiliser in East Asia.'

Certainly the growth of China's economy is making it harder for Beijing diplomats to tread so lightly on Southeast Asian sensitivities. China's claim to the South China Sea, in which Vietnam, Malaysia, Brunei and the Philippines also claim small territorial stakes, is not new. But Beijing has renewed these historical claims with vigour, insisting that China's claim to sovereignty was not negotiable. In 1974 and 1988, China used military force to seize territory in the South China Sea. In 1995, the discovery of structures built by the Chinese military on Mischief Reef, an atoll claimed by the Philippines, prompted a minor naval stand-off. The probability that China will one day enforce these claims grows with the size of its GDP. 'China will use its military force when it sees the opportunity. This irredentism must rank as the largest challenge to the status quo . . . ', writes Gerald Segal.[27] In 1979, China and Vietnam fought a border war in which China seemed to come off the worse. In 1988, the two countries skirmished in the disputed Spratly island chain. Memories of these conflicts, married to a much enhanced power projection capability, including the possible introduction of aircraft carriers and medium range missiles, have fuelled what one veteran Indonesian diplomat calls the 'historical uneasiness between China and Southeast Asia'.[28]

Though mostly unspoken in ASEAN official circles, suspicion

of China's strategic expansion is probably as great today as it was when Beijing was promoting hegemony in the guise of Marxist revolution. 'Historically, China has always expanded southward, never to the east or north', commented a senior Indonesian military officer in 1993.[29] But the texture of these perceptions varies from country to country. At one extreme, Indonesia argues that China is the chief threat to Southeast Asia's security. The Indonesian military sees China moving inexorably towards asserting its strategic interests in Southeast Asia, fearing that if Beijing's territorial claims were realised, China would become a Southeast Asian state – or vice versa. Thailand, which historically has always appeased China, tends to view Beijing's strategic manoeuvring as an inevitable, even understandable, response to the posturing of other regional superpowers – Japan, Russia and the United States – which seek to contain China. Nevertheless, all the countries of the region are concerned about the impact of China's emerging superpower status on the balance of power in the region.

From the mid-1990s, ASEAN officials watched nervously as closer ties between Beijing and Rangoon effectively gave the Chinese military access to the entrance of the Straits of Malacca. China established electronic listening posts on islands in the Andaman Sea just north of the straits. Burma also bought or bartered for arms from China worth over US$ 1 billion, and played court to China's fledgling forward policy in Southeast Asia. In return, Rangoon found a powerful ally and surrogate donor as Western countries shunned Burma's generals over their human rights record. Any move against Burma in the United Nations security council, for instance, would meet a Chinese veto. In Burma, China found a way to flex its diplomatic muscle. When Chinese premier Li Peng visited Rangoon in December 1994, he pointedly defended the military junta. Western diplomats in the Burmese capital compared the tenor of the Chinese leader's remarks to the way a US leader would behave in a client state.[30]

China's looming status as a regional superpower has made the ASEAN states nervous and helped strengthen moves towards regional cooperation. Though unspoken, this concern helped cement a policy of 'constructive engagement' with Burma in the early 1990s. ASEAN diplomats defended their contacts with the military junta on the grounds that it would foster economic security and therefore political change in Burma. In reality, they cared less about the pace of political change and more about checking China's growing influence in Rangoon.[31] The most obvious benefit to China was a land link to the sea for its South-western provinces. A 1985 article by former vice-minister of communications Pan Qi in the English language Beijing Review described a strategy of 'opening up Southwest China' in the following terms: 'Looking towards the South, we could find outlets in Burma.'[32]

If indeed this is China's long term aim, the signs are it is materialising. Physical contact between Southwest China and Southeast Asia will soon be established with the forging of road and rail links between Thailand, Laos, Vietnam, Burma and China's Southwestern province of Yunnan. The value of cross-border trade between Burma and Yunnan already exceeds US$ 1.5 billion a year. As well as acting as a conduit for cheap consumer goods flooding the markets of Burma, Laos and Vietnam, Yunnan is also a potential source of cheap labour for Thailand's more developed economy. Eventually, Yunnan will export better quality products at a lower price than Thailand because labour and materials are cheaper. 'A bit like dancing with a dinosaur', was how one Western intelligence source in Bangkok characterised the impact of Yunnan's relatively industrialised economy of 38 million people on Thailand's economy.[33]

'With the possibility that China will become the world's biggest economy some time in the next century', wrote Singapore's Minister for Information and the Arts, George Yeo in late 1993, 'old fears are bound to resurface. Thus a common East Asian consciousness can never be formed with China placing itself at the centre.'[34] But a common Southeast Asian consciousness is being spurred on by these developments. Fear of China, and to a lesser extent of a powerful Japan, helps explain why Southeast Asians are taking a more purposeful look at forging a common identity. Just as the thirteenth-century Javanese response to the threat from the Mongol empire was to forge alliances with neighbouring kingdoms, so the modern states of Southeast Asia are pondering closer cooperation to meet the challenge of local external powers. Any move in this direction is likely to have a significant impact on local notions of sovereignty and political autonomy, and inevitably on the process of political change.

## DREAMING OF ONE SOUTHEAST ASIA

We the undersigned citizens of Southeast Asia, meeting in
Manila, Republic of the Philippines, on 30–31 May 1994, do
hereby adopt and advocate the following vision of our region.
We believe that Southeast Asia should be a community. Collectively, this community should be a major, economic, cultural,
and moral entity on the world in the 21st century.'[35]

Citing a medley of reasons – from the need to avoid looking
inward as a region, to recognition of the region's common cultural
traditions – a group of nineteen prominent Southeast Asian academics and officials launched the concept of 'One Southeast Asia'
in mid-1994. This ambitious idea goes a step beyond ASEAN, in
that it focuses on the social and cultural dimension of regional
cooperation. Stress is laid on a common identity as well as
common interests. In diplomatic terms, the idea lays the groundwork for all ten countries of Southeast Asia to become part of
ASEAN. Yet by introducing the cultural dimension, the idea
comes across as rather inward-looking and defensive, cutting
against the grain of global trends towards open rather than closed
regionalism.

Southeast Asia has always been a cross-roads of cultures and
commodities. Why the need to erect cultural barriers? The strategic challenge posed by a resurgent China and pressure to conform with global standards of political and commercial behaviour
may help explain. Confronted by a world impinging on sovereignty and cultural norms, the response has been to shore up the
regional boundaries. As an earlier study of the concept opined;
'Integration is not a matter of choice . . . it is a necessity arising
from the fact of shared destiny.'[36]

For the time being the concept of full-blown unity – either in
institutional or social and political terms – remains a gleam in the
eyes of a handful of regional intellectuals. But the trend is unmis-
takeable. ASEAN has moved closer to forging free trade, freer
movement of people, and is getting accustomed to a free
exchange of ideas. 'The view has become more widespread than
outsiders imagine – and the groundwork for it has in fact begun',
notes Jose Almonte. Assuming this trend towards regionalism
develops, what impact will it have on the political landscape?
Judging from the sentiments expressed by Witoon from Project
for Ecological Recovery at the beginning of this chapter, it could

have a liberalising effect forcing states to adjust their norms to an acceptable regional standard or even universal standards. The question is what defines the standard – the soft-authoritarian style of Mahathir's Malaysia, or the muddled 'demi-democracy' of Thailand? Indeed, at first glance, Vietnam's accession to ASEAN in July 1995 did little to bring about political change: if anything, ASEAN officials saw Vietnam's membership as a move the Vietnamese Communist Party exploited to strengthen its legitimacy at home.[37] Closer contact between grassroots pressure groups will make it harder to deny liberal voices of dissent, but those voices will run up against the unifying effects of closer cooperation between ruling elites. More liberal governments will be less inclined to argue with their less liberal neighbours for fear of disrupting regional stability. This points to a dilemma: a society that supports the growth of a strong state, also acquires the potential to question the rule of the state.

Evidence of this dilemma can be found in contemporary Burma, where the pro-democracy opposition movement has drawn strength from its ties to like-minded Thai activists across the border. But at the same time, the Thai military has offered help or does business with the military junta in Rangoon. Burma, like Vietnam, has benefited greatly from the regional cohesion fostered by ASEAN. After two decades of sustained growth, the original six ASEAN states have acquired a modicum of economic clout in the region. Volumes of trade and investment from ASEAN helped sustain Vietnam's economy until the US lifted its trade embargo on Vietnam in 1994. The ASEAN states are beginning to offer modest amounts of aid to Indochina and Burma. Singapore has parlayed discrete defence contacts with Burma into more diversified technical assistance, which included running a domestic airline and building new hotels and an airport. Admittedly, the size of this aid cannot even begin to match the spending power of the World Bank or the International Monetary Fund (Thailand offered Burma a US$ 120 million soft loan to Burma for road improvement in the Northern Shan States in 1994.) But it suggests a willingness to fill the void in Burma, where Western governments maintain an embargo on multilateral assistance and talk about imposing economic sanctions. ASEAN's stance on Burma may seem distasteful to critics of the Burmese military junta; more objectively it lends substance to the idea of a common regional endeavour.

The diplomatic groundwork for 'One Southeast Asia' was in fact laid over the past decade, and began in earnest with the move to draw Vietnam into ASEAN. Vietnam did not need much persuasion. Hanoi first discovered how effective regional diplomacy could be when ASEAN took a strong stand against Vietnam's occupation of Cambodia after 1979. ASEAN diplomats coordinated and sustained a lobby supporting the Cambodian resistance coalition's occupancy of the country's seat at the United Nations. Sustaining this position prevented the Hanoi-sponsored government in Phnom Penh from acquiring international legitimacy, forcing it to negotiate with the Cambodian resistance factions in another ASEAN-coordinated initiative that eventually led to the 1991 Paris Peace agreement. The Cambodian peace process had to be endorsed by the Western powers and was eventually sucked into a huge United Nations bureaucratic vacuum, all of which diminished the regional dimension in forging the peace. Credit should be awarded to ASEAN, to Southeast Asians themselves, for initiating the withdrawal of Vietnam and a resolution of the vicious conflict between the Cambodian factions. It was a watershed in regional affairs, even if France and the United States were too arrogant or embarrassed to say so too openly.

Although scarcely realised, ASEAN's diplomatic experience with Cambodia, and more recently in Burma, has highlighted the region's potential to become master of its own political destiny. The practice of sending tribute to Beijing may not have had any appreciable impact on the sovereignty of these states, but it sustained the illusion of deference to the historical equivalent of a superpower that was only discontinued with the arrival of European colonial powers. The end of the colonial era was quickly followed by the onset of the Cold War and a new era of dependence on superpower patronage. Although taking a common political stand and the search for a more autonomous regional order were enshrined as basic principles when ASEAN was formed in 1967, it is only really in the 1990s that the region's economic dynamism, coinciding with the decline of superpower rivalry of the Cold War, has created an opportunity to begin asserting true regional autonomy.

## TOWARDS A SOUTHEAST ASIAN POLITY

If Southeast Asian states bind more closely together, what will the impact be on political systems? It is tempting to imagine that such binding will have a cathartic effect on the process of political change and foster more pluralism. There are signs that this is already happening. Non-governmental organisations are developing a regional network which allows circumscribed or controlled pressure groups in one country to tap support from the region. It has been easy for governments to paint NGOs as unpatriotic when they drew their support exclusively from Western sources, or to claim that they represent a foreign culture. It is rather harder to do so when the support comes from within the region. State control can also be eroded by economic liberalisation. The potential for doing just this comes from the ASEAN Free Trade Area, which is already dismantling the protective barriers used in some countries to protect state monopolies.

Tempting as it is to consider that 'One Southeast Asia' will be a freer Southeast Asia – that the process will help trim the banyan tree – there is as much opportunity for the branches of the banyan tree to be strengthened and spread out even wider with more regional cohesion. As we have seen, a major driving force to closer regional integration is the threat of external pressure – both from China and the West. And if it is political elites who fear the corrosive impact of external influence on their power, then quite possibly there is a political agenda backing moves for unity. Certainly, a more politically integrated Southeast Asia could evolve using the same principles that are applied in the diplomatic arena within ASEAN in its present form. Above all, this boils down to a commitment to deliberate and then reach a decision through consensus. Presumably, those states wanting to remain strong would block moves towards a regional parliament, or some statement of political principles that did not recognise their rules of the game. 'Regardless whether it is authoritarian or democratic, the deciding factor will be the quality of consensus', argues Jose Almonte.[38]

Another deciding factor will be the quality and outlook of the region's leaders once a more unified Southeast Asia emerges. Robert Scalapino argues that the coming generation of leaders will be more inclined to collective leadership because they will have sprung from the ranks of the technocrats who dominate policy-making. They will be less charismatic and therefore less powerful.[39] A more collective approach to leadership might also make them more inclined to cooperate regionally and take advice from their regional colleagues. But what if this new generation of leaders is also concerned about the preservation of the indigenous values claimed by the contemporary political elite? Elsewhere we have heard Malaysia's Deputy Prime Minister Anwar Ibrahim talk about preserving the best of tradition. Anwar is also a firm believer in 'One Southeast Asia'. In fact, the movement is relying on him to push along the agenda. But is Anwar interested in an Asian renaissance or preserving the culture of power and leadership he is likely to inherit? Only time and the long drawn out process of political succession, will tell.

Of course, the danger is that by searching for what the region has culturally in common, competitive urges may creep in and create alarming new divisions. Competing with 'One Southeast Asia' are more narrow concepts of closer cooperation between the Malay and Muslim or Buddhist parts of Southeast Asia. There are moves, for example, towards more interaction between the Muslim entrepreneurs of Indonesia, Malaysia and Brunei – a revival of the old 'Malindo' idea in a private sector context. Such pan-Malay sentiment worries tiny Singapore, once described in geographical terms as 'the nut between the two arms of the nutcracker'. On the mainland, Thailand dreams of becoming a gateway to the emerging markets of Indochina and Burma. Some planners go further and talk about a pan-Buddhist region encompassing Burma, Thailand, Laos, Cambodia and Vietnam. Significantly, some regional leaders seemed to be aware of the dangers of cultural bifurcation. In early 1995, Anwar Ibrahim addressed an international seminar on Islam and Confucianism:

here are two great traditions of the world whose adherents have generally been living, if not in perfect harmony with each other, certainly not in antagonism and discord, for the greater part of the last one thousand years. Indeed, through genial co-existence they have contributed, both in the past and the present, towards regional order and prosperity. One is reminded of the fact that centuries before the Enlightenment in the West, there had already been established productive engagement between the Muslim-Malay Sultanates of Southeast Asia and the Confucian Ming Dynasty of China.[40]

Although it seems unlikely that Southeast Asia will fragment along religious fault lines, realistically even the most optimistic scenario for a unified Southeast Asia is fraught with limitations. Despite the purposeful rearming that each country has undertaken in the past five years, the region has no effective military clout – the Philippines faced a threat from China to islands it claims in the South China sea with what one Philippine general described as 'an air force that can't fly and a navy that can't put to sea'. And for all the riparian economic behaviour, and slowly shifting patterns of trade, the region's economies are still dependent on external, principally Western export markets.

Doesn't this make Southeast Asia vulnerable to external influences for the foreseeable future? Is Anwar Ibrahim dreaming when he claims that 'the Asia mind has finally broken free from the intellectual morass' created by the quest for parity with the West. If so, doesn't this return us to the starting point of this book; the pressure to conform to Western standards of political behaviour? Perhaps for now. But this situation could change in the not too distant future. The only problem is that Southeast Asia may trade dependence on one cultural and commercial hegemon, for another.

# Epilogue

*Too soon to tell...*
*Zhou Enlai on what he thought of the French Revolution*

Democracy is an optimistic ideology by nature. 'One of the pleasures of membership of an advanced society', wrote American columnist Michael Kinsley recently:

> is precisely the knowledge that certain mundane aspects of life are shared by all. This gives reality to the otherwise abstract democratic ideal.[1]

The study of political change in Southeast Asia is deeply coloured by the notion that countries of the region are in various stages of transition from underdeveloped to more advanced levels of political development. The general assumption underlying the 'underdeveloped' to 'advanced' transition is that forms of autocracy are evolving into forms of democracy, and that if not voluntarily, then as a result of social and economic change, political elites in the region will progressively yield power to a more representative, pluralistic form of government.

By now it should be apparent that this is a simplistic, in some cases, even an optimistic assumption. The prevailing political cultures of the region are proving resistant to change. There is no simple, linear continuum of democratisation. In the recent history of Southeast Asia, there are more cases of retreat from democracy (Burma, Indonesia, Malaysia and Singapore). There are fewer cases, to date, where the direction of political change is strengthening democratic institutions (the Philippines and possibly Thailand). Neither are the more representative forms of government evolving in some instances duplicating the Western model. We have seen that strong leadership, supported by an enduring culture of patronage, remains a characteristic feature of some of the more economically successful states – in some cases reinforced or revived after brief periods of more pluralistic government. We have encountered a middle-class strata of society who prefer to support the authoritarian status quo rather than risk social upheaval; and we have seen how indigenous spiritual and religious values may replace imported secular ideologies as an idiom of political expression. Finally, it was suggested that a more integrated Southeast Asian community may also strengthen prevailing political values.

This more realistic perspective should not obscure demands for political freedom and democracy that breeds tension and demands for political change in the more authoritarian states of the region. The tension is real, if somewhat confined to a narrow spectrum of liberal intellectual activists. There is no doubt that more educated, economically enfranchised members of society in countries like Singapore, Malaysia and Indonesia yearn for more freedom to act and think for themselves. Although tempting to build into a wave for the future, it is important to remember that economic security also breeds complacency and support for the political status quo – particularly in a political culture where the heel of oppression is lightly applied, and the hand of patronage is often more evident. The media play up the trials and jail sentences endured by those who campaign for freedom. But democracy activists in these countries also have to combat apathy bred of material comfort, and a tenacious jealousy of one another's status and position that obstructs common efforts to push for political change. It is easier for ruling elites to trim the banyan tree at their convenience; harder for activists to muster the strength to hack off whole limbs.

At the threshold of the new century, the political complexion of Southeast Asia is not the mirror image of the West the departing colonial powers envisaged as their legacy 50 years ago. What of the future? For those bent on discerning a continuum, economics is seen as the key to change. One of the most persuasive arguments for the evolution of a Western-style civil society in Southeast Asia is that the region's commercial practices are beginning to resemble those of the West. The term used to describe this process is 'convergence'.

Governments in the region are framing laws that enshrine

aspects of standard commercial practice in the West, such as intellectual property and fiscal disclosure. As they do so they encourage more transparency in the commercial field, and hopefully build up more accountability in the political system. The so-called 'convergence' debate has a rather optimistic premise. It rests on the assumption that once Asians do business on the same terms and in the same way as Westerners, not only do Westerners stand to gain more in terms of market share and profit, but they also get to speak more English and live in countries that look and feel more like their own.

Viewed through the prism of political culture and the dynamics of regionalism, the prospects for political change in Southeast Asia along a continuum which projects parity with the West, look bleak for now. So how optimistic can we be that commercially Southeast Asia is on a convergent course with the old industrialised states of Europe and North America? Perceptions vary. There are those who are confident that convergence is inevitable as the region engages with the global trading system, and falls in step with the global rules laid down by the new World Trade Organisation. Their optimism is only tempered by acceptance of the fact that this is not a goal countries in Southeast Asia can attain in a single leap. Protectionist or nationalist sentiment runs deep in a region where most economies were freely plundered by colonial powers until half a century ago.

As Thailand grappled with a new copyright law and pressure to open up its financial and service sector in accordance with the WTO rules, there were howls of protest from domestic companies fearing the competition. They lobbied the government to slacken the pace of liberalisation and attempted to move the goal posts – proposing, for example, that foreign stock brokers be limited to a 25 per cent share holding in Thai subsidiaries. Government officials also dragged their feet. They suspected that freer trade principally benefited foreigners. 'The new rules are not made for foreigners to make money', warned a senior official at Thailand's new intellectual property department.[2] 'Ministers talk about liberalisation, but below them the senior officials are not supportive', complained a Thai entrepreneur. Happily for Western software makers and foreign financial institutions, governments in the region resisted these protectionist pressures and stood firmly behind policies of liberalisation. Clearly, they stood to lose a lot more by not adhering to GATT principles.

There are those who look at things differently, however. Malaysia's Prime Minister Mahathir is of the view that free trade is fine so long as it is not practised to benefit the stronger trading nations. That's why he wants to see Asian nations grouped together in an Asian trading forum – an insurance, if you like, against his suspicion that the West promotes free trade to erode the competitive advantages that Asia is blessed with. (He may also have been worried that Southeast Asian countries like Malaysia were in danger of losing some of these advantages as the cost of labour and other inputs increased.) The United States was not doing its best to dispel these fears when the Clinton administration chose to threaten Japan with trade sanctions over access to its auto market in mid-1995. America's huge trade deficit with Japan pushed Washington into bypassing the newly created World Trade Organisation – confirming Mahathir's suspicions about Western notions of free trade. Even less encouraging for the free marketers, was Mahathir's decision in 1995 to implement its own trade watch-list – though quite how a net exporter could impose sanctions on its own markets remained unclear.

Meanwhile, the economic landscape of Southeast Asia has undergone a quiet but major shift over the past two decades. High levels of trade with traditional Western markets have shrunk in comparison with levels of trade within the region, and with the greater Asian region. In fact, lower trade barriers and open markets have worked in Asia's favour. In the entire Asia–Pacific region, the percentage share of intraregional trade increased from 33.3 per cent in 1975 to 45.2 per cent in 1992.[3] These economic realities coincided with, and have to some extent supported, the confidence with which Southeast Asian states have defended their political systems against an onslaught of criticism from the West. The point bears repeating, as it may be hard for some people to grapple with. The plain fact is that Southeast Asia's more developed economies believe that they have secured a measure of self-reliance. By the year 2010, for example, a Japanese estimate puts Southeast Asia's share of the world's economy at 25 per cent – compared with 21 per cent for Europe and 27 per cent for North America.[4]

The prospect, if not quite the reality, of economic self-reliance, is already breeding new political attitudes towards the West. When the US congress voted to slash foreign aid in June 1995, a senior Philippine foreign ministry official observed: 'Ten years ago we would have been wringing our hands; today we don't really care because US aid is no longer so important to us.'[5] In 1991, the United States successfully blocked the appointment of a new Thai Prime Minister, Narong Wongwan, because he was suspected of involvement in narcotics smuggling. In 1995, when the State Department in Washington suggested that the appointment of cabinet ministers suspected of association with known narcotics dealers could impose a strain on bilateral ties, the incoming government of Banharn Silpa-archa reminded Washington that 'Thailand was not a colony of the United States'. An opinion poll in Bangkok revealed that this nationalist stance was endorsed by a majority, and a subsequent government inquiry into the allegations was led by a former foreign minister, Thanat Khoman, known for his staunch anti-American views. Times had changed. A US embassy official in Bangkok noted that once Thailand's exports to the ASEAN region overtook its exports to the United States in 1995/1996 'it won't be so easy for us to influence the government here'. The official wistfully remembered the days when 'all we needed to do was call up a general to get things done'.[6]

However, just as Southeast Asia has found the self-confidence to speak with a regional voice, its economic security seemingly assured, a new uncertainty is looming on the horizon. The end of the Cold War destroyed the old bipolar world and laid the foundations for a new world order that is optimistically considered global in outlook. Such optimism may be misplaced. As Henry Kissinger notes in his recent study of diplomacy, the world is now too complex to fit a definitive order of any kind.[7] And what if the world is on the verge of acquiring new polarities, also based on contrasting economic strengths and ways of managing society?

From a Southeast Asian perch, that's just how China's future role in the world is perceived. Few Southeast Asians subscribe to the comfortable notion that China's massive potential as a superpower will be defused by a chaotic fragmentation of the state. According to former Thai prime minister Anand Panyarachun, 'politically we regard China as a single nation, even if we tend to do business with 28 provinces'.[8] Like the myth of convergence, the chaotic China scenario is sustained by those who feel threatened by China's potential – one billion people living in an economy growing at 10 per cent a year. More realistically, since 95 per cent of the population are Han Chinese, Chinese cultural homogeneity can be considered a solid foundation for a national identity that could easily endure for another 2,000 years. Central authority has weakened in China (the central government's share of fiscal revenue has declined from 80 per cent before 1979 to 43 per cent in 1993). But few China-watchers, at least in Southeast Asia, can really imagine the richer provinces identifying themselves with anything other than the idea of China. Even fewer predict that China will develop a liberal democratic political system any time soon. Certainly, no one in Southeast Asia can imagine a China doing business in a way that disadvantages China or the Chinese, and only a handful of businessmen in the region envisage China doing business in the foreseeable future the way they do on Wall Street.

Strategic perceptions of China as an incipient superpower have helped Southeast Asian states find more in common in the interest of bolstering the defence of sovereignty, as we saw above. Not everyone in Southeast Asia sees the emergence of a powerful China as necessarily a bad thing for the region's well-being and security, however. Primarily, there are economic opportunities to be gained from access to the world's largest single market. Diplomatically, ASEAN is positioning itself to act as a mediator or moderator, to help China deal with the rest of the world – with all the commercial and diplomatic quid pro quos this might entail. In the process, Southeast Asia's traditional orientation towards the West is beginning to shift, swinging slowly and almost imperceptibly towards China – back towards China. 'With the advent of Western power, we turned our backs on long historical ties with China and India', reflects a Thai academic: 'Now, because of the market and opening up of China, that age of pre-Western contact is coming back; and coming back in a big way.'[9]

China has traditionally been viewed as a threat, but more ambivalently than that from the West. China's influence on the region through the ages has been principally cultural and commercial. The region has received knowledge and commercial gain from China, as well as demands for suzerainty. Southeast Asia's reaction to China has been ambivalent, compared to its ultimate reaction to European colonialism. This is because Chinese imperialism favoured indirect rule and preserved local sovereignty; Europeans eventually imposed direct rule on their Asian possessions. Arguably, this ambivalence will be felt again as China begins to play a larger role in Southeast Asian affairs. 'Thai society will adapt to aspects of China to balance Japan and the West', believes a Thai law professor. Even more surprisingly, he added: 'I would prefer to see China remain socialist to force our country's politicians to think about social policies.'[10]

Balance. The balancing of influences, views, and external forces, is the traditional hallmark of diplomacy in Southeast Asia. The syncretic impulse also lies at the core of Southeast Asian nationalism. 'Do we the Indonesian nation ... have only to choose between Pro-Russia or Pro-America?', asked Indonesia's founding vice-president Mohammad Hatta in 1948. He answered himself with a dictum that has so far served not just Indonesia but other countries in the region rather well in the post-colonial era:

> The government is of the opinion that the position we should take is to avoid becoming an object in international conflicts but remain a subject who has the right to determine our own position and strive for our own objective. . . . Our struggle must be based on the old motto: self-reliance and struggle on the basis of our own ability.[11]

The conventional view of the new global order is one that assumes the primacy of the West. But that's not quite how the world is beginning to look from a Southeast Asian perspective. We began this survey of political change in Southeast Asia by examining contrasting models of leadership and how they have been challenged in a Western context. To close, let's look at the next likely external influence these indigenous political orders will have to deal with – this time coming from the East – and gauge how easy it will be to maintain the self-reliance the region has managed quite well up till now.

## ETHNIC CHINESE: THE COMMERCIAL GLUE OF SOUTHEAST ASIA

Southeast Asia's longer-term economic security will depend less on foreign aid and export markets, and more on the ability of its entrepreneurs to generate capital and investment in the immediate neighbourhood. There may come a day when competitive pressures make the markets of Western countries and Japan less friendly for Southeast Asian businesses. At this point, the network of corporate ties and industrial linkages between local businesses and their ability to find new sources of investment will become important assets sustaining the region's growth. Singapore, one of the region's most advanced economies, is already looking at ways to enhance regional linkages as a way of maintaining the momentum of economic growth. Helped by a healthy current account surplus and a government offering incentives to those investing overseas, 'Singapore Inc.' is moving offshore. The fact that most of these businessmen are ethnic Chinese moving into other countries where they can deal with ethnic Chinese, helps a great deal.

Clearly, the ethnic Chinese of Southeast Asia already have a distinctive advantage in this respect. Their networks, based on bonds of clan or kinship, span the region more effectively than any corporate system or web of bilateral ties could devise. To take just one example, one of the lesser known dialect groups in Southeast Asia hails from the Fuzhou prefecture in China's Fujian Province. To other Chinese from this coastal area, they were looked down upon as country cousins. Yet as emigrants to the Malay archipelago and Indonesia, they have done remarkably well. In an arresting investigation of the Fuzhou network in Southeast Asia, veteran *Asian Wall Street Journal* reporter Raphael Pura discovered that the International Association of Fuzhous claims as members two of Asia's wealthiest tycoons: Malaysian Robert Kuok, and Indonesian Liem Sioe Long. The head of Malaysia's dominant ethnic Chinese political party is a Fuzhou; and the lucrative timber industry in Sarawak is dominated by Fuzhous.[12]

Ties like these are part of the human web that makes this region more integrated and interdependent than it often seems in either political or diplomatic terms. To cite Lee Kuan Yew on the subject:

> People feel a kind of natural empathy for those who share their physical attributes. Their sense of closeness is reinforced when they also share basic culture and language. It makes for easy rapport and trust, which is the foundation for all business relations.[13]

Rapport and trust, not only among themselves but with their hosts, have enabled the ethnic Chinese to virtually dominate commerce in almost every Southeast Asian country. There are approximately 23 million overseas Chinese in Southeast Asia, representing about 5 per cent of the population. Yet, in most countries of Southeast Asia, the minority status of the ethnic Chinese is greatly magnified by the fact that they control large proportions of the economy. If their population in Indonesia amounts to less than 4 per cent of the population, it is estimated that Indonesian Chinese controlled 70 per cent of domestic capital in the mid-1980s. In Malaysia, the Chinese account for 37 per cent of the population and control 65 per cent of the economy. In the mid-1970s, Chinese in Thailand, representing less than 10 per cent of the population, owned 90 per cent of all investments in the commercial sector.[14] One estimate of the total amount of capital controlled by the ethnic Chinese is in excess of US$ 85 billion. The top ethnic Chinese billionaires in Southeast Asia command a total net worth of around US$ 40 billion.[15] 'As a whole', wrote the Japanese scholar Yoshihara Kunio, 'Chinese capital seems to be a more important element of Southeast Asian capital than foreign capital.'[16]

This web of ethnic, kinship, or simply business ties, has helped insulate Southeast Asia from external economic shocks. In future it may act as a conductor of political and cultural as well as corporate influence. Feeling more integrated and assimilated with their host cultures, the ethnic Chinese in some countries of Southeast Asia are slowly abandoning their traditional role as political financiers in the background, and have begun entering the political mainstream. In Thailand the traditional Chinese approach to politics was to contribute to all political parties. In the mid-1990s, successful Chinese corporate magnates like Thaksin Shinawatra, who built a successful telecommunications empire and a personal fortune of US$ 2 billion in a decade, were leading political parties and aiming for the prime minister's office. Thaksin Shinawatra would not be the first Thai of Chinese descent to hold the office but he would represent the first of a group of Thai-Chinese who have built their political careers on the back of corporate activities which follow a traditionally Chinese cultural model.

In terms of political change, the trend towards more ethnic Chinese participation in government could well reinforce conservative political cultures. Reflecting the frugality and paternalistic tenor of ethnic Chinese corporate culture, the politics of someone like Thaksin boiled down to hard work and firm leadership. There is also a strong belief that money and connections, rather than debate and popular consensus, is the key to problem-solving. In the 1995 general election in Malaysia, large numbers of Chinese voters in the largely Chinese state of Penang aban-doned their traditional loyalties to the mainly Chinese opposition Democratic Action Party and voted for the Malay-dominated National Front ruling coalition. Here too, the level of comfort with the ruling establishment among Penang's traditionally sus-picious Hokkien community suggested that accomodation with the status quo was now preferable to dissent (although in a subsequent by-election in Penang, the DAP won a much increased majority).

Assimilation and integration have, over the past two decades, reduced the importance attached to the ethnic identity of the descendants of immigrant Chinese in the more advanced econ-omies of the region. But integration has also bred confidence and, paradoxically, less passivity about being Chinese. Confidence has bred a new sense of pride in Chinese culture. 'There is a new assertiveness among Chinese of the younger generation', noted Indonesian scholar of Chinese origin, Mely Tan. 'They are unen-cumbered by the baggage of the past. They say: we are Indonesi-ans of Chinese descent. What's the problem?'[17] Echoing this sentiment in Thailand, a young professional comments that 'these days it is chic to be Chinese'.

Another factor will reinforce this less passive Chinese identity – for rather practical reasons. With the rise of China as a major economic influence on Southeast Asia, it seems inevitable that ethnic Chinese who have spent the best part of half a century suppressing their ethnicity to integrate with their host societies, will begin to reverse that process in the interests of forging lucra-tive business ties with China. 'In the past we learnt Chinese because it was the language of our ancestors', suggests former Thai prime minister Anand Panyarachun. 'Now we are learning Chinese because it is an important business language.'[18]

The role played by overseas Chinese investment in China is hard to measure; most of the key players are shy about disclosing their exposure to China for fear that it will upset host govern-ments sensitive to capital flight. Official figures point to a pre-dominance of ethnic Chinese capital, though. In 1994 China attracted US$ 33.8 billion in new foreign investment. Hongkong and Macau accounted for 70 per cent of this; Taiwan 8 per cent.

By contrast, the US and Japan weighed in with 7 per cent and 4 per cent respectively. A large number of Southeast Asia's ethnic Chinese invest in China through companies in Hong Kong – although an increasing number are investing directly. Dhanin Chearavonont, the self-effacing president of Charoen Pokphand, Thailand's largest conglomerate, won't say how deeply the group is involved in China, but by 1995 the group had established joint-ventures in all but four of China's provinces. From livestock rearing alone, the company earned US\$ 3 billion a year. CP Group's Chinese operations, concentrating mostly on its traditional expertise in livestock rearing and animal feed production, made Dhanin an important figure in China. He has developed good access to the Chinese leadership. So good, that in Thailand he is frequently asked about the future of China. Like that of his ethnic cousins in Indonesia and Malaysia, corporate mega-players Liem Sioe Long and Robert Kuok, the contribution Dhanin is making to China's growth will almost certainly pay dividends once the Chinese economy takes off.

While some American and Japanese companies have experienced difficulties doing business in China, ethnic Chinese companies have managed to avoid many of the pitfalls. Partly this has been achieved by keeping their investment small and at the provincial level to avoid official scrutiny. But there is undoubtedly a degree of empathy with the Chinese authorities not enjoyed by non-Chinese companies. Charoen Pokphand executives, for instance, say that the Chinese authorities are happy to allow former civil servants to work for the company. This is how the Australian department of Foreign Affairs and trade summed up the advantage enjoyed by the ethnic Chinese in China:

> Networks are essential to foreign Chinese success in China. They allow access to the right officials at the township or village level. Local officials also can introduce investors to officials in other townships. Benefits flow both ways through the networks. On the other side, established foreign-Chinese business people can introduce new potential investors to the township, and assist the governments of townships with investments and bank credit in Hong Kong and beyond.[19]

In political, and to some extent cultural terms, the descendants of poor peasants who fled the coast of China to work as coolies in the great colonial cities of Southeast Asia may feel detached from the land of their ancestors. But whether they feel comfortable about this or not, they are poised to become the agents of a new era of commercial bonding with the great northern neighbour. According to a United Nations survey, the spectacular growth in China's world-wide exports and its heavy concentration in the region has been a major factor in the growth of intraregional trade.[20] Intraregional trade is making Southeast Asia less dependent on Western markets, and therefore on the West as a political and strategic ally. Some economists in the region believe that much of this intraregional trade is driven less by policies and more by the higher incomes and investment opportunities generated by the private sector – which is dominated by ethnic Chinese.[21]

The impact of China's economic clout in the region, has potentially far more than just commercial or economic implications. For ethnic Chinese this is a sensitive issue; it begins to make them less a population of 'overseas Chinese', but rather Chinese who happen to be overseas. Intellectuals dream of one Southeast Asia; but might the region's future more realistically be wedded to another thousand years of China's influence? The former Indonesian foreign minister Mochtar Kusumaatmadja reminds us that China's influence in Southeast Asia 'will always be cultural – never military in nature'.[22] How this affects the course of political change is a matter for speculation; but one worth exploring.

## CHINA: RE-ENTER THE DRAGON

Supapohn Kanwerayotin, a thirty-something Thai professional, remembers going to her Chinese primary school and being taught the *teochiou* Chinese dialect secretly. The teachers made them come to school around seven in the morning. They would hand out text books covered in brown or orange paper. The children could never take these books home, and they were carefully collected after class. Sometimes, for no given reason, the morning language class was abruptly cancelled. Although she was not aware then, Supapohn now knows this was because of a government school inspection. Teaching Chinese 25 years ago was frowned upon in Thailand. How things have changed. Today Supapohn is thinking of taking a job in China because, 'Thai-Chinese willing to work in China have a guaranteed job with the big Thai-Chinese conglomerates'.[23]

In the foregoing discussion, many of the assumptions about the course of political change were based on the weighting given to Western power and influence in the region. But what if this changes in the next half century? It is worth re-emphasising that from a Southeast Asian perspective, European influence has been but an interlude of effectively no more than 200 years, interrupting the much longer tradition of cultural and political influence exercised by China.

What kind of China emerges from the Deng era is of intense interest to Southeast Asians who feel, correctly, that it will affect their future too. In simple terms, a weak Chinese state, abandoning control to provincial kingpins, will offer tremendous business opportunities – as it did in the immediate aftermath of the collapse of the Qing dynasty. A weaker China might also encourage adventurism by China's neighbouring powers – as it did in the 1930s – and that could be destabilising for the region as a whole. A strong, unified China, on the other hand, will sustain its control over society, and maintain a forward diplomatic posture in the region. Both these aspects of a strong unified China could help strengthen the prevailing political culture in Southeast Asia and forestall convergence with Western standards of political and commercial behaviour.

For the purposes of this discussion, let us assume that China becomes, as is widely predicted, the world's largest economy by the year 2010. Economic growth marches along at a healthy clip of 10 per cent annually; the current account deficit remains comparatively low; yet China's market continues to open. The most important impact of an emergent China scenario will be on the Southeast Asian ethnic Chinese population. The conventional wisdom is that after almost half a century of steady assimilation with their host cultures, the region's ethnic Chinese have lost whatever bonds they had with the country of their ancestors. But this widely held view is being challenged by the emergence of China as an important regional market. China's market is said to be luring the Chinese Diaspora 'homeward'. Pragmatism has once again overruled the emotional ties of place and culture – this time to reverse or at least arrest the assimilation process. The general assumption, regardless of politically-correct statements periodically made by ethnic Chinese themselves, is that the Chinese of Southeast Asia are almost becoming even more Chinese, rediscovering their ethnic identity to exploit opportunities in China. Ahead of Indonesia's normalisation of relations with China in 1990, a move that greatly facilitated China's diplomatic push into Southeast Asia, Mely Tan feared that it would remind Indonesian Chinese 'of their own problem, that they are a foreign element in the country'. George Hicks and Jamie Mackie wrote in mid-1994: 'It may be excessive to suggest that we are now entering a phase of re-sinicisation, but it may well be that the phase of rapid de-sinicisation has ended.'[24]

It would be premature, and perhaps wrong, to predict any racial tension in the region as a result of a Chinese ethnic revival. However it can perhaps be safely said that China's influence over its ethnic emigrants has ebbed and flowed, but never really been extinguished. The declining Qing imperial dynasty, with its disdainful regard for emigrants, was reason enough for many Chinese to turn their backs on the homeland. But a politically resurgent China after 1911 sparked off a wave of pro-Beijing sentiment among Southeast Asia's Chinese community. If Deng's reforms and the flowering of China's market economy is once again restoring pride in China among the Chinese Diaspora, what will the implications be for Southeast Asia?

First, Western political and economic influence in Southeast Asia will increasingly find itself checked by China's sheer size and influence. Intangible as this may seem while the Beijing leadership struggles to rein in unruly provincial fiefdoms and cope with managing its market reforms, just consider the influx of Chinese immigrant workers – now over 100,000 illegally in Thailand; or the trade in cheap Chinese consumer products flooding Burma, and knocking at Thailand's door. In Burma's second city of Mandalay the visitor is assailed with complaints by local Burmese traders. 'We are treated as second class citizens in our own country', complained a retired Muslim schoolteacher, referring to the special treatment given Chinese businessmen by the city authorities.[25] If not a deliberate policy, China's probing of markets to the south on mainland Southeast Asia could easily help extend Chinese commercial influence. Cross border trade between Yunnan and Burma is estimated at an annual US$ 1.5 billion. A new corridor of trade with Southeast Asia is developing through Northern Laos, where the Chinese have been building a road link through to Thailand. Former prime minister Anand has publicly called for the old buffer states, that were designed to keep China at bay, to be turned into 'bridges' carrying commerce and trade.

Second, China's cultural influence in Southeast Asia is steadily growing and may be rather more important in the long run than the build-up of Chinese military strength. The process is subtle, and also rather sensitive in some countries. The need to do business with China is fuelling demand for Mandarin speakers in Thailand, for example. Enrolment in Mandarin classes increased by 30 per cent at Bangkok's Thammasat University from 1993 to 1994. Yet a dozen or so years before, Thai-Chinese were more furtive about learning the language of their ancestors; one of the few schools where Mandarin could be learnt was tucked away in the hills of northern Thailand in a community of former Kuomintang soldiers. 'The revival of Chinese studies in Thailand can be attributed to the fact that China, whose economy is ranked third largest in the world, has raised its doors to the world', commented a local Thai newspaper.[26]

Western diplomats are often confused because China's political profile hardly reflects the importance of its cultural and commercial ties – and perhaps also because they are convinced that a resurgent China will play by the global rules. Officially, China plays a low-key diplomatic role. Chinese embassies are mostly tucked away in the less fancy parts of town. Their diplomats maintain a low profile. Whenever senior Chinese officials visit the region, they are careful to stress China's policy towards people of Chinese origin: never to endorse dual nationality. 'As they are no longer Chinese nationals, they should fulfil their obligations to the country', intoned Chinese premier Li Peng during a visit to Jakarta in 1991. Yet Chinese embassy receptions draw thousands of the well-heeled and well-connected within the business community. In an address marking the twentieth anniversary of ties between Bangkok and Beijing in July 1995, the Chinese ambassador remarked that HRH Princess Maha Cakri Sirindhorn had made no less than six visits to China. In 1994, the Thai-Chinese Chamber of Commerce played host to a remarkable 278 investment missions from China. In Malaysia, the local Chinese business community pays the expenses of visiting Chinese provincial officials. Datuk Tan Gim Wah, the mayor of Penang, complained that it is often hard to keep up with the expensive tastes of Chinese officials. He has known local businessmen buy more expensive cars just to impress a Chinese official visitor.[27]

Even more subtle than China's official diplomatic thrust in the
region, is its cultural diplomacy. When the Chinese government
sent a holy Buddhist relic to Thailand in 1994, the Thai King
prayed at the temple where the relic, said to be a tooth of
the Lord Buddha, was temporarily installed. In Burma, another
Buddhist relic from China sent the same year attracted throngs
of devout Buddhists and the donation of many hundreds of thousands of dollars. Little by little, and for the most part without
fanfare, China is finding common cultural meeting points to
enhance its relations with Southeast Asia. 'We have enjoyed
friendly contacts for 1,000 years', Li Peng reminded his Indonesian hosts in 1991, usefully adding that 'both of our countries
underwent periods of colonial turmoil'. Here's how a Chinese
academic reflected on China's claim to the South China Sea, by
boldly claiming a common identity in the region:

> Countries and regions around this area have one of the fastest
> rates of economic growth in the world. . . . These countries and
> regions have their common interests and requirements, similar
> human backgrounds, and close links in history.[28]

Another Chinese academic quietly reminded the author about
the tradition of maritime trade existing between China and Southeast Asia. 'You Europeans have your Magellans and Cooks, but
you forget our own Admiral Cheng Ho', he quipped.[29] Where
the great European navigators left little other than maps and
place names, Cheng Ho, a Muslim eunuch of the Ming Dynasty
led half a dozen expeditions to Southeast Asia in the early fifteenth century. His fleet consisted of over 60 ships and some
27,000 men. By all accounts, the admiral's repeated missions to
the princely courts of Southeast Asia did much to repair the
damage to China's image done by Kublai Khan's marauding
Mongol invasions at the end of the thirteenth century. Cheng
Ho's contribution, not to say his influence, must have been considerable. For outside the central Javanese capital of Semarang,
there still stands a Chinese temple dedicated to the memory
of Cheng Ho. Another shrine exists in the east coast state of
Trengganu in Malaysia. Indonesian Chinese revere the Surabaya
shrine. But more remarkably, Chengo Ho, a Muslim Chinese, is
also believed to have played a role in helping Islamic missionaries
convert the Hindu rulers of fifteenth-century Java.[30]

A Muslim Chinese helping to spread Islam in the fifteenth

century; a modern Chinese government propagating the Buddhist faith at the end of the twentieth century. The effectiveness of China's cultural diplomacy has not lost much over the past 500 years. These cultural exports may not be as noticeable as a Michael Jackson concert tour, or another McDonalds restaurant but they draw a much deeper response. Anwar Ibrahim from Malaysia reads his history well when he speaks of the ties between the old Malay sultanates and the Ming Dynasty in the fifteenth century. And in one sentence, perhaps instinctively, he captures the essence of what drove China's engagement with the region then, and, in the author's view, what is very likely to be the engine of China's much closer engagement in the future: 'Trade, rather than war, was the governing mode of relations.'

The world has changed, of course. There will never be a hermetically sealed Asia revolving around the Middle kingdom of China as the mandarin scholars once fancied. There may even be a counter-reaction to a more assertive China; one that sees Southeast Asia look to the West for a strategic and cultural balance. But for now, it looks like China's growing influence in the region will help balance the perception that the rest of the world is on a convergent course with Western values. The closer integration of Southeast Asian states, and in turn with other East Asian states, principally China, will finally exorcise the ghost of Max Weber from the intellectual conceptualisation of the region's political culture.

The rhetoric of Southeast Asia's cultural renaissance has struggled to combat the notion that non-Western cultures are ill-equipped to progress economically or politically. It's ironic, that just as the proponents of Asian values began to turn the corner in the debate, by toning down their own distorted claims of primacy, and accepting more of the universal values enshrined in every one of the world's cultures, some of the pillars of Western virtue in Asia began to crumble. In early 1995, the US dollar lost 15 per cent of its value against the Japanese Yen, and former US defence secretary Robert Macnamara admitted that as early as 1963, he knew that America's engagement in Vietnam was a mistake. Do these symbolic markers signal an impending end to the Western interlude in Asia? Writing in mid-1995, Don Emmerson, an American scholar of Asian affairs, considered the future possibility that: 'Despite its geographic status as a Pacific power, the United States became a disadvantaged bystander on the rim, reduced to relying on Canada and Latin America in [a] tensely tripolar world . . . '.[31]

The argument in this book has focused on the ways Southeast Asian countries have preserved, recovered, and adapted traditional models of political power in the face of external pressure to change from the West. In the final pages the possibility has been raised that another, perhaps more familiar external cultural influence may prevail over the next few decades. But then it has always been the fate of Southeast Asia to serve as a crossroads of culture and trade. The beauty of this phenomenon has always been the diverse manner in which the impact of East and West has been felt. Like the mosques of the north Java coast where Hindu rites blend with Islamic orthodoxy, and a Muslim saint can be buried in a tomb alongside his Chinese wife. Or the Cao Dai church in Vietnam, which blends Taoist spiritualism and Christian dogma. This colourful, if sometimes baffling, eclecticism may cloud the political picture and confuse those interested in divining principles of governance, but it should alert the objective observer to a collective allergy to extremism and disdain for dogma. In a world afflicted by both, perhaps the region offers an example worth emulating.

# Notes

Any quotations from individuals, not otherwise referenced, are personal communications to the author, and of course I take full responsibility for their accuracy, for the reliability of data quoted, and for the opinions expressed here.

## PROLOGUE

1 Dr Kusuma Snitwongse, personal communication, Kuala Lumpur, May 1992.
2 Author's interview with Amnuay Virawan, Bangkok, June 1995.
3 *The Nation*, 20 May 1995.
4 Robert Bartley, Chan Heny Chee, Samuel P. Huntingdon and Shijuro Ogata (1993) 'Capitalism and the Role of the State in Economic Development', in *Democracy and Capitalism: Asian and American Perspectives*, Singapore: Institute of Southeast Asian Studies, p. 75.
5 *Financial Times*, 22 August 1994.
6 The pioneering work on ethnicity in Southeast Asia was done by Edmund Leach in his *Political Systems of Highland Burma* (1954) London: Bell.
7 Richard Robison, cited in William Case (1992) 'Semi-democracy in Malaysia: Pressures and Prospects for Change', Canberra: Australian National University Discussion Paper, series no. 8, p. 13.
8 Author's interview with Dhanin Chearavanont, Bangkok, November 1994.
9 Cited in *Washington Post*, May 1995.
10 Speech at Kuala Lumpur at 'International Symposium on Asia in the 21st Century', 24–5 January 1994.
11 Asian Development Bank, Annual Report 1994.
12 K.S. Maniam (1993) *In a Far Country*, London and Kuala Lumpur: Skoob, p. 126.
13 Interview with Wee Choo Keong, Kuala Lumpur, September 1991.
14 Jose Almonte (1993) 'Southeast Asia into the Twenty-First Century – "Philippines National Agenda" ', paper presented at Fifth Southeast Asia Forum, Kuala Lumpur, 3–6 October 1993.

15 Former President of Singapore, Devan Nair, in his Foreword to Francis T. Seow (1995) *To Catch a Tartar: A Dissident in Lee Kuan Yew's Prison*, New Haven: Yale University, Southeast Asian Studies, p. xiv.

16 Source: *Summary of World Broadcasts*, July 1994.

17 ESCAP (1995) *Review and Analysis of Intra-regional Trade Flows in Asia and the Pacific*, Bangkok: Economic and Social Commission for Asia and the Pacific.

18 David Steinberg (1995) 'The Burmese Political Economy: Opportunities and Tensions', paper presented at a conference on 'Myanmar Towards the Twenty-first Century', Chiang Rai, 1–3 June.

## 1  RECOVERING TRADITION

1 David K. Wyatt (1993) *Studies in Thai History*, Chiangmai: Silkworm Press, p. 285.

2 Cited in Scott Barme (1993) *Luang Wichit Wathakan and the Creation of a Thai identity*, Singapore: Institute of Southeast Asian Studies, p. 20, fn. 35.

3 Thongchai Winichakul (1994) *Siam Mapped: A History of the Geo-body of a Nation*, Chiang Mai: Silkworm Books, p. 3.

4 Rudolph Mrazek (1994) *Sjahrir: Politics and Exile in Indonesia*, Cornell: Cornell University Press, p. 482.

5 ibid., p. 486.

6 ibid.

7 Eric Hobsbawm and T.O. Ranger (eds) (1983) *The Invention of Tradition*, Cambridge: Cambridge University Press.

8 Ben Anderson (1983) *Imagined Communities: Reflections on the Origin and Spread of Nationalism*, London: Verso, p. 145.

9 Clive Kessler ( 1992) 'Archaism and Modernity: Contemporary Malay Political Culture', in Joel Kahn and Francis Loh Kok Wah (eds) *Fragmented Vision: Culture and Politics in Contemporary Malaysia*, Sydney: Allen and Unwin, pp. 133–57.

10 M. Nakamura (1983) *The Crescent Rises over the Banyan Tree: A Study of the Muhammadiyah Movement in a Central Javanese Town*, Yogyakarta: Gajah Mada University Press.

11 Francis Fukuyama (1989) 'The End of History?', *The National Interest*, no. 16, Summer, pp. 3–18.

12 Francis Fukuyama (1992) *The End of History and the Last Man*, New York: Penguin, p. 276.

13 Francis Fukuyama (1995) 'Confucianism is no Bar to Asian Democracy', *Asian Wall Street Journal*, 23 May.

14 Stanley J. Tambiah (1976) *World Conqueror and World Renouncer: A Study of Buddhism and Polity in Thailand against a Historical Background*, Cambridge: Cambridge University Press, p. 518.

15 In 1994, Rupert Murdoch's Hong Kong-based Star Television network replaced the US-owned Music Television (MTV) with a regionally-produced version called 'V'. MTV had been a source of considerable

criticism from governments in the region because of its brash, Western style. 'V', by contrast, brought audiences more Asian pop music, and toned down the presentation.

16  Ernest Gellner (1983) *Nations and Nationalism*, Oxford: Blackwell, p. 22.
17  Samuel Huntingdon (1993) 'The Clash of Civilisations?', *Foreign Affairs*, vol. 72, no. 3, pp. 22–49.
18  ibid.
19  Ruth T. McVey (1978) 'Local Voices, Central Power', in Ruth McVey (ed.) *Southeast Asia Transitions: Approaches through Social History*, New Haven: Yale University Press, p. 27.
20  Benedict Anderson (1983) *Imagined Communities: Reflections on the Origin and Spread of Nationalism*, London: Verso, p. 127.
21  Herb Feith (1963) 'Dynamics of Guided Democracy', in Ruth McVey (ed.) *Indonesia*, New Haven: Yale University Press, p. 317.
22  The survey was conducted by Dr Suvid Rungvisai of Chiang Mai University in the first five months of 1995. Personal communication, June 1995.
23  In 1992 and 1993, the author covered parliamentary by-elections in Kedah and Kelantan, which involved contests between the ruling UMNO party and the Islamic party (PAS).
24  George Yeo, cited in *Straits Times*, 20 December 1993.
25  Singapore's acting environment minister, Teo Chee Hian, on why the government needs to control information in the electronic age. Cited in *Far Eastern Economic Review*, 22 June 1995.
26  O'Donnell and Schmitter defined 'hard' democracy or *democradura* as involving democratic procedures without liberalisation; in other words, the scrupulous observance of democratic niceties such as convening parliament and calling elections, but never allowing an effective opposition challenge at the polls. 'Defining Some Concepts (And Exposing Some Assumptions)', in G. O'Donnell, P. Schmitter and L. Whitehead (eds) (1986) *Transitions from Authoritarian Rule: Prospects for Democracy*, Baltimore: Johns Hopkins University Press, vol. 4, pp. 6–14.
27  Augusta De Wit (1912) *Java: Facts and Fancies*, Singapore: Oxford University Press, p. 87.
28  Herb Feith, op. cit., p. 313.
29  S. Takdir Alisjabhana (1966) *Indonesia: Social and Cultural Revolution*, Kuala Lumpur: Oxford University Press, p. 154.
30  Author's interview with Nurcholis Madjid, Jakarta, April 1994.
31  John Ball (1981) *Indonesian Law: Commentary and Teaching Materials*, Sydney University: Faculty of Law, p. 359.
32  ibid., p. 371.
33  See Pramoedya Ananta Toer (1988) *House of Glass* (Rumah Kaca), London: Penguin.
34  Umar Kayam, '*Transformasi Budaya Kita*', inaugural speech at Gaja Madah University, Jogyakarta, May 1988.
35  J.M. Gullick (1989) *Malay Society*, Kuala Lumpur: Oxford University Press, p. 30.

36 *Far Eastern Economic Review (FEER)*, 24 December 1992.
37 Author's interview with a senior UMNO politician, Kuala Lumpur, 27 April 1994.
38 Personal communication, May 1994.
39 Harold Crouch (1993) 'Authoritarian Trends, the UMNO Split and the Limits to State Power', in Joel Kahn and Francis Loh Kok Wah (eds) *Fragmented Vision: Culture and Politics in Contemporary Malaysia*, Sydney: Allen and Unwin, pp. 21–44.
40 Federal Constitution of Malaysia, Article 150(1).
41 G.S Nijar (1989) *The Rule of Law in Malaysia. A Report of the Conference held at the European Parliament*, 9–10 March, p. 45.
42 Datuk Param Cumaraswamy, cited in *FEER*, 11 February 1993.
43 T.S. Selvan (1990) *Singapore: The Ultimate Island*, Melbourne: Freeway Books, p. 26.
44 Francis T. Seow (1995) *To Catch a Tartar: A Dissident in Lee Kuan Yew's Prison*, New Haven: Yale University Southeast Asian Studies, p. 251.
45 D.G.E. Hall (1968) *A History of Southeast Asia*, London: Macmillan, p. 171.
46 Donald F. Cooper (1995) *Thailand: Dictatorship or Democracy?*, London: Minerva Press, p. 369.
47 Likhit Dhiravegin (1992) *Demi Democracy: The Evolution of the Thai Political System*, Singapore: Times Academic Press, p. 231.
48 *FEER*, 31 August 1995.

## 2  *DEUS EX IMPERA*

1 Jomo Sundaram, cited in *FEER*, 4 May 1995.
2 *FEER*, 4 May 1995.
3 Author's interview with General Abdul Haris Nasution, 26 July 1990.
4 *FEER*, 5 March 1992.
5 Author's interview with Lim Keng Yaik, leader of the Gerakan Party in Kuala Lumpur, May 1994.
6 Personal communication, 18 May 1995.
7 Author's interview with Amnuay Virawan, leader of the Nam Thai Party, Bangkok, June 1995.
8 John Dunn (1992) *Democracy: The Unfinished Journey*, Oxford: Oxford University Press, p. 262.
9 Soeharto (with K.H. Ramadhan) (1989) *Soeharto: Pikiran Ucapan dan Tindakan Saya*, Jakarta: PT Citra Lantoro Gung Persada, p. 364.
10 In the late 1980s, Mahathir was infuriated by court judgments which overturned the expulsion of two foreign journalists from the *Asian Wall Street Journal*, and then ordered the release of an opposition politician under detention. In 1988, he amended the constitution so that, in his words, judges 'would apply the law made in parliament and not make their own laws ...'. Then in May 1988 the Lord President (Chief Justice) and two Supreme Court judges were dismissed after a judicial enquiry on the grounds of 'gross misconduct'

ahead of a controversial challenge in court lodged by a dissident faction of UMNO which they were scheduled to rule on. An amendment to the Printing and Presses and Licensing Act limits press licences to a renewable one year period. See Harold Crouch (1992) 'Authoritarian Trends, the UMNO Split and the Limits of Power', in Joel Kahn and Francis Loh Kok Wah (eds) *Fragmented Vision: Culture and Politics in Contemporary Malaysia*, Sidney: Allen and Unwin, pp. 26–7.

11 Anthony Reid (1993) *Southeast Asia in the Age of Commerce 1450–1680, vol. 2: Expansion and Crisis*, New Haven: Yale University Press, p. 169.

12 Satyagraha Hurip (1969) *Bisma: Warrior Priest of the Mahbharata* (translated by David Irvine (1990)), Jakarta: Pustaka Sinar Harapan.

13 A controversy rages in Thai historical circles over whether the famed Ramkhamhaeng Inscription genuinely dates back to the thirteenth century, or was concocted by King Rama IV of Thailand to support his notion of how Thai society should be conceived.

14 David K. Wyatt (1993) *Studies in Thai History*, Bangkok: Silkworm Books, p. 71.

15 Yoneo Ishii (1978) *Thailand: A Rice Growing Society*, Kyoto: Kyoto University Press, p. 33.

16 Anthony Reid (1993) op. cit., p. 202.

17 Kobkua Suwannathat-Pian (1993) 'Thrones, Claimants, Rulers and Rules: The Problem of Succession in the Malay Sultanates', *Journal of the Malayan Branch of the Royal Asiatic Society*, vol. 66, pp. 1–23.

18 *The Times* [of London], 23 December 1993.

19 *Cambodian Times*, Phnom Penh, 17–23 April 1994.

20 Neils Mulder (1992) *Inside Southeast Asia*, Bangkok: DK Books, p. 161.

21 Indonesia's 4 million civil servants were under an 'unwritten obligation to support only the ruling Golkar Party in elections'. Comment by Secretary General of Home Affairs Ministry, Suryatna, cited in the *Straits Times* [of Singapore], 1 December 1993.

22 Hamish MacDonald (1983) *Suharto's Indonesia*, Sydney: Fontana, p. 245.

23 The 'gratitude' incident is cited at length in Michael Vatikiotis (1993) *Indonesian Politics Under Suharto*, London: Routledge, p. 151.

24 Story as related to the author by Fikri Jufri, deputy editor of *Tempo* magazine in 1992.

25 Anthony Reid (1993) op. cit., p. 262.

26 Author's interview with Sarwono Kusumaatmadja, Jakarta, 26 September 1990.

27 Shahnon Ahmad's short story was published in Kuala Lumpur in the literary magazine *Dewan Sastera* in December 1993. Shortly afterwards, the magazine's editor Abdul Ahmad was moved to another position allegedly at Mahathir's request.

28 William Case (1992) 'Semi-democracy in Malaysia: Pressures and Prospects for Change', Canberra: Australian National University Discussion Paper, series no. 8, p. 9.

29 Mahathir Mohamed (1970) *The Malay Dilemma*, Kuala Lumpur: Times Publishing, pp. 8–9.
30 Quoted in 'One Happy Culturally Superior Family', *Time*, 21 November 1994, p. 37.
31 Personal communication.
32 Personal communication, July 1992.
33 Personal communication, September 1992.
34 Mahathir's assault on the courts in 1988 was widely reported. It revolves around the 27 May 1988 dismissal of the Lord President (highest judge in the land) Tun Salleh Abbas. Tun Salleh had been hearing an appeal by a group of political dissidents who questioned the legality of Mahathir's ruling UMNO party. Following Tun Salleh's dismissal, Mahathir told the annual UMNO assembly in October: 'What is so special about judges in Malaysia that they are considered to be above the law?' In January 1988 the attorney general Abu Talib Othman echoed Mahathir's impatience with the independence of the judiciary by saying 'independence of the court does not necessarily mean deciding a case against the state'. (All cited in Khoo Boo Teik (1995) *Paradoxes of Mahathirism*, Kuala Lumpur: Oxford University Press, pp. 292–3.)
35 David Steinberg (1981) *Burma: A Socialist Nation of Southeast Asia*, Boulder: Westview Press, p. 109.
36 Michael Vatikiotis (1993) *Indonesian Politics under Suharto*, London: Routledge, p. 51.
37 Soeharto (1989) op. cit., p. 288.
38 Edmund Terence Gomez (1994) *Political Business: Corporate Involvement of Malaysian Political Parties*, Townsville: James Cook University Press, p. 286.
39 ibid., p. 287.
40 *FEER*, 5 July 1990.
41 *FEER*, 22 June 1995.
42 Neils Mulder (1992) op. cit., p. 157.
43 Indonesia's State secretary, Moerdiono, cited in *Tempo*, 8 January 1994, p. 16.

## 3 DIFFERING ON DEMOCRACY

1 Tran Quang Co, a senior Vietnamese foreign ministry official, speaking at the Institute of Strategic and International Studies Round Table, Kuala Lumpur, June 1994.
2 Ralph Smith (1968) *Vietnam and the West*, Ithaca: Cornell University Press, p. 183.
3 V.G. Kiernan (1963) *The Lords of Human Kind: European Attitudes to the Outside World in the Imperial Age*, London: Pelican, p. 36.
4 Rudolph Mrazek (1994) *Sjahrir: Politics and Exile in Indonesia*, Ithaca: Cornell University Press, p. 486.
5 ibid., p. 486.
6 Smith (1968) op. cit., p. 187.

7  ibid., p. 185.
8  *FEER*, 2 December 1993.
9  Paper delivered at a seminar on human rights in Indonesia, organised by the Center of Strategic and International Studies, Jakarta, May 1993.
10 Pramoedya Ananta Toer (1992) *House of Glass*, London: Penguin. p. 218.
11 D.G.E. Hall (1968) *A History of Southeast Asia*, London: Macmillan, p. 669
12 Speaking at the 'First ASEAN Congress', Kuala Lumpur, 7–10 October 1992.
13 Paper delivered by Kishore Mahbubani in Kuala Lumpur, 1992.
14 Tran Quang Co in Kuala Lumpur, June 1994 (see note 1, p. 217).
15 Charles Maier (1994) 'Democracy and its Discontents', *Foreign Affairs*, July/August, pp. 48–64.
16 Mahathir, speech, 5 December 1993.
17 Robert Cullen (1992/3) 'Human Rights Quandary', *Foreign Affairs*, Winter, pp. 79–89.
18 Andre Gunnar Frank (1990) 'No End to History! History to no End?', in Ken Coates (ed.) *ENDpapers Twenty One*, London: Spokesman, p. 18.
19 Personal comunication, Kuala Lumpur, February 1994.
20 *Bangkok Post*, 20 June 1995.
21 *Time*, 14 June 1993.
22 Jaime Zobel de Ayala, speech at Pacific Basin Economic Council Conference, Kuala Lumpur, 22 May 1994.
23 Personal communication, Bangkok, May 1995.
24 *The Spectator*, 5 March 1994.
25 *International Herald Tribune*, 6 May 1994.
26 Author's interview with Anwar Ibrahim, 26 May 1994.
27 Seyom Brown (1988) *New Forces: Old Forces and the Future of World Politics*, Glenview: Scott Foresman.
28 Robert Scalapino, speaking at ISIS Roundtable, Kuala Lumpur, June 1991.
29 Jakob Oetama (1989) 'Socio-Cultural Aspects of Indonesia–US Bilateral Relations', paper presented at the Third Indonesia–US bilateral Conference, Bali, 27–31 August.
30 *The Straits Times*, 9 December 1993.
31 Khoo Boo Teik (1995) *Paradoxes of Mahathirism: An Intellectual Biography of Mahathir Mohamad*, Kuala Lumpur: Oxford University Press.
32 ibid., p. 47.
33 Cited in the *Straits Times*, 12 May 1991.
34 Mahathir's speech at *International Herald Tribune* Conference in Kuala Lumpur, 15 November 1993
35 Anwar Ibrahim speaking in Singapore, 19 May 1994.
36 Personal communications.
37 Anwar Ibrahim speaking in Singapore, 19 May 1994.

38 'A Conversation with Lee Kuan Yew', *Foreign Affairs*, March/April 1994, vol. 73, p. 118.
39 John Bresnan (1994) *From Dominoes to Dynamos: The Transformation of Southeast Asia*, New York: Council on Foreign Relations, p. 101.
40 Cited in the *Straits Times*, 14 August 1991.
41 'The Clash of Civilisation?', *Foreign Affairs*, vol. 72, 1993, p. 26.

## 4  CORE VALUES OR ELITIST CORES

1 Francis Fukuyama (1995) 'Confucianism is no Bar to Asian Democracy', *Asian Wall Street Journal*, 23 May.
2 Antonio Galvao (c.1544) *A Treatise on the Moluccas*, St. Louis: Jesuit Historical Institute.
3 *Bangkok Post*, 20 June 1995.
4 Personal communication.
5 Personal communication, May 1995.
6 Personal communication, July 1995.
7 Personal communication, July 1994.
8 Amnuay Virawan, addressing a lunch in honour of Malaysian Deputy Prime Minister Anwar Ibrahim, sponsored by Chulalongkorn University's Institute of Strategic and International Studies, Bangkok, 21 September 1994.
9 Sukhumbhand Paribatra addressing ISIS luncheon for Anwar Ibrahim, 21 September 1994.
10 Author's interview with Brigadier General David Abel in Rangoon, 15 January 1995.
11 David Steinberg (1995) 'The Burmese Political Economy: Opportunities and Tensions', paper delivered at a conference on 'Myanmar Towards the Twenty-First Century', Chiang Rai, 1–3 June.
12 Personal communication, May 1995.
13 Personal communication, May 1995.
14 Personal communication, Jakarta 1991.
15 Cited in *The New Straits Times*, 27 August 1993.
16 Personal communication, April 1995.
17 Author's interviews with foreign and Thai NGOs in Bangkok, October 1994.
18 For a good discussion of the Vietnamese Communist Party see Gareth Porter (1993) *Vietnam: The Politics of Bureaucratic Socialism*, Ithaca: Cornell University Press.
19 The author who penned these remarks, Bilahari Kausikan, was appointed Singapore's permanent representative to the United Nations in 1995. As a delegate of the Singapore Ministry of Foreign Affairs he issued this statement at the World Conference on Human Rights, Regional Meeting for Asia, Bangkok, 31 March 1993.
20 *Straits Times* [of Singapore], March 5 1994.
21 Interview with Malaysian rock artist Zainal Abidin, in *Mens Review*, May 1993.

22 *Jakarta Post*, May 1993.
23 *FEER*, 11 May 1995.
24 *Reuters*, 28 April 1995.
25 Personal communication, July 1995.
26 Author's interview with Sheikh Imam Ashaari Mohamad, Chiangmai, July 1994.
27 In August 1994, Arqam was banned by the Malaysian government. Ashaari was extradited from Thailand and placed in detention. He later denounced his own teachings and appealed to other Arqam members to return to society.
28 *Indonesia 50 Years after Independence: Stability and Unity in a Culture of Fear* (1995) Report of the Asian Forum for Human Rights and Development, Bangkok, p. 113.
29 Widely reported in Jakarta and personal communication to the author.
30 Author's interview with Liew Chen Chuan, editor of the Chinese language daily, *Sin Chew Jit Po*, May 1994.
31 Author's interview with Lim Heng Jim, managing director of Quantum, a hard-disk factory in Penang, November 1993.
32 Andrew Macyntire (1990) *Business and Politics in Indonesia*, Sydney: Allen and Unwin.
33 Benny Subianto (1992) 'The Indonesian Middle Class and the Idea of Democracy', paper presented at the Conference on Indonesian Democracy 1950s and 1990s, Centre of Southeast Asian Studies, Monash University, 17–20 December.
34 Morton Abramowitz (1993) a paper presented at the Institute of Southeast Asian Studies in Singapore, 25th anniversary, 30 August.
35 Chai-anan Samudavanija (1994) 'Bypassing the State', draft paper in the possession of the author.
36 Sukhumbhand Paribatra, op. cit., September 1994.
37 Lee Kuan Yew cited in the *Straits Times*, 11 May 1991.

## 5 THE RELIGIOUS CHALLENGE TO AUTHORITY

1 The author is indebted to Ike Ong for this point.
2 Personal communication, July 1995.
3 Rudolph Mrazek (1994) *Sjahrir: Politics and Exile in Indonesia*, Ithaca: Cornell University Press, p. 149.
4 M.B. Hooker (1988) *Islam in Southeast Asia*, Netherlands: E.J. Brill, p. 35.
5 The Hanoi government insists that all religious and social organisations belong to a state backed umbrella group called the Fatherland Front. The Unified Buddhist Church of Vietnam, which claims to be the sole legitimate Buddhist church of Vietnam, has refused to join.
6 Sulak Sivaraksa (1988) *A Socially Engaged Buddhism*, Bangkok: Inter Religious Commission for Development, p. 47.
7 Hussin Mutalib and Taj ul-Islam Hashim (1994) *Islam, Muslims and*

the Modern State: Case Studies of Muslims in Thirteen Countries, London: St Martin's Press, p. 3.

8  'A Conversation with Lee Kuan Yew', Foreign Affairs, March/April 1994, vol. 73, p. 118.

9  Author's interview with M.R. Sukhumbhand Paribatra and M.R. Ruchaya Abhakol.

10  Author's interview with Surin Pitsuwan, Bangkok, 29 September 1994.

11  Surin interview, 29 September 1994.

12  Personal communication with a Malay stockbroker in Kuala Lumpur, May 1994.

13  Cited in 'Converging Harmony', The Nation, 5 August 1994.

14  Vasan Sittiket, quoted in Manager, no. 60, December 1993, p. 85.

15  Tempo, 16 April 1994.

16  By doing so he upset local forestry officials and the police. In December 1994. Phra Prajak gave up his struggle to protect the forest, and left the monkhood under what press reports said were mysterious circumstances. Rumours abounded that he was a conman; but many suspected that he was the victim of a powerful blend of business and political interests behind the logging operation in the area.

17  William Klausner (1993) Reflections on Thai Culture: Collected Writings of William J. Klausner, Bangkok: Siam Society, p. 201.

18  Mark Jurgensmeyer (1993) The New Cold War, Berkeley: University of California Press, p. 21.

19  Surin Pitsuwan, speech in Kuala Lumpur, 25 January 1994.

20  Author's interview with Anwar Ibrahim, Kuala Lumpur, June 1994.

21  Surin Pitsuwan, speech in Kuala Lumpur, 25 January 1994.

22  Author's interview with General Chavalit Yodhmani, Bangkok, April 1995.

23  Cited in The New Straits Times, Kuala Lumpur, 18 May 1994.

24  Tourabi opted to collaborate with the military junta of Jaffar Noumeri. I am grateful to K.S. Jomo for making this point.

25  Personal communication, Bangkok 1995.

26  Bangkok Post, 12 November 1985.

27  Author's interview with Thaksin Shinawatra, Bangkok, June 1995.

28  V.S. Naipaul (1981) Among the Believers, London: Penguin, p. 215.

29  Kuntowidjoyo's speech in Malang, East Java, at the inauguration of Ikatan Cendekiawan Muslim Indonesia (Association of Muslim intellectuals) (ICMI), December 1990.

30  Personal communication.

31  W.F. Wertheim (1974) 'Islam in Indonesia', in Oey Hong Lee (ed.) Indonesia After the 1971 Elections, Oxford: Oxford University Press.

32  Power and Impunity: Human Rights under the New Order, published by Amnesty International: London, 1994, p. 91.

33  Author's interview with Nurcholis Madjid, Jakarta, 30 April 1994.

34  Personal communication, 1991.

35  S. Gordon Redding (1993) The Spirit of Chinese Capitalism, New York: de Gruyter.

36 Author's interview with Nurcholis Madjid, Jakarta, 30 April 1994.
37 Author's interview with Alyamsyah Ratu Prawinegara, Malang, December 1990.
38 Author's interview with Amien Rais, Malang, December 1990.
39 Author's interview with senior Indonesian staff officer, Kuala Lumpur, 10 June 1994.
40 Author's interview with Adi Sasono, Jakarta, May 1994.
41 Rehman Rashid (1993) *A Malaysian Journey*, Kuala Lumpur: published by the author, p. 89.
42 Mahathir speech, Kuala Lumpur, 14 September 1993.
43 Ibrahim Zein, personal communication, Kuala Lumpur, 18 June 1994.
44 Rehman Rashid, op. cit., p. 115.
45 Author's interview with Fadyl Noor, October 1993.
46 Document from Institut Kajian Dasar, a think-tank set up under the patronage of Anwar Ibrahim in 1993.
47 Author's interview with Marzuki Darusman, Jakarta, May 1994.
48 Author's interview with Abdurrahman Wahid, Jakarta, May 1994.
49 Author's interview with Nurcholis Madjid, Jakarta, April 1994.
50 Harry Benda (1958) *The Crescent and the Rising Sun*, The Hague and Bandung: W. van Hoeve, p. 13.
51 Syed Adam Al Jaffri, speech given on 18 June 1994 in Kuala Lumpur, at a conference on 'Political Culture: The Challenge of Modernisation'.
52 Author's interview with Nurcholis Madjid, Jakarta, April 1994.

## 6  COMING TOGETHER

1 Author's interview with Witoon, Bangkok, August 1994.
2 The proposal was made by Thai foreign minister Kasem Kasemsiri at the ASEAN Ministerial Meeting in Brunei, July 1995.
3 Cited in 'Asia Goes on Holiday', *Economist*, 20 May 1995, p. 65.
4 Views gathered from residents of Chiangmai during the author's doctoral research in Chiangmai, 1981–3.
5 Lucian Pye (1985) *Asian Power and Politics: The Cultural Dimensions of Authority*, Cambridge, Mass.: Harvard University Press, p. 1.
6 ibid.
7 Author's interview with Jose Almonte, National Security Advisor to the President of the Philippines, 4 September 1995.
8 Cited in Edward Said (1993) *Culture and Imperialism*, London: Chatto and Windus, p. 246.
9 Dewi Fortuna Anwar (1994) *Indonesia in Asean: Foreign Policy and Regionalism*, Singapore: ISEAS, p. 18.
10 See Michael Vatikiotis (1995) 'A Giant Treads Carefully: Indonesia's Foreign Policy in the 1990s', in Robert R. Ross (ed.) *East Asia in Transition: Toward a New Regional Order*, Singapore/Armonk: ISEAS/ M.E. Sharpe, pp. 216–34.
11 Anwar Ibrahim, keynote speech at the Eighth Asia-Pacific Roundtable, Kuala Lumpur, 6 June 1994.

12 Dewi Anwar, op. cit., p. 5.

13 Personal communication, Bangkok, May 1995.

14 Dewi Fortuna Anwar (1993) 'Towards One Southeast Asia: Modalities and Agenda for Action', paper presented at the Fifth Southeast Asian Forum held in Kuala Lumpur, 4–5 October 1993.

15 C.P.F. Luhulima, 'The Performance of ASEAN Economic Cooperation', draft paper in author's posession dated 25 October 1993.

16 *The Defence of Thailand* (1993) The Ministry of Defence: Bangkok.

17 Personal communication, Bangkok.

18 D.G.E Hall (1968) *A History of Southeast Asia*, London: Macmillan. p. 73.

19 Gerald Segal (1990) *Rethinking the Pacific*, Oxford: Oxford University Press, p. 30.

20 Sarasin Viraphol in his (1977) *Tribute and Profit: Sino Siamese Trade 1652–1853* showed how Siamese tribute to China was driven more by the fact that tributary trade was exempt from duty rather than any acknowledgment of China's sovereignty over Siam. (Cambridge, Mass.: Harvard University Press, p. 244).

21 Cited in George Hicks and Jamie Mackie (1994) 'A Question of Identity' *FEER*, 14 July.

22 Author's interview with Dhanin Chearavanont, December 1994.

23 Figures from Hicks and Mackie in *FEER*, 14 July 1994.

24 Australian Department of Foreign Affairs and Trade, 1995.

25 General Jose Almonte, speaking at a conference on 'Asia–Pacific Security for the Twenty-first Century', sponsored by the Asia–Pacific Centre for Security Studies, Honolulu, 3–6 September 1995.

26 Chen Qimao (1995) 'The Security Issue in the Asia–Pacific Region and China's Security Policy', paper presented at 'Message from Asia', Bangkok, 5–6 July.

27 Gerald Segal (1990) op. cit., p. 389.

28 Hashim Djalal, Indonesian Ambassador at large, addressing SEAPOL Tri-Regional Conference on Maritime Issues, Bangkok, December 1994.

29 Personal communication.

30 Personal communication.

31 See 'The Great Game for Burma', editorial in *The Nation*, Bangkok, 26 December 1994.

32 Pan Qi (1985) 'Opening the Southwest: An Expert Opinion', *Beijing Review*, no. 35, 2 September, pp. 22–3. (I am indebted to Bertil Lintner for bringing this article to my attention.)

33 Personal communication.

34 George Yeo (1993) 'Creating Co-prosperity in East Asia', *The Daily Yomuri*, 26 June.

35 Opening statement of 'Southeast Asia Beyond the Year 2000: A Statement of Vision', Manila, 31 May 1994.

36 *Shared Destiny: Southeast Asia in the Twenty-first Century: Report of the ASEAN–Vietnam Study Group*, February 1993. The report, which contained a section titled 'A Vision for Southeast Asia', was a dry

run for the Manila declaration a year later, and was put together by the same group.
37 The author is indebted to Kavi Chongkittavorn for this point.
38 Author's interview with Jose Almonte, 4 September 1995.
39 Personal communication, Honolulu, September 1995.
40 Address by Anwar Ibrahim at the opening of the international seminar on 'Islam and Confucianism: A Civilizational Dialogue', University of Malaya, Kuala Lumpur, 13 March 1995.

## EPILOGUE

1 Michael Kinsley, Time essay, *Time*, 4 December 1994.
2 Interview with Lt. Suchai Jaosividha, director general of the intellectual property department, Bangkok, 24 May 1995.
3 *Review and Analysis of Intra-regional Trade Flows in Asia and the Pacific* (1995) Economic and Social Commission for Asia and the Pacific, Bangkok.
4 Cited by former Japanese foreign minister Nakayama Taro at 'Message from Asia' conference organised by Yomiuri Shimburn at the Oriental Hotel, Bangkok, 6–7 July 1995.
5 Personal communication, June 1995.
6 Personal communication, April 1995.
7 Henry Kissinger (1994) *Diplomacy: The History of Diplomacy and the Balance of Power*, London: Simon and Schuster.
8 Anand Panyarachun, keynote address at a seminar marking 20 years of Thailand's diplomatic ties with China, Bangkok, 1 July 1995.
9 Author's interview with Professor Umporn, Panachet, 13 September 1995.
10 Personal communication with member of the Law faculty of Chulalongkorn University, Bangkok, April 1995.
11 Excerpted from speech by Mohammad Hatta before the national committee of Indonesia, 2 September 1948.
12 Raphael Pura writing in the *Asian Wall Street Journal*, 8 June 1994.
13 Speech by Lee Kuan Yew at the Second World Enterprise Convention, Hong Kong, 22 November 1993.
14 Estimates of overseas Chinese control over local economies drawn from S. Gordon Redding (1993) *The Spirit of Chinese Capitalism*, New York: de Gruyter.
15 *Overseas Chinese Business Networks in Asia* (1995) Report of the Department of Foreign Affairs and Trade, Canberra, p. 120.
16 Yoshihara Kunio (1988) *The Rise of Ersatz Capitalism in Southeast Asia*, Singapore: Oxford University Press, p. 52.
17 Author's interview with Mely Tan, Jakarta, 6 August 1990.
18 Author's interview with Anand Panyarachun, July 1995.
19 *Overseas Chinese Business Networks in Asia*, op. cit., p. 204.
20 *Review and Analysis of Intra-regional Trade Flows in Asia and the Pacific* (1995) Economic and Social Commission for Asia and the Pacific, Bangkok.

21 Author's interviews with Dr Niphol Poapongsakorn and Dr Wisarn Pupphavesa, Thailand Development and Research Institute, Bangkok, July 1995.

22 Mochtar Kusumaatmadja, personal communication, Kuala Lumpur, 9 June 1993.

23 Personal communication, Bangkok.

24 *FEER*, 14 July 1994.

25 Personal communication, January 1995 in Mandalay.

26 *Bangkok Post*, 12 April 1995.

27 Personal communication, Penang, November 1993.

28 'Advancing Regional Cooperation in Asia', paper by Yan Zhang of the Fujian Academy of Sciences, delivered in Kuala Lumpur, 24 January 1994.

29 Personal communication, Kuala Lumpur, January 1994.

30 Lee Khoon Choy (1977) *Between Myth and Reality*, Singapore: Federal Publications, p. 95.

31 *International Herald Tribune*, 28 June 1995.

# Index